CODE
ETERNAL NIGHT SHIFT SERIES
BLOOD

BOOK TWO

LENA NAZAREI

Copyright © 2022 Lena Nazarei

All rights reserved. No part of this publication in print or in electronic format may be reproduced, stored in a retrieval system, or transmitted in any form or by any means, electronic, mechanical, photocopying, recording, or otherwise without the prior written permission of the publisher.

This is a work of fiction. Names, characters, organizations, places, events and incidents are either the products of the author's imagination or are used fictitiously. Any resemblance to actual persons, living or dead, or actual events is purely coincidental.

Design and Distribution by Bublish, Inc.
Published by Nurse Lena Books

ISBN: 9781647045340 (Paperback)

For my real bosses & co-workers ~ thank you for
letting me be creative. I know I talk about my
books too much and you always let me.

For the real "Olivia" & "Ellie" ~ thank you for your tireless
support and encouragement. You love me exactly as I am—
weird, obsessed with vampires and dreaming big.

For the real "Tom" ~ thank you for taking the girls when
I need to write, work or do homework and still not
laughing when I told you I was writing another book.

For Emily ~ thank you for believing in me more than I believe in
myself. I wouldn't have made it through many days without you.

For Jeremy ~ thank you for your expertise, your support,
your ideas and your inspiration. You let me pull you into
this crazy, vampire existence and I'm never letting you leave.
And, Logan, thank you for your patience with us!

For the real aides, nurse & doctors all over the world. You are real,
actual heroes. I do not do you justice in my books. We have worked
so hard the last two years with no end in sight. It's exhausting and
impossible tasks we face. I am so proud to be among you. Thank
you for everything you have done and will continue to do.

I love all of you so much.

So, it sounds like you guys did not get enough with the first story. I am still trying to wrap my head around the idea that people are interested in my life. For the most part, I don't feel all that exciting but I do admit that I have had an adventure or two since my little cemetery picnic and near demise. I was shocked when someone actually wanted to publish my journal. My friend Monica told me that her therapist said writing things down can help you grasp the reality of it and come to terms with your feelings about it. I never thought it would go anywhere but my nightstand drawer.

For those of you who didn't read the first book, I am a vampire. Yep, an honest-to-goodness walking corpse. I am also a mom, a nurse and a student. Obviously, I changed my name, and the names of all involved. I am not quite ready to come out of the coffin for the whole world. Vampires, for the most part, like to hide. We do not want everyone knowing about us- as a matter of fact it is against our "law". The only reason my kind is not "shutting me up" is the fact that I have changed names, locations and kept the really juicy things to myself. Most of the readers think it is just a fantasy and the imagination of a bored woman.

I am happy to let it stay that way.

Luckily, my family and co-workers do not like these "types of stories" and are too busy to even notice a little book on a shelf. Let's face it, most nurses are too exhausted to read after work! At the time I'm writing this particular part of my life, we are in the midst of a global pandemic. It's been way too many months of non-stop illness and a never-ending line of patients. Everyone I know is working more hours than any human should. I've been picking up as many night hours as I can, since I know I can't catch the virus. But, all those people in my hospital, and around the world, are goddamn heroes. My ex, Tom, is a police officer. He's out every day protecting people. They're all human and putting their lives on the line to help- never knowing if the next shift will be the last one. I am so lucky to know them.

Okay, I have to stop thinking about it. I am tearing up and already have a bunch of bloody teardrops on my keyboard. I don't know how I would explain that to Best Buy if my laptop stops working.

Moving on–my first journal was well received by a few of you and it sounds like you want more. To be honest writing all that down did help me cope with what happened. Writing down some more can only help me. And, if you guys want to hear it–I am happy to tell.

Just don't come looking for me. I would hate to have to get rid of you.

Let's see, where did I end the last time? It was after the night in the barn. I had introduced Rhys to the girls, and Frozen (worst decision ever). I had just really started to accept my feelings for Sorin. My powers were emerging fast and strong. I didn't know how to control them or my blood lust. Alex was kind enough to write a doctor's note for the hospital so I could take two weeks to deal with everything. The girls were going to be with Tom and Sarah for that time so they would be safe while I learned how to handle it all.

Oh yes, and I had promised Sorin a 24-hour date. I remember now–vividly. Just thinking about it may require a cold shower.

For those of you who need a recap–just a few days before this story will start, I was attacked for the second time by the same insane serial killer. I still feel the blood all over me even though I know it is not still there. If you have been through something traumatic, I don't have to tell you how long it takes to believe it is over. I can assure you it is the same for vampires. Thankfully we don't dream so I don't have to worry about nightmares.

Spending the night after the attack making amends and the next with my daughters was what got me through. Those girls are literally my reason for living–or whatever you call my continued existence on this Earth. Being 14 and 12 meant they were somewhere between child and adult but certainly not ready to know what happened to their mom. The middle and high school years are some of the roughest ones. If you think facing a psycho vampire, the endless reaches of eternity and my uncontrolled powers is scary—it is nothing compared to teenaged girls. I would fight crazed creatures of the night over a hormonal high schooler any day.

That being said Olivia and Ellie were–and still are–my everything. Nothing short of those two would have kept me fighting my way back from death.

At that time, my ex-husband Tom and their step-mother Sarah knew I had developed solar urticaria. The condition makes the sun like poison to the unfortunate souls who develop it. With this diagnosis the hospital was forced to keep me on nights only or face a lawsuit.

Oh, yeah! For anyone who doesn't know me–I was a full-time nurse on a cardiac unit at a small Pittsburgh community hospital when the tale I am about to tell was unfolding. A brilliant hematologist named Dr. Alex Kitchner was a coworker and partner in crime. He has known about the existence of vampire since the late 1980s, when his 17-year-old sister Sheena was turned and disappeared. Since then, his life's focus has been finding a cure for vampirism. The false file and diagnosis that protect my secret were his doing. In exchange, I provided him with my blood to use for testing.

Also working by my side in the hospital was Monica. She was my best friend and the only other human to know my real condition. Seeing me use my powers to kill the monster that had kidnapped her was how she had learned about my condition. Sadly, instead of a nice heart to heart she saw me naked, fangs out and covered in blood. You couldn't blame her for needing some time to come to terms with it all and decide if we were still friends.

Last but not least–tucked away in the blood bank–was the shy and boyish Rhys. Only myself, Alex and Monica knew he was my 240-year-old vampire maker.

When the story starts, I was saying goodbye to my beautiful children….

October 2019

Olivia and Ellie were wrapped in their favorite blankets as we walked down the street to their Dad's house. A small suitcase in each of my hands slapped against each thigh as I stepped. Honestly, they were really unnecessary. Their rooms at his house were just as full as the ones at mine but if something was missing it was only a four-house stroll between the homes. Outvoted by the girls–the little suitcases were packed and travelling with us. I made a big show of pretended they were extremely heavy and they laughed at my dramatics. They didn't realize that I could now bench press a car and not be out of breath. The thought brought on the usual guilt I felt when I remembered I was keeping a huge secret from them. But the memories of the horror on Monica's face and her recoiling from my touch was all I needed to know my daughters would never see my darker side.

Tom opened the door as we walked up. The October wind stirred up dried leaves on his porch and made the girls shiver so I hurried them up to his warm living room. Instinct made me hesitate at the doorway but I remember that his wife Sarah had invited me in once. I was okay to enter without an invitation until they rescinded the invite. Here's to hoping it would never come to that.

Stepping through the threshold was followed by a quick look for his German Shepard, Tank. Last time I saw the canine he had wanted me dead. That's not me being dramatic I assure you. The look in that dog's eyes above his bared teeth was not playful. He had seen me for what I had become and he didn't want me around his family. Tom must have known what I was searching for.

"Sarah took him for a walk. I am sorry about last time. I don't know why he acted like that."

I laughed, trying to sound like I didn't care. "Maybe I smelled like something weird. Who knows!"

The girls dropped their blankets on the couch and threw themselves down. Simultaneously, they extracted their phones from their back pockets and pulled open the YouTube app, becoming lost in videos before the suitcases were set down.

"They're mad at me," I said to Tom. "They want me to stay longer but I can't. I need a little time to get my head right."

Tom touched my shoulder. "I get it, Kate. Your whole life has been flipped on its head. If someone told me I'd never see the sun again I'd need some time to accept it all, too. You know they'll be fine."

Walking over to the couch I took in the sight of my two daughters. Olivia looked the most like me having inherited the same noticeable cheekbones. Tom's brown eyes and olive skin had been passed to them both—negating my pale Irish skin and blue eyes—but the almond shape of my eyes was same as the two pair avoiding me. Olivia's hair was chestnut brown and mine black but both of us had thick waves down to the middle of our backs. Ellie had the same shade of brown as her sister but her thick hair stopped at her shoulders and the bangs, she had recently cut herself, framed a round face that was a mirror of Tom. The brown of her eyes was lighter than her sister's or Dad's. The wisdom in them, when she looked up at me, made it evident she had been on this Earth before in a previous life. Despite being two years apart they were often mistaken for twins but I knew they could not have been more different.

"Can I have hugs before I go? I love you and I will miss you more than you know."

Begrudgingly, they stood up and each one wrapped a single arm around me. I used my arms to pull us all together. "When I get back, I should have this all figured out and we can start this new chapter, okay? I love you guys so much."

"We love you too," Ellie spoke into my stomach. "I wish you weren't going."

"I know," I answered. "I'll text you every morning before I go to bed and call you every night when I wake up, okay?"

"Okay," Olivia answered. "Mom?"

"Yes," I said as she pulled away from me.

"When you come back, can we do our night picnic?"

The words 'night picnic' made me flash back to the last meal I had eaten outside the hospital in the moonlight. I saw flashes of the attack and felt my throat being torn at. I shoved the images away and gulped down my fear.

"Of course," I said. *Because, when I get back, I'll be over this and that picnic will be a good way to start the new part of my life.*

A sound hit my ears–faint but clear. Tank and Sarah were a block or so away and heading for the house. I knew I needed to get out of there before the we found out if the dog or I were stronger.

"Gotta run, guys. It's 10. I'm heading to a friend's house and you need to get to bed soon. You can text me on my cell. If it's not daytime, I'll be awake." I kissed the tops of each girls' head, patted Tom's back and made my way to the door.

"Do you want to wait for Sarah? She would love to see you."

I shook my head. "I really need to go. I'll text when I get safe to my friend's house."

Once the front door was open, I focused my hearing. The woman and dog were one street up. I fought the urge to move at a vampire's speed to my house but made a point to move as quickly as a human could have. As I turned up my driveway Tank began to howl. He knew something dangerous was nearby and he didn't like it. I couldn't blame him but I wished it could be different. Sad to say it but I would miss that dog being my friend.

Inside my house, I made a final walk through. I didn't know how long I would be at Sorin's or Rhys' but I didn't plan on being back at my place for a good chunk of the two weeks I'd requested off. I needed time with my kind and to get a handle on my powers. The last two days I'd lived in fear of something happening that I couldn't explain. If some power had come out and hurt or scared my kids, I never would have forgiven myself.

Without the girls there, I didn't need to pay for heat so I turned the thermostat down to 60 degrees. Vampire or not, I was stingy with the utilities. Even death couldn't change that!

Next, I checked every lock and every window, reflecting on how being almost murdered twice will make you paranoid about your home security.

My bedroom was last. The curtains were pulled back to show the plywood that Tom had nailed in over my window when I was first "diagnosed". They had colored all over it and written messages to me. I hated closing the curtains and covering the words but there was no reason to leave them open while I was away. A search under my bed revealed a large duffel bag that I had bought months ago with a plan to use it as a gym bag. The tag on the zipper was proof that it had never made that planned trip. I ripped it off and started to fill it with 14 days' worth of personal needs. Toothbrush and toothpaste were first because, yes vampires brush their teeth. I didn't know if I really needed deodorant anymore but I threw it in. I knew Sorin and Rhys had shampoo and conditioner so I only added a brush and hair ties for my hair. I almost tossed in contacts and solution but remembered I had perfect vision in light and darkness now so I moved onto clothes. I chose a mix of casual and dressy- ranging from yoga pants and tank tops to jeans and tops to dresses. Black pumps, a pair of sandals, some boots and a pair of sneakers were thrown on top since I didn't know what I would need but I wanted options. I really didn't need a bra thanks to the effects of vampire blood on the body but I threw in a couple just for decency.

My stomach twisted and reminded me I had not eaten. The small fridge at the end of my bed was still full courtesy of Sorin. The padlock that kept out curious children was opened and my choice for the evening was AB since I hadn't tried it yet.

Three minutes later, the microwave beeped and I extracted a Mason jar from the cabinet. A violent flash hit me- a vivid memory of the man who had brought the jar to my home… I saw the barn, the blood everywhere, the flames ripping through him.. heard the screaming.

He is dead, Kate. It is just a jar. Breathe. I threw the Mason jar into the garbage can and pulled out a wine glass instead—centering my thoughts and bringing myself back to my kitchen.

Sipping at the warm blood, I started to forget Will's face and breathe again. The AB was a little sweeter than the A. So far O negative was my favorite. However, it is the most needed blood in the hospital and only in like 6% of the population, so I feel extremely guilty when I drink it. The nurse in me thought I should only drink the most common types. That being said if someone offered me O, I would totally take it. I mean, if it is already in a vampire's fridge, it was not like I was taking it from a donor that needed it, right?

I finished my meal while I made one more walk through the house. Washing the glass, I dried it and put it away. I ensured my tiny bedroom fridge was locked tight and no signs of blood drinking remained. With my duffel bag in one hand, I pulled the garbage bag out of the kitchen trash can and flipped off the last light in the house. I turned the front door knob once it was closed to be sure it was locked and made my way to the driveway to dump the trash bag into the big outside can.

Pointing the fob at the shiny black BMW, I pushed the unlock button and heard the car chirp. It would be a sad to hand that car back over to Sorin. I had taken the girls for a night ride after the previous sundown. We had each window down and the sunroof open. The fall night air wrapped around us while we cruised around the neighborhood in our fancy car. They had squealed and begged me to try and buy one just like it. I don't think they understood what they were asking. After taking 400 selfies with the car, they had finally walked away from it and accepted it was not ours to keep. Tonight, I threw the duffel bag into the seat that Olivia and Ellie had sat in the night before.

My little house looked so alone when I glanced up at it. Without the joyful noise of my daughters and the usual chaos that my human life had filled it with, it was lost. A pang in my gut matched my worry that no part of my life would ever go back to the way it was before my turning.

You have to let go. You can't keep holding on to what used to be. Look forward, Kate. Stare ahead and make it work.

"I'll see you in my next chapter, house."

Climbing into the car I resisted the need to look one more time. There was no point. The woman that had bought that house was dead and a new owner had taken over.

3

I took my time on the drive to Sorin's manor. It wasn't because I wasn't excited to see him–I was but I was also nervous. I still needed to come to terms with the way he made me feel on top of everything else I was dealing with. First, I had only been a vampire for two weeks. Second, I had likely lost my best friend since she was terrified to be in the same room with me. Third, I had a maker who I was still getting to know. Next, I was manifesting more powers that most vamps get in 1,000 years and no idea how to control them. A couple of those powers killed someone just days before and I hadn't really accepted that I had done that. That was all before you added on the overwhelming desire I felt for a man I met 13 days ago. The person I was with him was strong, sensual and desirable. I needed to get to know that woman before I could let her completely give herself to someone.

So, I was using that car ride as my chance to think before Sorin's presence took over my ability to.

Using the handsfree, I asked the car to call Alex.

After one ring his voice filled the air of the car and danced out the open windows. "Hello?"

"Hi, Alex."

"Hi, Kate." I heard the relief in his voice. He was happy to hear from me. My instinct was to wonder why. *So paranoid, girl. Have some semblance of self-confidence.*

"Are you okay? Have you seen Monica?"

"I'm fine. Yes. I saw her today at the beginning of my shift and I just left her a few minutes ago. She's doing better. I think she'll be moved out of ICU to stepdown tomorrow. All your co-workers are thrilled that she may be on your floor soon."

"It's her floor, too," I reminded him.

"You're right. They asked about you. I told them that it wasn't my place to say but that I recommended you take some time to deal with your new diagnosis. They think you're in therapy. I didn't work to dispel that rumor."

"Thank you, Alex. I heard that everyone's calling you a hero. They all think you saved Monica from a psycho killer."

He was quiet. I didn't have Sorin's power of empathy but I was pretty sure he was embarrassed. I could practically feel his blush. I half-smiled at the thought. Two weeks ago, I was convinced he was the biggest douchebag around. Most doctors fell into a few categories: cool doctor who is one of the people, smart doctor who helps the nurse when they are in a pinch, the never-around doctor who will give you anything you ask for if you can only get him on the phone and giant asshole who thinks he is smarter than everyone in the room at all times. Some doctors are a mix of cool and smart. But the dicks are not cool or smart. I would've put Alex in the "douche" column.

I would've been wrong.

"I'm sorry, Kate. Everyone is praising Rhys and me for saving Monica. You're the one that saved us all and no one knows."

Shock overcame me. I had not seen that coming. "Alex, honestly, I don't care. You were dying. You couldn't have done anything. But as soon as you were back, you two protected her and got her to the hospital. You sat at her bedside. You fought for her to get the best treatment. You deserve the praise. I wish I could be the one taking care of her but I am so glad it's you."

Another pause.

"I never really thanked you. I would have been dead if it weren't for you. I really want to hear the whole story when you are ready."

I let out a long sigh. "I don't know when I will be ready to retell everything but I promise when I am, you will get the exclusive. Are you really okay? I mean—like–you have no lasting effects from all of that?"

"No," he laughed. "Honestly, I have felt better in the last few days than I have in a long time. I have energy. I feel strong and healthy. I actually ran a CBC and H/H on myself and everything is perfect. How close to death was I?"

"Pretty close," I answered. I hadn't told him yet just how close. I knew one day I was going to have to be honest with him and tell him everything that had been done to him. He deserved that much.

"I'm headed to Sorin's," I continued, changing the subject. "If you need me, text me. I'll get back to you as soon as I can. In the meantime, please keep me updated on Monica. I owe you big time for watching out for her. And thank you again for getting the hospital to give me this break."

"Of course," he answered without thought. "You should've taken more time to adjust. You need this time after everything you've been through. I'll take care of Monica. And, when Rhys is here, she is letting him visit. That's a good sign. If you don't hear from us assume that everyone is okay. Relax, Kate. Take some down time."

"Thanks, Alex." I hit the button on the steering wheel that ended the call.

The silence in the car gave me a chance to regroup. Monica was moving to stepdown and that was good. Alex was healthy and that was good. I had saved them both and that was good.

Enjoy the good news, Kate. Stop second guessing everything and waiting for bad news.

I dialed Rhys next. His voice replaced the silence. "Hello. Girls dropped off?"

I couldn't help but smile. I had always enjoyed the faint hint of Scotland in his speech, even before we were more than casual co-workers. But, now that we were family, it sounded like home. I know that's weird. I just don't know how else to describe it.

"They're not happy but they're safe at their Dad's house and I'm in the car. I hope they forgive me for being so absent for the last two weeks and the next two to come. We've never spent so much time apart."

He sighed. "Kate, you have to stop being so hard on yourself. You're doing this for them. Once, you have your powers in check and deal with what you have been through you'll come back. Then, you'll be right back to being the same awesome Mom they're used to."

He always knows what to say.

"Thanks, Rhys. How's work?"

"Boring without you. Gotta say though, I have come to appreciate boring."

I raised my hand to my heart. "Boy, isn't that the truth! I should be at Sorin's soon. When will you come by?"

He chuckled. "Try not to plan ahead so much and just exist in the moment. I'll see you the day after tomorrow or the one after that. I haven't decided."

No planning, huh? That will be a tough one. "Fine," I resigned. "I'll see you whenever."

The phone clicked dead seconds before Sorin's mailbox came into view. My nerves started to get the best of me. I thought about turning around but knew how stupid that was.

Stop, Kate. You've slept with him, bathed with him and killed a man with him. What is there to be nervous about???

There was no time to ponder it as the front door opened and Tamela came into frame. I hadn't known her long but I had become fond of her. She oozed strength and confidence. It wasn't just that she was 6 feet tall and could break a man in half. It was the way she carried herself, like underestimating her could be fatal.

Tonight, she had her long dark hair gathered in a high ponytail. The hair had been turned into a long braid that touched her lower back. Knowing her, she could use that braid like a weapon in some way. Her red sleeveless turtleneck was made of silk and made her dark skin shimmer in the light of the house behind her. Her black leggings hugged her legs and ended in leather boots. A gold cuff wrapped around her right bicep.

She looked ready to either go on a date or kick some ass.

She motioned for me to stop the car in front of the main entrance and I followed direction- cutting off the engine and stepping out of the BMW. We met each other in the driveway and she wrapped her arm around mine in a gesture of either friendship or protection. "Someone will park the car and take your bag to your room. Come and drink with me. Sorin has someone in his office but has been awaiting you."

The familiar foyer was warm and the lights were dimmed when we entered. I was surprised to not see Sorin's other two bodyguards, Edwin and Naseem. But they were likely upstairs with Sorin. I was sure I would see them eventually as they were never far from the lord of the city. I wondered if there was a ranking among bodyguards. If there was, I was certain Tamela was in charge.

Instead of walking straight ahead into the kitchen, we turned right and made a path through the dining room and into the solarium. I had seen the room before but had never spent more than a few seconds in it. Several vampires sat, stood and lounged around the large circular room. The faint music was instantly recognizable as *Hotel California*. It was a big change from the jazz I heard in here last time. A massive bar graced the far wall but I imagined it was there for the prior owner. Vampires don't drink alcohol. It doesn't have an effect on them so it would just be a waste of money.

It had been explained to me that the vampires of the city often congregated in the manor for a place to be themselves. It seemed to be rare that there was not a group hanging around the home at night. I hadn't really met many vampires yet. Rhys, Sorin and his staff were the only ones I'd spoken to. After Sorin's ex-assistant Will had turned out to be a lunatic, I was a little gun shy.

Shocker, right?

This evening there we're less than a dozen, one of the smaller parties I had witnessed. Tamela crossed to the bar and then slid behind it. "What can I get you?"

It took a minute for me to realize she was talking to me. Only when I saw her staring at me did I register the question. "Oh, I ate, thanks."

"After what you went through, I don't think some extra sustenance would be a bad idea. You need to always be at your strongest, if you can be."

I didn't need to ask her what she meant. I was guessing that Sorin had confided in her that I was manifesting more powers than normal. He'd warned me that it could make me a target. Knowing him, he wanted his strongest ally to be mine too. Arguing with her seemed futile.

"Do you have O negative?"

"I do," she smiled.

Moments later a glass was on the bar and smelled delicious. I stepped up to the bar and had just brought it to my lips when I heard someone move up next to me. I turned to face the new person and had to adjust my sight up a little. I had chosen to wear a black dress that Sorin had given me for my birthday and–after agonizing–picked black sandals over heels. I regretted that choice when I saw the woman at my side.

By my measurement, she was 5 or 6 inches taller than my 5'8". She had heels on but without them she was probably only an inch shy of Tamela. Her honey blonde hair fell in thick curls around her face. It was the kind of hair you see in shampoo commercials and try to convince yourself is not real. The white cocktail dress looked like it was painted on. She clearly had zero body fat when she was turned. She had to be a model or an actress. Her hazel eyes seemed almost cat like and what I saw in them confused me. Irritation was evident across her face. She seemed familiar to me but I couldn't place her and wondered if I'd offended her previously only to forget.

"You must be Kate." She didn't offer a hand or anything so I assumed I was correct and had pissed her off.

"Do I know you? I'm sorry, I don't remember."

"Play nice, Evelyn." Tamela was still behind the bar but her voice seemed to be in the space between this woman and me.

"Stay out of it, Tamela." The model named Evelyn responded without breaking her gaze from mine. "Last time I saw you, you had an adorable set of leggings and some knockoff boots. At least tonight you have chosen a dress."

That was the clue I needed. I knew where I'd seen her.

The night I'd come to tell Sorin my suspicions about Rhys, he'd been surrounded by three women. She had laid her hand on him and stirred up a quick jealousy in me. It was the first time I'd felt that kind of jealousy and I hadn't liked it. I don't want to be someone who turns against another woman over a man. I'd always believed that girls should be lifting each other up, not clawing at each other. I'd felt guilty for my reaction to her touching him.

Tonight, I stopped feeling bad because she was clearly a bitch.

"Ah yes," I sipped at my drink and tried my best to look confident. "I remember you. You were trying desperately to get Sorin's attention but weren't getting it."

The look that crossed her face reminded me that vampires had a wild beast inside of us. Imagine a time when you were at a zoo and saw a look in an animal's eyes that made you happy for the bars. That's what she wanted. She wanted to tear me apart.

Stand in line, sweetie.

I continued to work on my warm drink and turned away from her like I was looking for a friend. I felt her power roll at my back. I steeled myself and mentally prepared for a fight but I knew she was much older than me and probably knew how to actually control her powers.

Tamela stepped in, cutting off the power scratching at my spine. "You know the rules, Evelyn. No fights. Everyone is safe here. I'll be happy to throw you out if you would like."

"I apologize. I don't know what came over me." Her voice had changed. She sounded more like a lady from those 50's commercials now.

I turned back to see what was happening. Evelyn's eyes had lost the desire to maul. She had turned into the vision of class and grace. I didn't necessarily believe it but I was relieved to not have to face down another attacker in the matter of days. She turned toward a crowd of women in the back corner and made her way to them. But not before a quick look back to inform me that this was far from over.

4

Staying at the bar to talk to Tamela was my best chance at a calm night. I didn't really need to get to know anyone- figuring I had enough vampires in my life as it was. Tamela was telling me about her time living in New York City when the air shifted and the familiar electricity danced up my legs.

I knew he was in the room before I turned to face the entryway.

Sorin's black hair fell just below his shoulders. The bluish tint was harder to see in the lighting but I knew it was there. His eyes, however, were impossible to miss. They were the only grey eyes I'd ever seen and they sucked the air out of my chest every time. They caught light from a source I wasn't sure of and danced with it.

And, they were looking straight at me.

The black shirt he wore had billowing sleeves with buttons that stopped mid sternum. It had to be from a time long before now because I hadn't seen anything like it outside a turn-of-the-century film. It was untucked from the black leather pants that I was certain he'd been wearing first night we—well you know.

All black to match my dress. Had he known?

Evelyn walked up to him in a way that reminded me of the boa constrictor from Jungle Book. She looked predatory and hungry. Her hand rested on his left shoulder. He turned, half-bowed, lifted her hand to his mouth and kissed gently.

"Good evening, Evelyn. You look lovely," he spoke to her in the way a person tells their friend's little girl that she looks pretty in her new dress. She either didn't catch the tone or didn't care. Her eyebrow arched and she let loose a million-dollar smile. The next words had that fake smile faltering. "Have you met our newest vampire?"

I fought the urge to laugh out loud and decided to take the high road. I spoke up, knowing they could hear me from across the room. "She just introduced herself. She's very welcoming."

I heard Tamela whisper, "Nice."

I liked that she approved of my decision to give the fly honey and not vinegar.

"I did," Evelyn took the opportunity to please Sorin. "I wanted her to know exactly how I felt." Her words were dripping with kindness but I took their true meaning and tucked it away for later. She continued, "That all of us are treated the same here."

What does that mean? Is she trying to tell me that she has been in Sorin's bed, as well? That they all had?

There was no time to fall any further down that dark rabbit hole because Sorin had released Evelyn's hand and was heading towards me. I took a second to watch the beautiful woman's face fall and then set my gaze on the man walking towards me.

Walking is not the ride word–gliding is much closer to Sorin's way of moving. If you'd asked me what he did before the turning, I would have guessed dancer by the way he moves. But, somehow, I knew that wasn't right. His scent reached me as he stopped to shake the hand of two male vampires. They exchanged words but I was too intoxicated by his smell to focus on his words. Describing it to a human is difficult but, I will try.

Think back to being in the woods in the morning. The mix of dew, spring water, the extinguished campfire and pine? That's Sorin. It's primal and fresh.

He finished his conversation and one of the men followed him on his path to the bar. The men flanked me, one on each side. My eyes were on Sorin but I was acutely aware of the vampire at my back. Sorin leaned forward and laid his lips on mine. It was chaste but enough to awake every cell in my body. My power jumped to life and reach for his. I felt aroused and exposed–like a teenaged boy must feel when he realizes he has an erection in class and can't hide it. But it was quick and I felt the electricity of Sorin's magic gently pressing mine back into me.

"Later," he whispered in my ear.

"I felt that," the man behind me said, reminding me that he was there. He sounded like he was happy to have been a part of something that others had not been invited to.

I turned. "I'm sorry. I'm still trying to control it."

"Don't be sorry," he answered. "It felt great." He extended his hand and I hesitantly laid mine in his. He matched Sorin's gesture with Evelyn and raised my hand to his lips in a sort-of bow.

"And, they said chivalry is dead," I quipped.

"Most of us are," he answered just as quick and gave me a quick wink. "These humans have forgotten how to treat beautiful women."

When he stood and let go of my hand, I could really look at him. He was an inch or two taller than me but his shoulders were broad and his arms told a tale of someone who had worked out up until the day he was turned. His chestnut brown hair was sprinkled with the perfect amount of grey and a little too long with no discernable style. A subtle scruff highlighted his prominent jaw line. His wild hair reminded me of Rhys, giving me an instant fondness for the new vampire. His eyes were the bright blue of a summer sky and they made me ache for daylight. A row of perfect white teeth put Evelyn's smile to shame. I could only surmise that he and she must have modeled together. I was suddenly worried that I was not good-looking enough to be a vampire–not in this crowd anyways.

"Kate," I figured the least I could do was tell him my name after he had felt my metaphysical lust.

"Jeremy," he responded. He had dressed down for the evening in a black t-shirt under a black suit jacket and dark blue jeans. "The man that was next to me? The one with his back to us? That is my partner, Logan."

I glanced at the man in a navy jacket looking like he wanted to do anything but acknowledge me. He was making his way to the group of women that Evelyn seemed to control and looking more like a man walking to the electric chair than a person going to see a friend. I returned my attention to Jeremy and his smile. He appeared so kind but I couldn't fight back the fear washing up my throat. My brain frantically made connections between the man in front of me and the one I had met here and instantly liked, the one I thought was my friend, the one who had brought me blood when I was alone and hungry—then had tried to kill my friends and rape me. The icy wave of fear slid over me and threaten to pull me back into the memory of the barn.

I fought it.

Not all men are Will. Jeremy is not Will.

Sorin laid his hand on the small of my back and I knew he was sensing what I was feeling. I pulled my thoughts back to the room I was in and the man in front of me. As far as I knew, he was not a psycho killer and I needed to believe that I was safe. He was looking at his partner with adoration in his eyes—I had to focus on that and not let my fear get the best of me. I followed his gaze back to the man now talking to Evelyn.

"He seems nice." I said and shoved the impulse to shake deep down.

"Normally, he's not rude. But, you see," he leaned in a whispered quietly in my ear. I guessed he did not want the others to hear. "Evelyn and he own a business together. He doesn't want to be on her bad side. And talking to you would make his eternity very unbearable. I must apologize for him."

"Tell him it is totally fine. I completely understand," and that was not a lie. My own fear of what people were truly capable of was fresh in my psyche.

"He'll be relieved," and he flashed that brilliant white smile. "He loves what he does but, not who with."

Sorin joined the conversation, "What is fine?" His hand slid from my low back around to my hip and the familiarity of it sent chills through me. *He won't let me get hurt again.*

"I'll tell you later," I turned to him, raising the volume of our conspiring back to a conversational level and smiled. *Can he really not see what is going on here?*

Jeremy moved around so I could face both men at the same time. "What does your partner do?"

He took a sip of the blood in his hand and licked his lips to remove the remaining drops. "Fashion. He and Evelyn have a clothing line together. They're quite talented. I would tell you to come to the next show but, well, you know."

Of course, she's in fashion.

"And, you?" I asked him, trying to steer the conversation away from the evil witch across the room.

"I'm embarrassed to say I am one of their models."

Guessed it. "Why embarrassed?" I asked.

He bobbed his head and chuckled to himself. "Well, for decades I was a well-respected professor of literature. Unfortunately, my masking skills are minimal and it became difficult to explain why I was not retiring. So, I did. We moved here, met Evelyn, Logan started his fashion line and I grew bored. Enough time has passed, and their line is hardly globally recognized, so it seemed safe to start modeling. At least, I get to see him every once in a while. He's at the office most nights." He laughed again. "I have unloaded my sob story on you and you asked a simple question. Please forgive me."

"No!" I answered. "Actually, I've been thinking about earning my masters so I can teach nursing online. I figured I can't stay in the hospital forever and this will buy me some time before I have to give it up. I'd love to talk to you about being a teacher."

He lit up. I had the suspicion that not many people asked him to use his brain anymore. *A curse of being attractive, I guess.* "I would love that, Kate. Truly."

I found a napkin and pen behind the bar, quickly writing my number below eye line and laid it on the polish wood. I gave Jeremy a wink. "Grab it when you can, so 'you know who' doesn't know we are friends." He winked back, conspiratorially. During the charade, Sorin watched me with amusement. I wished for his power of empathy so I could know what he was thinking but reminded myself I had more than enough powers to try and handle.

A few minutes of casual conversation amongst the three of us and Jeremy moved to drop his empty blood glass on the bar. He snatched up the napkin, dabbed his mouth and slid the incriminating cloth into his pocket.

"Logan has given me the look and I must go save him from the leeches. It was fate that I chose to speak to you, Kate. I look forward to our talks of academia."

"I'm glad you decided to talk to me, too." And, that was also not a lie. I needed to move on from what happened and couldn't blame the whole bushel of vampires for a couple bad apples.

With that, he moved to the group of women and laid his hand on the navy shoulder of his partner. They turned like they had rehearsed the exit before and disappeared out of the solarium. I looked around and realized that most of the vampires had left. Only Evelyn and the woman on each side of her remained. I didn't know where Tamela went or when she had left but she was nowhere in the room.

You have to get better at sensing people coming and going if you want to survive.

Morbid thought but true. I added it to the list of things I wanted taught.

To my dismay, the three vampire brides were walking towards Sorin and me. I braced myself for what may be coming. The man at my side appeared to be expecting it. The look on his face was hard to read.

"Sorin," Evelyn stopped in front of him and the other two vampires halted to each side of her. All three were blonde but neither was quite as breathtaking as their leader. She towered over them and had an aura that would make any female feel "less than."

"Eve," he responded.

Oh, she has a nickname with him? How appropriate. Eve. The first woman and the reason mankind was cast out of Heaven.

"I was hoping to walk with you in the gardens before I go–like we used to." The last half of the sentence was said with her hazel eyes locked on me.

"I am sorry but I have much to do before sunrise and I have no time for walks. Perhaps, another time." She took that as an invitation and while she was disappointed, I could see the hope in her eyes that she still had a chance.

"Then, I will ask for my car and return to the mansion. I wish you would come see it one night." She stepped into him and laid a hand on each of his shoulders. "It is something to behold."

Her movement forward had pushed me away from him and I wrestled the desire to do something very un-ladylike to her. I had noticed the word "mansion" like I knew she wanted me to.

Don't stoop to her level, Katie.

Sorin held each of her wrists and brought her hands together in front of his chest. "I will try to come and see it soon. I am familiar with the estate but I am sure you have done wonders with the interior."

If she smiles any bigger, her face will split in half.

He leaned forward and kissed her cheek then to my relief, dropped her hands and gave a kiss on the cheek of each one of her "groupies." He snapped his finger and without a sound Edwin appeared in the room.

"Please see to it that each one of these lovely ladies makes it safely to their cars."

"You got it," he answered his master and opened his arms to invite the women to follow him. They did but Evelyn made sure to look back at us. Obviously, she was looking to see if I was leaving too.

I wasn't.

"Come with me." It was a whisper but I followed the man pulling me towards the door to the outside.

Every drop of uncertainty was gone. I wanted whatever came next.

5

He moved so quickly. At first, I thought I couldn't keep up but I found that I could. I matched his pace and the yard around us was a blur. It only came back into focus when we stopped. The white twinkling lights in the trees were the same as before. The little brook under the bridge was louder this evening so the recent rain must have kicked up the pace of the water's movement. The little black bench was still nestled in the center of the ring like it had been the night I had sat here and awaited my fate.

Only tonight a new smell was in the mix. The air was filled with the rose bushes around the grove. Music crept out from a speaker I couldn't see. A piano played something I didn't recognize but immediately felt moved by. Sorin stepped towards the bench and reached his arm to me.

I moved to meet him and slid my hand into his.

He didn't sit down as I had anticipated but instead pulled me into him and his free arm found its rest on my back. He swayed and I knew what this was. It was the dance he had promised me. The dance in the place we had first seen each other.

I had once heard a Native American legend about the origin of soulmates. The lore goes that we were once a creature made of four arms, four legs, two heads but one soul. The Gods, in their jealousy of our happiness, sent lightning bolts to split us all in two. So, we walk the Earth with two legs, two arms and one head but only half of our soul. We spend the rest of our time on this land searching for the one that holds the other half of our soul.

With my body pressed into his, I had the sensation of two halves coming together; like our beings fit together to repair something broken. My head rested just below his shoulder and our feet moved in synchronicity. The notes of the melody told our muscles what to do.

"I have counted each second until I could have this dance with you," he spoke just above me. "Since the moment I saw you here, alone in the protection of the trees, I knew you were bringing change."

I looked up at him, continuing our dance. "You didn't tell me who you were."

"I didn't," he agreed. "And while I regret starting our courtship with deception, I would not replace that encounter for my life. What I felt in you, what I saw when your blue eyes looked at me, was the truth. You didn't desire me for my status or my abilities. Your body ached for me; your power touched mine; just me—the man–not the master of the city."

We glided across the lush grass with only the leaves and roses to witness us and I didn't know what to say. The music transitioned into a piano melody. All I could do was look into his eyes while we danced around the little oasis; the rest of existence melting away. My head fell back into his shoulder, finding its place to rest while I fought to focus my thoughts.

I can't think. I need to think.

He slowed our dance, stepping away from me. I felt a hand slide under my chin and lift my gaze to his. What I saw was a mixture of desire and fear. *He is afraid? Of me?*

I hated the yearning and uncertainty that I saw in those grey eyes. I hated seeing this strong man with distress on his face. My feelings for him were complicated to say the least but one was clear; I didn't want him to hurt.

I closed the space between us and raised onto my toes to lay my lips onto his. It was the invitation he had been hoping for. He returned the kiss like a man dying of thirst who was given his first taste of water. I knew without a word spoken that he had worried while I was away. He had worried that I would reject him, hate him for the lies, the deception and, worst of all, not knowing that he had invited my killer into my life. I wondered why he didn't use his empathy to just read me. But, considering the chaotic mix of emotions I was feeling, I knew it was not enough to just read me. If I didn't know how I really felt then how could he?

The night we met; I had thought he was a party goer who had come to hit on the "new girl." I'd felt things for him that I didn't think I'd ever felt. He had brought something in me back to life. I'd stopped feeling like a woman at some point in my life and didn't notice it until it came back that night. I was no longer just a mom or a nurse; I was someone to be desired and cared for. I was something of worth.

But it had been a trick and I knew it. He hadn't told me who he was. He allowed me to open up to him and had seen the look in my eyes and felt my desire but still had lied. It had been too easy for him, like a game. I didn't think I was completely over that yet.

I stepped back and dropped his hand. "I'm sorry. I need a minute."

"You can speak to me, Katherine." Just the sound of my name on his lips was enough to bring a reaction from my body. I ached and all he had done was say my name.

"In the last two weeks, I have been tricked and lied to, almost murdered twice, had everything I know changed or taken from me and fallen into bed with a man I barely know. My head is spinning. I can't think around you."

He stood still–the kind of still only vampires can display. He didn't breathe, blink or sniffle. He looked like a beautiful mannequin. I think he was waiting for me to continue.

I did. "I'm not mad about you not telling me who you were that night. I don't regret anything that has happened between us. I just need to wrap my mind around all of it and what it means."

Mercifully, he moved. I think I would have gone insane if he had stayed like that much longer. It was too inhuman, too otherworldly.

"Tell me what you need from me and it is yours." There was no emotion in his voice. The words came out like a rehearsed speech. I couldn't tell what he was hiding or why he would keep it hidden but I didn't want to push.

"I would like to sleep alone tonight." Even as I said it the voice in my head screamed *nooooo*. "I would like to start training tomorrow and learn more about what I am. I think, once I get to know the new me, I can focus on whatever may be real between us and start to get a handle on what I'm feeling."

I was prepared for a fight. I half expected him to throw me over his shoulder and carry me to the bed like a caveman. Honestly, I don't think I would have fought him but, thankfully I didn't need to find out. He bowed and when he rose I saw that he was still hiding his feelings.

"May I walk you back to the manor and see you safely to your room?"

He sounded so formal. His speech was like something out of a historical romance where the young man comes to court a young lady and chaperones must accompany the lovers. It reminded me that he was from a time long before me. I suddenly felt so far from him, so ordinary. *He won't want you in the end. He will need someone as old as him, as powerful.*

He extended his arm, bent at the elbow and I smiled at the old-fashioned gesture. I slid my arm around his and fell into step with him. This time, we weren't rushing. We took our time in the immense lawn, with the sound of the brook and the moon to keep us company. Neither one of us wanted to end the night but I knew I was right. I needed a night without children or makers or lovers so I could think clearly. While my mind reinforced that I was making the right choice, the fibers of my body fought me for control. My flesh wanted his, my heart wanted his, my need wanted his. I could feel the weight of him on me like it was less of a memory and more of a present event.

He spoke and broke the silence. "My strength is not limitless. If you continue to feel that way, I will break and bring you to my bed."

I blushed. *Empath, he's an empath you stupid girl. Shut off the porno movie in your mind.*

"I'm sorry," was all I could think to say.

"Don't be sorry. I try to not pry but sometimes your feelings are too strong to not sense. Truthfully, I am pleased to know you still yearn for me."

We reached the door to the solarium and he turned to me. He opened his mouth to speak but I spoke first. "Sorin, there isn't a man or woman who meets you and does not fantasize about you."

"But I only care about you desiring me." He brought my hand to his lips again but, this time, it didn't feel gentlemanly. I quivered.

"What about Evelyn?" *Why would you say that???*

His left eyebrow arched in confusion. "What about Evelyn?"

Well, I started it. I needed to end it. I swung open the door and stepped into the now quiet room. The echoing of our shoes on the floor was reminiscent of clapping. *I don't think it is applause for you, Kate. This was an epically bad call.* He followed at my back and I was grateful I didn't have to see his reaction.

"She practically clawed my face off tonight. She's called dibs on you and she doesn't want me anywhere near your bed."

I reached the base of the stairs and started up them, no clue which room I was heading to. I heard him move behind me but I think if I hadn't been a vampire, I wouldn't have heard anything. He was shockingly calm. I hoped it wasn't the calm before the storm. *Or, he's trying to think of a lie to tell you.*

"She has been in my bed."

Nope, not a lie. He went for truth. Dammit.

"So have many others. But she means no more to me than the rest. We found comfort in each other one night and I had no desire to repeat it."

I resisted the urge to cringe or run. I kept walking at a human pace to the second floor. As my foot landed on the solid floor, his hand grabbed my upper arm and spun me to face him. I wasn't prepared for the face I met. He was serious and I saw the man that ruled this city.

"What I felt with you, what I feel with you–it has never been that way with another. I have waited 500 years for what occurred in that office and in my bed with you." To drive the point home, he took several steps forward while I moved back to match the pace. Our journey was ended with a wall at my back. Once the wall was there to support me, Sorin's hand found the curve of my buttocks. In tandem, he crushed his mouth on mine and lifted my legs to wrap around his torso. I'd only seen the man that vampires feared for a second but it'd been enough to scare and excite me.

Heat filled my rib cage and slithered up my throat. It had been waiting for its mate and wouldn't be disappointed. The warm lightning poured from his mouth into mine. The mixture of powers danced in our kiss. My breathing increased and the heat waves matched the rhythm of my respirations. With my legs around him, the dress had risen up to my waist but I didn't care. With my lower half holding onto him, he was able to run his hands up each side of my body to slide his fingers into my hair and fill his fists with it. He broke the kiss and met my gaze. The air between us wavered with our powers. His irises had swallowed the pupils leaving bright grey orbs in each eye. The shades of grey rolled around each other and created the illusion of clouds on a stormy night. His fangs peeked out from his swollen upper lip.

"Tell me to stop," he said in a voice similar to the growl of a large cat.

"Stop." It was out before I could make the conscious decision to have him carry me down the hall to the bed I wanted so badly.

Without hesitation, he stepped back, placed his hands under my thighs and gave me the second I needed to slide my legs down his.

Once my feet were on the floor, I felt a little stronger. My breath was still coming in pants but I was not shaking and that was something.

We stood there for minutes, staring at each other. Each one was waiting to see what the other would do. He was still again, guarding his thoughts with a lack of movement. I closed the distance and laid my hands on his solid, unyielding chest. He lowered his head so we could make eye contact. His still swam with the threat of an imminent downpour.

"Please don't hate me," I whispered.

It was answered with the simple movement of him laying a hand on each of mine, then kissing the tip of my nose. The one-word response allowing me to breathe again.

"Never."

He stepped back and the air between us felt so cold. "I am afraid I must say our goodnights here. I cannot follow you to your room. I fear I wouldn't be able to stop again."

"I understand. Which room is mine?"

"End of the hall. On the left. Next to mine." Breaking our eye contact and shutting down his power was the response I needed but wasn't sure I wanted. My own magic had retreated into my chest when I had said no. The leftover air was frigid and empty.

"You will be close enough to call out should you need me. I will see you when you rise."

With that, he was in his office with the door closed before I could take in a shuddering breath. *Go to him and finish what you started.*

But even as my brain railed against me, I knew I wouldn't go to him.

I prayed it wasn't the wrong decision.

6

The bedroom was just as big as Sorin's which made me think all the bedrooms were master bedrooms. In place of his Asian design, the walls in this room were covered in a forest of birch trees. Tall, thin white trees against a grey sky created the feeling of being in winter woods. I imagined gathering firewood to bring back to a cabin and keep the cozy fire going. I loved the beautiful forest- pleased he had chosen this room for me.

My duffel bag lay on the end of the king-sized bed. It was nowhere near the size of the bed next door but it was big enough for just me. The comforter was the grey of that winter sky around me and made me ache for the eyes of the man that I had rejected. I carried the bag to the long white dresser that sat opposite the bed. A mirror rose from the top of the dresser to the ceiling. The reflection revealed a woman I still didn't recognize.

Since my turning, my black hair had become thicker and caught the light when I moved. The skin that I had battled with moisturizers and wrinkle cream was as flawless as it was pale. My lips were full and pink from the blood I had drunk earlier. By comparison, the biggest change had happened in my eyes. They had always been the color of sapphires and were often complimented. Now, as a vampire, they held the sparkle of the gem, ensuring that very few would be able to look away. I had ordered contacts to dull them. They should be arriving soon. I felt sad knowing I would have to hide the color of my eyes around humans but knew it was necessary to keep my secret hidden.

I unpacked my few belongings into the drawers, leaving a sleep shirt out. It was one that I used when I wanted to be comforted. The black tee hit my knees and proudly exclaimed "I will start working when my coffee does." I didn't need coffee anymore so the joke was no longer applicable but I liked the shirt.

My dress went into a closet that was the size of my kitchen. It looked so lonely in the space so I shut the door and set to my nightly routine. *Well, I guess it's my morning routine now.*

Once clad in the faithful sleep shirt, I gathered up my bathroom supplies then hesitated. I knew where the room was but didn't want to be so close to the office and risk seeing Sorin again. I couldn't bear whatever look was on his face thanks to me. I wrestled between the chance he'd be out of the office and the thought of sleeping without brushing my teeth.

The teeth won. I couldn't lay there for the day with blood still on my teeth. I doubted I needed to worry about cavities but hygiene is something you can't skip. I didn't want to find out the hard way that not brushing gives you nasty old blood breath.

I slowly opened the door and tiptoed down the hall, knowing full well I was being ridiculous. *I am a grown adult. Not to mention he has super hearing, dummy.* But the thought didn't stop me from ninja slinking down to the bathroom.

Once safely inside, I turned on the water and worked on cleaning the teeth I would have for centuries to come. Even if I didn't need to do it the ritual was calming. My hair was pulled into its usual ponytail so flying paste doesn't end up in my waves. The messy style and scrunchie made me feel a little human, which I liked. *I bet Sorin could say no to you now, toots. You are looking quite unsexy.*

"I am no Evelyn," I said to the mirror as I shut of the water and returned my items to the little zippered travel bag they had come from.

Once my mission was accomplished and I wasn't distracted, I looked around the space. The huge white tub in the center brought an involuntary smile. I could almost smell the rose shampoo that Sorin had washed my hair with. He had helped me wash the blood off my body. He had been so gentle, so unlike the man I had just seen in the hallway. I stepped up to it and ran my hand along the cool porcelain. I couldn't believe it had only been four nights since that bath–since the barn.

"Nope," I said to the empty room. "We are not going there tonight."

I opened the door, marveling at the fact I hadn't turned on any light and had done all of that with perfect night vision. The marveling didn't last long. It came to an abrupt stop when I faced the large oak door of the room that Sorin was currently in. I focused my hearing and knew that he was pacing. I could hear each step across the room and back. Without thinking, I was in front of that solid wood with my hand lying flat against it. The pacing stopped and I ran for my room.

With the door between the hallway and myself, I threw the bathroom bag across the room. It landed with a thud and fell to the ground. I threw myself onto the end of the bed and pulled my knees up to hug them. I was utterly aware of the fact that it was stupid to try and not make a noise or move. Every person in the house was a vampire with super hearing and the one I was actively trying to stay away from was the most powerful of them all. What did I think he would do? Run in and pounce on me?

That's what I want him to do isn't it?

But, I didn't. I knew what I wanted but not how to get there. I wanted to be sure of myself, to be confident and not second guessing every word he said or move he made. I wanted to figure out who I was. I wanted the confidence I had seen in Evelyn's eyes—to be so sure of my value. To be honest, I was having issues trusting people long before Sorin lied to me and Will tried to kill me. But I didn't know why or how to get over it. That was what I needed to do. Then, once that was all figured out—then I could offer my full self to him. I wanted that for me but also for him. Because that is what everyone deserves; to have someone give themselves over completely without reservations.

I wasn't afraid of Sorin loving me. I was afraid of him loving me, getting to know me and then falling out of love with me. That was why I had stayed away from men for so long—why I used humor and a rough exterior to keep everyone at arm's length. I had to learn why I believed I was not lovable.

And, until then I needed to keep things with Sorin outside of the bedroom. Because let's be honest—the man was utterly overwhelming.

A human probably wouldn't have heard the slight click of his office door opening or the light steps down the hall to my door but I had. Just like I heard him stand there for an eternity that was really half a minute. The invitation for him to come in was just behind my lips. My hesitation resulted in him entering his bedroom, shutting the door and climbing into a bed alone. I pictured him there and how easy it would be to join him but knew I was making the right choice.

When it is the right time, I will know it. Let's just hope it wouldn't be too late.

7

I snapped awake before I had realized that sleep had taken me away. The birch trees overhead confused me for a few seconds until it came rushing back that I was at Sorin's, the girls were safe with their dad and I needed to start learning how to be a vampire. Stretching my arms above me felt utterly human and very good. Every time I woke up and hadn't had a nightmare vision, I was grateful. This evening was no exception. The clock on my phone let me know that the sun was going down and it was safe to leave the room. Like all the bedrooms at the manor this one had no window but I had quickly made it a habit to be sure night was falling before I left a room.

My first move was to text the group chat that had Tom, Ellie, Olivia and myself. I let them know I was up. Olivia and Ellie both said "Good morning" with a moon next to it. Tom let me know that my mail was inside and that my contacts had arrived. I thanked everyone and promised to call before I went to bed and they went to school.

Without knowing what was on the agenda for the next twelve hours I wasn't sure what to wear. I figured I couldn't go wrong with active wear so yoga pants, a long t-shirt and sneakers were the winners. By the time my hair was brushed and braided I was acutely aware that I had to stop procrastinating and face whatever may come.

My travels to the kitchen were blissfully uneventful, giving me time to gather my thoughts and muster some confidence before opening the swing door. Tamela, Edwin, Naseem and Sorin were gathered around the island with glasses of blood in front of them. The discussion felt important so I thought about backing out of the room but was stopped by Tamela waving me in.

"Good evening, Kate." Edwin pulled out a stool next to him and poured me a glass. "We were all just discussing what we thought was a priority for your training.

Surprised, I looked at Sorin for clarity. I had thought that he was not sharing all of my powers with anyone and felt betrayed. He gave a slight shake of his head in something that looked like "later" so I dropped it.

Tamela picked up the explanation. "Each of us are trained in a different style of combat. We were discussing what style we thought you could pick up the quickest so that you would be able to defend yourself. The other styles you could be taught over time. I think grappling is the best for a woman needing to get out of a struggle. Edwin and Naseem want to train you to throw punches and kicks in the hopes that you could keep the attacker from ever grabbing you. Finally, I told everyone that we should let you choose."

In the silence, four sets of eyes locked onto me for an answer. Sipping on the blood I tried to think of what to say. I had never been taught any kind of self-defense and hadn't the slightest idea what the right choice was.

"Tamela, you're the only other woman here and I know you can handle yourself. What do you recommend?"

She sauntered up to me and threw an arm around my shoulders. "Good answer, Kate and I say you learn to get out of holds before you worry about anything else. I am sure you know how to kick someone in the balls but do you know how to free yourself from a grab?"

Man, was she a freaking badass.

"Let's do it, then." My response had Edwin and Naseem looking disappointed so I continued on. "Then you guys can teach me your stuff and I will be unstoppable."

They appeared the like the plan so I took my win and finished my drink just as Sorin came into my space. I smelled him before I saw him or felt his lips on the top of my head. His breath was warm in my ear. "Can I speak to you in the living room?" he whispered and left the kitchen.

Following behind him, the door shut off the sound of the bodyguards planning my training and I found the living room to be silent. Sorin was on the couch bringing on hot and clear memories of what had happened on the couch in his office so I chose to stand in front of him. His voice broke the silence. "I have not told them of all your powers. I would like to set aside time for training with them and time training with me. Lilias will be here tomorrow to work with your far-seeing but I can help with the rest. I do not have all of your powers but know how to control them. Have any more arisen since I saw you last?"

He was being so business-like it was a little hard to take in what he was saying. My mind was racing with thoughts like *Are you mad at me? Have you moved on? Why aren't you flirting with me?* But I reminded myself that was what I has asked for. He was not being cold, he was being respectful.

"No, nothing else. The healing, ghost thing and fire were the last to happen- you were there."

"I was. So, flying, far-seeing, visions of the future and past, psychic abilities, healing, communing with spirits and pyrokinesis. Did I miss anything?"

Just hearing them listed made me a little queasy and I took a seat next to him. "When you say it all out like that—it's just—I'm—I feel so out of control."

The business man demeanor faded and was replaced by the Sorin I had fallen for. His empathy shone in his eyes; he was feeling my fear, my uncertainty and my desire to be normal again. There was something comforting in a person you never have to try and explain your feelings to. Yes, it can feel intrusive but it was also exhausting to tell people what you were going through and I didn't need to waste that energy with Sorin. He really did know.

He laid his hand lightly on my cheek directing my eyes to his. "I know you are sick of hearing this but it does get better. Whether developing one power or ten, all new vampires feel out of control and scared. Everyone thinks that it would be delightful to suddenly be a preternatural creature with magic inside them but it is not—it is terrifying. And, you are dealing with all of this only days after being kidnapped, assaulted and having to defend yourself against a monster. You are the most extraordinary woman I have ever seen. You *will* get through this and master your new powers. In a year, this fear will be a memory."

It felt entirely natural for me to lean in to him and brush my lips against his. He was frozen in place as if he worried that any motion would send me running. Before anything else could happen, the doorbell ripped through the moment and he backed away just as the door was opening.

"Hello?" The chipper voice filled the house and was followed in by a woman I knew all too well. Evelyn entered the living room and Sorin stood- like the gentleman he was—to greet her.

"I am a little early," she chimed, extending her hand for Sorin to take and kiss.

Using the moment to really take her in, I realized that I had been wrong the day before and I actually could hate her more. The soft pink pantsuit fit her in a way to suggested it was made for her. The result was that her legs looked six feet long- which reached to her perfect, tiny waist—which turned into a chest that would fit in on Baywatch. Her hair fell in curls around her long neck and onto her exquisitely postured shoulders. Pink stiletto heels peeked out from under the slacks, suggesting she was about 5'10" without them—6'2" with them. It allowed for her and Sorin to be eye to eye.

I wondered how long it would take that gazelle to hit the ground if I kicked her in the back of the knee.

Sorin's voice brought me back. "Evelyn, I did not expect you this evening." I was pleased that his voice sounded dry and he wasn't using his power to make it crawl up your body like he sometimes did.

She faked an expression of embarrassment. "Oh, I am sorry. I meant to call and make an appointment but it must have slipped my mind. Shucks, am I ditzy sometimes. Can you fit me in?" The last part was said as she leaned into him and I heard the flirtation in the words.

"Of course," he responded. "Meet me in my office, please. You know the way."

"I do" she said looking over to me. I answered with a smile—refusing to allow her to see my jealousy.

Sorin turned to me when she was gone. "I am sorry but it is time for you to train with Tamela and I do have much to accomplish this evening. Can we meet in my office in two hours?"

"Sure," I answered, hoping it didn't sound as petulant to him as it did to me.

Honestly, though, it didn't matter if he heard it because me brushing past him and walking abruptly out of the room without a word certainly got the point across.

8

Training with Tamela started out pretty easy. She was trying to judge what I knew, how conditioned I was and if I had any natural talent. So, like I said- easy—since the answer was that I knew nothing, was completely unconditioned and had zero martial arts skills within me. Poor girl was probably second guessing her offer to train me!

She was the picture of natural fighting talent in the center of a workout room in Sorin's basement. The brown tank top and workout pants were only a shade darker than her skin, giving off the impression she was 100% muscle. Every inch of her was toned and vibrating with a promise that she would make you regret any move you made against her. The braid in her hair was wrapped into a bun but I knew it reached her low back. Her gaze ran up and down my body like she was deciding if the tool in front of her was the right one.

"Let's start simple and work up, shall we?"

I wholeheartedly agreed.

She pulled out some mitts and slid one on each hand. They were black flat circles and I was confused when she held them up. She held the pose for a second then realized I was clueless. "They're for punching, Kate."

"But I thought we were working on me getting out of holds?"

She dropped the mitts with a sigh. "I need to know what I am working with- your strength, speed and coordination. Think of fighting like a dance. You don't know the first step and I don't know if you have two left feet or one. Trust me, okay?"

The pads were back up at her shoulders so I assumed I didn't really have a choice but to trust her. The first punch was awkward and I was mortified that she had felt my wimpy hit.

"First problem, Kate. Hitting doesn't really come from the fist. The power comes from your core and your legs." She stood up, got into position and hit at the air. Each air punch looked like she was a snake striking out. Her speed did not hinder her grace or the overall effect of a deadly opponent.

"You make it look so easy," I quipped without being able to hide my disappointment in myself.

She stood up straight and I looked up to meet her face. "Kate, you can do this. Your problem is not skill or speed or ability, do you know what it is?"

I laughed "Not really."

"It's that," she responded not matching my humor at all. "It is your determination to hold back. You make jokes and walk around like you have failed before you have tried. I don't understand why someone who saves lives *for a living* doesn't believe she is strong."

It is a rare moment when I have no response but this was one of those. I don't know what hurt the most- the disappointment in her face or the fact that she knew me so well in such short time. I was having to come to terms with the fact that my social circle was now full of beings that had been on this planet for a very long time and could read people in seconds. It would be impossible to fool anyone who had experienced every type of human time and time again.

So why was I trying? What did I have to lose?

"Because I feel like a fake." It wasn't more than a whisper but she heard it and followed me down to the ground as I let my legs give way. We sat there facing each other with our legs splayed out and me fighting back tears. Anyone who walked in would look at us and think of two school friends telling secrets during recess while the others played. She chucked the mitts to the side, laying her hands on the mat to each side of her and waited for me to continue.

"Every day since as long as I can remember I move through my day waiting for someone to realize I have no idea what I'm doing and call me out. I'm scared every time I walk into the hospital. I'm scared of making a mistake or missing something that costs someone their life. I'm scared of being a mom and worried I'm actively messing up my kids. I think I'm actually relieved when they are with Tom because I know it is one day that I'm not screwing up or hurting them. I feel like I am faking my whole life. And, now I get to add on faking being human. Now, I get to worry about someone finding out that I didn't survive an attack that no one even knows about. So, I live each moment just trying to get through it without losing everything I have when someone realizes that I don't deserve it."

I didn't need to see the fresh drop of blood on the mat to know that I was crying. I had been fighting back tears since I woke up so it was bound to start eventually. I just never could have guessed it would be my sparing session with Tamela that would bring it on.

She took a deep breath and let it out. "I wish I knew the right thing to say to you; the thing that would make you see what we all see. But, Kate, you have to see it for yourself to really believe it. All I can tell you is that I think everyone feels like that sometimes. Maybe it isn't all the time like you just described but I know I have felt that way."

"Really?" I looked up to see her and gauge her honesty.

"Sure. I'm the head bodyguard for the master of the city. It is rare to see a female in this role, with men who answer to her. I spent a long time feeling like at any moment Sorin would look at me and say 'Why did I choose you? You are not worthy of this position.' But he never has and over time I came to see that I was the right person for this job. You know why? Because I am doing it for the right reason. I am here to protect Sorin because he is a good and just man. Without him, chaos would reign and vampires would be hurt. So, I think what you need to do is not focus on the minute to minute or the little decisions but focus on the reason you do these things. If your reasons are good, then you are worthy."

All I could do was nod. It was a lot to take in.

She grabbed the mitts and stood up. "For now, trying punching these mitts. I promise it is therapeutic."

I stood and mimicked the stance I had seen her use moments before. Tightening my core, I locked my sight on the mitt in her left hand and focused all my negative feelings into it. This time when my fist connected with the mitt, her arm jerked back in response. She smiled and whooped in celebration.

And, she was right—it felt great!

Thirty minutes later I realized that I was covered in sweat and breathing heavy but could have kept going for much longer. But I was getting bored and wanted to learn something else. I stood up straight, "So, vampires can sweat?"

"Yep," she answered while she removed the mitts and tossed them to the corner of the room. "Feeling tired?"

"Not at all," I responded. "This is awesome! I used to get winded walking up the stairs. Now, I could run a football field! What's next?"

"Well," she pondered. "I think we could try some grappling just to see where we are and what I need to teach you. Sound good?" She walked past me and I heard the small fridge open. I assumed they had blood down here too and was suddenly ready for a drink.

"Heck yeah!" I agreed and started to bounce up and down on my toes, punching at the air like I had seen so many boxers do in movies. I felt like I could go 20 rounds and not quit.

That confidence was gone the second I felt arms come from behind me and wrap around my torso- pinning my arms to my sides. The air was sucked out of my chest and I was pulled back into the barn. My mind was racing. The scent of old hay bales filled my nostrils and I felt the floor fall away. I could hear Monica's soft whimpering and the beat of Alex's slowly dying heart. The sharp edge of the knife was cold against my throat.

Will is back. He survived.

"Kate!"

Tamela's voice violently ripped me out of my flashback. I wasn't in the barn. The weights around the room reminded me that I was in Sorin's basement with Tamela and we had been training. Will was still dead. Monica was in the hospital.

Each fiber in my body was quivering with the memory of what had happened. *Had it only been a few nights ago?* In some ways it felt like a moment ago but also felt like a lifetime had passed.

"Kate, I'm so sorry. I wasn't thinking. I thought I would grab you when you weren't prepared and just see what you did. It was so insensitive. I didn't think about how it would affect you so soon after everything that happened. Are you okay?"

It was clear in her expression that she felt horrible and my instinct was to take away that hurt. I opened my mouth to speak but nothing came out. It was like my brain couldn't form words yet, like it needed to reboot. My mouth opened and shut a few times before sound emerged.

"I'm okay." That was the best she was getting because the next thing I knew the world was black.

9

Sounds and sunlight filled the little park by my house. We'd walked there a hundred times before today. Pittsburgh rarely had sunny days and it was even rarer to enjoy one in the fall or winter time. I'd forgotten so quickly what the sun looked like and felt like on my skin. It was the smell I had missed the most- the smell of warmth. That familiar smell was mixed with drying autumn leaves and a nearby fireplace. Someone not too far from me had apple cider and the aroma revealed there was a little bourbon in it. Guess they needed a little daytime drink. I could hear Olivia and Ellie playing- their feet bumping against the soccer ball and their squeals of delight.

Wait. Why am I outside?

I was halfway to the trees for coverage when my skin started to react. It was like hot irons running up and down the exposed flesh of my arms and face. I had to get to the shade and figure out what to do next. I couldn't remember getting here or why I would come to the park in the daytime. All I knew is that if anyone saw me, I was screwed. No one could know- especially not the kids.

How long do I have until I burn?

The answer was that I didn't have long. I knew that when smoke started to rise off my forearm. The trees were getting closer but I still needed to find a shed or a place to hide until nightfall. I looked around to see that I was drawing attention. Several adults had stopped talking or pushing kids on swings to stare at me. I was seconds away from being the next front-page story.

One man raised his finger in my direction and was talking to the woman next to him. Concern covered his face. I didn't know what I looked like but I was sure I wasn't masking my distress very well. The smoke was thick now–rolling off of both arms and up into my face. It was blocking my vision and felt like walking through a fog that was only around me. The burning on my skin was becoming agonizing. I was having trouble thinking through the pain and fought the urge to drop to the ground and let the flames take me.

Staggering, I reached out and felt my palm hit the bark on the tree trunk. At least I could get out of the sun and take a minute to plan my next move. But that relief was washed away when the pain in my hand ripped out of my skin and the flames started.

The screaming was still in my ears when I opened my eyes to see Sorin above me. He was talking but I couldn't hear him. Seconds went by before the sounds from my vision were replaced by his voice. "-let me know you are okay."

"I'm okay." I repeated the same phrase for him that I had uttered to Tamela, hoping I wasn't going to black out again. Sorin's face retreated from my line of sight so I could see the ceiling in the gym and take notice of a spare lightbulb. It seemed so out of place in the opulence of the rest of the manor. The silliness of the thought in the midst of everything that was happening let me know that my brain seemed to be returning to normal.

Sitting up brought on a quick moment of dizziness but then my usual sharp focus returned and it appeared I was actually okay instead of just saying it. Tamela slid her arms under one of mine and Sorin matched her on the other side. They lifted me gently to my feet, maintaining their hold in case I passed out again. When it was clear that my legs were going to continue to hold me, the two let go.

"Tell me what happened," Sorin demanded.

Tamela answered. "I grabbed her from behind to see how she would respond. I thought it would give me an idea of what I needed to teach her and what she knew instinctually. I have done it to so many trainees before. When she froze, I knew something was wrong. That's when it hit me that she had just been abducted and it was too soon to try something like that. Before I could really assess the situation, she fainted."

The breath that Sorin let out was a clear indicator that he was angry. I wanted to come to her defense but was still wobbly and unsure what to say. The memory of the barn was all mixed up with the vision I had while I was out. I didn't know if I saw the park because I blacked out or blacked out because the vision was coming on. Up til that point the visions had always happened while I slept during the day. This was the first nighttime one. *What did it mean?*

I stopped my line of thinking to focus on what Sorin was saying to Tamela.

"I asked you to help her learn to fight, not re-traumatize her."

"I know, my lord. I'm sorry. It was a bad call," she sounded so different. Like a soldier talking to a commander, not the girl I had been opening up to just moments ago.

"You're right, it was a bad call. I trusted you to use your judgement and you acted impulsively. You should have known better than anyone."

"Whoa," I found my voice. "She didn't know. She wasn't there. How could she have known that he grabbed me like that? How could she have known it would make me flashback?"

His eyes were filled with anger. Tamela's gaze remained on the ground. Both of them hadn't expected me to speak. I thought I would have to keep going or continue in the thick silence but Tamela spoke.

"Because I have been a victim and I know what it's like. I should have put myself in your shoes but instead I tried to rush you into learning to fight. I was so intent on making you a warrior that I didn't worry about giving you time to heal."

With that she straightened her posture, turned and walked out of the room. I stared at her back with no idea how to respond. I figured it was something we would have to talk about later but didn't feel like that was the time.

Her departure left me alone with Sorin. His grey eyes were brighter than usual but didn't have the swirling energy that I had seen in other moments- more heated moments. He was holding something back and I wasn't sure I wanted to know what.

"Why don't you shower and take some time to rest? We can work on your powers in an hour or so, if you feel up to it."

"Sorin?"

"Yes," he responded shortly.

"I think I had a vision while I was out." It wasn't the best way to phrase it but I was too overwhelmed to worry about how I came across.

His left eyebrow raised in an arch that I was familiar with and told me I had his attention. I was happy to see the anger disappear in his eyes but didn't like the worry I now saw. "Tell me."

So, I did. I told him exactly what I'd seen and felt- from the second my eyes closed to the sounds in my ear when I awoke. I explained where the park was and how I knew that my daughters had been there. He hung on every word and stayed quiet until I finished.

"I think–given your history–that we should take this seriously as a vision of the possible future. Do you know why you were in the park during the day? Any reason why you'd risk being exposed?"

"No clue," I answered. "I think they were just playing soccer. There was no obvious reason for me to be there and I had no way of knowing how I got there. I didn't see Tom or Sarah. Just other parents."

He blinked several times like he was trying to clear his thoughts. Running his hands through his hair he let out a long sigh. "Let's just keep this to us and in the back of our minds until we know why you saw it. In the meantime, go shower and I will meet you in my office. I want to do some research before our meeting."

It was the word "meeting" that reminded me of the one he had just left; the one with perfect Evelyn. "How did the last one go?"

He waved his hand in the air in a gesture of dismissal. "Usual business, nothing exciting."

I hoped the relief didn't show on my face but even I noticed the relaxing of all my muscles with those few words. I don't know what made me do it but I closed the distance between us and slid my arms around his chest, laying my head on his sternum and hugging him. He wrapped his arms around me and rested his chin on my head. "I don't like not knowing what is happening and like even less that it is happening to you. I promise we will figure it out, *regina mea*. I won't stop until I know how to harness your powers and know that you are safe."

"Thank you," I whispered. "I believe you."

10

An hour later, I faced my reflection in the bedroom mirror. The bed behind the mirror image was inviting me to curl up and avoid everything in my life. Freshly brushed, damp hair laid on the back of my royal blue tank top and bare feet peaked out from under the matching peasant skirt. Curling my toes under, I found a slight comfort in the soft light grey rug below my feet. It was soft, clean and simple- all the things that my existence did not feel like at the moment. I yearned for the days when juice spilled on a carpet was the worst thing that could happen in a 24-hour period. But alas, those days were long gone and never to return. So, I gathered some courage and started the journey to an office I knew intimately.

Flames crackled in the fireplace and I knew before looking up that Sorin would be sitting on the long green couch with an antique coffee table in front of him. This time the surface was not home to crime scene photos but a scattering of ordinary paperwork. I found relief in that, knowing that the photos were put away because the bad guy was gone.

Snapping out of whatever thought train he was riding, Sorin smiled and waved me in. "You look much better."

"It's the shower. That water pressure—absolutely therapeutic." I had expected to hear the slapping of my bare feet on the hard wood as I crossed the room but it was silent. It made me wonder if I was now moving in that same graceful, dancer-like way that the other vampires did, almost weightless.

Standing to greet me, he extended his hand and I laid mine on his. The kiss on my back of my hand was chaste and quick, like a reflex more than an invitation. It was such an old custom but I loved the chivalry of it. However, if we are being honest, I was sad that he was controlling himself so well around me. As much as I wanted time to breath and process, I didn't want him to become bored and immune to me either.

Vampire or not—emotions and desires are damn complicated.

"Please," he waved to the spot next to him. "Come sit."

I did, allowing our thighs to touch as we both sat. Looking over the papers on the table before us, I was pretty sure it was all business related. There was a day planner that was full of appointments and scribbled to-do lists, a mix of Excel spreadsheets with figures larger than I'd ever worked with and a variety of legalese and contracts.

Sorin must have seen the confusion on my face. "Until I have a new assistant, I want to try and stay on top of things."

The mention of his previous assistant brought on a sudden awkwardness that neither of us wanted to address. Sorin started to gather up all the paper and arrange it into a stack which he took to his desk and deposited before returning to me. He faced me when he sat and laid his hand on my thigh. "How do you feel?"

"Fine," I said. "Good as new."

"Well then, I am pleased to hear it. Would you like to try a lesson?"

I wasn't really sure what I was agreeing to but I knew I was willing to do anything that would get my focus off of his warm skin on my thin skirt. "Better now than never. What do I need to do?"

"Start by telling me what you know about your magic? For instance, how do you feel when you are using your abilities? Can you bring them on at will?"

"Rhys told me that some powers are like breathing and others are like punching. When I have visions or information comes to me or I fly—it's like breathing. When I—with Will—when I brought fire—it was a punch. Same when I healed Alex. It came out of me like I was hitting them. Does that sound dumb?"

"No," he leaned back, sliding his hand off my leg. "I like the way he explained it. But I would like to explain it a little differently and hope I do not confuse you. Do you know music? Read it or play an instrument?"

"I did in high school and college–the flute. And, yes I read music."

"Power is like a frequency. You can control the volume, the base, the treble—once trained. When not actively using it, magic is at a frequency you can just barely sense but no one else will notice. When needed–you turn it up."

"You lost me," I said.

He leaned into me. "Have you ever tried to cry when you weren't sad? Conjure up tears with a thought."

"Yes."

"It is like that. Pulling up something inside of you that is not tangible but it's there."

I chuckled. "Okay maybe instead of trying to explain it you could teach me."

"Close your eyes."

I laughed again. "Why?"

"Just close them and listen to what I say. Try to let go and just hear me."

I let my eyelids drop while I laid back against the couch, seeing no reason to resist when I was the one asking him to teach me. After all, he was my best shot at not vamping out in front of my kids or at work every time I pulled out an IV and saw blood. The subsequent silence felt like minutes but was likely only a few seconds. I focused my hearing on all the sounds- the crackling fire, the creak of a step somewhere else in the manor and a light fall breeze on the other side of the window. A frog ribbited just beyond the rustling leaves just before Sorin softly laid a finger on inside of my left wrist. Before he would have found a pulse but now there was none. The pressure laid there for several seconds and began a slow trail up towards my shoulder. Each centimeter took a millennium and the cells in my arm reached to meet his.

"As my journey up your limb continues, I want you to picture your flesh gathering and following it up- like the skin is congealing into one as my finger passes."

So, I did. I imagined his touch was magnetic and I was made of a soft metal. As his finger slid up—my metallic essence was grabbed and pulled. The slight pressure of this finger was exhilarating, like his miniscule touch forced my electrical impulses to follow his commands. A tingling arose in my core as if my trunk had fallen asleep while I was focused on my extremities.

"Now, imagine your energy is passing my finger and will meet my touch when it reaches your shoulder."

I did what he said and pictured the gathering sensation in my arm sped past his touch to my shoulder to await him. With this thought, the tingling in the center of my body spread out to fill my neck, face, each arm and down. My body was a mass of live wires. I felt euphoric and couldn't tell anymore where his finger rested.

"Open your eyes."

The sight that met my rising lids was the office but different— because I was taller than before. *I'm floating.*

Recognizing that I was now several feet off the couch brought all that tingling to a sudden stop. Sorin caught my falling body and pulled me into him. My face halted an inch from his.

"Now," he said. "We try again with your eyes open so you can control the rise and fall."

Being in his arms and within kissing distance made it almost impossible to think clearly so I slid backwards to sit in the same spot I had begun the exercise. I was proud of myself for willing my muscles to escape his embrace but my eyes were still locked with his. Neither of us glanced away as his finger returned to my wrist and start its long journey up my arm again. I repeated the imaginary pull of my flesh to follow his trail, feeling the familiar electrical sensation in my abdomen return. Those grey irises started to ripple like they were made of sparkling, diamond-filled water and someone had thrown a stone into them. I knew once the swirling began that I wasn't strong enough to resist what was coming.

Rising to my knees on the couch the live wires under my skin spread their heat up and down my torso. Sorin mimicked my action, ending on his knees, continuing his finger up my arm and staring into my eyes. Our lips met without a thought and he wrapped each of his hands around my upper arms. I could feel my electricity reach out to his hands like his flesh was conducting it. Our kiss rose from innocent to passionate as the pressure of my knees on the couch sank away from my kneeling. Sorin's hands slid from my arms, around my back to embraced me. He wasn't holding onto me because I was keeping him in the air. I somehow knew that my power had entered him; his arms encircled me only because he needed to feel me. His legs relaxed and mine wrapped around his hips to feel him pressed against me. Slowly, our entangled bodies began to spin.

I never wanted to stop kissing this man but recognized that we needed to return to the Earth safely. I gingerly pulled back from the kiss and placed a hand on each side of his face, holding his gaze to maintain my concentration. Without needing to hear from him how to lower us down, I instinctually imagined the "pulling up" sensation in my body reversing to "pull down." Seconds later, my knees gently returned to the evergreen upholstery.

"Can you fly?" My voice was just above a whisper.

Sorin smiled "Not until this evening and perhaps only when I am with you. I am very excited to see what else we can share between the two of us."

The knock at the door interrupted any chance of us continuing to work on powers. And, the face that popped into the room assured the mood was destroyed for anything else.

"So sorry to interrupt," Evelyn's overly sweet voice chirped. "I left my bag."

Sorin dropped his arms and stood to greet her. I was always so impressed when a man was good-mannered, especially when a woman came into the room. However, this evening—with this woman—I was not thrilled by Sorin's chivalry. He met her in front of his desk as she sauntered into the room.

I tried to leave the couch in the same flawless way that Sorin did but I was too annoyed to focus on grace. Looking around I saw a designer bag resting in one of the merlot chairs and decided I would need to throw the furniture away now—it was ruined for good. Evelyn was laying her hand against her sternum in an "oh, I'm so silly" gesture that was obviously a lie. I'd bet money she didn't make a move without calculating every possibility and had probably never forgotten a thing in her life–or afterlife. She'd left the purse for a reason. From what I saw in her eyes when they flicked to me, I'd guess her plans hadn't involved me being in the room.

I was tickled pink to have messed up her perfect moment.

I stepped up to Sorin's side in a gesture that told her I was more than willing to partake in this particular battle. The fact that I didn't grab his arm or pee a circle around him was a testament to how badly I didn't want to sink to her level. But I'd make it clear that I was onto her game and had no intentions of backing down.

She feigned a large glance around the room to find the bag like she didn't know exactly where she'd left it and giggled when her eyes landed on it. Moving to the chair, she bent to retrieve her prize. Was she tall? Yes. But did she need to make such a dramatic bend to get the purse? Nope.

It had the intended effect. The outfit clung in all the right places, accentuating curves and adding a layer of fluidity to the motion. She glanced back before standing up but not at him, at me.

Game on, Evelyn.

Returning to us in that same fluid way she reached her hand out. Sorin took it as we all knew he would and brought it to his mouth. I used that second to meet her stare and hoped my eyes showed every word I was thinking. Both of us returned to our lovely selves when Sorin's head rose to look at the women in front and beside him.

When she turned to make her way out of the office, I was preparing to pat myself on the back for holding my own with a worthy adversary.

"Oh," she chimed without looking back. "Sorin, when you come to dinner make sure to wear the blue suit. It is absolutely my favorite."

And just like that—the air was sucked out of my lungs.

11

"What dinner?" I tried desperately to sound nonchalant. Women that got jealous, clingy, controlling and/or obsessed with their man we're horrible. I never understood why anyone thought it was okay to insist that their partner never go anywhere with anyone but them or went through their phones and emails. If you'd told me that I'd ever have pressed someone to explain what their plans were with another adult, I'd have called you a liar—until tonight. I told myself that it wasn't because I was controlling or had really low self-esteem but that I didn't trust Evelyn. I tried to make myself believe that I was just being curious. Especially because the man in question can read emotion and can experience my feelings.

"You're upset."

Shit. Serves you right, Kate. Trying to fake it with a freaking vampire empath.

"Not upset just curious."

"Katherine, I can feel the jealousy and anger. So, let's try again. Why are you upset?"

Dropping down into the same chair that'd just been home to a Prada bag, I focused on the fire. "I don't like her. She wants you all to herself."

Silence.

I looked back but his face gave away nothing so I kept going. "Say something."

"She has asked me to attend a charity dinner she is hosting in her home. It is nothing more. As Lord, these are the kinds of things I am asked to do."

Yep, he's annoyed. I've pushed it too far.

"You confuse me, Katherine. You are hot and then cold. You push me away and pull me in—only to push me away again. You said you need time to understand what we have and I would never not respect your needs. But what we have feels like finding a piece of me that I was missing. It feels more natural than feeding or sleeping. Do you not feel the same?"

Fear and submission played tug of war inside of me. I knew he was right. Us together felt like drinking water when you're thirsty—the answer to a question I'd been asking my whole life. So, what was I scared of? What did I need to figure out?

"I just need to be sure."

"Sure of what?" he pressed. "Sure of me?"

"I want to trust you, I do."

With that one sentence his face changed. The desperation and transparency that were there for a moment vanished under a blanket of stoicism. The unreadable expression told me everything I needed to know—I'd hurt him.

"I see," he responded. I wanted to take it back but it was too late. He had heard that I didn't trust him and there was no such thing as erasing moments. I stood and took a step towards him, my arm outstretched but he didn't take it.

"Sorin, I—what I meant was"

He stopped me mid-sentence. "Please don't apologize. Honesty is valuable and you gave it to me. No need to regret. You're right. I lied to you at our first meeting, sent you to find a crazed killer, allowed a maniac to be in my home- even befriend you and was unable to destroy him when he had you in that loft. He was at the home your children sleep in. How could you trust me?"

"Sorin, please."

"Katherine, I am sorry. I did not know you or what you would mean to me. If you never trust me, I will understand why."

I stayed silent, unsure of what to say.

"I think we have accomplished much this night and already expected too much of you. Get some rest. I will be in my room should you need me. Please take all the time you need."

In a blur, he was gone from the room and I was standing alone. *Do I follow him?*

No! You've done enough.

Walking the hallway distance with my head down I felt like I was a kid who had been sent to their room without dinner for misbehaving. That big bed amongst the birch trees seemed impossibly empty and sad. I didn't want to be in this bed. I wanted to be in his bed.

So why aren't you?

"Ahh!" I screamed into the empty room when my door was closed. Venting my overwhelming emotions, I punched the pillow on my bed over and over until I couldn't anymore.

The truth was I didn't know what I was thinking or feeling or what to do. Chances were that I'd just done some real damage. Sorin had looked genuinely destroyed and it was me doing the destroying.

But you're just being honest. That's okay! Stop apologizing. Hiding your feelings and your truth is why your relationships fail. You try to be someone else to please everyone around you but it just ends in you utterly miserable, choosing to be yourself and them not loving the real you.

And there it was. My trust issues had nothing to do with Sorin's deception on my first night or that fact that none of us knew that Will was a sociopath or the flirty, perfect Evelyn or even my lover's decision to use me as bait to lure in my attacker. It was simple—I knew I needed to be myself from the beginning so that Sorin could fall for the real me and our relationship could last an eternity. But deep down, I didn't believe Sorin would love me exactly as I am so I held back—like I always did. When he started to push deeper or I felt myself opening up—I freaked and retreated like usual.

When Tom and I divorced, I swore I would work on myself, get some therapy and heal from all my past shit before getting into any more relationships. But I'd been so busy raising kids and at the hospital that I'd put all that "self-care and working on me" on the back burner. Then as the years went by, I figured I would just never fall in love again.

Oh, I'd wanted to! I'd dreamt about it alone in bed when the kids were sleeping. I'd watched all the Hallmark movies and wished the perfect man would waltz into my life with some "meet-cute" moment. True I'd envisioned bumping into him and spilling my peppermint latte on him or finding out our kids went to the same ice-skating camp when we inadvertently switched their backpacks at pick-up. In the fantasy, I'd been witty and charmingly cute and utterly confident- not afraid to be myself.

And yes, Sorin walking into the Christmas light-covered grove and handing me blood when I was dressed in Rhys's sweatpants wasn't too far off from those silly romance movies.

The only thing is in my fantasies I hadn't felt any fear or uncertainty at all. And, in my fantasies I was safe because I really believed it would never happen for me.

But, then it did. And contrary to my fantasies, reality had been hard. I hadn't been sure of myself. I was drowning in fear. I questioned every word I said and gesture I made. I wanted to run far and fast to a place where I never put myself out there and allowed anyone to love me. Why?

Well, boys and girls because then no one can reject the real you and tell you that you're not lovable.

So, what was I going to do? I had a couple options. I could go into Sorin's room and tell him everything I was thinking and allow him to choose. Or, I could continue to push him away, finish my time here, go home, let Evelyn win him back and be safe from hurt but also not possibly have the love of a lifetime.

Behind door number one was the chance that he would love me, understand all of my insecurities, be patient with me as I worked it all out, listen to my stories and painful memories so he could truly know me and we could spend eternity healing each other. But he could also push me to points that I was uncomfortable and would have to be honest and grow. We could fight. We could break up. I could have my heart broken. He could realize I had way too much baggage to carry until the end of time.

Behind door number two was the definite extensive time period it would take to get over him and most likely an eternity of wondering if I should have taken door number one. I could run into him at vampire functions and see him with other women over the decades and centuries. I would likely have to move away from Pittsburgh when the girls were grown so I could avoid him altogether—but would Rhys go with me? Could I leave my girls? But, upside—I would save myself from having to be exposed and vulnerable when I let Sorin into all the dark parts of my soul.

"Fuck you, Hallmark," I said to the empty room. "I never see this in the movies. Nope. They just get over all their issues when someone gives them the right ornament and snow falls and they happen to be at the same town square on Christmas Eve!"

But I wasn't going to get that kind of luck. I wasn't a Christmas movie—I was a Halloween one—the kind you see on HBO at night.

Creatures of the night don't get magical, happy endings.

But the truth was I wanted that—the storybook romance for the horror movie monster.

12

I must have fallen asleep without even realizing. The transition from waking to sleep to waking was getting less sudden and becoming more seamless. Rhys had once told me that some older vampires could stay awake in the daytime if they needed to. I mentally added to the to-do list in my mind to ask an older vamp about how they controlled the "on and off" part of their existence. I didn't want to keep falling into a coma every time morning arrived.

The texts on my phone reminded me that I was supposed to call the girls before I fell asleep each dawn. I Facetimed the oldest and both faces were on the screen when she answered.

"Mom!" Ellie yelled. "You didn't call us before school. You promised."

"I know, kiddo. I suck. I am so so sorry. I basically passed out." *Not a lie.*

"Everyone was worried. What if you were back in the hospital?"

"You are totally right. This was totally my bad. I am going to set an alarm to remind me."

This must have appeased them because they stopped chastising me and started to relay their days to me. Addison, a friend of Olivia's, had joined the girls' soccer team. Apparently, she had become close to the sisters and Tom had agreed to a sleep-over at his house. They were obviously excited enough to have already planned the snacks, movies, sleeping arrangements and topics of discussion because they honored me with the details of each. Half an hour later they informed me that it was time to run to the store with their dad for the necessary rations and made me swear to call the next morning- which I did.

When their faces disappeared from the screen, I felt a brief moment of grief. I was never going to see them play outdoors or have sleepovers or pick them up at school again. That was 100% for Tom now. It was sad but true. But I reminded myself, that had been the cost of them not attending my funeral and it felt like a small price to pay.

Being a vampire and "snapping on and off" means that when you awake for the evening it's like whatever was happening when you fell asleep was two minutes ago. Unless I have one of my visions, I feel like I blinked and it went from day to night. Which means- that night- my internal turmoil over Sorin was feeling nice and fresh.

Another point in the "con" list for vampirism, if you're keeping track.

Honestly though, I was so mentally exhausted from my breakthroughs the previous night that I truly didn't have it in me to keep agonizing. Instead, I decided to take a hot shower, get dressed and find some blood. Whatever was going to happen that night was going to need clean hair and a full stomach. Any requirements above those would have to be handled as they arose.

As a result of my decisiveness, an hour later I walked into the solarium with freshly blow-dried locks, a glass of blood and no care in the world. Looking out into the backyard was surreal; this room was so rarely empty. I took the opportunity to really enjoy the estate that I was currently a guest in. The walls seemed like they were aching to spill their secrets—vibrations were in the floor and the drywall. I imagined all the gatherings in this space, the vampires who came on their first night and the ones who had come a hundred times. Holding the glass in my left hand, the fingertips on my right played over the lightly textured walls, the smooth bar top and the cool glass of each convex windowpane. My bare feet enjoyed the aged floor and wondered how many steps had been taken on the wood over the years. I pictured the dancing—ranging from slow to lively as the decades fell to time. How many had found refuge here since Sorin had taken ownership?

Bodies materialized around me. I could see them but not completely. Most of them were on the softer edge of solid. Some of them were almost ghostlike; just apparitions. The most solid of them were the ones I examined first. Their clothes were recognizable having come from recent time periods; go-go boots were besides bell bottoms which mixed with leg warmers which mingled with shoulder-padded jackets. Sounds emanated from moving mouths and the volume of the music from the surround sound speakers started faint then rose to join the conversations. The music was jumbled; as if someone had turned on three different songs at once. Bodies faded in and out—flapper dresses turned into cocktail dresses and then back to Victorian gowns. Faces of the party goers transformed as they changed and shifted. My brain tried to rationalize what it was seeing. It was like I had one of those flip books in front of me and someone was letting the pages fall through their grasp to replace the picture on each page with another.

A strong voice—thick with accent—overtook the symphony of sounds.

"Focus on one," it lovingly demanded. "Just pick a face."

The feminine command was motherly and I held onto it for clarity. The man in the corner, at the end of the bar was not old enough to drink alcohol but the blood in the glass told me that he would never look older. I knew from the pressed uniform that he was a soldier but my years of blowing off history classes meant I could not pin down a time period or war. Somehow, I knew his name was Daniel and that he was 18 when he lay dying on a battlefield, surrounded by dark trees and thinking of his mother crying into her sewing when her son never came home. A beautiful girl with red curls piled high on her head had come from the trees and carried him to a log cabin somewhere. It was a blur because he had passed in and out of consciousness as she hurried him through the forest. When he finally regained full awareness, her blood had already been in his stomach and his turning was quickly approaching. I had a moment to wonder if he regretted it or what he had seen during his change when a sight stopped my train of thought. The red-haired girl came from the periphery of my vision to join him at the bar. Her hair was no longer up but cascaded down her back and he lit up with the sight of her. She took the glass from his hand, whispered in this ear, gulped down the remaining blood and they left together to find a place in the manor where they could be free from prying eyes and kiss for the thousandth time. I knew without question that they were still together and living somewhere in the Midwest.

"Extraordinary," the motherly voice cut in and wiped the room clean of music, sounds, visions and smells. Reality returned so I could turn to witness the woman belonging to the guidance. Her white hair fell in waves, swept to the left side and down to touch her hips. The dark eyebrows were a striking contrast to the ivory strands and rose high above brown eyes. The next thing I noticed after that amazing hair and those wise eyes were her feet—bare like mine. She stood in the doorway of the solarium with eyes locked on me. She arms were crossed in front of her, her stance wide and planted and her head just off to the side like she was appraising a piece of art.

"You saw the past—but not as a vision really—you really saw them. They live so they are not ghosts, per say. But you saw them as they were; the energy imprint they left behind. Tell me- what do you know of them? Quickly- without thinking or filtering."

"He is Daniel. He was supposed to die in battle but she saved him. She had seen so many die before that boy and not cared. But him—he was different. She had to save him—risk exposure for him. Her name is Kelly. They live out west somewhere—it's like a ranch—and they are still in love."

I couldn't believe the words coming out of my mouth but they were out and she seemed intrigued. She looked at me like I was the most interesting thing she'd ever seen. I had so many questions to ask her like *Who are you? What's your name? Did you see what I saw? Did I really see what I saw? How old were you when you were turned? You're a vampire, right?*

But there was no time for an interview because she started up again. "When he said you could far-see I did not believe him. It is too rare and it does not come to a newborn. But here you are." Her voice was like something straight from a fairytale. I had heard it faintly in Rhys but this was so rich. You could almost smell the Scottish air every time a word spilled from her lips. "You've seen the past, drawn information from it and come back. How is this possible?"

"You tell me. I don't even know who you are, let alone how you know what I saw." The usual instinct to shut down and use sarcasm to protect myself was rearing its ugly head.

"Oh my," she laughed and it tinkled in the room like a bell. A joyous feeling overwhelmed me with that laugh. I was drawn back to a childhood memory of swearing I heard Santa's sleighbells on the rooftop of my home one Christmas Eve night. The utter belief of holiday magic had filled my young days for years to follow. Her voice felt the same way. "What a first impression I've made."

I loved her, embarrassing but true. Despite my experience with previous vampires in this home I instantly adored the woman before me. She felt like what I think a mother should feel like. I was 100% certain she would have made me chicken noodle soup when I was sick or French braided my hair if I asked.

"I believe Sorin has told you about me, dear. I am Lilias. I've come to teach you to travel around the world without ever leaving your room. That is, if you truly possess such power. Shall we begin?"

"Let's do this." I sassed back and knew we were in for a wild ride together.

13

Lilias turned, retreated into the living room and I dutifully followed. It gave me a second to appraise her. That magnificent hair swayed with the rhythm of her steps. I've told you how graceful Sorin moves; like a ballet dancer. Lilias was somehow even more delicate in her movements. She made me think of fairies, fliting through a green, whimsical forest to escape the eyes of village children. You could almost see the magical swirl around her. For the hundredth time since I made the choice to live in darkness, I asked myself if I was really experiencing this or just lost in a long dream.

"It is not a dream, Kate." That revelation was followed by her tinkling laugh.

"You read minds," I accused.

"As do you," she responded.

In the living room she made a sweeping gesture towards the recliner and I obliged by sitting into its cool leather. Effortlessly, she pulled the other one to face me and sat. Meeting her eyes, I tried to understand the curiosity I read there. Somehow, I knew without question that she had been around for a very long time. She felt older than anything else

I'd ever been near—older than Sorin—yet she looked utterly interested in me.

"What are we doing?"

She rested her hands on my knees and leaned in. "*We* are not doing anything, child. *You* are going to show me that you can far-see, as Sorin reports."

"Fine," I conceded. It was true that I was completely enamored with this woman but I was also annoyed by her insistence that I couldn't leave my body. *What a stupid thing to lie about.*

"Tell me about the first time you did it."

She was still staring at me and I didn't like how close her face was but it also didn't seem like she would back down so I figured I should just do what she asked.

"I was in my bed," my face started to flush. I suddenly remembered the first time and was embarrassed to know what I was about to divulge to this stranger. I decided to just do it quickly and get it over with. "I was thinking of Sorin, imagining his bedroom and bed and how he would look. I used to think if you imagined something vividly enough right before sleep then you would dream about it. That's what I was trying to do. Then, I imagined standing in his bedroom at the foot of his bed."

"Had you been in his bedroom?"

My blush deepened. "Why?"

"Don't be offended," she answered quickly. "I care not if you have shared a bed with him. I am trying to establish if you knew what it would look like or if you travelled there without truly knowing."

"I had been in his room but not in his bed," I gulped. "Yet."

She waved her hand like she was shooing away a fly. "Proceed with the tale."

"I was in my bed, in my house. I was thinking of him and imagining him. Then I was standing in his room. I thought it was my imagination and then he reacted. He looked up from the book he was reading. He spoke like I was there. He couldn't see me but he knew I was there. When he called me, the ringing phone brought me out."

"Yes," she interrupted. "He told me you were able to describe his room, what he was doing and wearing—or not wearing—and that he felt you."

I felt no need to respond. I was there and didn't need her to tell me.

"And the next time—you were in danger."

Impulsively I drew back in a physical representation of my brain trying to avoid the memories. "Yes," I responded, coldly. I remember my desperate attempt to reach Sorin after Will had kidnapped me. "I was in danger. But it didn't work or last long enough. We all almost died. What good is this power if no one can hear me or see me?"

"Kate," she reached out a hand to rest on my cheek. "I mean you no harm. If I do my job well, then you will be able to speak to anyone—anywhere in the world—and they will see you. Please believe in my teaching."

I reached up to meet her hand, wrapped mine around it and pulled it off my skin. "Let's do this, then. I don't ever want to be that vulnerable again."

"Close your eyes," she whispered and I did. "The man you reached for that night is somewhere in this vast residence. Try to focus on him as it is more important that you learn to reach a certain person as opposed to reaching a specific place."

That old familiar fear was resting at the edges of my brain. She was sending me to find Sorin but I didn't know if I was ready to see him or if he would even want to see me. I'd been cruel last night. If I'd been on the receiving end of my issues as many times as Sorin had dealt with them, I think I'd have run for the hills. Maybe I'd find him only to realize he was finally over my brand of crazy.

Lilias sighed. "Your thoughts are too chaotic. Try to calm yourself and just focus on the image of him in your mind. Forget all the complicated feelings. Just picture him in your mind's eye and imagine standing in front of him."

How easily I see him in my head. Starting with the part of him I was most afraid to live without—I conjured the image of his eyes. They blinked and sparkled in the darkness of my imagination. Next, his face grew around the eyes and his long hair fell to each side of a smile that held a hint of mischief. *Oh God, his smile—please tell me I didn't take that smile away forever.*

I saw his shoulders emerge under the smile, just barely brushed by the bluish-black hair. Those shoulders had taken on the weight of me when the arms below them carried me up the stairs. The hands at the end of those arms had washed my hair in a bath of dried blood. They'd only ever protected me, touched me with love and never hurt me. The chest between the arms had taken blows for me, let me rest on it and carried the heart that wanted me. The legs had carried the man who carried me.

The air around the man wavered and came into focus so I could start to remember the room. It wasn't the office we'd collided in or the bedroom we'd danced in or the grove we'd met in -but a simple, cold garage we'd said goodbye in. Resting against the black BMW, Sorin's arms were crossed and his gaze was up. He was close enough to smell and I knew I would never be sick of that scent.

Without looking down he spoke, "You've found me but you've more to do. Don't lose focus. Hold onto the thought of me but pull yourself into the room—try to touch me."

In an uncharacteristic moment, I didn't even think of arguing or questioning him. Reaching out my arm to him, I tried to touch the man but simply passed through him.

"Don't reach out here with your physical body. Plant your feet onto the ground there and reach out in your mind," Lilias' voice broke through.

I re-centered my focus before I could slip away from the garage. *Glue your feet to the floor*, I screamed in my head. The sensation of glue oozing down my legs and onto the floor followed the words, locking me into the room for the moment. Tapping into all my years of hospital experience, code blues and sixteen-hour shifts, I pulled my remaining energy into my core—like it was magnetizing me to the floor.

Sorin's line of sight dropped from the ceiling to me. "I see you," he exclaimed in wonder.

I laughed and felt myself waver. Using the energy I'd pulled in, I brought my figure back into a solid. "Can you hear me?"

That heartbreaking smile lit up his face. "I can."

My respiratory rate started to climb. I knew I wasn't going to be able to hold this for every long. The time to speak was now. "I can't move to you or touch you; not yet. I need time to practice."

"You are doing very well," he answered. "I continue to be awed by you."

Now, I thought. "I don't have long," I started and could hear how weak my astral voice was. "I'm too weak to hold this yet."

"You are far from weak, Katherine."

"Stop." I held up my arms to see that I was already fading away. "Just come and find me," I managed to whisper just before my spirit was pulled back into the living room to be reconnected with my body.

Lilias' face came into focus in front of my own when I returned to my physical body in the recliner. She threw herself backwards and clapped, kicking her feet into the air. "Far seeing! I truly believed I was the last—yet here you are. It is miraculous."

There was zero seconds to respond to her glee when a wind threw me back a few steps. Several small candles in the back of the room were extinguished by the force of Sorin entering the small room. Stopping just inside the room, his head was cocked to the side like he was confused by me. I froze at the sight of him. *What do I say after last night?*

Lilias looked back and forth between the two of us. Stepping into him with that same fairylike elegance, she laid her hand on his chest. "She is unexpected, just as you said. I will leave you two to talk about what you need to and I will remain in the manor to continue to teach her."

Gratitude filled my chest when she left the room. Normally I would want to ask a hundred questions but now wasn't the time. I could speak to her later but Sorin needed to hear what was on my mind before I lost the courage. And if I was going to be brave, I might as well get the scariest part out first.

"I love you."

14

When you say those three little words to someone for the first time you hope they will respond in a positive way. I'd said it before to people: my kids, Tom and Rhys. But I'd never been so terrified to say it or so invested in the response.

Just because my heart didn't beat, doesn't mean it can't be broken.

Sorin could've done several things. He could've laughed, walked away, told me I was crazy, said it back—anything. But I didn't let him do anything. I kept talking in a desperate attempt to postpone his reaction.

"And, I do trust you. I don't trust myself. I don't trust that you'll fall in love with me or if you do that you'll stay in love with me. I'm afraid that I'll do what I always do. I've always tried to make people love me by acting the way I think they want me to. Then, when I get tired or frustrated with that and start to be myself—well, they don't like me. Then, they want me to continue to be that fake me so I shut down and everything inside me dies for them. I always wanted someone that I could be myself with and speak my mind to and show all the broken parts to. But in reality, I just thought I was going to be alone for the rest of my life. I didn't see you coming and once we'd slept together, I figured you were done with me."

He opened his mouth but I stopped him and continued my rant.

"But you weren't. You kept coming after me, to my work, to my home. You sent gifts and impressed my co-workers. You bought me a dress and washed my hair and listened to me talk. But weirdest of all, you didn't run away. And, Sorin… I've always been myself with you. For the first time ever, I showed someone the real, flawed person I am from the very beginning. And, you were still interested. I finally had what I dreamed of and I'm scared shitless. So, I pushed you away and you stayed patient and respected me, even though I could see it was killing you. I mean, it was killing me too. I wanted to be in your bed—want to be in your bed. I want to be with you until the end of time. But I'm so freaked out and convinced that you'll reject me. Worse than that, I'm scared you'll love me but only for a little while. And, Sorin …"

I made sure he was looking into my eyes so he could see that I meant the next few words. "If you stopped loving me, I think I'd die. But I can't die, so I'd just live forever with a broken heart."

I'd said it. It was out and I couldn't take it back. With trembling hands, I pulled my hair in front of my shoulders, then threw it back; trying to keep myself busy so I wouldn't reach out for the man in front of me. I wanted to give him the chance to choose and not feel pressured. The silence between us was agony but I knew I had to let him think and not push so I remained quiet.

My answer came when he reached out a hand and pulled me slowly into him. My right hand continued to shake in his left as he raised it up to the side of his face and slid his other hand behind my back. Our eyes never lost each other as the next few minutes unfolded. Swaying to nothing, he began our dance—the dance I now knew well—the dance to music only he could hear. We were close enough to kiss but he didn't move in. He stared and swayed while all of what I just verbally assaulted him with ran just behind his eyes.

"Katherine." It came out like a sigh almost too faint to hear. "For hundreds of years I have moved through this world with purpose, power, strength and a mission but no fire. My fire died so long ago that I thought it was only a dream. I wake to the same thing each night–protecting the vampires of this city. I have had many partners in my bed to fill the time. I have given refuge to vampires who would have died without us. I have donated millions to good causes. But none of that brought my fire back."

He leaned in to lay his lips on the edge of my ear. "Then you walked into my life and flames have consumed my nights ever since."

Wind kicked up around us and I was in his arms being carried up the stairs. Nothing could have stood between Sorin and the end of the upstairs hallway. Even in the rush of emotion I noticed he hadn't made his bed. Oddly that little thing gave me comfort and made him more endeared to me—the knowledge that he was not "all put together" either.

Setting me down on the floor at the end of that messy bed, he picked up exactly where he'd left off in the living room. Slow dancing to nothing, I flashed back to the first dance we'd shared in this same room. That woman had been so unsure of herself and using any excuse to avoid the feelings bubbling up inside her. But the woman in that room was now certain of what she wanted and had found the courage to speak it out. And, the man holding her had not run screaming.

Dipping me down, Sorin laid his lips onto mine. This kiss was different than any of the others. It was just a little hesitant and so careful. I knew his uncertainty was because he was unsure of the words I had just shared and I wanted desperately to show him I was serious. Answering the kiss with a flick of my tongue, his mouth opened to match my pace as he lifted me up. When I started to work at the buttons of his shirt, he knew all he needed to.

With each of his hands on the side of my face he lifted my gaze up to the gathering storm in his irises. "I love you, Katherine. Everything I have to give is yours. Forever."

No more words needed to be spoken that night. When his shirt was on the floor and my dress was next to it, he lifted me so I could wrap my legs around his torso. The heat that was rising in my core was against that bare skin and reached out for him. Laying me onto the bed, he pulled the last piece of clothing off of me, stood back and just looked. I should have felt exposed or vulnerable but I was too enthralled by him to care. His gaze trailed slowly down my naked form and back up to meet my eyes. He didn't need to say what he was thinking—he was enjoying the moment and looking forward to what was to come. It was not our first time together but it would be the first time since we committed to each other and he was going to make it memorable.

And, I was 100% in.

The sound of his remaining outfit hitting the floor sent an electric shock from my toes to my head. Energy swirled in my stomach and started to spread out from my center. When he dropped onto his knees at the end of the bed, some of that energy rushed to meet the hands that he'd laid on each thigh. Each kiss that landed on the inside of my thigh felt hot and caused the ache inside me to throb harder.

The first orgasm came when his tongue slid up the wet center of my need and flicked over the epicenter of that throbbing. I screamed and pressed back into the mattress, grabbing his hair with each hand. He didn't stop but continued that slow, stroking of his tongue and I struggled to catch my breath. The mixture of sensations overwhelmed me. I felt the stroking of his tongue, the electric crackling of his power as it slid from him and started to dance over my skin and the heat of my power rolling off of me and onto him. All of it danced in and out and over and around us—mixing with the gathering need in my abdomen. I sat up and pulled his face to mine. I wanted to see him, I wanted him inside of me and I wanted to take a second to focus. I wanted to be in the moment not lost in sensations.

He must have seen what I needed because he nodded, pulled me into him and stood. Turning to the side of the room, he walked us into the wall—using it against my back to brace us. I remembered the night before in the hallway when he had done this same thing and I had stopped him. But I ended that thought spiral immediately and reminded myself that the only thing that mattered was now.

One last questioning look into my eyes was answered with a slight nod and Sorin slid himself into me. Crying out, I held onto him and we froze for a moment to live in the sensation of him hard inside of my core—two bodies made one. Then he moved out inch by inch only to drive into me again. The magic around us pulsed with each thrust. I was almost visible on the edge of my vision—like the Northern lights—dancing and swirling with each motion. I allowed him to move at his pace, giving myself over to him completely and motivated only by the desire to fulfill his need—knowing this would be the first of centuries of lovemaking.

He rested his face onto my shoulder, lost in my hair and his shift allowed for his pelvis to rub against my heat. As he rocked his hips, the friction against me was perfectly placed and my breath came in quick gasps. Whether lost in his own need or completely attuned to what I was feeling—he didn't lean back but continued the rocking that moved him and rubbed me. Holding onto him like an anchor, I felt that cramping build in my center and knew I would have done anything to satisfy this desire. The dancing lights around us grew brighter and matched the pulsing of our power. Sorin's pace increased and I braced myself for what was to come.

The release of that growing constriction throughout my body threw me back into the wall at the same time Sorin arched back and cried out. Our powers shot forth from our joined bodies into the room and bounced between walls, ceiling and floor to eventually seep through the crack below the bedroom door or return to us. Panting, Sorin took several shaking steps backwards to find the bed so we could fall onto it and let our muscles recover.

We each lay on our side, facing each other and not able to speak. I didn't know what I would have said if I could have spoken but there really was nothing we needed to say. We had said it all. So, instead of talking, I reached out and laid my hand on his sternum. He laid his over top and we stayed like that until our breathing returned to normal.

He was the first to speak. "Stay with me tonight. Don't return to your room."

"I won't," I answered. "I want to wake up next to you any time I can."

"We still have much of the night. Would you like to do this a few more times?"

"Yep," I giggled.

And that is exactly how we spent the rest of the night.

15

Waking up next to Sorin was never going to get boring. I could do it for 1,000 years and still lose my breath when I opened my eyes to see him. The night before had been magical. We'd spent hours exploring each other, laughing, sneaking to the kitchen for blood like teenagers, and then exploring each other again. He'd stayed quietly in the corner of the room when I had called the girls at 5 am; listening to us talk about mundane things. Lying down next to me after I'd hung up, we'd talked until the dawn or exhaustion had taken us away.

Gazing at him now, it was hard to understand how I'd ever thought of walking away from him—existing without him in my life. I took that quiet moment to revel in the knowledge that he loved me, that I'd said to him and he had said it back.

The buzzing phone pulled me out of my thoughts and brought Sorin out of his sleep. Expecting the voice of Olivia or Ellie, I hit the answer button on my phone and brought it to my ear. I knew Sorin would stay quiet but brought my finger to my lips to ask for his silence anyway.

"Kate?"

Nope. It wasn't my kids—it was the hospital. My heart sank and I couldn't keep the frustration out of my voice.

"Yes?"

"Oh, thank god." It was Jerry, the director of nursing and he sounded way too happy to hear my voice. "Listen, I know you're on vacation and I know you need this, I do. But we have a situation and it's an all-skate."

I stayed silent. I wasn't agreeing to anything until I heard what he had to say. Looking over to Sorin, I saw the curiosity in his eyes but knew he could hear everything so I didn't feel the need to repeat anything. I just shrugged.

"Kate, I need you to come in tomorrow and the next few nights. Please. I am begging. Then you can take all the time you need, I swear."

"Why," I asked. I still wasn't agreeing to anything. I needed this time off to get my life together and I'd just finally admitted all my feelings to myself and Sorin. It didn't really seem like a good time to run off to the hospital and back to overnight shifts.

"We got a call today. There was a complaint and the department of health is coming to investigate. The guy's getting here tomorrow to look at charts then he wants to be on the floors on night shift."

"Why night shift?"

For those of you that don't know, surveyors from the DOH or the Joint Commission come to the hospitals sometimes to check things out. It's a necessary part of being in medicine but they *never* come on night shift.

"I guess the complaint was about the night shift. That's why I need you. You and Monica are the best and I need one of you when this guy shows up. You know all the policies, the procedures, the best way to answer his questions and what to tell the other nurses to do. Monica's still inpatient and I can't ask her. That's why I'm begging you to please come in."

The mention of Monica's name brought a visceral reaction out of me. I sat up straight and my shoulders tensed up. The truth was that Monica was in the hospital because of me and I felt extremely guilty about it. If she hadn't been pulled into my shit, she wouldn't have been kidnapped, munched on and almost killed. It would've taken a lot to get me out of that manor and away from Sorin. Unfortunately, Monica was one of those things. If I said no, I wouldn't put it past the hospital to see if they could get Monica discharged and back to work.

"Fine," I relented. "But, as soon as the DOH is gone, my two-week clock restarts. I need time off, Jerry."

"Great! Whatever you need. Just be here tomorrow and every night until the complaint is resolved and then you're off. I promise. I'm sure he won't find anything and it'll be quick."

He may have still been talking but I didn't need to hear anymore. I'd been through enough joint and DOH visits to know what to do. I hung up the phone and turned to Sorin.

"You don't need to work you know. I will provide for you."

The old Kate would have gone on a feminist rant but this new Kate recognized that he was trying to help, not be a caveman. "I appreciate that. Rhys has offered the same. However, I like being a nurse and I'm not ready to walk away just yet. I'm sorry I have to go but we have tonight and if you're going to love a nurse you might as well get used to the whole 'being called in' thing."

"Well," he replied as he pulled me into him. "I do love a nurse so I will concede to this small thing. Shall we find food and then work on some more of your powers?"

"Sounds like a plan."

Half an hour later, we were in the office with full glasses of blood and a roaring fire. I heard the text alert on my phone and picked it up to see Rhys was messaging me.

RHYS: Get called in tomorrow?

ME: Yep.

RHYS: Me too. I'll pick you up from there to take you in so you can get your van.

ME: Good thinking. Forgot all about that! XO

RHYS: See you tomorrow after sundown. XO

I laid down the phone and saw Sorin's eyebrows raised in question. I alleviated the curiosity. "Rhys got called in too. He's going to get me tomorrow and take me in so I can pick up the van."

Sorin smiled. "At least he will be there with you."

"True," I answered. "I'll feel better going back if I know he is downstairs."

"Are you going to be okay going back?"

I hadn't had time to really think about. I hadn't worked since Will had grabbed me in the parking lot. I'd been in the hospital to visit but hadn't worked. Would I be able to put that all behind me and just "get back to work"? I didn't know. But I was going to find out.

I didn't want to waste the time we had worrying about the next day so I changed the subject. "What power should we work on?"

He either didn't recognize that I was derailing the conversation or didn't mind because he answered. "I would like to work on your psychic abilities. Now I do not possess that power specifically by empathy is much like reading minds. Are you open to that?"

"Sure," I conceded. "Let's do it."

He concentrated his gaze just off to the side of my gaze then looked back just as quickly. I wasn't sure what he was doing but didn't need to ask when Tamela walked into the room. "Did you just call her?"

"Yes," he answered without any explanation.

"Can you do that because your lord of the city?"

"No," he responded. "All makers can call their progeny."

I jumped back. "Wait! You turned her?"

Tamela was the one to respond this time. "He did. Many years ago."

The word 'shocked' didn't cover what I was feeling. I think I was surprised I hadn't somehow known but then I didn't really understand how the whole maker-makee thing worked. Were you supposed to be able to tell? Were they supposed to introduce each other as maker and child? I didn't know so I wasn't sure if they'd really held anything back from me. I decided to ignore all my questions and go for something practical.

"What does it feel like when you get called?"

Tamela chuckled. I don't think she had expected that particular question. "Like his voice in my head and a pull on my body that I have to answer. I assure you, if Rhys should ever call you, you will know."

"Okay, so what are we doing? Why does Tamela need to be here?"

Sorin stepped forward and stopped next to her so they were both facing me. "Because," he smirked, "you need to read her mind."

I let my eyes lock with Tamela. We hadn't really talked since she'd run out of the gym and I wanted to have that conversation but not with Sorin around. So, I made the choice to play along. I started to focus my thoughts on her but she held up a hand.

"Wait Kate. I don't want you aimless roaming around my head. We're asking for you to focus on one particular thought. I've hidden something in the home. Can you find what it is and where it is?"

Sorin picked up where she left off. "Ask the question in your mind. Ask yourself what did she hide and then find the answer inside of her."

What did she hide? What did she hide? What did she hide? I looked into those dark eyes and set my intentions on answering my own question. For a while all I saw was her eyes looking at mine. Frustrated I repeated the question in my mind—*what did she hide?*

His necklace.

That voice in my head had not been mine. In the midst of my repeating question, Tamela's voice had weaved in and out without her ever moving her lips. With that one answer, I changed the question in my head.

What necklace? What necklace? What necklace?

The brown eyes before me faded and a red jewel replaced her pupil. A red jewel that grew a chain from each side. The gold chain was worn and clearly an antique. The ruby at the center was also showing the signs of time. When it was new it hadn't been extravagant or polished but she had thought it was the most beautiful thing she'd ever seen. I felt the weight of it against her chest when he'd fastened the clasp behind her neck.

"Your father gave you that ruby necklace and you've kept it this whole time. It's the only thing you have left from when you were human." The words were out of my mouth before I had known that the thoughts had come to me.

Tamela's eyes grew wide. "Where is it?"

"You didn't hide it," I was continuing to speak as the thoughts came to be and didn't take the time to think before they came tumbling out. "You lost it and you hoped I'd find it this way but didn't really believe I could."

Her hands came to her mouth and a tear slid down her cheek "I didn't. Do you know where it is?"

I closed my eyes, trying desperately to see more than just the necklace but where it lay. "Grass," I revealed as it came to me. "On grass, under dead leaves. It's by a bush. You were fixing a light outside. The chain broke and it fell to the ground but you didn't realize it. Now, leaves have fallen on it."

"I know where that was. That was weeks ago. How?"

Sorin laid his hand on her back. "I am not pleased that you used her power for your benefit but I am thrilled that she was able to find something that even you didn't know the location of. Go retrieve your jewelry and we will talk later."

The bowed head gave her the appearance of guilt but the smile on her face told me she felt it was worth it to find her treasured ruby necklace and she'd take whatever punishment came. I thought about telling Sorin to go easy on her but knew that getting involved in a sire-progeny bond was probably off limits. Plus, he was the master of the city and I didn't need to step on his toes.

Pick your battles, I thought. It was a favorite motto of mine.

I decided to lighten the mood and crack a joke. "Need me to find any lost things for you? We could start a whole business!"

He didn't look amused as he walked towards his desk. "Katherine, you must keep these abilities to yourself. No one can know how strong you are. You still have no real control over these powers. We are still at the beginning of your training."

Contrary to popular belief, I do know when to stop joking so I did. "You're right."

That stopped him in his tracks and he froze on his path. Clutching his heart, he turned to look at me. "I'm sorry. Could you repeat that?"

"I said you're right."

"That's what I thought you said. This is momentous. I may write this in my journal."

"Hysterical." I let the sarcasm drip off my response. "It wasn't like I was going to print out posters to hang all over the city."

The levity left his face and the serious side of Sorin returned. "If you listen to one thing I say Katherine, then may it be this—if the wrong vampires hear of your powers, you will be in great danger. If they discover you can merge those powers with masters, I fear for you. Please remain as ambiguous as possible."

There was real fear in his eyes and that was the scariest part of all. "Okay," was all I could muster. "I promise."

16

A doorbell shot through the manor. Sorin didn't seem surprised and I reminded myself that he had a lot to do as the master of the city. I was sure it didn't all stop just because I was there. I could only pray it wasn't "perfect Evelyn" again. If I was lucky, it was a vampire looking for a place to hang out for the night or someone new to the area.

Of all the things I'd guessed it would be, I didn't even consider it was a human—until Dr. Kitchner appeared in the office behind Tamela.

"Alex!" I squealed and ran to hug him. The embrace was strong, the kind of hug you give to someone who almost died in your arms a weak prior. He reciprocated the squeeze. It was still hard to believe I had despised this man only weeks ago.

It's amazing what becoming a vampire and being kidnapped by a Nazi will do for a friendship.

To Sorin's credit, he didn't react to our long embrace. I attributed that to two things: he didn't seem like the jealous type and he'd seen the shape Alex had been in before I'd healed him—no, we'd healed him. The two men shook hands when our hug ended and Sorin took his place next to me.

"What are you doing here?" I asked.

"I called Sorin," he answered. "To ask how you were doing and if I could do anything to help you with your powers. He invited me to come by."

"How's Monica?"

"Well" he pulled off his gloves, held them in his right hand and unzipped his coat with his left. "She was moved down to your floor today. Everyone's watching out for her. I'm hoping she can go home in a week or so but she's got a long road ahead."

Nausea rose up in my gut. *My fault.*

"I came to talk about you, though. How is your training? How are you adjusting?"

"Oh boy, well I'm not sure. I don't really have anything to compare it to. One minute I feel like I've always been meant to be this way—like I've been training to be a vampire my whole life. Like destiny almost. But the next minute I feel like this awkward kid going through puberty and wish I was human again."

Alex looked over to Sorin. "And, what do you think?"

Sorin's eyebrows raised. I don't think he expected to be asked but I was learning that Alex was great at gathering information wherever he could. "She is like nothing I've ever seen. I don't remember what it was like to not be a vampire. Being human is more of a distant dream than something I lived. Nevertheless, I have seen many transitions from mortal to immortal and have never seen anyone come into their vampire selves as quickly as she has. If you had told me about a new vampire fighting off an older one with the kind of force she did, I would not have believed it. Yet, I saw it with my own eyes."

"And your powers?"

I looked to Sorin to be sure I could answer. He nodded. "I trust him."

"Nothing new," I answered. "Working on the ones I have. It is actually easier to use them then I expected. But I have good teachers so that's a part of it."

Alex nodded. "Well, as your doctor I recommend you keep doing what you're doing. You look great. Take the time off to recover. I can tell the hospital you need more time if you decide you do."

So, he wasn't one of the ones called.

"Actually," I quipped. "I am back tomorrow."

"What do you mean?" He asked, looking confused and annoyed.

I raised my hands. "Not by choice, not really. I was sort of voluntold. DOH is coming tomorrow for a complaint investigation. I don't know what floor and what the complaint is. All I know is it's night shift. Jerry wants me or Monica and I can't let them pull Monica out of bed and throw scrubs on her."

"What is the point of me writing a medical necessity form for a leave of absence if they're just going to call you?"

"I don't know," I laughed. "But this is the gig so I'm going in tomorrow. Once the investigation is over, I can take time off. It's okay, Alex."

"I'll be there tomorrow night, then. Rhys?"

"He'll be there, too."

"Good," Alex said, pleased and relieved.

"Normally I'd tell you that I'll be fine and don't need anyone. Truth is, I'll be glad to have some allies in the house. I'm not sure how I'll handle being back."

Alex started to zip up his coat and put his gloves back on. "I'm going to head out. I really just wanted to stop by and make sure you were okay. I'm going to get some sleep and I'll see you tomorrow."

Sorin stepped into him and placed his hand on his shoulder. "Can I get you something for the road? I'm sure it is cold. Edwin makes—what I am told—is very good coffee."

"No thank you," Alex responded. "I really do need to sleep tonight. Next time?"

"Of course, I will see you to the door."

Both men left he room and I was grateful for the moment to reflect. Did I mean what I had said? That it felt like I was destined to be a vampire and hadn't known it? It had come out of my mouth without me realizing I was thinking it. If it was true, did I love being this way? Would I want to go back if I could? I didn't know. When Alex had told me he was looking into a cure I had been desperate for humanity. I just wasn't anymore.

Sorin returned to the office and broke my train of thought. "You feel very serious. Everything okay?"

I moved to the couch and sat. Sorin joined me. I carefully planned the next question so it would come out right. "Would you go back to being human if you could?"

He sat back, giving the question the serious thought that it deserved. "I would not. I meant what I said. I do not remember being human. But I see their vulnerability, their weakness. I feel them aging when I am around them. They have so much to fear—violence, illness, accidents. I do not desire that existence."

I wasn't surprised by his answer. "You don't miss the sun?"

He shook his head. "I don't remember it. I see it on television and in paintings but I don't recall how it felt so why it would be something to grieve? I may have in the beginning but it is no longer a part of my world."

He turned to me. "Do you? Would you return to human if you could?"

I took in a deep breath and let it out. "I don't know the answer to that anymore. At first, yes. I wanted to go back. I don't want to be a threat to my children or miss all their daytime stuff. I feel so apart from them now—so different. So much has changed."

He stayed quiet and let me continue. "But like you said. I see now how frail I was then- how easily I could have died. I like that I could protect them if I had to. I could lift a car off of them. I don't feel pain in every joint or need to take naps to get through each day. And, I like the power I feel inside of me. Plus, I know it's shallow but I like looking this way."

I looked into his grey gaze. "And, I want to be with you."

That was when he raised his hand to interrupt. "Katherine. I would still be with you- even if you were human. I am not in love with your power. I am in love with you. But I would of course need to be much gentler with your body."

I felt a tear slip out of my eye and run down to my chin. "But I'd grow old and die. So, either I become human and you bury me or I stay a vampire and bury my children."

He wiped the tear from my face. "*Regina mea*, first off you are trying to make a choice that is not available. Without a cure, you are torturing yourself for nothing. Secondly, I would treasure 60 more years with you and take that over you outlasting your daughters. If the choice ever arises, do not consider my feelings. Do what is in your heart."

I kissed him for that.

When the kiss ended, I stood and reached for him. "No more talking about depressing things. Let's go for a walk outside."

17

The rest of that night went way too fast and before I knew it I was waking up in Sorin's bed thanks to the alarm I had set. He didn't stir and I let him sleep while I showered. I hadn't brought scrubs because I hadn't planned on going into work. So, I threw on some clothes I brought into the bathroom and planned to grab some out of my locker at work. Every good nurse has spare scrubs in the hospital. You can't imagine the things that may get on us at work and no one wants to wear that for the rest of their shift.

I was getting better at using the makeup to tone down my beauty and finished the look by pulling my hair up into a bun.

Sorin was sitting up when I returned to the bedroom. "I see that you are ready to leave. No point in trying to talk you out of this, I assume?"

"Nope," I said, climbing onto the bed to crawl to him and lay a kiss on those lips. "I have a duty."

"I suggest then that you do not kiss me again, and get out of this bed. My will has its limits."

Almost like it was timed that way, I heard Rhys calling out from downstairs. "Katie?"

"Coming," I yelled down. Getting off the bed and onto my feet, Sorin followed. I remembered that he had fallen asleep naked and groaned at the sight of him. "If Monica weren't hurt…"

He arched his eyebrow. It was one of his favorite ways to respond to me and it was getting to the point where that arched eyebrow stirred something in my stomach. I had to walk away pronto or I was never leaving.

So, I turned and pulled myself away from the most beautiful nude man I had ever seen.

Rhys was at the bottom of the stairs with a thermos. "Dinner?"

"Yes," I chimed, reaching the bottom, snatching it out of his hands and hugging him like he'd been gone for months. "God, it's good to see you."

He squeezed as hard as he could and broke off the hug. "Let's scoot. We can catch up on the way. Scrubs?"

"In my locker," I responded. Then yelled into the house, "I'll be back everyone."

Walking out of the house, I was faced with Rhys's little Civic. A flash across my brain showed me that same Honda parked next to a dark barn. I shook my head to clear it of the memory and Rhys noticed.

"Katie?"

"Rhys, do you have flashbacks? I mean, from that night?"

"Sure," he answered. "I think that's normal. Especially because we can't process it through dreams, right?"

"Yeah, I guess. Okay. I'm just glad I'm not the only one. I won't be thinking about it and then—WHAM—it's back in my brain like I'm living through it again."

He walked to the car to open my door for me. "You can talk to me, you know."

"I know." And, I did know I could. But I really just wanted it to go away. *Healthy, right?* I climbed into the car and jumped at the sound of the door shutting.

On the way to Pittsburgh Medical Center, I caught him up on the work we'd done with flying, reading minds and far-seeing. He was intrigued by Lilias and said he couldn't wait to meet her. It reminded me that I hadn't told her where I was going. That seemed pretty rude since she'd travelled all this way for me. I texted Sorin asking him to please pass my apologies to her. He assured me he would.

The sight of the hospital didn't bring the gut punch that I was worried it would. It was just the same old building I was used to and I was relieved to not have to suffer through anymore flashbacks. Then, we pulled into the parking garage and across from my van.

The flashback show began.

Me reaching to close my van door. The feeling of a blow to the head. Waking up in a trunk. The sound of Alex being drug over gravel. And, the shadow that loomed over me when the trunk was opened.

"Stop," I yelled out.

"Katie." Rhys threw the car into park and cut the engine. "This is a bad idea. You're not ready. Call Jerry and tell him he can't force you back when you're on an approved leave."

"No," I said. "This is going to happen whenever I come back. Doesn't matter if it's now or two weeks from now or a year from now. The memories are gonna come back and I have to deal with it."

"Yeah, but to deal with a trauma at work during a DOH visit with Monica on your unit... seems like more stress than necessary."

I had forgotten that Monica would be on my unit. I was going to see her on top of everything else that was going on. How would I act? Would she ask me to get out? How would I explain that to everyone?

Didn't matter because I was going in. I made up my mind. Finishing off the blood in the Thermos, I opened the door and stepped out of the car into the garage I had been abducted from.

Totally normal day, right?

Rhys followed me past the van and I didn't look at it. Wasn't ready for that part, yet. But I did make it into the hospital and to the elevator. After making me swear I'd call him for anything, Rhys and I said our goodbyes in the lobby before he jumped on the elevator to go down to the basement and I picked the one heading up.

I thanked all the gods above when I made it to the breakroom to put on scrubs before anyone saw me and I had to face a barrage of questions. Coming out into the unit, I was shocked to not see anyone. They obviously knew the DOH was in the house. Whenever we get surveyors or investigators the staff tend to scatter and try to not be seen.

The assignment board revealed that I was working with one of the Tiffanys, Jackson and someone named Diana. I was hoping she was a new hire—we needed more nurses—but she could have been pulled from a different floor.

I also saw that Monica was in 502. But, I didn't really need to read it. I could actually smell her. Yep, you heard that right. I could smell her.

My senses were getting sharper by the day. At first, I was so overwhelmed by all the sounds and smells and sensations. But, recently I was able to pick different things out and turn certain things down—like turning down the volume on a radio. And, when I walked into the unit, I had smelled Monica. I made a point to focus on it. The scent of cigarettes was gone which made her essence even easier to pick out. I'm not sure how to describe it really so I will do my best without sounding weird.

She smelled like sugar cookies.

That's the closest I can think of. She smelled like warmth and simple sugar. It was the scent that I knew was my best friend—or ex best friend. I didn't know yet what would happen when she saw me so I pushed that off for the time.

Instead, I used the unexpected alone time to focus on other smells. I could pick out Jackson. He smelled like cologne and something metallic. Tiffany's smell was also sweet but much sweeter than Monica's—like cotton candy. I knew it was Irish Tiffany and made a mental note to figure out her last name.

"Hello?" The voice behind me sounded irritated and very suspicious.

I turned to see a woman in scrubs that I didn't recognize. The blue scrubs set off her caramel-colored skin and made her eyes look more amber than brown. Her dark hair had red streaks running through it and it was down. She must have been an agency or travel nurse because there is no way Jerry would have allowed an employee to have their hair down, let alone red. And, definitely not when a DOH was in the hospital. Maybe she didn't care. Which, honestly, would have made me very impressed.

I smiled to try and put her at ease, pointing at my badge. "I'm Kate. I work here. You?"

She let her gaze drop to the badge, to the assignment board and then back to me. I expected the mistrust in those eyes to disappear but they didn't. It looked to me that it actually dialed up a notch when she realized I worked on the unit. Clearly, she had been burned at some previous jobs because this girl was cold as ice.

You could even smell it on her. Much unlike the scents I had just been focusing on, hers was far from sweet. She smelled more serious. The closest thing I can think of is a campfire. Her essence was like the outdoors. Sorin smelled like the outdoors but in a fresh way—like outside a cabin after a storm. This nurse smelled like the outdoors after rough camping.

She cleared her throat. I stopped thinking about her smell and brought my attention back to her scowl. "So, you're the reason I had to take extra patients until you could get here? Babysitter issues?"

"Something like that." Now, I was getting annoyed. I saw no need to explain myself to her. I didn't know what her problem was with me but it was quickly becoming an issue on both sides. I will give anyone a chance. Her chance was up and my mind was decided.

She was a bitch.

"I am happy to take those patients off your hands. It sounds like it is too much for you." I let the sarcasm drip off those words.

"Well, you are taking 501 and 503 off of me. Sounds like 502 specifically asked for you to not be her nurse."

That hurt. I was sure Diana didn't know why Monica had requested me to not take care of her but it didn't matter. Anytime anyone asks you to not be their nurse it hurts. But when a co-worker asked it looked like you were incompetent and they knew it.

"That's fine. Just give me your papers. I don't need report." I didn't give her time to insist that I do a full report. I snatched the papers out of her hands and went to find Jackson.

18

After getting report from Tiffany and Jackson, I found a computer and made a plan to hide in the family lounge for a few minutes. I needed to get myself together and fight the urge to run into Monica's room and beg her to forgive me. Part of it was the need to lay eyes on her and know she was alive, part of it was to find out if she was my friend anymore and part of it was to get the inevitably pain over with when she rejected me.

That plan was thwarted in its tracks when two men turned the corner, onto the unit and into my line of sight. One was Jerry. The other, I could only assume, was the investigator. The badge on his shirt let me know but I wouldn't have needed it. The clipboard in his hand was a dead giveaway that he was DOH. The man was easily 6'4" as he towered over Jerry. Salt and pepper hair was cut short to his head, more like a soldier than a government employee. He was close to 50 years old if not just over it. The white shirt was buttoned up to his throat, pressed within an inch of its life and tucked into grey slacks. If that didn't tell me how uptight he was, the shiny wingtips would. They were polished and perfect. I knew instantly that this guy wasn't going to leave any stone unturned or any detail uninvestigated.

I gulped and fixed a fake smile onto my lips before stepping forward to meet them. I had to look up to meet his eyes. Extending my hand, the inspector gripped tight and pumped once before dropping it. "Hi, I'm Kate a nurse on the unit."

"Head nurse," Jerry quipped and gave me a look that told me not to correct him.

"Henry Kunsman," he responded. The voice was so deep it was on the edge of a rumble and the tone was definitely in line with the whole "military" vibe.

I really didn't have time to fluff an inspector. I had enough on my plate so I tried to rush the exchange. "What can I do for you Mr. Kunsman?"

"Direct? I like it. And, it is Henry. I need to look at the charting on this unit for the past two weeks. I am specifically interested in night shift since the complaints were directed at the night nurses."

"Complaints? Plural?"

"Yes," he answered and clearly didn't want to expand.

"Follow me." I waved for him to follow and took him into the unit director's office. Last time I had been in here, Monica had been talking to me and Sorin had shown up behind me. Fighting back the emotions that stirred up in me, I opened the door and turned on the computer. Accessing the charting system was quick work. Henry sat down at the desk, looking huge in the small office.

"I will find you if I need you," he said without looking at me. Jerry nodded that it was okay for me to leave, so I did.

The next few hours were tense on the floor. Everyone knew that Henry Kunsman was digging through charts and didn't look like he was going to go easy on us. No one knew what the complaint had been or if it had been our unit specifically, just that it was nights. And, since we were all on nights, we were all nervous.

I made a point to avoid looking into Monica's room as I moved from 501 to 503. Though I did focus on her heartbeat and breathing a few times to be sure she was okay. I may have even peeked at her monitor at the nurses' station to watch her heart rhythm for a minute or two.

Diana was taking care of her so it wasn't even like I could casually ask her nurse how she was doing. It was evident that Diana hated my guts. I wondered if Monica had told her something that made her hate me. I knew in my heart that Monica never would have shared my big secret but maybe she'd said something else like "it's her fault I'm here" or "I will never look at her the same" or "I don't want her near me." She may have even said something under the influence of pain killers without realizing it.

Whatever it was, Diana was not my fan. And frankly, I didn't care. I had enough to worry about without trying to make a friend out of enemy. I just wish I could find out how Monica was doing.

When Henry came out of the office, I stopped worrying about my friend and started to worry again about the investigation. I reminded myself that as soon as he was done, I could go back to Sorin and spend 14 days with him. Henry's face was a mix of frustration and concern. I didn't like it.

"Miss Murphy?" He waved me over.

"Yes."

"Are you familiar with the night staff?"

"Yes."

"Good. I would like to interview you. Come into the office please."

I followed him into the cramped room and tried to not react when he clicked on the overhead light. It felt too much like being interrogated and I had no idea what he was about to ask me. I found the chair on the other side of the office. Instead of sitting back behind the desk, he leaned back onto the desk, facing me with his arms crossed. It was reminiscent of a principal who was about the lecture his student about responsibility.

"You've been here a long time."

"I have."

"Tell me about some of the newer staff. How well do you know Dr. Kitchner?"

"What do you mean?"

"Do you feel he is competent? Do you see him outside of the hospital?"

"Yes, he is competent. We wouldn't have him here if he wasn't." I didn't know where he was headed with this line of questioning but I didn't like it. Whatever complaint he had received, I hoped it wasn't about Alex. "And, no. I don't see him outside of the hospital. Plus, he has been here five years so I wouldn't really call him new."

"How about Jackson Hutton? He has been here less than a year. How well do you know him?"

"Not well, Mr. Kunsman. We work together. I don't see them anywhere but here. I know them as well as you know anyone you work with. But, as far as competency goes, I trust everyone on this floor with my life."

He turned, retrieved his clipboard from the desk and furiously wrote on the papers. Everything in me wanted to get up and walk out but I resisted. No need to make this worse than it had to be. When he looked up, I put the smile back on my face.

"How about breaks?" He asked. "How long of a break do you get when you work?"

I had been in DOH investigations before and this one was getting weirder by the second. "We are supposed to get two 15-minute breaks and one-half hour lunch. But it never happens."

"And does anyone ever put that together and leave their assignment for the full hour?"

I laughed out loud before I could stop myself. "Never. Whether you want to believe me or not, we never get a full break and no one leaves that long. The last time-" I stopped myself. The last time was when I had gone outside to eat and died. Probably best to leave that out.

"Is that the complaint?" I asked. "Did someone say we abandon patients for an hour at a time? And what does that have to do with Alex?"

"Who?"

"Dr. Kitchner," I corrected.

"Nurse Murphy. I don't need to tell you the complaint at this time. When I have my findings, I assure you the issue at hand will be known. Until then, I expect you to answer the questions honestly." He stood, opened the door and gestured, which I happily complied with. Between Diana and him, I had enough attitude for one night.

This is what I get for agreeing to come in.

19

The rest of the shift was spent avoiding any one that I could. I checked in on patients, made sure their meds were caught up, filled up all the med carts with supplies so the day shift would be set up and cleaned the break room. As my end time approached, I decided I had to at least say hi to Monica. She may kick me out but I would choose that over her wanting me to visit and I didn't.

From the doorway I could see she was sleeping. She looked so much better than the last time I had seen her. Then she had been in the ICU and so many lines had been coming off of her. Now, I saw the heart monitor lying to the side of her and an IV in her arm that wasn't hooked up to anything. At least I knew that she was healing—physically anyway.

Fading bruises on her face told the story of what had happen to her. Everyone in the hospital thought she'd been abducted and assaulted, then rescued by Alex and Rhys. Only a handful of us knew the awful truth.

She opened her eyes just as I was about to leave the room. To my relief she didn't look horrified like she had when she'd seen me in the unit. She took a moment to focus her eyes and thoughts before the voice of my dear friend filled the room.

"You look more human."

I shut the door before someone could walk by and overhear our conversation. "Makeup helps. And dry shampoo kind of dulls my hair. Plus, scrubs make everyone look worse."

She laughed weakly. "Isn't that the truth."

An awkward silence followed. In all my years as her friend I don't think we'd ever had silence between us but it was thick in the room. "Can we start fresh?" I asked her sheepishly.

She looked away and stared at the wall. After a minute, I prepared myself to leave. She looked back and I saw a mix of sadness and hope. "I'll try."

Smiling, I took a tentative step further into the room.

"What do you think of my nurse?" She was trying to start a normal conversation.

I groaned and rolled my eyes. "She's rude. Is she a new employee?"

"No," Monica answered to my relief. "She's a traveler. Here until the new year to help for the holidays. I think she's good. She wasn't rude to me at all but I'm also the patient not a peer. How are the girls?"

"Good," I said, soothed by the normality of the conversation. "They're having a sleepover with a new friend at Tom's house."

"And, you? Anymore sleepovers?" I could tell she was forcing the conversation but I appreciated it and loved that she asked about Sorin. Monica was a hopeless romantic and I knew she actually wanted to hear about everyone's love life.

"Oh my god, Monica. You have a one-track mind."

"Take pity on me, Kate. I'm so bored here. Everyone's treating me like I'm glass."

I sighed. She did deserve all the juicy gossip. She'd almost died because she thought I was in love with Alex—the only man she'd loved for the last five years. Hearing me talk about Sorin would probably do more for her than any of the medicines she was getting. "Yes. I am currently staying at his manor. As a matter of fact, I left him naked in bed to come here."

She sat up and winced. "What? Tell me everything." She had a little of her old spark back. I started to hope that we could really stay friends.

"I told him I loved him and he said it back."

She clutched her heart. "Kate, I'm so freaking happy for you."

"What about you?" I asked. "Alex has been by your side practically every day."

"Yeah," she said. "He actually was here not too long ago. He had to go see patients and get some work done. But I think we're just friends. He really hasn't given me any sign that he's interested in more."

"Monica, you're in a hospital bed after being attacked. If he had made a move, I would've punched him in the face for being a jerk."

"I guess," she sighed. "But, him being here every day has just made me more in love with him. I feel like I'll die from the size of the crush I have on him. Like I can't breathe when he walks in."

"Trust me, I understand that." I sat on her bed next to her and she pulled back. I know it was instinct and she didn't mean to do it. But I still saw it and knew what it meant. I stood and stepped back to give her space.

"I'm sorry. I just—I need some more time."

"I get it," I said and tried to sound understanding. I didn't want her to see the hurt in my face.

The normality that she'd being trying to force fell away. I looked in her eyes and realized that things were not going to be okay after all. "Kate, I don't know how to be around you. You look like my best friend but you're not. You're someone new—something different. You're not human." She paused and I knew she was about to say something I wouldn't like. "I saw you in the barn. You had fangs and you were covered in blood. You ripped out his throat like an animal."

I held back the crying that was threatening to start. No need for her to see that running down my face. She clearly saw me as a monster without the blood tears.

"I want to be friends again someday. But I don't know if I'll ever able to hang out with you guys and watch you drink blood like its normal."

"You're totally right," I conceded and started to back out of the room. "Please don't feel bad. I totally get it, really." Just as my back reached the door, I felt the need to say something and didn't see why I should hold back. "You know. I didn't ask for this. It happened to me. Just like what happened to you happened to you. He took my life away from me but Rhys gave it back. The alternative was me in a wooden box. We take care of people everyday and never treat them like their disease. I'm just asking that you do the same for me."

Before she could respond, I was out of the room and on my way to report off to the other nurses. I was extremely done with that shift.

Jackson and Tiffany made the report easy. I just updated them on anything that had happened during my time. I left out the conversation with the inspector. There was no reason to get them worried about what he was looking for.

Diana was a different story. When I walked up to the nurses' station and stood beside her, she didn't even look up at me. She continued to type into the chart like I wasn't there. I threw my handoff report for 501 and 503 onto the keyboard in front of her.

"Listen, I don't know what your issue is with me but I need to give you report."

She finally looked up to acknowledge my presence and glared at me. "I think you know what my issue is with you. You don't belong here and you know it. They may not see you for what you are but I do."

With that she stood and walked away from me, leaving me speechless. I quickly grabbed my things from the breakroom and headed for the garage with thoughts chaotically bouncing around my head. I knew deep down that there was no way Monica had told her. However, there was always a chance she let it slip somehow. But that logically didn't make sense. If she knew I was a vampire, she'd be more freaked out than rude. Something else was going on.

I saw Rhys in the parking garage and ran to him. "Hey! I'm happy to see you. Did you meet the inspector?"

"No," he shook his head. "But it sounds like he'll be heading my way tomorrow night. You?"

"Oh yeah, what a delight he is. I don't know what the complaint is but I can tell he's one of those ones that won't leave until he finds something to get us on. He was asking a lot about the staff so the complaint is about one or more of us—not the hospital."

"Great."

"But I have something possibly worse. There's this new nurse, Diana. She hated me before I even walked onto the unit. It's like I pissed her off in a previous life. And she said something that's making me paranoid."

He looked worried. "What?"

"She said that I didn't belong here and she could see me for what I really was."

"Did she look scared?" he asked.

"Not at all. If looks could kill I would have dropped dead when she said that."

"I don't think it's anything but maybe mention it to Sorin. I think we're all a little on edge since Will but I don't want to ignore something that could be important either. I know Alex wouldn't say anything and I have a hard time believing Monica told a stranger. Do you want me to come meet her tomorrow?"

"Yes, please. If she's nasty to you too then it's just her personality. If she's nice to you then we may need to dig deeper to find out what her problem is with me specifically."

"Let's head out and get home before sunrise. We have a plan so rest today and don't worry. Love you."

"Love you too. I'll see you tomorrow." And with that I jumped into the van I had not missed at all to head back to the man I missed immensely.

20

When Sorin's manor came into view relief washed over me. It meant that the night was over and I had survived the first shift back. It also meant I was minutes away from being in his arms. Suddenly, the last few hours didn't seem that bad. It's funny how the right people can do that for you.

I shot a text to the girls to tell them I was heading to bed soon and loved them. I waited a few minutes for a response but was sure they were probably sleeping in. They would see it when they woke up. A rush of grief washed over me. I missed them so much and couldn't figure out how this was all going to work. I never saw them anymore. They deserved a mom who was way more present.

But this is the mom they have and at least you're here.

I agreed with the thought. It was just so sad that they had to constantly work around my whole daylight aversion thing. I don't know what I would have done without Tom and Sarah taking over like they had. I was lucky that the girls had them but it didn't stop the wish I had that I was the one playing fulltime parent.

The front door of the home opened to reveal Sorin. There was no one in existence that could look that good in a tshirt, jeans and bare feet. Only this man could stop your breath with $30 worth of clothing. I climbed out of the van and ran to meet him. "God is it good to see you."

"Rough shift?"

"That's an understatement. Let's grab some blood and I'll tell you everything."

We were on the couch in his bedroom when I finished the whole story. The conversation with Monica, Diana's words and thinly-veiled hatred of me and the DOH inspector from Hell sounded really bad when told all together. Sorin listened to the sordid tale without moving a muscle. I didn't know if all old vamps could freeze like he did or it was just him but it was going to take awhile to get used to it.

When he did speak, his tone was business like. "Let's start with the obvious—do you think Diana knows what you are?"

"No," I answered. "I thought about it the whole way here. She'd be way more scared than bitchy. I think it's more likely that she's heard hospital gossip about me. Maybe Monica said something that made her think I'm a bad friend or somehow to blame. Monica told everyone she doesn't want me as her nurse so maybe Diana thinks I'm a bad nurse. Maybe everyone knows we hooked up in the supply closet at work and she thinks I should be fired. All of that is way more likely than her knowing."

"I would like to meet her to be sure."

I laid my hand on his shoulder. "Please don't take this the wrong way but please don't come to work until I know what everyone is saying. Rhys is coming up tomorrow to meet her—like a 'welcome to the hospital' thing. He'll get a read on her and let us know. She doesn't know him or my relationship to him so he may get more out of her."

"I am trusting you to let me know if I should worry." He laid his hand on mine. "We're partners now so this city and its people are your responsibility as well."

I tried to not panic. I hadn't thought about what it would mean to date the master of the city. Was I willing to take on all that responsibility?

"I will," I answered.

"Next," he continued. "Monica still needs time. The attack was not long ago. If you are having flashbacks, I am sure she is as well. Just keep visiting her and giving her space. When she is ready, we can invite her here to ask any question she may have. It may put her at ease to be able to speak freely and know what we really are—as opposed to what she is afraid we are."

"Good point. Thank you for that. I'll mention it."

"Lastly, Mr. Kunsman sounds like a man on a mission. You are very smart and capable. I'm sure he will find you to be reliable and honest."

"Yeah, but I worry about who he's after. He was asking about Alex and Jackson. I'm seriously worried about who will take the fall for whatever the complaint is. Hospitals don't exactly have your back when stuff like this happens. Unless the complaint is found to be unsubstantiated, someone usually has to take the blame. If we lose anyone, I may have to work every night until they replace that person and I don't think I can take much more."

"Then quit. I will provide for you."

"I know!" I was getting annoyed and trying to not lash out. "I like being a nurse. I don't want to lose it yet. Someday I'm gonna have to leave the hospital because I can't hide anymore. But I'm not ready for that day. But, I also can't work every night. I need a life."

Sorin lifted his hands in surrender. "Then let us worry about it if it happens. Do not worry about something that may not occur."

"True," I conceded. "I have enough to worry about without creating drama in my head. Can we just head to bed? I'm kind of over tonight."

He kissed my forehead. "Go to bed. I will join you soon but I still have much work to accomplish."

"But, the dawn?" I asked.

"As you age you will be able to stay up later into the day, be patient. I will be next to you when you arise."

"And then I just have to go back to work. This sucks."

He tilted his head and I knew what he was thinking. *Then don't work.* But I wasn't having that conversation again. I either needed to accept that this was the crappy hand I was dealt for now or lay it down and let Sorin pay my bills. So, I sucked it up and started to get ready for bed.

I heard him walk into his office when my phone dinged. It was Alex.

ALEX: Sorry I missed you tonight. Way behind in work. Back tomorrow?

ME: Yes.

ALEX: Can I get another sample?

ME: Sure. Did you meet the inspector?

ALEX: No. Why?

ME: Just be careful when you're talking to him. Talk tomorrow?

ALEX: Sure.

Lying in bed I tried to not let myself get overwhelmed with worry but all my thoughts wouldn't stop. What if Alex was fired? What would that mean for him finding the cure? Would it mean Rhys and I couldn't use him to stay on night shift? Depending on what the complaint was, would Alex be able to get another job, even?

I was picturing what it would mean for all of us if Alex was fired when I snapped off for the day.

21

Vampire or not- waking up to an alarm is awful. The only difference for us is when you wake up you aren't groggy or confused. You open your eyes and are ready to go. That's one check in the pro-vamp category.

Sorin woke at the same time and the sight of him instantly sent my whole body into one big cramp of need. He looked over at me with a smile that told me that he knew exactly what I was feeling. *Damn empathy.* "Is there time?" he asked.

"Do you have enough blood?"

To answer my question, he rolled on top of me to press himself hard against stomach. The aching grew desperate and the throbbing at my core reaching almost painful levels. I spread my legs in response and was thankful that we'd both made it a habit to sleep naked. Sliding slowly down my body, his erection caressed each millimeter and brought me to the edge of insanity.

"Please," I cried out.

When he found the right spot, I could feel my body react and ready itself for him to move into me. And when he did, I instinctively clenched around the solid length of him. He moaned and froze to gather his control before continuing. His pace started slow but quickly grew with the desire to satisfy our needs. Our breathing came out in tandem as we moved against and with each other until the orgasms washed over us.

When he collapsed onto me, I was still shaking. Buried in my hair he spoke into the pillow, "Don't go."

"Tempting but we both have work to get done. You can't rule a city from bed."

He groaned and rolled off of me to look up at the ceiling. "So practical. Perhaps you are right. We must be responsible. However, I request we do this again when you get home."

Home. He had called this home—like both of ours' home. It was all moving really fast. First, we'd said the three big words then we'd talked about forever and he'd told me I was sharing his position as protector of Pittsburgh. Now he's calling this home. I'm sure he didn't mean anything by it but wanted to be sure he understood that my daughters came first.

Looking into his eyes I didn't think it was the time to have that conversation so I smiled. "I would never deny you, my Lord."

With that I jumped out of bed to get showered, dressed and on my way.

It wasn't until I was pulling into the hospital that I realized I'd dressed in civilian clothes thinking I had scrubs in my locker but in reality, those were lying in Sorin's hamper. So, I was going to have to go steal some from the OR. I really didn't like their scrubs but it'd get me through the shift and I'd wash mine when I got back to the manor.

When I walked into the pre-op area to find a nurse and ask for some, I saw a back and head of hair I recognized. "What are you doing here?"

Rhys turned. "Hey! I'm delivering blood. What are you doing here?"

"Getting scrubs," I responded and gave the nurse he was talking to a pleading look. She walked over to a cabinet and pulled out a set for me.

"Wait for me," I asked Rhys and went behind a curtain to change. When I came out, he was patiently in the corner and the nurse had left with the blood.

"I don't know if she's working but do you want to go up and see if Diana is there?"

"Sure," he answered. "Aren't you worried about people realizing we're friends?"

"No. Why?"

"Well, you know. Because I'm the weird guy downstairs."

I threaded my arm through his so we were side by side and laid my head onto his shoulder. "No way. I'm proud to be next to you. Let them gossip. It's their fault for not getting to know you."

We walked arm in arm to the elevator and hit the button for five. That's when I remembered our mission. "Oh wait", I said. "We don't want her to know we're friends. I want you to get a read on her before she knows we know each other. Figure out why she said what she said."

He hit the pause button on the elevator to buy us time. "What did Sorin say?"

"He wants to hear what you think. I stopped him from charging down here. I honestly think it's nothing. But he's waiting for a report."

Rhys hit the button again to continue our journey to five. When the doors opened, I stepped off after him and watched his head tilt up. His body froze and his head rolled slowly back and forth. He looked like he was smelling the air. I didn't have time to tell him he looked very not human when I heard someone come around the corner.

Of course, it was Diana—because that's my luck–and she had seen us together so there was no point in lying. It was obvious from her face that she had seen Rhys looking weird. Her whole body froze the same way Rhys' had and she dropped down like she was getting ready to pounce. Rhys turned to her and held up his hands. "Hold on. I mean you no harm."

"How many of you are there?"

"Only us two and we are not here to hunt. Why are you here?"

My head was bouncing back and forth between the two of them and my "freaking out" level was at its max. Rhys looked angry and concerned. "What the fuck is going on?" I whispered to him.

Diana looked like she didn't believe any word out of my mouth. "Like she doesn't know?"

"She's new," Rhys answered. "You're her first."

Diana cautiously walked towards us and lowered her voice. "You're her maker?"

"I am."

Now, I was really upset. They just kept talking like I wasn't there and I was quickly getting furious and terrified all at once. I controlled the volume of my voice but let my anger show. "Someone better tell me what's going on before I lose it."

She sneered at me. "You don't tell me what to do, vampire."

Rhys put his hands between us. "Whoa. Calm down."

I turned to him. "Do you know her? How does she know?"

"Because," she answered. "I can smell you. Just like I know you can smell me."

Rhys grabbed my arms and turned me to him. It was clear on his face he was trying to deescalate the situation as quickly as possible. "Diana's a werewolf."

22

We all agreed to meet in the blood bank so we could talk without anyone hearing us. Rhys and I took the elevator and Diana had taken the stairs. She said she wouldn't be "trapped in a box with corpses."

Rude.

I hadn't said a word on the ride down or during the walk to Rhys' office. I didn't know what to say. My brain was racing with questions and thoughts but no coherent sentence could be put together. When Diana walked into the room, we'd been standing silently waiting for her.

"A vampire in a blood bank. Nice." Every word out of her mouth was dripping with distain. I honestly didn't know how I was going to make it through the night without throat punching her.

"Why are you here?" Rhys asked. For the first time, Rhys' power washed over me. I felt how untrusting he was of her and knew that he'd fight to protect us if he had to. I suddenly felt his age and that he'd been holding back this whole time.

"Don't bother trying to glamor me. It doesn't work on us."

"I'm not trying to use any power on you, Diana. I'm merely making it clear that this is my territory and my progeny. I may protect it. That's clear in the pact."

"I know the pact," she snarled. "I'm not here to fight you or break the pact. I'm working, just like you."

Rhys laughed. "I didn't think there were any packs left in Pittsburgh. You just happened to come to a city with no others like you and pick a hospital with two of us?"

"Not that I have to tell you but there is a pack in Ligonier. My family, actually. So, I came home and happened to be assigned to this hospital. I didn't pick it. But," she chuckled "to my defense, you guys are like cockroaches. Pick up a rock and vampires crawl out."

Man, I hated this chick.

I interrupted. "Wait, I have questions. What pact? And what is your issue with me? I've never met you."

"The pact," she sneered "is a little agreement between us and you where you guys win and we're under your thumb. And, my *issue* with you is that you put humans in danger by being here. I thought you were playing dumb when I met you yesterday. You really didn't know what I was?"

"No, I didn't. I knew you smelled different but not what you were. And, why would I care if I did?"

She had to think about that. "Because we're enemies."

"But, why?" I asked.

Rhys chimed in. "It is a long, complicated history."

"No, it isn't," she challenged. "You almost wiped us out and took over all the cities. Then you made us sign a pact with you as the beneficiaries. So, we get to hide in the country and live off of scraps while you sit in huge houses."

"Speaking of the pact," Rhys interjected. "Have you introduced yourself to the lord of the city?"

She crossed her arms. "No. Why should I? It's a big city. I only drive in for work. I'm not living here."

"That doesn't matter and you know it," Rhys's power was starting to die down so he must've been letting his guard down. That made me feel a little more at ease.

"Unless you two tell him, he won't find out. I only signed a 12-week contract so I'll be gone before he knows. Plus, I hear he's a dick and you two aren't exactly top-notch vamps so I'm guessing you don't even know him that well."

Rhys and I looked at each other. Neither of us knew what to divulge to her but we knew we'd have to tell Sorin. Did she deserve the heads up?

"What," she asked.

I looked back at her. "I'm dating him."

"What?" She covered her face with both hands. "Are. You. Fucking. Kidding. Me?"

"No."

Her hands dropped. Her bravado was gone and for the first time she looked nervous. "I thought you were new."

"I am," I answered. "Like a month."

"Seriously?" She dropped heavily into the chair behind Rhys's desk. "Of course. I try to sneak into the city to make some money for my family and I'm assigned to the one unit with the master vamp's girlfriend. Just great."

"How long have you been coming into the city?" Rhys stepped towards her.

"This is my first week. Got called when two nurses had to take leaves."

She was talking about Monica and me but I didn't think it mattered.

"You still can announce your plans to him. It isn't too late."

"Yeah," she responded defensively. "But, he's gonna be pissed that I waited and my pack is gonna be pissed I didn't follow the pact. I told them I'd presented to him when I took the contract. If he refuses me entry, what do I tell them? What do I tell the hospital?"

"Cross that bridge if you have to," I answered. "I don't know anything about the pact but I know Sorin. The longer you wait, the more upset he'll be."

"I have to work tonight and tomorrow night. When I am supposed to go? You bloodsuckers can't exactly have daytime appointments."

I tried to not be offended but was seriously over her insults. "Call him. Tell him what's going on and see what he says. You can do what you want but I'm trying to help you here."

"Fine," she agreed.

"Do you want me to call him?"

She took in angry breath but nodded her head in submission. Clearly between a rock and a hard place, she was going to have to accept our help. I dialed and he answered on the first ring.

"What a delight," he answered.

"Hold that thought," I interrupted. "You're not going to be happy. I am here with Rhys and Diana."

"Clarify." I felt that electricity seep from the phone and across my ear. His power was radiating across phone lines- not a good sign.

"Rhys came to meet her like I said and we discovered something unexpected."

"Spit it out, Katherine."

"She's a werewolf."

The electricity became hot and tingled over my skin. Pulling the phone away gave me some reprieve and I thanked the gods that anger wasn't directed at me. Hitting the speaker button, his voice filled the room.

"Explain yourself," he roared.

She was trembling when she took the phone from my hand. "I was given a contract for this hospital two weeks ago and began this week. I only come into your city for work but I should've come to you sooner." She took a breath and steeled herself. "I'm sorry."

When she apologized, she looked like she was regurgitating razors. Obviously, accepting fault was not her cup of tea. I totally empathized with her on that. It was equally clear that she wanted to get out of this mess unscathed.

"I will be there later. I expect a very good explanation as to why you broke the pact and why I should not declare war on your pack."

The phone went dead and she dropped it onto the desk top. It chimed so I retrieved it and opened the message.

SORIN: Do not trust her. Tell her nothing.

ME: Okay

I was too shaken to argue or ask questions. I'd never really seen this side of Sorin. I'd seen him fight Will in the barn and I'd felt his power before but never really seen how he ruled when he was crossed.

Diana looked back and forth between us. "I'm going back to work. If this is my last shift, I need to make as much as I can."

I couldn't help but feel bad for her. I wouldn't have wanted Sorin mad at me and I definitely understood wanting to support your family.

"I have to go up too," I told Rhys. "When we have time, I want the whole story."

"Agreed. I thought I had more time for history lessons but it seems we don't. Let me know when Sorin gets here. Although, with how angry he is I will probably feel him arrive."

"I wouldn't want to be her."

He nodded. "Me either."

23

The same crew from the night before met me when I walked onto the unit. They were all annoyed that I was so late. Only Diana knew why. She acted like nothing had happened but I knew she was worried. I remembered what it'd felt like to know I had to present myself to the head vampire of the city. I was so nervous and I hadn't already pissed him off. She was clearly one tough cookie to be acting so calm.

I peeked in on Monica and saw a huge bouquet of flowers next to my sleeping friend. The fragrance filled the room. She looked peaceful so I left her dreaming to go see my people. I was introducing myself to my last patient when I caught Mr. Kunsman's scent. It was pipe tobacco, bar soap and musky- like cologne. The groan escaped my lips before I could hold it back. To be honest I'd completely forgotten about him in the chaos of Diana and her big secret.

I straightened up, met his eyes and smiled. Walking down the hall in my direction, the clipboard was firmly gripped in his hand. I wish I could see what he'd written there. Toying with the idea of reading his mind, I let it go. Until I could actually control my powers, I shouldn't be using them in public.

"Nurse Murphy," he called.

"Yes, Mr. Kunsman."

"Call me Henry," he responded as he reached me.

"Call me Kate," I used the same tone he did. Somehow, he missed that I was mocking him.

"I'll be following each of your nurses for an hour. Is there any reason I can't?"

"No," I answered. "But please stay out of their way. May I ask something?"

"I may not answer but go ahead."

"Was the complaint on this unit?"

"I won't answer that yet. All I can tell you is that it involves night shift staff and is very serious." Then, he turned and walked back to find one of the nurses.

So, not only had he told me nothing helpful he'd turned my anxiety up a notch. Whatever was going on, it sounded like people really could be losing their jobs. I knew there was no point in losing my mind until something bad actually happened but that was easier said than done. This was the last thing I needed on top of dealing with trauma, learning to be a vampire, a new relationship and werewolves. Since everything was out of my control, I decided to just do my job.

Two hours later, Rhys texted me that Henry was in the blood bank. I wished him luck and said a plea to the universe that Rhys wasn't the one in trouble. Jackson hurried up to me, clearly out of sorts. "That guy is intense," he sighed.

"What did he say?"

"Nothing," Jackson exclaimed. "He just watched me and kept scribbling on that damn clipboard. Tiffany was almost in tears when he left her. The new girl is off the hook since she wasn't here when" he made air quotes for the next three words. "The incident occurred. That was all the guy said to me for an hour."

I let out a breath and rubbed my temples. "So, we know some kind of incident occurred then. It wasn't a complaint about behaviors or the hospital in general. Think—what has happened in the last couple weeks that could bring DOH here?"

"Dude," Jackson leaned back against the wall and crossed his arms. "I've racked my brain. I can't think of anything. Do we know it was this floor? I heard he's watching people on every floor."

"True," I agreed. "He's in the blood bank now. So, it may not have been us. He could be watching us to see how nurses should act and then comparing it to whatever happened."

"I sure hope so. I've seen people get fired over investigations. And, for him to be here multiple nights is not good."

"I hate to admit it but, I agree with you. Just keep your ears open and do everything by the book."

"You too," he patted my back and jogged off to his side of the unit.

Walking towards Monica's room, I heard her giggling. It was late for visitors so I knew it had to be Alex. Entering 502, I stopped when I saw Sorin at her bedside. He had the biggest vase full of daisies I think I've ever seen and her face was lit up as she laughed again. "Well, hello."

They turned to see me in the doorway and Sorin set the flowers next to the others. "Katherine. I was going to find you next. I wanted to see how the lovely Monica was doing."

"That's very sweet," I smiled. I admitted to myself that I was happy to see her grinning but was hurt that she was so wary around me but comfortable around everyone else. Sorin and Rhys were just like me but she didn't seem to be scared of either.

But she hadn't known them before they turned and hadn't seen them rip out someone's trachea. The thought startled me. For the first time I really had to consider the possibility that she and I would never be okay. Until then I'd held out hope. But, seeing her reaction to Sorin in comparison to how she looked at me made it hard to ignore the truth.

He gave his attention back to Monica and gave a little bow. "I will leave you to rest. I do hope to get to know you when you are feeling better."

"I'd like that," she said.

He joined me in the doorway and whispered in my ear. "Where is Diana?"

I smiled one last time to Monica, told her I needed to get back to my patients and led Sorin out into the hallway. "Can we go some place private, please? I know you're mad but the inspector is here."

"Where do you suggest?"

"Outside," I answered. "In the back. Where… you know. By the graveyard. No one goes back there. I'll find her and bring her down. Do you know where it is?"

"I do," he responded and left the unit. The fact that he was so controlled was making me nervous. I was learning that this was his 'calm before the storm' behavior.

Diana was in the break room. Her eyes told me that she already knew but I said it anyway. "He's here."

24

Walking down those stairs and out the back door was much harder than I had anticipated. Images and sensations threatened to flood my brain. I was acutely aware that the last time I'd walked through that door was the last few minutes of my humanity. The nurse that had carried some leftovers to the bench was murdered. What remained was someone the same but so different.

And, she was freaked the hell out.

Stepping out into the night air, I wondered if werewolves needed a jacket but figured it was not the time to ask. Sorin stood with his back to us, next to the bench I'd died on. Thankfully, it had been long enough that the smell of my own blood wasn't there.

Had anybody seen the remnants of my attack? Had there been any sign that someone had taken their last breath there? Or had it just seeped into the ground and was lost to time?

His power filled the air. It worked with the autumn breeze to dance up, down and around us. It was so much stronger than what I'd had a taste of. In the moments of passion, his magic was sensual, strong, electric and playful. Tonight, that power was hot and serious—a promise of dominance if tested.

Turning to face us, his eyes shone in the dark. I don't mean that they glowed like a flashlight. His eyes were like stars—moving and luminescent. My breath caught at the sight of him.

His voice was in my ears without his mouth moving. *Come to my side.* I didn't know how he'd spoken into my head but I listened. Moving to him, I turned and stood to his right to face Diana. Clenching every muscle, she stood her ground and didn't waver. After a few seconds of thought, I saw the decision cross her gaze and she dropped to one knee.

When she spoke, her voice was steady. "I am Diana Salgado from the Castaneda pack. I have come into your city for work but do not intend to stay. I plan to finish a three-month contract and leave. I ask you permission to be here and swear to follow your laws."

"Rise," he said and that one word cracked through the dark like thunder.

She did, with her head high and made eye contact with him. I was blown away by her bravery and couldn't help but be impressed. Anyone else would have peed their pants by now.

"Castaneda wolf. I know your pack leader. He has never broached the city without respecting the treaty. Why have you?"

"That's my grandfather and he doesn't know. It's not his fault. I did this alone."

"Again, I ask. Why have you not followed the agreement? Do not make me ask a third time."

She pulled down her shoulders and straightened her spine. "Because I don't like vampires and thought I could slip in and out with no one noticing. I thought I could avoid you guys all together. My bad."

The wind around Sorin kicked up and dried leaves bounced away. Only then did I see that the wind wasn't a normal fall breeze but had been him this whole time. "You defy me, disrespect my authority and mock the treaty that brought death to both our sides?"

Diana raised her hands and dropped down to both knees this time. She'd finally understood just how big she'd messed up. "Please, forgive me. I shot off my mouth without thinking. I'm begging you to let me work for three months and I'll be gone for good."

Dying down, the wind subsided and the leaves came to rest on the ground. I bit my tongue knowing that I shouldn't interject or undermine anything Sorin was saying. But man, did I feel bad for her. I knew exactly what it was like to run your mouth when you shouldn't.

"I am allowing you one chance, Diana. And, this only because I respect your grandfather. If you break another of our laws, your pack will be sent out of state. Speak the laws so I know you are aware of them."

With her head bowed she spoke to the ground. "Do not reveal our species or yours to humans. Do not hunt in your lands. Do not shift in a part of your lands that is not approved."

"Rise," this time his voice was normal—I mean normal for Sorin.

She did, revealing dirt on the knees of her scrub pants. A dried leaf sat in her hair but she didn't touch it or brush at her knees. She froze, awaiting his response.

"You have permission for three months entry to Pittsburgh. Know that Katherine is my partner and you are to treat her with the same respect as me. She and Rhys will be watching you. Do not defy me again."

"Yes, sir." She turned and marched into the hospital. When the door shut behind her, I let my body relax.

"Remind me to never get on your bad side," I quipped.

He rubbed his hands down my arms. "You did the right thing telling me. I meant what I said. Watch her and do not trust her."

"Okay," I responded. "I will."

"Can you be off tomorrow night?"

The sudden change in the subject surprised me so I took a second to think. "I don't know. This DOH guy is on the war path. I don't know what he's looking for but I think he's after some of the staff."

"I will agree to whatever you need to do but I was hoping you would be my date to Evelyn's dinner."

In that case, I thought. Screw the staff. I wanted to see her face when I walked in with him. "Well then, I would be honored and will make sure to be off. I can stop by my house to grab a dress."

"No need," he stopped me. "I ordered you one today in the hopes you'd say yes."

I smiled. "You think of everything. Shoes?"

"I let Tamela pick the shoes. I cannot be perfect at all things." He leaned into me and brushed his lips against mine. "How long until you return?"

"Not long," I sighed. "But I need to get back up there. I've spent more time off the unit tonight then I should have. Any more of this and I'll be the one getting fired."

"Go back, then. I will see you at home."

There it was again—home. As I walked away, I realized that every time he said it I was getting less and less freaked out.

25

It was harder to track down Jerry than I'd hoped and took longer than planned to convince him to give me the next night off. He'd eventually conceded, admitting that the plan for Mr. Kunsman was to be on the 3rd and 4th floors the next two days so they really didn't need me. I swore that I only needed the one shift off and would be back for the following night. Henry had told Jerry that after seeing the other units he would interview doctors and release any findings. With any luck, the DOH would be out of the hospital in three days maximum and I could be back to my vacation.

When I pulled into the driveway of the manor, I could almost feel the sun behind the trees. I rushed into the house and up the stairs. It was eerily quiet so I assumed everyone was settled down for the day. Sorin was at the end of the hall when I turned the corner.

"Cutting it close," he said.

"I know but I got the okay to be off tonight and you have yourself a date for dinner."

Wrapping his arms around me, I dropped my bag onto the floor and didn't care if it stayed there all day. It had been a very long night and all I wanted was to climb into bed with him. "You worried me," he said into the top of my head.

"Sorry," I answered into his chest. "Worst case scenario, I could have slept in my van in the parking garage."

He opened the bedroom door, lifted me up and shut the door behind us after stepping in. Tossing me onto the bed, he started to pull off my sneakers and I pulled the scrub top up and off of me. Undoing the tie of my pant, he pulled them down and off. With extraordinary speed, he stripped off his clothes while I crawled backwards up to the top of the bed and under the covers. He was next to me before he responded to my comment. I didn't like how serious he looked.

"Katherine, you put yourself in danger when you work. When I stood before that cemetery, I could not look at the bench. You were killed in that spot. Then taken from the parking garage you just spoke of. You've encountered a werewolf without knowing and almost not beat the dawn home."

I opened my mouth to dispute but he silenced me with a look.

"You are powerful but you cannot control the power. You don't know yet what you smell or hear. Sleeping in your van would expose you. What if someone saw you and knocked on the window only to realize that you were not breathing and your heart not beating. What would they do?"

I thought and answered. "They'd call a code and try to save me."

"Correct," he said gravely. "But in saving you they would expose you for what you are. Expose all of us. Each time you work you risk not making it out in time or meeting an enemy without knowing it."

I sat silently, thinking about everything he'd said. But then I thought of Jeremy. He'd been a professor—respected and happy in his profession. Eventually he had to walk away and now his brilliance was lost to a runaway and he was nothing but a pretty, moving mannequin. I wasn't going to stop being a nurse and start being Sorin's eye candy. "I'm not quitting, Sorin. Not yet. If it gets to the point where I have to, I will but I still have a lot of lives to impact before I slink away into the shadows."

"I know why you want you work, Katherine, I do. But it puts you at risk. I will provide for you and your children. There are other ways for you to help people. You can work with me. Help me run charities, maintain a safe space here for the vampires of Pittsburgh, come to functions with me.."

"Wait," I pulled back from him. "Are you asking me to be your new assistant?"

"No. I am offering you my city. Be my queen, at my side."

I let my anger show. "First off, I can't be here full time. I have kids that need me too. Secondly, this is what you signed up for. You fell for a nurse. No offense but this is not 'Pretty Woman'. You can't throw some dresses at me and make me an accessory."

He looked confused. I could only assume he hadn't expected me to turn down the offer. "That is not what I was asking and I know you have children. I thought you would be happy to work by my side. And, I don't want to worry every night that you might get stuck in the hospital and not make it out. You and I both know that they cannot promise you will walk out of the building when you need to. What if you are in a code blue? Will you stop CPR to leave before sunrise?"

He was right but I couldn't think about that yet. I couldn't accept that I may have to lay down my stethoscope forever. I turned my back to him and lay there. "Katherine."

"I can't talk about this now. Please just let me think."

To his credit, he let it go and I felt him lay down. In the silence, my mind was racing. Was I done at the hospital? Was he right? Every time I walked in there, was there a chance that I'd be discovered? All vampires would be discovered? What would I do if, like he said, I was in the middle of a code and had to walk out? Could I? And if I didn't leave in time and the sun was up, what would I do?

I could hide in Alex's office, I thought. But what if he wasn't there and it was locked? Or, I couldn't control the onset of sleep and I just snapped off in the middle of the unit? They'd assess me and think I was dead. Then they'd attach a monitor to me and see a flatline. How long before they realized they didn't have a corpse but a real-life undead creature? What if the sun rose while they worked on me and the daylight streaming into the unit fried me to ash?

But if I quit—what would I do? How would I explain that to the girls? To Tom? How would I explain being able to pay my bills? I guess I could fake having a work from home job but for how long? And how many more lies did I want to tell them?

And, the big question—could I be content just being at Sorin's side? Because once I did it, there was no going back. And, did I really want to put all of my eggs in this one basket already? We had just said I love you only days before. Wasn't this all moving a little fast?

Rhys worked at the hospital and had for years with no issues. But, it was different and I knew it. He was in the basement where no one saw him. He was much older than me and able to control himself. Plus, he wasn't a nurse. He could literally walk out anytime he needed to.

Maybe I should talk to him, I thought. *See what Rhys says.*

And if he agrees with Sorin? I didn't know and I didn't want to think about it anymore. I willed myself to fall asleep so I wouldn't have to deal with my thoughts anymore.

And, that's exactly what happened.

26

When I woke up there was no one next to me. I didn't think I'd ever be relieved to not see him beside me but that's what I felt. I didn't know what to say so I was thrilled to have a few more minutes to think. I pulled on my dirty scrubs and left the room preparing myself to see him but saw Tamela at the top of the stairs instead.

"Kate," she said and came towards me. "Sorin wanted me to pass something onto you. He said that he had to get on this call and he is sorry. He wants to finish your talk later. I assume you know what that means?"

"I do," I said.

"Also, be ready for the limo at 11. I can help you with your hair if you want. The dress is downstairs. I'll bring it up if you want to get a bath."

"Should I?"

Tamela smiled. "You smell like the hospital. And, I am sure you will want to be at your best for this evening. I would wager my life that Evelyn will be."

I tapped the side of my head. "Smart thinking," I told her. "Any help will be appreciated."

"Truthfully," she leaned in. "I despise her. I would love to see her knocked down a peg or two. Don't wear makeup. You are breathtaking without and she will put on too much. Go light on any perfume as we can be overwhelmed by scents easily. Trust me with your hair, shoes and jewelry. Sorin chose the dress and it is exceptional as always."

"Love it," I exclaimed. Heading for the bathroom, she spoke to my back. "Leave the scrubs in there. I'll throw them in with my clothes tonight."

"I owe you," I yelled back and slid into the bathroom without looking at the closed office door. I knew he could hear us but didn't care. I wanted some time and was going to be sure I got it.

The bathwater was starting to chill when I climbed out of the huge tub. For those of you curious- yes, vampires have to shave. Our hair still grows.

So, I had shaved, washed and conditioned my hair, loofahed every inch of myself and brushed each tooth. I had nothing else to postpone leaving the safe bathroom. I found the black satin robe I'd grown to love and the hair dryer I knew was under the sink. Tying the robe around my waist I swung the door open to face whatever awaited.

The still closed office door awaited so I figured I had more time and that was fine with me.

What awaited me in the bedroom, however, was unexpected. Lying across the bed—protected by a clear, plastic garment bag—was a long red satin gown. It looked impossibly long and way too elegant for me. I had the sudden urge to back out of the dinner. The gown was too fancy and I was 100% certain I was in way over my head. Combine that with the strain and unspoken issues between Sorin and me meant this dinner was doomed.

Before I could rush down the hall, Tamela stepped in with a large bag in one hand and a chair in the other. "Let's get ready in your room. There's a better mirror there and I don't want Sorin to see you until you're ready. Every woman deserves the big reveal before a fancy party."

"I don't think I should go."

"Bullshit." Tamela kicked out a hip in defiance. "You're going."

I didn't argue. I was nervous, not dumb.

Carrying the dress into my birch tree lined bedroom, I was not unaware of the weight of it. Yes, I was super strong but I also knew what a dress should weigh. This one was heavier—which meant it was not cheap. Tamela sat the chair down facing the large mirror and pointed at the bed. I lay the dress across it and dropped the hair dryer next to it. She then pointed at the chair and I followed the command.

Unpacking the bag, she lay each tool on the dresser. I saw bobby pins, a curling iron, a straightener, several types of brushes, some sparkly clips, a necklace box and a shoe box. Fighting my nature, I trusted her decisions and didn't ask any questions. The hair dryer was deafening with my new hearing so I focused on trying to the turn down the volume. To my delight, I was able to do it and the whoosing died down to a muted whisper.

"Thank you for doing this. You really don't have to. I'm sure it's not in your job description."

"You're welcome," she answered. "And, I want to do this. I've been surrounded by men for too long. Secretly, I was excited to do some hair and pick out shoes. I'd had been crushed if you said no. It gets lonely among the testosterone."

"Don't you have friends?" I asked.

"No," she responded very frankly. "Women use me to get to Sorin. Men treat me like one of the guys because I'm a bodyguard."

"That's sad," I said as she flipped off the hair dryer and plugged in the curling iron.

"Not really. I've never been one who needs friendship."

"Oh," I tried to change the subject. "So how do you know how to do hair?"

"I like knowing how to do things. I get interested in something and then look up everything there is about it. I watch videos and read manuals and train online if I can. Hair was an obsession in the 70s and 80s but I've stayed on top of new styles and techniques."

"Lucky me. I guess I don't have to worry about heat damage or anything like that."

"You do not," she answered.

We stayed quiet while she curled, twisted, brushed and pinned. It was soothing to have her play with my hair. I thought about the night Sorin had washed my hair for me and it brought a pang to my gut. *Was he mad at me?* It didn't really matter because I was going to find out soon and have to face whatever he was feeling.

"Tamela? Can I ask you something? You don't have to answer if you don't want to."

"Go ahead."

"Sorin said something about you knowing what I went through and you'd been a victim. What did that mean?"

She didn't stop what she was doing but the air around her changed. I felt horrible for asking. She was having a good time doing hair and I'd ruined it. "Never mind. It's none of my business."

"No, it's okay. I planned on telling you. Just wasn't sure when or how to start."

She cleared her throat and unplugged the curling iron, picking up a hair pick and a handful of the gemmed clips. "A long time ago, I was sold to a man who was cruel. At first, he had me working around the house and it wasn't bad. I stayed in a small cottage on the property with my father and mother at night. I'd seen what he did to anyone who messed up so I made a point to not mess up. I was quiet and careful."

She sounded more like a soldier reporting than someone telling a story. "As I got older, it was harder to not be noticed."

Going silent, she continued to fluff curls and push on pins. I stayed quiet out of respect, allowing her to go at her speed or stop the story if she needed. She didn't stop. "One night, he pulled me out of my bed and carried me to the house. I heard my parents scream and I screamed but no one helped. He locked me in the basement with a mattress and a bucket. When his family was asleep, he would come down to the basement."

She stopped talking again. I didn't need the details to know what she meant. My heart ached for her–a young girl locked in a basement with no way out.

"One night I heard this commotion upstairs. There were men yelling and crashing. When the door opened, I was sure he was coming down, drunk and in a rage, ready to take it out on me. I prayed that this time he'd kill me. But, in his place was a man with black hair and grey eyes and the palest skin I'd ever seen. I thought he was a ghost at first, or an angel. I never asked how he knew I was down there or why he saved me but he did."

"And your family?"

"Gone. I begged him to stop by the cottage before we left but it was empty. I never knew what happened to them."

"Did you ask the man?"

She looked into the mirror and I found her eyes in the reflection. "When Sorin carried me up the stairs, he shieled my eyes but I saw enough. There was blood everywhere and more bodies than I could count, we were moving too fast."

"I'm so sorry."

"He brought me here to Pennsylvania where I healed and grew and was turned into the vampire you see before you."

"That's why you said you understood what I was going through?"

"Yes. To be at the mercy of another—to wish for death—to flash back again and again. I know it well. I'm sorry I grabbed you the other night. It was so insensitive."

I turned to face her. "What I went though was nothing like what you did. I'm so sorry to hear that you suffered like that. Please don't feel bad. You were trying to help make me less vulnerable. And now I totally get why."

"Kate, this isn't a competition. No one's suffering is more than or less than another's. Suffering is suffering. But I'm stronger for mine and it's clear that you are too. Now turn around so I can finish."

This time I turned around and really looked at my hair. Half of it was up in a mass of twists with sparkling gems peeking out from all over. The other half fell around my shoulders and down my back in soft, long curls. It was everything I hoped for and weirdly emboldened me.

As I marveled at the intricacy of the style, she opened the necklace box and placed the item within around my throat. A choker of diamonds and rubies graced my neck and every time I moved or swallowed the gems twinkled in the light.

"I'm keeping your ears and wrists bare to showcase the necklace, which showcases your face."

"I'm in way over my head," I said before I realized it would be out loud and not in my head.

"Listen to me," she laid a hand on each of my shoulders and caught my gaze in the mirror again. "He's already chosen you. Remember that. Hundreds have yearned for what is yours. He wouldn't have fallen for you if you weren't deserving. So, own it."

"Tamela?"

"Yes?"

"Can I be your first friend?"

She smiled faintly and then pulled it back. "Of course."

27

"Katherine?"

I heard him call up to me from downstairs as Tamela was zipping the dress up behind me. She handed me the silver, strappy heels and nodded. "You are worthy," she said. I inhaled, took the heels and slid them on before starting my walk into the big, reveal moment that all women deserve.

The dress was ruby red and off the shoulder. The bodice was formed by the two pieces of fabric crisscrossing over the torso. At the waist, the fabric opened up to create a large, flowing skirt with a slit up to the middle of my thigh. Every time I took a step in those heels, my leg peeked out and returned to be lost in the skirt. I'd been afraid when I'd seen how long the dress was but the slit meant it flowed backwards like a train on the ground and created a stunning effect when you walked.

The final moment unraveled perfectly when I became visible at the top of the stairs and looked down at my date. We both took a moment to stare. He was in a tuxedo and looked every bit the distinguished gentleman that I'd expected. It was the first time I'd seen his hair pulled back and it made him look older, more regal.

As I descended the stairs, his eyes watched my every move like a child who sees something magical and is afraid it will disappear should they lose sight of it. I saw the clouds gathering in his irises.

"Katherine," he whispered. "I have no words for your beauty."

"Thank you," I responded. When I reached the bottom, I took his outstretched hand and curtsied. It'd been what I was supposed to do the first time I met him but I'd botched it and bowed instead. He couldn't hide the delight in his eyes when I looked up.

"Shall we?" He led me out of the house and into the black limousine that awaited us in the driveway. Edwin stood by the opened back door in a black uniform. Sliding into the leather seat, Sorin joined me and the door shut. The decanter in the back held blood so I assumed this wasn't was a rental from a human company. Since Sorin's bodyguard was our driver, I guessed this was his private car.

He tentatively laid his hand on my thigh and I laid mine over his to show him we weren't at war. "As much as I'd love to now ruin this perfect moment, I do want to finish our conversation before we arrive."

I sat quietly looking ahead and preparing for another argument.

"I want us to enjoy this evening and not have anger between us so I will skip straight to honesty. Do you remember when you told me that it would destroy you if I did not love you and you would exist for eternity without me?"

"Yes," I whispered.

He reached for my chin and turned me to face him. "If you died, I would walk into the sun and await death."

The air was sucked out of my lungs. I knew he wasn't lying. He would walk into the daylight if I left him—voluntary or not. Did it scare me or make be happy?

"When you leave me, I worry that some evil will befall you and you will not come back to me. I have not felt this penetrable in centuries. So, I selfishly want to keep you safe and with me, where I can control everything around you and protect you every moment."

I swallowed as air returned to my chest and I could breathe again.

"But it *is* selfish and I see that," he took his hand from my chin and ran it down my arm to my hand, gripping it. "If you must work then work. If put in the same position, I don't know that I could walk away from my duties either."

I took a shuddering inhale and tested my voice. "Thank you."

"You're welcome," he laughed. "But it was terrible of me to even ask it of you. I spoke out of fear and worry, without considering your feelings."

"I've been thinking, too." I let out a sigh and leaned into him. "You have very good points. Every time I go in, I do risk a lot. I put all of us, my livelihood, my kids and everyone I love in danger. I'm not ready now but I do think I need to find another way to be a nurse and soon."

"I will take that as a compromise and promise to help you do whatever you choose to do."

"And, in the meantime," I said. "I would love to learn more about what you do and how I can help you take care of the other vampires in our city."

He was pleased which made me extremely happy. "Well, consider this evening your first lesson in leadership. This evening we are attending a dinner for charity. The wealthier of us in this city and some surrounding ones pay for an invite to the event. The money goes to a fund to help new vampires or those in need to get whatever is necessary. Recently we were able to sunproof a home for a young man who was sleeping in a dirty garden shed. He was turned against his will in another area, found his way to us and we've been caring for him."

"A vampire charity? I thought I'd heard it all."

"We care for our own," he answered. "Misfortunate can befall anyone–living or non."

"How is this a lesson for me? And why would you pay to go to this party?"

"You will need to be civil and mingle with the group here this evening. It is important that we maintain peace among us. We represent this area. I believe the lord of DC and the ladies of Philadelphia and Baltimore have traveled in for this. They are interested in creating a fund like this for their lands. You pay for the invite for two reasons: to give to charity and to be able to rub elbows with the most powerful around. At this event will be masters but also those who are leading their industry. Fashion, architecture, business.. there is no telling the connections you could make at one of these parties."

Everything in me wanted to crack a joke but I was recognizing the inappropriateness of my humor more often. I guess I really could learn.

"Katherine." It was his serious voice so I prepared for a lecture on being respectful, instead he gave me a warning. "Remember that these other masters cannot know of your powers. Please stay close to me. I will stay tuned into you. If you think something may happen that you cannot control, leave the house and return to the limo. I will meet you there."

Now, I was officially panicked. I hadn't even thought about my out-of-control magic. What if something did happen?

"Breathe," he said making it clear he was already in tuned to me. "You controlled your rise and fall in my office so you know you can do it. Just keep your emotions in check."

"Can we practice in here? One last night? Something quick like the reading minds thing."

"We cannot."

"Why," I pleaded.

"Because we are here."

Showtime.

28

Evelyn had the same half-circle driveway that Sorin did and like his manor, this was tucked back in thick trees and far from any main road. That's where the similarities stopped. When I'd first seen the manor, I'd thought it was extravagant. Now that I'd seen *Chateau Evelyn*, Sorin's house looked like a guest house. This place was an actual mansion. A large, white marble torch sat on each side of the walkway to the front door. The house extended to each side further than I could really gauged and peacocks walked around the property.

Yep, fucking peacocks.

We stepped out of the limo and I felt very exposed when I felt it pulled away behind us. I didn't know where it was going but it couldn't be far because that was my hiding place if stuff got bad, right? Sorin's hand rested on my low back and he laid his mouth against my ear. "Breathe."

I took a big inhale in and audibly let it out. Head held high, I walked to the massive entrance with Sorin at my side. Feeling the skirt flare behind me gave me a feeling of being a badass so I used it to bolster my confidence.

I belong here.

The white marble continued into the foyer of the mansion giving it a stark, classic appearance. It was more like a museum than a home. Sounds from the vast rooms to each side of the entryway mixed together in a symphony of talking, laughter, clicking glasses and a string quartet. The trill of a peacock came from behind me which brought an eyeroll from me.

Peacocks. The woman is ridiculous.

Sorin kissed me on my cheek and pulled my thoughts back into focus. "Let's get through this so I can take you home and get you out of this wonderful gown."

My body clenched in response to his proposal. I'd have turned and left that moment to return to the limo and get started early but a tuxedoed man in the corner of the foyer called out. "Lord Sorin and his guest."

Too late. We'd been announced and now we had to mingle. Damn manners.

We turned to the right and followed the sound of the violins. Each room was impossibly big and way too white for my taste. A long table graced the opposite wall with a row of crystal decanters. Each one was filled with blood and an equally neat row of crystal rock glasses stood empty in front of them. My gut churned at the sight. I had forgotten to eat. Without needing to say anything, Sorin led me to the glasses. A woman in a long black dress stepped up. "What type do you prefer?"

"Um, anything."

She curtsied, poured from the one in front of her and handed the glass to me. Refraining from gulping, I swallowed back the warm liquid and suppressed a groan. Sorin took the next glass from her and we headed for the adjoining room. This was where most of the sound was coming from. Musicians sat in the far corner playing something beautiful and haunting. At least a hundred people were split up into groups, lost in conversations and stories.

From across the room, I heard the telltale fake giggle of our hostess. "We must go say hello" Sorin said and I knew he was right. I finished the blood, set the glass on a nearby table and squared my shoulders. With the heels, Sorin stood only an inch taller than me. I tried to imagine what we looked like side by side. From the faces that turned to us as we passed, I was assuming we looked pretty damn good.

To my dismay, when she came into view, she was absolutely gorgeous. A white gown trailed behind her and lay on the ground like someone had positioned it that way. It was streamlined up her body like someone had painted it onto her and the lack of straps showed off her long arms, just like her pinned hair and dangling diamond earrings showed off her long neck. She looked like the human version of a swan princess and I hated her guts.

The only thing that gave me an ounce of joy was when she turned to see him, then me and her face fell. Within a second, her composure was back and the vehemence in her face was a memory but I'd definitely seen it.

"Sorin," she squealed as she stepped in to kiss each of his cheeks.

"Kate," she said in a sweet voice but shockingly didn't step in to give me air kisses.

"Evelyn," I said mimicking her sweet tone. "What a beautiful home you have. Thank you for inviting me this evening."

She paused to carefully consider how to respond. To her credit she went with "Of course and thank you."

To my right, I saw someone in my periphery step away from her group and to my side. Just as Evelyn pulled Sorin away to the left, Jeremy stepped into my view. "Excellently played," he said.

We hugged and I made sure Sorin stayed within yelling distance while we spoke. "Boy, am I glad to see you. You might be the only one here that actually knows me and doesn't want me dead."

"So, let the people here get to know you then. Evelyn may not have invited you but this is a great chance for you. Take advantage of it."

He actually had a good point. Why let her ruin the night? I had a stunning dress, a strikingly attractive date and was among the most influential of my kind. Plus, I was interesting and smart. The worst that happened was no one wanted to get to know me and I was okay with that. What I wasn't okay with was not trying and letting Evelyn win.

"Wait," I leaned into him. "Before I mingle, can I ask you a question?"

"Sure."

"Do you regret walking away from your career? I mean, do you feel like being a model is less.. I don't know what I'm trying to say. No, I do–what I want to know is does Logan respect you less as his employee than he did when you were a literature professor?"

He raised his eyebrows. "I need more. Why do you ask that?"

"Sorin wants me to quit nursing and help him, I don't know, rule this city, I guess. He wants me to not work and to pay my bills."

"Wow. That's a lot to unpack. I'm going to assume you need to talk about much more than we can truly discuss here in a few minutes. I don't want to give you advice or an opinion that may affect what sounds like a big decision without knowing more. Can I do this? Can I invite you to my home on another evening when it's just us and listen to everything you have to say? Then, I will give you my thoughts. Does that sound good? Do you need to choose tonight?"

"Actually, that's a way better idea. Yes, that would be great and no I don't have to choose tonight."

"Wonderful. I have your number and will text you before I leave while it's fresh in my brain. I think we've been put in each other's path for a reason my friend. Now, go meet and impress powerful people. Know that the more you make people laugh tonight, the more it will eat away at Evelyn."

29

Evelyn was talking Sorin's ear off but at least he was within eye sight and shouting distance. When Jeremy walked away, he and she were speaking to a short, round man about something that looked important. He had glasses on but I knew from experience that vampires no longer needed glasses. So that meant that he was wearing them for show. Odd.

I snatched a glass of blood off a tray as a black-clad waiter walked by. Approaching a group of men, I heard one saying "without their quarterback, they're sunk."

Nope, not my group.

The next was comprised of a few women who looked like they'd all been turned in their early twenties. The conversation was heated and one was arguing with another about "the power of polka dots."

Pass.

Finding Sorin to ensure I'd not wandered too far, I discovered him still with Evelyn and the bespectacled vampire. A younger man had joined their group and tried to look interested in their conversation but kept sparing furtive glances in the blonde's direction. He had it bad for Evelyn and she didn't seem to know he even existed.

Before I could sidle up to the next group and eavesdrop, I heard a woman behind me. "Terribly boring conversations, aren't they?"

Turning around, I had to look down to find the owner of the voice. She was less than five feet tall and I was gauging it was several inches shorter than that. Her dark brown hair was cut into a bob with sharp bangs across straight across a young face. She was so small. I wondered if she had been scared when she was first turned and so much smaller than everyone.

"Not boring," I said. "Just ones that I can't meaningfully comment on."

"Very political answer. I respect that. I am Akila."

"Katherine," I responded. She hadn't extended her hand to shake or anything so I just let the introduction hang in the air.

"The lord of the city's Katherine?"

Oh boy. Word was already out. What did that mean? "Yes," I answered very carefully.

"They are right, you are very beautiful."

"Thank you." It was awkward to be around someone who just speaks whatever pops in their head but it was good practice for being civil with everyone so I fought the urge to just walk away.

"What subject could you comment meaningfully on, Katherine?"

I responded without thinking. "Medicine."

"Excellent," she beamed, grabbing my arm and pulling me over to a long couch that was—you guessed it—white. She sat and I took the place next to her. "I was a medicine woman a long time ago before women should have known of such things. I have stayed knowledgeable on the subject and would love to discuss it with someone. How do you know of medicine?"

It was an odd way to ask so I answered honestly. "I'm a nurse."

She clapped her hands together. "Now? You mean you practice medicine in this time?"

"Yes," I said. "I work as a nurse in a hospital." *Shit, am I giving too much away?*

"Oh," she squealed like kid on Christmas morning. "To be you, to be in the modern hospitals and see what has come to art of healing. You must love your work."

"I do."

"Do you work in a specific area of medicine?"

"Mostly cardiac, I work on a telemetry unit."

"Please," I was just able to set down the glass before she grabbed both of my hands and squeezed. Thankfully, she let go right away because I thought she was going to break my hands. She was strong. "Tell me what you have seen on your most recent shift. Have you seen an open-heart procedure? What about a catheterization? A TAVR?"

"I have seen them all. We just have to ask and we're allowed to go in and watch any procedure we want to. The really good docs will teach us as they work. Some even let you scrub in."

Her face was a mix of awe and incredulousness. You would have thought that I told her I flew on a dragon to sit on a star. "Tell me. Have you done cardiopulmonary resuscitation on a human and brought them back?"

"Of course," I laughed. "I do that about once a week. Sometimes more, sometimes less. But I don't think a month goes by without doing CPR on someone."

"Amazing, truly amazing. You are doing things we only dreamed of. And, how is it being around all that blood and all those humans? Do you not struggle?"

"No. Not at all." But that wasn't true was it. I'd almost vamped out in front of a patient when I'd hung blood the first time since turning. It'd been really soon after and I hadn't eaten so that was stupidity on my part but it'd happened nonetheless.

I was getting a little worried about the line of questioning when I felt the electricity tingle over my chest and knew my knight had arrived just in time. "Akila, I see you've met my beautiful partner."

She reached up a hand and Sorin dutifully stepped up to the couch to take it and kiss it. Evelyn, unfortunately, was at his side still. I stood and so did Akila. She reached up to lay the freshly kissed hand onto his chest. "Do not lose this one, Sorin. She is magnificent. Please plan a trip to see me soon and bring her. I could talk to her for days."

Akila flitted away into the crowd and Evelyn looked shocked. Clearly what Akila had said upset her but I didn't know why. Sorin laid his hand on my back and his touch instantly put me at ease. "I would like to introduce you to a few more and then we will leave."

"So soon?" Evelyn quipped, not hiding her disappointment.

"I'm afraid so. Katherine only has this evening off and we do have plans for later." He let his hand slid down to the swell of my backside and back up to my back.

"Make sure you say goodbye before you go." She slithered away and back to her crowd of cronies leaving me pleased.

"I don't know what's gotten into her but I do kind of like it. Is that bad?"

"Oh my, Katherine. I do like this jealous side of you. She's upset because an invitation to Akila's home is very coveted and rather rare. Yet, you got one in minutes. I don't think you will ever cease to amaze me."

"And, why would everyone want her invitation?"

"A few reasons, I assume. One, she is the lady of New York City—a powerful spot to rule over as an international vampire must come through her city for passage into our country. Two, she is the wealthiest vampire in the world. And, third—no one knows for sure–but she is somewhere around 2,000 years old."

I laughed and he looked confused. "Why is that funny?"

"Wait. You're serious?"

"I am. You've managed to woo an extremely powerful and very old master in minutes. That is why Eve is upset. The best part is that you didn't even realize what you did. You just sat and spoke to someone without knowing what was in it for you. That is likely why she liked you."

30

For the next hour, we met more vampires than I could really remember. There were a couple lords and one more lady. They all were nice enough but, I didn't really hit it off with anyone like I had with Akila. By the time I was done smiling and greeting and meeting everyone the word was out because all the questions were the same.

Did you really get a personal invitation to the lady Akila's home?

The love of gossip and the speed with which it travels is something that humans and us have in common. Even death doesn't stop someone from spilling tea.

Sorin and I were talking to the vampire with glasses again. His name was Stanley, I learned and he was incredibly dull. He was discussing the recent trend in mortgages when my date leaned into my ear. "Go to the foyer. I'll tell him I need to find you and come meet you."

"I'm going to go powder my nose," I said to the men and Stanley grunted like I wasn't even there.

Reaching the lobby, I was thrilled for the break in the noise. The night had gone so much better than I'd hoped. I'd been the consummate lady, laughing at the correct time and the correct level. Using my manners and managing to walk through the room like I'd been born in heels and a ballgown. I thought the vampire grace was finally showing up and I was loving it.

"You aren't fooling me."

I groaned before I could stop myself. Evelyn appeared from the room I'd just exited. Had she been waiting for me? "What do you want, Evelyn?"

"You may be able to throw on a dress and not trip over your own feet for a few hours but we both know you are not going to be able to sustain this. He needs a real woman to rule at this side, someone who can host things like this with their eyes closed. Eventually, he'll see you for the independent, sloppy, complicated wreck that you are. You'll say the wrong thing to the wrong person and make one mess after another. And, he'll grow bored with cleaning up after you. It's exciting to save a woman once or twice. Men thrive on the whole damsel in distress thing. But it grows tiresome eventually. He'll shove you aside and come back to me like he always has when his relationships don't work out."

Be classy, Kate. Don't call her a bitch.

I took two graceful steps towards her, ensuring the dress flew up and out behind me. Every word I uttered next was said calmly. I let my seriousness come through in my eyes not my tone. "Listen up, Evelyn because I don't repeat myself. He and I are forever. You have two choices: back down, accept it, we can be casual acquittances who are cordial at events or you can keep this up and declare war. And, you will lose. Why? Because I am an independent, sloppy, complicated wreck who will fight to the death for the people she loves. Someone has tried to kill me twice and been unsuccessful. Why do you think you wouldn't be?"

Unfortunately, she did not back down. She closed the distance between us. "I choose the latter. But I have no desire to kill you, Kate. I'm just going to take all that you have and leave you to wish you were dead. No one takes from me. No one."

Heat rolled in my stomach and boiled up my throat. Her eyes grew wide but she didn't back down. Instead, I felt an icy wind hit my face.

She was answering my power with hers. I was starting something that I was close to not being able to stop.

Sorin rushed into the room and between us. He may have been feeling both powers but his eyes were locked on me alone. "Stop." He said and the voice cracked in that foyer with the threatening storm tone I'd learned to listen to. It snapped me out of it and the heat behind my teeth retreated back into my stomach. I grabbed his hand and had no words. He and I both were very aware of how close I'd gotten to blowing it and showing Evelyn that she was right.

"Thank you for a lovely evening, Evelyn." I spoke out without losing Sorin's eyes. "My lord, I think we should leave for the night."

"I agree." He turned to Evelyn while stepping backwards. I was already at the door when he bowed. No kiss on the hand for her this time. "Good evening. Thank you for the invitation and the generous donation to the vampires of Pittsburgh. Due to this event, several other cities will be creating a similar fund. I'm sure they would love your insight on how to throw a party this successful."

Reaching the entryway, he laid his hand on my back and we left the mansion to the sounds of her returning to her guests. But I knew that she was far from done. We'd both fired our first shots and started a war. For this night, at least, the fighting was over.

When it would begin again, I didn't know.

Safely inside our limo, I laid my head back against the leather and sighed. "That woman."

"Katherine, you almost gave her exactly what she wanted."

"I know!"

"How did things escalate things that quickly?"

"I don't know. She just pushes my buttons." No need to tell him that I'd basically thrown down a gauntlet and she'd picked it up. I'd pretty much offered up battle so it was totally on me that now I had a real-life arch-nemesis. It was possible that she was all talk and she wouldn't really come after me but even as I thought it, I knew that wasn't true. That chick would rather die than let me have Sorin.

"You cannot let her get to you. You have to control yourself. Anyone in that party knowing about your powers is dangerous… all of them knowing… I don't want to think about it."

That reminded me. "Do you trust Jeremy and Logan?"

He looked over, curious. I'd managed to get his focus off my little catfight so that was a win. "Why do you ask?"

"Jeremy invited me to come over and talk. I'm thinking about eventually becoming a nursing professor at a college. He taught at a university. Figured he can talk me through the pros and cons."

"I like them," Sorin answered. "And, I do like the idea of you teaching and not being in the hospital. You know that Logan works with Evelyn."

"I do. But he wouldn't even be there. It would be Jeremy and me. And I wouldn't tell him anything I'm not supposed to, so there'd be nothing that could be leaked to Evelyn."

"*Regina mea*, you are smart. I don't need to tell you what to do or give you permission to speak to someone. I trust them and you. But, will you take one of the guards with you? They can stay outside the home."

It seemed like the best I was going to get and I really wanted to talk to Jeremy so I agreed. My concession did wonders to lighten the mood so I took advantage of the rest of the ride home to run my hand up and down his leg, knowing exactly what effect it would have on him. By the time we reached the manor, I didn't know if he'd be able to stand.

He did of course and led me quickly up the stairs.

31

It wasn't the bedroom where he ended but the bathroom. Trusting him and too overwhelmed by lust to care where we were I watched him turn on the shower. The black jacket and cummerbund were tossed to the corner without him letting go of my gaze. Crossing the tile back to me he turned me to face the mirror and stood behind me to slowly unzip the dress. The sounds of the fabric falling to the floor and his groan when he saw I had nothing on underneath were lost to me. I was watching the creatures in the reflection. They were magical with the palest skin that almost glowed in the dimly lit room and eyes that couldn't be real. The man started to pull at pins in the woman's hair so it could fall in waves to her shoulders and down her back. As he worked, the look on his face was one of pure need.

When the last twisted tress was freed, I turned to face the man in the reflection. I had to touch him to know he was real. Unbuttoning each button revealed the chest that was the center of his power; that had shielded me, carried me, been a sleeping place for me and held the heart that wanted me. Adding the shirt to the pile, I ran my fingers over each muscle of that chest and let them play over every ripple and swell. My heels were still on so I slid them off and let my eyeline drop to this part of him—my favorite part of him. I knew the teasing was going to test both our patience so I only allowed myself a few seconds of exploration before I looked up to him and smiled.

Breaking away from him, I walked to the shower, through the steam and stepped into the stream. The pressure felt like a massage against my tense muscles. Letting go of the stress of the night and looking forward to what was about to happen, I let the water run down my skin. Moving to line the pounding water up with the tops of my shoulders, I laid each hand on the wall, dropped my head and enjoyed the sensation of the water on my upper back. That's when I heard his pants hit the floor and felt him step in behind me.

Hands kneaded my shoulders and a moan escaped my lips. They slid up to each side of my neck, down my back, around my hips, across my stomach and up to grasp a breast in each hand. Leaning back into him, he took the weight of me and I felt him ready against my low back. His hands squeezed, released, rolled and played until my nipples were throbbing. The sensations of him and the water running down the front of me were almost too much to take. Simultaneously I wanted to rush this and also have it never end.

His mouth found my neck as he ran his lips over the place my pulse had been, only to move to my earlobe and nip. I felt the quick scratch of his fangs and ran my tongue over my teeth to find that mine were also down. I'd had much better control over them the last few days but this had proven to be too much and they'd been triggered by need.

Grabbing my hips, he turned me to crush his mouth against mine. The water ran over our kiss while our tongues tangled in a passionate dance. My fangs were throbbing, a new experience for me and he pulled back. Those grey clouds were furiously swirling in his irises and I thought I could see actually lightening in his eyes. "Feed on me," he said. "Bond to me."

I didn't need him to repeat. I struck at his neck and sank my teeth into his flesh. The tightness of his trap muscle relaxed when my fangs slid in. His arms wrapped around my back and pulled me into him.

Until that moment, I'd never drunk from a living donor. I'd only known blood from bags. I didn't know if what I was tasting was what all fresh blood tasted like or if it was just because it was a vampire but I didn't think I could ever stop.

What ran down my throat was the sweetest honey and the most expensive bottle of wine. It was like drinking a sweet nectar from a peach off the tree on a warm summer day. My magic exploded in my stomach and was shot out into Sorin. I sucked at his neck and his grip on me was like a man trying to save himself from drowning. Pulling my mouth away from him was the strongest thing I'd ever done and his lips were on mine instantly.

Tasting him in the kiss was ecstasy.

He broke the embrace by turning me back to face the water and pulled my hair to the side. That's when he struck at my neck the same way and I cried out with the orgasm that shot through me. It bent me over as the waves of pleasure rolled over my body. Holding his arm around my center, he sucked at my throat and slid himself into me, making me cry out again. As his mouth left my neck, I saw the drop of blood fall to the shower floor and wash away. Then, my senses were lost to the awareness of him moving in and out of me. I placed my hands on the wall to steady my shaking muscles and give me the ability to move with him.

When the orgasms hit us and reality had seeped back in, I was worried we'd broken glass with the mixture of our screams and the power that erupted from us. I figured we'd hear soon if something in the house was damaged.

I realized the water had turned cold so I turned it off and turned to see Sorin leaned back against the shower wall. I stepped into him and laid a kiss on the two small fang marks on his neck; my marks.

"It's a shame that'll be gone in a couple days."

"Yes," he smiled wryly. "But we will forever be bonded."

"I like that."

"As do I."

Forever.

32

I knew the building in front of me even though I rarely saw it at night. Olivia and Ellie's school looked so different without the sights and sounds of kids everywhere. You could almost smell the exhaust of the buses, the cafeteria and fresh paper. I couldn't remember why I'd come here. The dark windows told me everyone had left so it wasn't like there was a practice that I needed to get them from. The band had just had a concert so it wasn't that. Perhaps they'd forgotten something they needed for homework and I was supposed to be getting it. But, how? There were no cars in the parking lot so no one was here to let me in. Plus, it didn't seem like it was freshly dark; it was very dark so it was late in the night.

A howl ripped through the air and sent chills down my spine.

"Girls, run!"

Sorin shot up in bed and was over me when I opened my eyes. "What?" he asked.

I grabbed his arms. "The girls."

"What? I don't understand. Did you have a vision?"

I looked around and saw that I was in bed, in Sorin's room, at his manor. I wasn't in front of the school. Looking at the clock I saw that I would have heard the alarm in a few minutes so I had been sleeping.

"I did. I don't know what it means, though."

I sat up and he wrapped his arms around me. "Start at the beginning. What did you see?"

"Their school. It was night time. No one was there. I didn't know what I was even doing there. Then, a wolf howled. Last time I had visions I didn't know what they meant until it was too late. By the time I saw the barn I was already in serious trouble. Now, it's about the girls. They were in both visions. I can't afford to find out what it means when they're already in danger. What's the point of seeing this stuff if I don't know what to do?"

"But the girls weren't really in either one. You thought you heard them in the park but you didn't see them."

"Sorin, think about it. The park and the school are both places I only go with them. In the barn vision, I heard Monica scream and saw Rhys's car but didn't see them. It didn't stop them from getting almost murdered."

"You're right. So, what else do we know? You were in daylight in the last one and at night in this one, what else?"

I pulled back. "The howl. C'mon. There's a wolf howling in my vision and we just happened to have met a new werewolf in our city who hates me."

"That's a stretch but I see where you're going with this." The alarm went off and ended his thought.

I took my frustration out on the off button, stopping the alarm but also crushing the clock. Its retirement had come early. "I can't let her get to my kids."

"I will make sure she is watched closely. Tell Rhys what is going on and use him to help you keep an eye on her, too."

"Sorin," I said but stopped short. I was afraid to say it out loud. "She can be out in the day and we can't. How do I keep them safe when I can't even leave the house?"

"Talk to Tom," he reassured. "Think of a way to raise his awareness and caution without alarming him. Just make sure he drops them off and picks them up until we figure this out. We all have human allies that can do things for us in the day. You have Alex and Monica; I have my own. I can use them to watch your children, as well. But, start with Tom and Sarah before we escalate to a level we can't draw back from."

I nodded, feeling a little more at ease. "Okay. I will on my way to work. It's probably good we showered last night so I have a little extra time." At the mention of the shower, every nerve in my body came alive. He reached out and ran his fingers over the base of my neck.

"Speaking of which," he smiled. "You will need to wear something under your scrubs to cover that."

I ran my fingers over his matching mark. I knew from past experience that these bites took longer to heal that most injuries. He'd given me one on my chest only a few days after I'd met him. Then it'd felt slutty, now I looked back on it with pride. I think it had lasted until the third night but all of that was lost in the memories that I'd suppressed of my trip to the country in a car trunk.

"You will need to actually button your shirt all the way up for a change to hide yours."

He laughed. "On the contrary, I will proudly display this to anyone who would like to see it. Among our kind, this is a sign of commitment. I would no sooner hide this than hide you. Think of it like an engagement ring."

"Whoa," I responded. "I had no clue."

"Do you regret it?" He looked genuinely worried.

"Absolutely not. It felt like the most natural thing. Like I had to bite you."

That brought a light into his eyes. "As it should feel. I know you must go. Please do hurry back to me. I will see what more I can find out about our Diana."

Rolling myself out of bed, I spotted my clean and folded scrubs on the couch. I'd have to do Tamela's laundry for her one of these nights. Or, better yet, find out what chore she hated and do it for her.

Shuffling to my room, I raided the drawers and found a long-sleeved white tee that would cover my bite. I stared at it for a second in the mirror. His bite was bigger than mine and this one had been more substantial than the one he'd given me on my chest. It was like that one had been a test run and this one was the big show. It hurt my heart to cover it up but there was no way I could explain that to anyone at work. A hickie was hard enough to live down—imagine an actual vampire bite!

Once the shirts were on, I found that it was invisible and tried to not linger on the fact that he would get to proudly display his. Truthfully, the full vamp life was mine for the taking. He'd offered it several times and I was the one who wanted to continue among the humans. So, I had to hide my boyfriend's mark and keep it to myself.

The makeup was applied, hair was up and phone was in my pocket with plenty of time to eat and call Tom.

He answered on the third ring just and I was gulping. "Hello?"

I finished the swallow and responded. "Hey, Tom."

"Hey Kate. What's up? I'm not with the girls. I'm at work."

"No. That's good, actually. I wanted to talk to you. But you have to listen before you say anything."

"Oh boy. Let me pull over."

Taking a breath, I said a silent prayer that he'd believe me and not ask too many questions. "I have this really, really bad feeling. You can think I'm crazy or whatever but I'm going to ask you for a favor."

"Shoot."

"Please, can you or Sarah drop the girls off at school, pick them up and not let them go anywhere without you until this feeling goes away?"

When he spoke, it was his cop voice. I was not going to be lucky enough to have him just listen and agree. "Kate, if you're in some kind of trouble, tell me and I can help."

"I'm not, I swear." I was lying and I knew that lying was putting them all in danger but what was the alternative? Tell him the truth? "I just keep seeing teens come into the ER and I just have this sick feeling like the girls aren't safe."

"I get it. Cops have an instinct just like nurses do and I've learned to trust them. I promise to do what you ask but, Kate?"

"Yeah," I braced myself.

"If I find out that you've done something that put any of us at risk and you're not being honest with me, I will not forgive you."

"I know," I managed to respond with what little air I had left. "I'd do the same thing to you."

The line went dead and I dropped to my knees. Sorin had told me last night that he was being selfish but was he really? I was the one putting everything and everyone on the line so that I could have a "normal" life. Only, I was anything but normal. Maybe I should accept that I was dead to this life, walk away from my daughters and my job, and live a new existence with Sorin. It would be painful at first but over the decades or centuries, the pain would fade. I could show off Sorin's bite, run extravagant parties with him, visit millennia old vampires in NYC, help those in need and never have to set an alarm again.

But, I'd be a mother with no children to hold and a nurse with no lives to save. Could I really do that and look myself in the mirror? Or would I slowly die inside and grow to hate the men in my life: the one who'd turned me and the one who'd made me love him?

I wasn't going to figure it all out that moment.

What I did have to do was get up off that floor and go to work.

33

The sounds of the hospital hit me when I walked into the hallway of the doctors' offices. With my new hearing, I could adjust how the noises hit, which ones hit and which ones I could turn off. I was still working on it so I took a moment to turn down the beeps of monitors and IV alarms and turn up voices. I heard Alex's right away. He was in his office and talking on the phone.

Tapping on his door, I hoped he'd hear me but didn't want to interrupt his phone call. I figured he would just open the door when he was done. Instead, it swung open and the first face I saw was not his but Henry Kunsman, DOH inspector.

God, was I sick of this guy. *Give me my hospital back!* I screamed in my head.

He turned to me and smiled. Until that moment, Alex was the tallest guy I knew but he had to peek out from behind Kunsman. He let his stoic expression fall and showed me that he was equally as frustrated with the intruder.

Henry bounced his chin at me like he was saying hello. "Nurse Murphy, what a pleasant surprise. Are you here for business or pleasure?"

I ignored the obvious implication and chose to be overly professional. "Actually Mr. Kunsman, Dr. Kitchner is well respected in the hospital and I would love his professional advice on something. Obviously, I can't discuss it with you as that would be a HIPPA violation."

He looked back and forth between us. I didn't think he was buying my excuse but I didn't really care. I just wanted him to go. He must have decided not to push the issue because he retrieved his upside-down clipboard from one of the chairs and brushed past me.

"I will see you later, Nurse Murphy. I am coming back to your floor tonight."

When he was gone, I shut the door to the office. "I hate that guy. Why was he here?"

Alex dropped into the chair. I saw now how tired he looked. All of this was getting to him. He'd been sitting with Monica every day, plus doing his regular work, plus his research and now the DOH surveyor from Hell was in his business. I was reminded that he was human. How quickly I'd forgotten that some of the ones closest to me were not as resilient and bulletproof as I was.

"Alex, you look awful."

"Thanks," he said and dropped his head into his arms on his desk.

"What can I do to help?"

Looking up he shrugged his shoulders. "I honestly don't know. After you healed me, I felt like I could go weeks without sleep and lift a bus. But, with everything going on…"

"You're pushing yourself too hard. Take a day or two off. Get some sleep and eat a hot meal. Seriously, Kitchner. You're worrying me."

"I can't take a day until this guy's gone, first off. And, I feel like I'm so close to a breakthrough for the cure. Plus, Monica. I'm the only one who can visit in the day."

I felt like utter garbage. "I know. I'm sorry."

He stood. "That's not what I meant. It's not your fault or Rhys'; just is what it as and I can't stand that thought of her alone in that room."

Did I see something in his eyes?

"Alex? Do you like her?" Silence. I kept going. "Because if you don't, stop going to her bedside. She's madly in love with you and you're making her fall even harder." Again, no response so I finished my thought. "But if you do, tell her. Take it from me, time is so short and we have no idea what day is our last. Don't waste time."

Finally, he spoke. "I didn't think I'd ever be able to talk about these things with anyone; share a life with anyone. I resigned myself to solitude. Then, Rhys arrived and I had a confidant. Then, you became a friend. Now, Monica."

I waited, fighting the impulse to shake him or squeal.

"I feel like I didn't see her until now, not really. She is nothing like what I thought. She's warm and bright and funny. We like the same music. I told her about my sister and my work. She told me about her parents."

"And?"

"Kate, our kiss."

I gulped. I was hoping to never talk about this again, that it would just go away. But, not with Alex. He had to research everything. "What about it?"

He stepped into me. "I felt- something. It was something I can't explain."

"Power," I answered. "You felt my power. I couldn't control it and it flared up. You were the one in the room, nothing more." Even as I said it, I knew that wasn't exactly true. I had been part power but more than that. We'd been the much-needed presence of hope to each other. So, in that moment in that room, we'd found comfort in each other and tried to feed a need. I'd been confused afterwards but my time with Sorin had cleared it up.

He, on the other hand, hadn't had someone to hold onto.

"Take my advice, Alex. Forget the kiss. That was nothing compared to what you can feel with the right person. And, you'll never find it if you don't start getting honest with yourself and her. Now, do you need blood? I gotta go."

"Oh, yes! Thank you. I'm so exhausted, I completely forgot."

The process was almost routine at this point. Ten minutes later, six test tubes were being labeled and laid into the fridge. He'd given me a band-aid out of habit. I'd never stopped him. I didn't need it, the puncture healed almost instantly but, seeing what band-aid I got was quickly becoming my favorite part of being a guinea pig.

He asked the usual questions: any new powers? Have you feed? Writing in his journal as I answered, his head popped up when I told him I'd fed on Sorin.

"Wait, what? Can you guys feed on each other?"

"It's not for sustenance," I answered, repeating the way Sorin had explain it to me. "It's a bonding, like marking territory. Now, I can sense him if I need to and he can do the same with me."

"Interesting. Can I see the bite?"

I pulled down the top to reveal the clean punctures. "Why isn't it healed?"

"I don't know. Bites from other vampires take longer. The last one took a few days."

"Last one?"

I blushed. "This is the second time he's marked me. I've only bitten him once."

"And, when did that happen? The first time?"

I didn't know I could blush harder but there it was. "Actually, the same night as our... you know."

I thought he'd freak out or call me a name or something. He picked up his journal and started to flip back. *Had he written about it in his journal?* "Kate. Did your powers start before or after he drank from you?"

"Before. It was the first night. I was at the Hole, the night I saw you there. I was reading the bartender's mind without realizing it. I knew her name, that she had a pendant from her dad in her pocket and that she wanted me."

"That quickly? Okay. I will need to ask more about exactly when your powers emerged. I thought for a second, I'd figured something out.

Never mind. Well, congrats on you marking or bonding or whatever it's called. Seem like it's moving fast but you look happy so..."

He was suddenly acting weird, like he was trying to rush me out of the office. I figured he had a lot to do and was noticeably exhausted so I said my goodbyes and left for the fifth floor.

Climbing the stairs, I asked the universe for one, normal, boring shift.

34

I didn't have to look at the assignment board to know Diana was there. I smelled her when I stepped out of the stairwell. Hard to believe I'd never noticed how different she smelled than everyone else. But, to my defense this was all still really new.

I should bottle different scents so new vampires could be introduced to the smells and told what they were on day one. That would save a lot of baby vamps from a lot of embarrassment.

Actually, I thought, that wasn't a bad idea. Maybe I could really be a good sidekick for the master of the city. Bring new ideas to the table as the youngest one in the bunch. Most of those guys didn't remember what it was like to be new. I could bring a different perspective to it.

Diana was standing in the back of the unit with the inspector. I didn't know why they were talking since she'd only been here a week. I went to the break room to drop my things off and grab my stethoscope. I noticed new pictures decorating the front of one of the lockers. It was red-haired Tiffany next to a man at what looked like a pumpkin patch. They looked happy and for a second, I was jealous of her, in the autumn sun with hot apple cider and scratchy hay under her. But that was quickly replaced with relief that one less nurse was lusting after Sorin. Which meant I'd only need to deal with passive-aggressive comments from one now. Examining the nameplate on the locker, I could now differentiate the two Tiffanys by last name instead of their appearance. Irish Tiffany was actually Tiffany O. Scanning the lockers, I found the other one and now knew that her friend was Tiffany H.

Awesome! Already learned something this evening.

Making my way to the board, I found Diana was no longer with Mr. Kunsman but at the station. So was Tiffany H and a woman I didn't recognize. "Hi," I extended my hand to her. "I'm Kate."

She grabbed it and shook. "Susan. From four."

"Well, Susan who am I taking off of you?"

Report was quick and I was piling supplies into my med cart when I heard Alex's voice. Following it, I stopped outside of Monica's room. The conversation was wrapping up so I waited. When he came out, he was looking much better than he had before. Some of the weight seemed to have come off his shoulders. He patted my shoulder and kept going.

Walking in, I saw Monica smiling in a way that was normally reserved for Christmas morning. She saw me and to my relief the smile didn't falter. It was a faint whisper but I heard it. "He asked me out to dinner."

I dropped down to sit on her bed and she didn't pull back. "He asked me out to dinner," she repeated like she needed to hear it again.

"When?"

"When I get out of here and feel up to it. Anywhere I want to go."

"Mon, I'm so happy for you."

"I'm still in shock," she breathed out. "I imagined it a thousand times. And, just like that, it happened. For real. What do I wear?"

"Well, let's worry about getting you out of here first. Then, I think you deserve a new outfit for this."

"Yes!" She exclaimed, laid her hands on mine and then pulled them back.

"You're not cold," she said, more curious than freaked out.

"I'm full. That helps."

"Oh," she said. "You mean you had…"

"Donated and totally voluntary" I answered before she could ask.

"Right. I mean, I didn't think you—I mean I know you wouldn't—I mean I know you have to but to hear it so nonchalantly. It's weird."

"I know," I soothed. "It's okay. You can ask whatever you want. It's a lot to get used to." Before she could say anything that would break my heart, I took the subject back to Alex. "So where do you want to eat?"

"Oh, wow. Well, he said anywhere. And, I only get one first date with him so I want it to be perfect. I'm thinking Capital Grille downtown."

"Good choice," I nodded. "Amazing food. I've only been once but I remember the lobster macaroni and cheese very fondly."

"I bet Sorin would take…" she trailed off. She laid her hands back on mine and this time she didn't pull back. "Sorry. I keep forgetting."

"Mon. Stop saying you're sorry. You're my best friend. If it takes you 50 years to get used to this and be okay with it, I'd wait."

"Thanks," she said, laying back onto her pillow. "I gotta get out of here. Diana's great and everyone's taking good care of me but I gotta go."

The mention of her name brought back the wolf howl in my vision. "Hey, Monica? Has Diana said anything about me?"

She sat up looking suspicious. "No. Why?"

"Nothing," I reassured her. "She just really doesn't like me and I couldn't figure out why."

"Not at all," Monica returned back to her resting position. "She doesn't talk much and she hasn't said anything about anyone here. She's very focused on the job."

"Speaking of which, I better get back to it. Congratulations, again. I really am so happy for you." I stood and left her beaming in bed. I knew her well enough to know that she was picturing the whole thing in her head right down to the dress she was wearing and the menu.

35

The patient assignment this shift was particularly heavy so it was three hours before I stopped to text Sorin. I snuck off to the elevator lobby and pulled my phone out of my pocket. I'd missed a call from a local number I didn't recognize and a text from Rhys asking me to come down if I could. I texted Sorin.

ME: Remind me to tell you the good news when I get home.
SORIN: I'll take good news anytime. How's work?
ME: Awful but done soon. See you in bed.
SORIN: Deal.

I checked my watch and figured I could spare a few minutes. Dashing down the stairwell, it occurred to me that it was getting easier to walk down this corridor or through this hospital without having flashbacks. With that realization and the memory that Monica seemed less revolted by me every day, I felt confident that things really were getting better.

Opening the door to the basement, I expected Rhys' music to hit my ears but was met with silence. That was very unlike him so I prepared for something bad. But, turning into his office nothing really seemed off. He was behind his desk as usual.

"No music?" I asked and his popped up.

"Not with DOH in the house, by order of Jerry."

"Ah," I said. "And how did your time with the lovely Mr. Kunsman go?"

"Very uncomfortable. He asked a lot about our policies for checking blood and what we do during codes. He looked in a ton of charts and watched me deliver a few bags. Do you know why he's here?"

"No, I was hoping you knew more. So far, the most I got was that there was an incident."

"Yikes. Not good."

"What would you do if you got fired?"

"Why?" He looked alarmed and I wished I'd phrased it better. "Did you hear something?"

I held up my hands. "No! Sorry. I was just curious. Like, if you weren't working here, what would you do? How would you get blood?"

"Oh, well I have money so I don't really need to work. As for blood, there's always ways. I mean I could ask Sorin how he gets his. We'd be fine, Kate. Why? Are you worried you'll be fired?"

"No, just curious. What would you do every night?"

"I don't know. Read, I guess. Go online. But, I'd get bored pretty fast."

I wanted to talk about something else. It was making me think about what Sorin had proposed and how I'd eventually have to leave the hospital and I didn't want to go there. "Why did you ask me to come down," I asked.

"Sorin called. Told me to keep an eye on Diana and that you would explain. Did she mess up?"

"Ah, yes.. that." I spent ten minutes telling him about my visions and the conversation with Tom. He listened and didn't say anything until I was done. "So, I just think there's more to Diana than we're seeing. She showed up and now there's a wolf howl in my vision."

He came out from behind the desk and leaned back to sit on its surface. Crossing his arms, he sighed. "I don't like her at all. She snuck in and lied, she's got a terrible attitude and hates vampires. But, devil's advocate for a moment, there are wolves in Pennsylvania and the howl could be symbolism. If you remember, when you had the barn vision there was a howl and no werewolves showed up."

I threw my hands up in exasperation. "What is the point of this power? It doesn't show me anything helpful!"

"One thing at a time. Tom has the girls and Diana is here so everyone is safe tonight. With Sorin, you and I watching her she'd be a fool to make a move. She'd start a war between them and us. Our numbers are far greater and we are much more powerful."

"I sense a 'but' coming."

"But," he conceded. "When they shift, they are strong and fast. I don't truly know how many of them are left or if their numbers have grown. The last time, they killed a lot of vampires before they were subdued. And, there were far less humans in the mix that time."

I felt a little weak in the knees. Had I turned my family into cannon-fodder? Would they be casualties in a battle that had nothing to do with them?

"Katie, stop. You're jumping right to the worst and we're nowhere near that. Sorin is looking into her pack. We're watching her here and Tom's not going to let those girls out of his sight. Get through tonight and go home. You have a whole army around you."

"You're right. I have to get back up there. We can all meet up at the manor and talk more when we get a night off. Let's get through this inspection and deal with that first."

He kissed the top of my head and I left his office to the sound of him humming. He'd have music one way or another.

Climbing the stairs two at a time, I froze when I heard a door open and shut forcibly. I was on the second floor and they were definitely on the top floor. I didn't hear steps down so they were using the stairwell to hide. Someone hissed into the stairwell and I realized it was a harsh whispering. Pressing myself back against the wall, I focused my hearing on that hiss to turn up the volume. As it became louder and clearer in my ear, I knew it was Henry and he was agitated.

Hell yes, I thought. *Maybe I'll get a clue about who he's after.*

"Don't send someone else yet," he hissed into what I assumed was a phone and paused for the response. "Sir, with all due respect, I've been doing this a long time. I'm confident that I can have this closed in days."

Great. Days more with this dick poking around. Just what I need.

"Sir. I'm certain there is only one or two involved. Nothing more. I've shut whole groups down; I don't need help with two at most."

Oh my god. He could actually shut whole places down? I tried to not breath too loud, then reminded myself that he didn't have the hearing I did. Thankfully, I thought, he's only after one or two but I was worried about who that was. Jackson? Alex? Rhys? But, then again, he was on other floors. It could have been nurses I don't even know and I could be freaked out for nothing.

"We saw the pattern and it leads to here; I'm certain I'm right. I can feel it, I just have to find them. They're here or frequent here. You have to trust me."

Silence as the voice on the other line barked. I couldn't make out the words but the tone was angry. What was he talking about? What pattern?

"If you pull me, it will be a mistake. More will die."

I was getting more confused. As far as I knew every death in the hospital in the last month had been standard codes with no red flags. Maybe, I thought, it was something in the ER. They got a lot of deaths that could result in an investigation. Up on the units, our deaths were usually the result of injury or illness and rarely did anyone look into them. They were "open and shut."

"Thank you, sir." His relief at whatever the other person just said raised the volume of his voice despite the attempt to not be heard. "A week is more than enough. I've been hunting for thirty years. It may not be an employee but someone is using this hospital as their hunting grounds. If there is a vampire here, I will find them and destroy them."

Fuck.

36

Every muscle in my body turned to ice. Waiting for the sound of him returning to the floor felt like an eternity. When he did, I bolted up the stairs and onto my unit. Running to the break room but being sure to not use more than human speed, I slammed myself into the corner and dialed Rhys with shaking hands.

"You just left," he said.

"Rhys, we got a big problem. Shut everything down and meet me in the parking garage. I'll be there ASAP." I didn't wait for him to respond before cutting off the call. Grabbing my things from my locker, I tried to pull myself together and walk out to the nurse's station.

They were all there when I threw my papers in front of them. "I have to go. Emergency. Take your patients back; my info is on the papers."

Tiffany and Susan looked pissed. Diana looked like she didn't care if I died or laughed. I didn't let any of them ask questions, I turned and calmly walked off the unit, to the elevator and slammed my hand against the button to close the door.

Rhys was in the parking garage when I got there. "No time," I said. "We're taking your car and going to the manor. Now. We'll talk on the way."

To his credit, he didn't ask questions. Once we were out of the garage, I let out the breath I'd been holding. "Can I tell you and Sorin at the same time? I don't think I have it in me to say it twice."

"Sure but, Katie, at least tell me the kids are okay." His voice was shaking.

"Yes, they're okay."

The rest of the drive, he gripped the wheel tight enough to snap it. I replayed the words I'd heard in the stairwell over and over in my brain. You couldn't interpret those words in any other way. He'd said what he'd said and we were in trouble—not the doctors or nurse or staff—us.

Sorin was sitting on the manor steps when we pulled up. I didn't know how he knew but he'd known and I was grateful to see him. If anyone knew what to do, it would be him.

I headed straight for the stairs and knew the men would follow. Every fiber of my being was shaking when I sat on the long green couch. They chose to stand side by side in front of me. Concern was evident on their faces and I knew I was about to change their nights for the worst.

"I was in the stairwell and heard someone on the top floor on the phone. I wanted to practice controlling my hearing so I did. I knew it was the investigator and thought I'd get some details on what he was looking for or who he was after."

"And," Sorin prodded.

"It's us. He's after us. He's a vampire hunter."

They looked at each other and back to me. "How do you know?" Sorin asked.

"He said 'I've been hunting for 30 years, if there are vampires here I'll find them and destroy them.'"

Sorin moved to sit behind his desk and Rhys dropped heavily into one of the chairs behind him. Both of them were thinking but neither was sharing his thoughts. I was going insane waiting to hear what they were going to do.

"You and Rhys left abruptly, together. What did you tell them for why?"

Rhys answered first. "I don't really need to check in with anyone. I just tell the lab to cover blood requests and leave."

They both looked at me. "I said there was an emergency."

Sorin didn't look pleased or worried. He had that blank expression he gets when he doesn't want to give anything away. "What are the chances he heard or saw you in the stairwell?"

"Zero," I answered. "I don't think he'd been so open if he knew someone was listening."

He steepled his hands and rested his forehead on them. "This was what I feared when the murders were occurring. I worried that someone would put them together and it would lead them to the hospital. That is why I asked you two to find the person behind the murders."

He had. He'd mentioned it when we first met; that the killings put as at risk of being found out. We'd thought that Will's death had ended it, but we'd been wrong; it'd been too late.

"How bad is this" I asked.

Sorin looked up and at me. "Hunters are very good at what they do. There are not many but those that remain are still here because they are experts. A hunter on your trail is not something any vampire wants, no matter how powerful they may be. It puts us in a precarious position-either we kill him and others come or allow him to kill us."

"He's hunting for the vampire that killed all those women. That's not us. It was Will," I rationalized.

"Yes," Rhys joined in. "But he doesn't know Will's dead nor would he care. He's looking for *any* vampires. The murders just brought him to us. He won't bother with asking if we kill humans or not. When he figures out what we are, he won't stop until we're dead."

"So, we don't go back."

Sorin stood when I said that. "You cannot break from routine. If you're due to work, you work. If he asks you questions, you answer. Don't change anything, it would only make him look harder at you." He turned to Rhys. "Same for you."

I was just finally putting it all together. "So, there was no DOH complaint?"

"No," Sorin answered. "I'm sure if we call, there is no inspector for our state by his name. That's likely not even his name. These hunting organizations have fake badges for any department they need. Hunters are like ghosts. They are gone as quickly as they arrive and no one is the wiser."

"So, what if we call the DOH and let them know we have an imposter?"

Rhys stood now. "No, Kate. That would only tell him he was close and he or someone like him would dig deeper."

"He's right," Sorin agreed.

The doorbell rang through the house and we all checked the clock. Only an hour until dawn. Who'd be here? I didn't need to wait because I heard the giggle when the door was open. Evelyn was literally the last thing I needed but she was here anyway.

Might as well make this night even shittier.

She appeared in the office doorway looking like million dollars. Taking it all in, she was surprised to see anyone but Sorin in the room. I realized that we probably looked as frazzled as we felt but she didn't seem to miss a beat.

"I brought the check from the proceeds of the gala. I figured it was important to get to you right away so you can continue to help those in need."

Sorin crossed to her, took the envelope she was offering and politely laid the kiss on her cheek that I knew she was waiting for. She was beaming when he pulled back and her eyes landed on the base of his neck. In all the chaos, I'd forgotten about the bite. At the beginning of the night, I'd delighted myself by imagining her face if she'd seen it. Now that it was happening it seemed so unimportant when compared to everything else we were dealing with.

He must have noticed where she was looking because he froze. Her face contorted. I expected her to come after me but she only had eyes for him. The betrayal and shock filled her gaze.

"You let her mark you?"

37

"Are you bonded?" She yelled on the edge of a howl. "Evelyn."

She didn't let him finish. She shot across the room in a blur and ripped at my scrubs. The shirts tore under her grasp, opening to reveal Sorin's mark. He was behind her and pulling her back with equal speed but she'd seen all she needed to see. Rhys had moved between her and me when Sorin managed to get her a safe distance from me.

"Why her?" she whipped around to face him and broke away from his grip.

"I've chosen her as my mate, Evelyn."

The rage was replaced with sorrow. "What? Why? Because Akila likes her? So, what."

"I marked her only days after I met her, Eve. We only bonded last night but I knew our first night that we were fated."

She threw herself in him, wailing in agony. "Please Sorin. Choose me. We are meant for each other, I know it."

He gently but firmly pushed her away. When she saw that blubbering and begging wouldn't work, she let the sobbing stop and the fury return. Cold wind kicked up in the room and bit at my exposed chest.

"Not in my home, Evelyn. I speak as your lord not as a friend."

The wind halted but she locked eyes with me. "This isn't over." She moved too fast for me to see her leave but the front door slamming told us all we needed.

Sorin slipped his shirt off his arms and brought it to me. I pulled it around me to hold together in the front. I'd felt like it was important to not give Evelyn the satisfaction of me covering up when she was there. Once she was gone, I didn't want to stand with my breasts out in front of Rhys. I wasn't embarrassed, really. It was more out of respect.

Rhys called for Sorin to join him in the center of the room and I saw something I'd never seen in my maker–confidence. He almost looked like he was challenging Sorin. "According to our ways, you should have asked me before bonding with her and choosing her as mate."

I could hardly believe what I'd just heard but Sorin responded to the words in the same formal way. "For that I ask forgiveness. I wanted to but did not plan for it to happen when it did. I was going to ask you this evening but it was forgotten in all the events."

To my shock, Sorin dropped to one knee and placed Rhys's hand on the top of his bowed head. "Rhys Selkirk, I ask to be mated to your progeny Katherine Murphy. I will lay down my life for hers if asked. What say you?"

I was motionless as I stood witness to something that looked completely archaic and utterly romantic at the same time.

Rhys bent down and moved his hand from Sorin's head to his back. They both rose to face each other. I saw a tear run down Rhys's cheek when he spoke. "Lord Sorin I can think of no one that is more suited for her. I know that you will protect her and cherish her. Together, I think you two may humble the most powerful among us. However, as I may in our laws," he turned to look at me. "I forfeit my right to give her away and allow her to choose. If she wants you as mate, she may have you."

Rhys crossed back to me and laid a kiss on my forehead. "I am very happy for you. I'm heading to bed but will find you when I arise. I'm sure you want time alone. We will figure this all out, okay?"

I kissed his tear-streaked cheek and he left without another word. Sorin reached his hand out to me. Still clutching the shirt in front of me, I covered the small distance between us and took his hand with my free one. "Are you going to ask me the same way?"

"No," he said. "When I do ask, it will be perfect. But Rhys had a right to force me this evening. I should not have bonded with you until I spoke to him."

"So, what are you asking exactly? What is mated? Is it like married?"

He started the walk to the bedroom, swinging my hand as we walked. "Not exactly. With human marriage, there is divorce or death. But mating is eternal. We do not die so when we say forever, we mean it."

"But," I said when we walked into his room. I pulled off his shirt and the destroyed clothing underneath. "We can die."

"Yes, we can." He matched my movements, undressing and throwing everything to the corner. Moving to the bed, we split off to our sides and pulled down the cover. "And, if your mate dies then you do not mate again. You do not lie with another or bind to another or mark another."

Lying next to him with the weight of the covers on top, I was understanding what he was saying. "You're saying you never want to be with anyone else? You?"

"I am," he answered. "Is that what you want?"

I smiled teasingly. "I guess you'll have to wait until you ask me to find out."

He arched his eyebrow. "Fair enough."

"Sorin? What are we going to do about everything? About the hunter and Evelyn and my visions and Diana?"

"Don't worry about Evelyn. I've seen her temper before. She blows very hot and burns out quickly. I did look into Diana's pack and will tell you more tomorrow. As for the visions, did you speak to Tom?"

"I did," I relented.

"So, the girls are safe for now. We will keep watch on everything from our end, be extra cautious and aware. Follow my direction about not breaking from your routines and not raising any red flags until I can come up with a plan for the hunter."

He reached over and pulled me into him so my head rested on his chest. He wrapped his arms around me. I felt his breath on my hair. I inhaled the scent of him.

"I just realized something," I said. He answered with a *hmm*. "You're talking about forever and I don't even know your last name."

"When I was given a surname, we were referred to by our father's name or their profession."

I lifted up to look at him. "Okay. So?"

"My surname is Popescu." He said it like it should get a response out of me. When it didn't, he smiled and that eyebrow arched back up. "It means my father was priest."

Now, he got a response. My eyes widen and I cocked my head to the side. "There's a story there."

"For another night, my love. We have centuries to tell stories." Before I could press, he changed the subject. "Weren't you supposed to tell me good news?"

"Oh yes," I said, sitting up straighter. "Alex asked Monica out to dinner."

His smile was genuine. "Wonderful. I do think they would be a lovely couple."

I relaxed and laid my head back on his chest. "They really would. They both deserve someone. They're such good people."

"Then, why do you feel sad?"

No point in hiding from him. "Because I don't think Monica is ever going to really be my friend again. She's trying but she just doesn't look at me the same anymore. She's fine with you and Rhys. She's adjusting to the idea that vampires are real. But she can't relax around me. She saw me in the barn; she saw what I did to Will. It's like I've really died and I'm haunting her. I wonder if it's better for her if I go away."

"Ask her what she wants," he spoke into my hair.

"Yeah, I guess."

But the truth was I didn't want to hear what I knew she'd say.

38

When I woke the memory of the broken clock came back to me and I panicked. We hadn't set an alarm. Reaching for my phone to check the time, I saw two things: I was fine on time and I had a missed call from the hospital.

Hitting play, I listened to the voicemail. *Kate, its Jerry. I heard you had an emergency. Hope the kids are okay. Listen, the guy is in the emergency department all night so we don't need you in tonight. I know I pushed you to come back and I really do appreciate it. Take tonight off and we will see you tomorrow. Hoping it's the last night he's here.*

Thank goddess! A night off. I needed it more than anyone knew. I remembered the missed call from the night before and played that voicemail.

Hey, it's Jeremy. This is my number. Text me and let me know when you can come over. I'm home every night this week basically. Can't wait to ask you about the gossip I'm hearing.

Perfect. I rolled over to lay a kiss on the sleeping man next to me. Just as I was about to slip out of bed, his arm snaked around me and pulled me into him. He wasn't going to be satisfied with a chaste kiss so I matched his intensity. When we broke it off, I'd almost forgotten my mission for the night.

"I don't have to go in tonight."

He sat up. "We talked about this."

"No," I raised my hand to stop him. "They cancelled me. It's called down-staffing and it happens. No red flags. What's you plan for the night?"

"I want to get you and Rhys to the kitchen with Tamela. I'd like to report everything I've learned so far and see no need to repeat it. Then, I have some calls to make and business that I can no longer postpone."

"I'm going to go to Jeremy's then. Whenever you plan on being free, I'll plan on being back."

"Good," he answered. "I want you to work with Lilias on your far-seeing. She cannot stay much longer and I think it's important you learn this. You never know when you may need to get a message to me or Rhys."

"You're right. I'm sorry. I forgot all about her."

"She is enjoying the sights of Pittsburgh so it is not a wasted trip. But I do want you to utilize her knowledge before she goes. Go get Rhys. I'll get Tamela."

With a last kiss, we were moving. I slipped into my room for unripped clothes and knocked on Rhys' door. He opened it and I ran my hand over his bed-head. "Meeting in the kitchen. Do you gotta go in tonight?"

"Yeah," he answered. "You?"

"Nope, got cut. Kunsman is in the ED all night."

"Great. I'll be down soon."

When he walked in, the rest of us were sitting at the island pouring our breakfast from the heated pitcher. I had Rhys' already poured and at the chair next to me.

Once we were all drinking, Sorin started. "I spoke to a few contacts. Diana's grandfather has passed recently and there is a struggle for pack leader going on. She came home to represent her family as she is the oldest of her father's children. She has younger sisters but there is no male offspring from her parents. It will come down to her and the oldest child of each of her father's four brothers. They have allotted time for everyone to arrive and for anyone outside of the family who wants to challenge to do so."

"Why did no one tell you when he passed," Tamela asked.

"I don't know," he answered. "I should have been made aware of this as it's in the pact and I am the closest vampire ruler."

"So, what do you think," I asked. "Why wouldn't they tell you?"

He thought about it while he drank. "I saw Diana. Her hatred of us is clear. I do not blame her given her history. But, if she wanted to do battle, she wouldn't have come into the city. I do believe she is working to provide for her family. The youngest of the pack will look to her for food. I worry about what will happen depending on who takes over as leader. Whomever it is should meet with me to sign a new treaty. Some say that a few of Diana's cousins want to start a new war with us."

"Can we ask Diana," I offered.

"No," Rhys interjected. "Part of the pact is that we stay out of pack business. We shouldn't even know this much. If they knew we were looking into it, we'd be in breach of the treaty."

"So why ask?"

"To protect your children," Sorin answered. "If you truly thought your vision was warning you that Diana meant them harm, I believe you and would find out anything I could to stop it. Even if means a war between wolves and us."

Rhys chimed in. "I'd die for those girls."

"Me too," Tamela echoed the sentiment.

"What do we do with this info, then? It doesn't seem like it is connected to Olivia and Ellie at all."

"I agree," Sorin responded. "And for that I am relieved. Let's hold onto this for now. We know that she had a legitimate need to work. That explains her motive for coming into the city and lines up with what she says. It doesn't mean I trust her. I want to invite her to the manor and warn her about the hunter. It puts them as much in danger as us and it will go a long way to getting the pack on our side. I can't stress this enough. We do not want a war."

I took a shuttering breath. I had to trust him and believe that he knew better than me but I felt like I was gambling with the girls' lives. "Okay."

Rhys checked his watch and kissed me on the cheek. "I have to head in. I'll call you when I leave okay?"

"Okay. Love you."

"You too," he said and left the room.

Sorin looked at Tamela, then turned to me. "We have work to do, also. Go see Jeremy. I should be free in two hours, three at most. Take whatever car you need. Keys are in the garage."

He laid a kiss on my other cheek. "And I also love you."

"And, I love you."

I texted Jeremy that I unexpectedly had the night off and asked if he was free. As I washed and dried the glasses, I thought about what I would do if he had plans. What did the girlfriend of the master do when she wasn't working or taking care of kids?

I didn't know.

Thankfully, I didn't need to find out. The return text had an address and told me to get over there when I could.

Nice, now all I had to do was choose the car I wanted to play with for the night.

39

Turns out I'm utterly boring and I chose the BMW I was already familiar with. I didn't want to risk wrecking one of his cars. Since I was comfortable with this one and knew how it drove, it seemed the safest bet.

Pulling up to the address on the phone, I double checked to make sure it was the right place. Could you imagine trying to explain to a nice, suburban family why you showed up on their doorstep in the middle of the night?

I was starting to see the trend amongst vampire homes. Rhys, Sorin and Evelyn all had homes far from other neighbors. Anyone else who passed the driveway probably didn't notice it or figured some rich person lived up there. Jeremy and Logan had the same vibe. I'd almost passed the driveway myself but saw it right as the trees opened up to reveal the asphalt. Turning up the drive, I passed weeping willows in each side. Part of me expected some huge mansion like Evelyn's but I was pleasantly surprised.

It was bigger than Rhys's little cottage but smaller than the manor. This style was much more my taste. It seemed out of place in

Pennsylvania, looking more like a southern plantation than a northern home. The wrap around porch held rocking chairs and swinging bench seats. I could imagine rocking outside with a book and listening to the sounds of the woods around me. I made a note to tell Rhys he needed a swinging bench. It wouldn't fit on his porch but we could get a free standing one for out by the flowers.

Jeremy swung open the door before I could make it up.

"I am dying to know everything. I'm a patient man but I can't believe the things I'm hearing until you say they are real."

We hugged and I took in his scent. It was the beach at night- saltwater and sand and moonlight. Pulling me over to the porch swing, he left the door open. Guess there was no time for home security when gossip was hot.

Sitting side by side, he let his leg touch the ground to slowly rock us back and forth. It was probably meant to put me at ease but I didn't care since it was working. It felt like all the craziness of the last few nights was far away in a different life. Here on the porch, it was just a story to work through.

"Where do I start?"

"Where do you want to start? The last time we spoke you were talking about leaving nursing and weren't sure he'd respect you. But, from what I've heard things are much more serious."

I looked over at him. "Let's start with what you've heard and go from there."

"Did you get an invitation from the lady of New York?"

"I did."

"And, did you and Evelyn display power at the party?"

I let my confusion show. "I'm not sure what you're asking."

Jeremy sat up straighter and leaned in. "Evelyn was in a tizzy after you left. She told Logan that you displayed power and challenged her."

"I mean, if I did, I didn't mean to. She kept pushing me and needling me until something flared up inside of me. Then, I felt her power too."

"Well, doll. You challenged her and she has no plans of backing down. Then, she called Logan before we we're even out of bed and told him she needed him, pronto. Whatever you did last night, she's throwing a fit at work. She's ripping apart clothes and insisting that it all has to be redone before next week's show. He said she's acting insane."

"It's probably this." I pulled my shirt to the side and let Jeremy see the fading bite.

His eyes widened and he slapped his hand over his mouth to contain his gasp. "That'll do it," he said through his fingers.

When he dropped his hand, the smile told me he was Team Kate. "Did you bind?"

"We did," I whispered and giggled like a school girl. I don't know what was getting into me but I felt silly, like I didn't have anything to worry about.

"Oh, sorry!" The giddiness left me like a slap to the face. The silliness was suddenly replaced by my usual undertone of anxiety.

"What was that?" I asked.

"One of my abilities. I forget you're new so I didn't really make the effort to control it."

"It was like being full of Xanax. I think you could have pulled a gun on me and I wouldn't have cared."

"It's called waking dream. I can manipulate emotions- turn them up or down. As an aftereffect, whatever feeling you crave will be brought on. You must have needed to be calmed. I pulled it in. Again, I'm sorry."

"No, it was great to not be stressed out for a few seconds. What others powers do you have?"

Instead of answering, he waved his hand at the front door and it slammed shut. Giving a quick nod to the nearby windchimes, they began to dance in a non-existent wind. Turning his attention back to me, he said "Telekinesis. Your turn."

"What do you mean?"

"I mean," he quipped. "What power have you manifested?"

Panicked rolled through me. I wasn't supposed to be telling anyone. I promised Sorin I wouldn't share anything with Jeremy that I shouldn't. Honestly, I didn't know him that well and really should trust Sorin.

"Nothing as cool as that," I answered, hoping he'd let it go.

He didn't. "To hear Evelyn tell it you are bursting with more power than she's ever felt."

This is exactly why Sorin told me to control myself, I thought, so someone wouldn't be aware of what I could do. Now, not only was someone aware but it was the person who most wanted me dead.

He knew I had a power so I had to pick the most innocuous thing. I knew I shouldn't have been able to fly or far-see. Admitting I had visions was dangerous. I definitely didn't want to tell him I spoke to ghosts or set a man on fire. "I can read minds."

"That's pretty cool. So, you know what I'm thinking?"

"Truthfully," I made a point to lie as little as possible. "I still need to learn how to really use it. I'm a work in progress. I can try, though."

"Okay." He sat up straighter and looked into my eyes.

I met his gaze and tried to focus on looking *through* his eyes instead of into them. I started to repeat a question in my head—*what is he thinking? What is he thinking?*

"How can you remember the sun so well? I'm only a month old and I feel like I can barely picture it anymore. Yet, your memory is so clear. How long has it been? Where is that cabin?"

Jeremy hadn't expected me to really be able to do it. His reaction said it all when his pupils dilated and his mouth dropped open. "How? You're so young."

Oh no. Maybe I ended up picking one of the powers I shouldn't have had yet.

"I mean," he continued. "Lots of vampires can read minds but most aren't able to get such a clear picture so quickly. Bravo."

I let out a sigh and tried to move on. "So, where's the cabin? It's pretty."

"It was in Maine but that was 200 years ago. I'm sure it's long gone."

"It looked peaceful. Why didn't you stay?"

"It was time to move on. You'll see over the years, no matter how hard you try there comes a time when what you're doing no longer works. Too many people become suspicious or you need to change professions. Then, you find a new life elsewhere."

"I hope someday you'll tell me your story. But my time is short tonight and I came here for a reason. Where was I when we got distracted?"

"Ah yes, you bonded to the most eligible bachelor in our state and Evelyn hates you. So, the major question. Will you quit nursing and join his side as a fulltime lady or will you balance the two worlds?"

40

Looking at Jeremy I wanted to just tell him everything that was on my chest and get it all out. I wanted the opinion of someone who was unbiased and didn't really have any skin in the game. I couldn't talk to Rhys because he'd never given anything up for someone else, as far as I knew. But I also didn't know how much I could tell Jeremy. I couldn't mention Diana, my premonitions, the hunter at the hospital or the rogue vamp I'd torched with my mind after he attacked me at the hospital—twice. So, I decided to just tell him my feelings and ask him about his experience.

"I've always been a nurse and I love it. I save lives and get to be there for people in their worst moments. I'm respected and proud of where I'm at in my career. But everything is different now. It's going to get harder and harder to stay there. Plus, I have two kids."

Jeremy grabbed my thigh. "I had no idea. I guess I just didn't really think about it. How old are they? Where are they?"

"It's okay." I laid my hand on his and squeezed. I lowered my head to look at our hands and try to not be overwhelmed. "Twelve and fourteen. They're with their dad and stepmom. They all think I developed a rare disease and can't be in the sun. That's the other thing- all the lying. I lie at work and to my kids. I feel so disconnected from them now, like we're getting more apart by the minute. Not working would mean more time with them. Especially since I only have a few decades with them...."

Less than a month as a vampire and I was talking about decades like they were months. Time seemed so precious and so abundant at the same time. I was acutely aware that the girls wouldn't live forever like I could. In that moment, nights with them became the most valuable thing in the world. Heat trickled down both cheeks.

A white handkerchief appeared in my vision. Wiping at those hot tears, I continued. "I mean I feel so selfish thinking about everything I lost or could lose, when I also was given so much. I'll live forever and never get sick or old."

"But?"

"But, I'm not ready to lose my identity."

"Why do you think you'll lose your identity?"

"I won't be a nurse anymore. Then, eventually I won't be a mom." I let that thought linger in the air because I wasn't ready to go down that road. "I'll just be Sorin's girlfriend."

"And, why is that bad?"

"It's not. That's not what I meant. It's that I'm afraid I'll lose respect."

Jeremy pulled his hand back and I looked up at him. He looked genuinely interested. "I understand what you're feeling. I had the same thoughts. When I left the university, I was lost. So much of myself and my time had been wrapped up in teaching. I'd been awarded, applauded, published and celebrated. Once it was all gone, I was certain I had nothing to offer."

"So, what did you do?" This was what I came to hear. I wanted so desperately for him to say something that made my choice easy.

"I stopped grieving what used to be and started to get excited about what was going to happen. I focused on my relationship and did things I'd never had time for when I was working all the time. We traveled and learned things we'd always wanted to. Then, I put my energy into helping him in his work."

"But, are you fulfilled or do you feel like you lost yourself?"

He appeared kind and stern at the same time, like a big brother who caught you doing something bad but wouldn't tell. "I think you need to ask yourself a few questions. First, is being a nurse and a mom really all that there is to you?"

"Well, no."

"Okay, so leaving the hospital or not being with your kids doesn't mean you lose yourself. Secondly, do you respect yourself?"

Surprising myself, I answered without thinking. "Yes."

"Okay then others will respect you. And, why do you respect yourself?"

"Because I'm reliable, a hard worker, smart and capable. I'm a good mom. I'm a loyal friend."

He stopped me. "So, why wouldn't you bring all of that to whatever you do next?"

"I would. But-"

He waited a beat then encouraged me to not stop. "What aren't you saying?"

The tears started again. "Every part of my human life that I walk away from gets me farther and farther away from them. Once, I quit the hospital and work with Sorin, I'm afraid I'll fall in love with the ease of it and give up on them. And what if that's what's best for them anyway?"

Letting out a huge breath, he sat back and rocked the bench. "Kate, I don't envy how complicated your life is but I do have some advice."

I waited, holding my breath and hoping for a grand revelation.

"You have to trust your gut."

That was it? Trust my gut? That didn't help at all. I wanted him to tell me it would all be okay or that I was crazy to leave the hospital or that he'd regretted his choice. Anything would have given me clearer direction. But instead, he told me to trust my gut—which was totally confused.

He kept talking. "When the time is right, your instinct will tell you what to do. In the meantime, you have to stop overthinking everything. You're trying to plan for any possible outcome or problem or negative consequence. None of us know what will come or what's in store for us. You'll make yourself insane with worry and, like you said, you only get so many years with your daughters. Don't waste them worrying. Follow your gut. Love on your kids when you can. Let Sorin be by your side and be by his. Everything else is out of your hands, my dear."

"Have you ever thought of going back to teaching? Like at a different university with a different name? Have you ever regretted leaving when you did?"

Rolling his head to face me his face lit up with that thousand-watt smile. "Nope." Before I could ask another question, headlights flashed across his face and I heard a car pull in. "This will be interesting," he said to no one.

Behind me a car door opened and shut. I stood to see Logan walking towards us with a mix of curiosity and horror on his face. "Kate?"

I wasn't sure from his tone if he was more mad than scared or vice versa but I was going to start with sweetness and see where I got. "Logan. I'm so happy to finally get to meet you. I've heard great things about you. I know this puts you in a bad spot. I can leave."

Logan's reservations seemed to thaw and it looked like manners would win. He came up to the porch and extended his hand. I took it and was pleased he gave mine a firm squeeze, treating me like an equal. "No," he said. "I'm sorry it's taken this long for me to introduce myself. Evelyn is at the shop so this is a good chance for us to speak openly. I'm sure Jeremy's explained."

"He has," I looked to him and then back to his partner. "I'm sorry you're in the middle of it."

"It's not your fault, not really. Whoever won over Sorin was going to face Evelyn's wrath. You happen to be the lucky winner. You had no idea the hornet's nest you were kicking."

I laughed and he didn't. That stopped me.

"Seriously, Kate," Logan stepped into me. "She's insane. When she wants something, she'll stop at nothing to get it. I've seen her ruin competing business, destroy people's livelihoods and that was business. With you, it's personal."

If he was trying to scare me, he succeeded. All I could think of was getting back to Sorin and his bodyguards. "Well, on that note. I think I better go. I don't want to risk her finding me here. You've been kind to me and I don't want to repay that by getting you in trouble."

Jeremy leaned down to kiss me on the cheek. I remembered the tear-streaked handkerchief and handed it to him. He waved it off. "Keep it. And, text me if you need anything. You'll get through this. You have more friends than enemies."

When I pulled away, I looked back in my rearview and saw them kiss. Whatever magic they had, I hope Sorin and I had it too.

41

When I returned to the manor, I found Sorin still in his office. It was a nice night so I figured a walk around the property was exactly what I needed. Stepping through the back door off the solarium, I was surprised to see that Lilias had the same idea. She was in a long white dress walking aimlessly towards the little grove that I'd come to love. I called out to her and she turned. Motioning me to come to her, I did.

"I was hoping I'd see you this evening," she said when I reached her. "Are you up to a little lesson this evening?"

"Sure," I responded. "And, I'm sorry I haven't been available. You came all this way."

"Nonsense," she smiled. "What's meant to happen, will. No sense in fighting it. Let's go sit on that lovely bench. I love this spot and am I to understand it means a great deal to you as well?"

Shocked, I locked eyes with her. "Are you reading my mind?"

"I am," she admitted without shame. "You met Sorin here?"

There was no point in lying so I didn't. "I did. Only, I didn't know it was Sorin at the time." I followed her to the very spot I'd sat when he'd wondered up to me. Sitting, I could recall that moment with perfect clarity.

She stood in front of me, looking down to me. "The energy here is strong for you and that's what I want you to tap into. The emotions and sensations it conjures can be tapped into. So, I want you to focus that energy and find your maker."

Lilias was right. Being in that spot was making so many thoughts and feelings swirl around inside of me. The excitement of that first sight of him, the lust I had felt and the betrayal from discovering who he was all danced inside my chest. Focusing on that, I closed my eyes to pull the energy together, imaging it was a bright ball behind my sternum. Every time I inhaled and exhaled, I imagined the light in that ball flaring and dimming. Then, I thought of Rhys. I remembered his face as he rushed up to us and then dropped to one knee before Sorin. I remember the feel of his hand in mine.

"Rhys," I whispered into the night air.

The darkness of my closed eyes was filled with the blood bank in the hospital. Rhys was behind his desk. I chuckled when I realized he had music on. The volume was very low but it was there. He'd defied Jerry and turned on his beloved music. My love for him was overwhelming. I knew without a doubt that I would die for him.

He was working on a stack of papers- looking at one, typing on his computer, then throwing that piece into the garbage to repeat with the next one in the stack. His head bobbed to Dolly Parton while she told the story of Jolene trying to steal her man. My viewpoint told me I was likely standing just inside the room, where most of the nurses stopped when coming for blood. They were all scared of him and tried to get in and out as quickly as possible.

"If it is safe, try to make yourself solid and speak to him," Lilias' voice floated into my head.

Looking around, I saw we were alone so I repeated my actions in Sorin's garage. I imagined the glue rolling down my legs and holding me to the floor. Holding my hand up in front of my face, I saw my hand was solid.

"Rhys?"

He jumped up, stunned to see me in his office. "Katie?"

I held my finger to my lips. "I'm practicing. Can you see me?"

He nodded his head and gulped. "I knew you could do this but to see it.... wow."

I smiled. I'd already held it longer this time than I had with Sorin. Excitement shot through me when I realized the ways I could use this to help. "Cool, right?"

He stepped towards me and reached out a hand. I mirrored him, feeling myself waver when I moved. His hand passed through mine. "You look solid but you're not."

"Don't ask me to explain it," I laughed. "I can't hold it long but I'm happy to see you."

"You'll see me soon. I'm about to cut out and come over. I want to be there when Diana is."

"She's coming? When?"

"Talk to Sorin."

"Okay," I said and felt myself fade back into the darkness. Opening my eyes, I blinked to refocus on the twinkling lights of the grove. Lilias' white dress started as a blob but was back to a dress in seconds. "It's hard."

She sat next to me. "Of course. Any new skill is hard. Think of anything you have mastered. Were you good at it immediately?"

I thought of nursing school and all the nights in the skills lab trying to learn how to put in IVs or read a cardiac strip. She was right, it had taken a lot of practice. But I was finding it hard to compare those things to the ability to astral project, or whatever it was I was doing. "I guess not," I conceded.

"Continue to practice," she said, sounding like a teacher giving a lecture. "First you went room to room. Now, you have traveled miles. Someday, you will be able visit me across an ocean and stay for hours. But you must be careful. When you far-see, you leave behind an unprotected body and you do not know who will be in the room that you appear to. I suggest you do it from a locked room and do not solidify on the other side until you know it's safe- like you did tonight."

"How many more lessons do I need?"

"I leave tomorrow evening. I can't stay. But, you know how to do it. You only need to practice, like any new thing. You can call me if you have any questions. And, I will come back when I can."

"Oh," I said, hoping she didn't hear the disappointment in my voice. "Okay. Are there other people nearby who could keep teaching me?"

She laughed and it was such a magical sound. I didn't want her to stop. "Kathrine, as far as I know you are the only other vampire in the world who can do this. And, Sorin is clear he wants no one else to know about this so even if there were others, this is a secret. Remember?"

I sat back against the bench. "You're right."

I turned to Lilias to ask more but a sound hit my ear. It was a car slowly rolling up the driveway. We both jumped to our feet, waiting to see the vehicle. Lilias sniffed at the air but I didn't need to—I knew that smell already.

Diana was here.

42

I left my teacher in the grove and was on the front porch before she brought the car to a stop. Stepping out, her expression hid nothing. "I hate when you guys do that. Can't you just walk normally?"

"Why? You know what I am. Why pretend otherwise?" It was the first time I'd said something like *what I am* but I didn't allow myself to dwell on it. I was too busy trying to look tough and match her annoyance.

"Why do I have to be here? Is he pissed or what? Just tell me now."

"I'll wait for him." I opened the door and was relieved to see that Tamela was already there. Waiting for Diana to walk up to the entrance, I could see the fear in her eyes. I wasn't sure what to do. I didn't know if hearing about Kunsman was going to relieve her or upset her even more. But, I couldn't control that. It was happening so I might as well just go along with Sorin's plan.

Diana stood in the foyer with every muscle tensed. I knew she wasn't dumb enough to try and fight us but I could tell she was attempting to be ready for anything. Tamela gestured towards the living room. "Would you please sit? Sorin will be down shortly. Can I get you anything??

"I don't drink blood," she snarled.

Tamela held her composure. "I am aware. We do have other things. Coffea, tea, water, soda?"

Diana shook her head, choosing not to sit but to pace the room. I was pretty sure she could be on day ten without water and still not take a drop from us. She was so freaking stubborn but I also admired her pride.

"I can sit with you while we wait." I sat in one of the big chairs and waited to see if she'd speak. Tamela left us in the silence. After minutes of walking around, Diana finally sat on the couch. She somehow looked more uncomfortable sitting than when she was moving.

"So," she started without looking at me. "How do you end up the master's girlfriend when you're brand new? Did you volunteer to be made a vampire so you could be with him?" The disdain dripped off her every word.

I was still new to vampire etiquette but I was pretty sure that was a rude question. "That's a very long story and none of your business. I wouldn't ask you who made you a werewolf."

She turned to me now, locking eyes with me and showing me how disgusted she was. "I was born a werewolf. I didn't have a choice."

"Well," I answered with the same level of snark. "Neither did I."

"Except that's not true," she challenged. "I heard about how you guys are made. You have time to choose to turn or to die peacefully. Must be nice. With us, you're born this way or you get scratched or bit and boom—werewolf. There is no other option."

Knowing that I had to control myself, I gulped back rage. She had no right to talk to me like she understood the choice. "To be clear, I didn't have a choice. I couldn't leave my daughters without a mom. And, you have no idea what you're talking about. If you want to get ugly, you do have a choice. You could choose to kill yourself rather than be what you are. That's basically the decision we get faced with."

I prepared for a snarky comeback but there wasn't one. Her eyes were wide and could hear her heart rate speed up. "You have kids?"

Shit, I thought. Why couldn't I keep my mouth shut? "Yes." That was all she was getting.

"You can't be around kids for chrissake. Bad enough you're around bleeding humans at work. You can't put your own kids at risk."

I stood. "How dare you. You don't know me or my kids. You have no idea what you're asking."

She raised her hands up. "Whoa, fang down. I'm not saying forever. I'm just saying you have to learn control before you go back around your kids. You're so new. What if they cut themselves and you haven't eaten?"

I took a breath and fought back the heat rising in my throat. I knew if we kept this up, Sorin was going to burst into the room and make things worse. I wanted to show him I could handle tough situations. "I know. Don't you think I know?" I sat back down, slowing my breathing.

"Listen, Kate. I know I can be a bitch. I get it. But, I feel for you. Family is everything to us and I get the sense that you're the same. Can I tell you something?"

"It better be good," I snapped.

"Shifting is different for true born werewolves like me and those that start human. When you're born this way, it happens around puberty. You have time to be prepared and everyone is around you. It's basically your nature, so shifting comes on like anything else natural. But, when you start human and this thing is forced upon your body—it's like you'll always have two sides fighting to be in control. Their shifts are brutal."

"What are you saying?"

"What I'm saying is, we take them in and teach them. We talk them through it but ultimately, they have to accept it. They have to stop fighting it, stop wishing it hadn't happened. Once those two sides start to harmonize, the shift is less traumatic and they remain in control once they're in wolf form."

"And?" I was trying to follow what she was saying but she'd hit a raw nerve and I was vibrating with anger.

"I've seen new wolves totally lose it and hurt someone they love. I don't want that for anyone, not even a bloodsucker."

The room felt like it melting around me and the floor was giving out. She was right and I knew it. She was saying out loud what I was so afraid of but didn't want to admit. "I can't do this."

"Do what?"

"Talk to you about this. I can't." I gripped the chair and felt the solidness of it threatening to give way. I loosened my clutch before I broke the furniture. She already thought we were freaks, no reason to give her a show.

"Hey, I get it. I'd rather jump off a cliff than hurt my family but I'd also have a very hard time walking away from them."

This was the change of subject I wanted. "But, didn't you just come back? Where were you?"

"How did you know that?" Her gaze squinted at me, curious and untrusting.

I had to think fast. "You said it at the hospital. That you'd just come back to the area and needed a job. That you didn't know who the head vamp was."

She relaxed and in response so did I. "Right. Yeah. I was away for a while. Had a falling out with everyone and needed some time alone. It killed me but it was the right move for all of us."

"And, what brings you back?" I hoped I wasn't pushing too hard.

"Sometimes family needs you even if they don't want to see you. It wasn't the easiest thing but it was the right one."

She didn't give anything away but she also didn't lie. I applauded her skill at walking a very thin line. I figured I was still safe to push. "Will you stay?"

"I don't know. Depends on a few things. Why? Don't want the wolf in your city?"

"I didn't say that. I'm just trying to make small talk. You know, like normal people that don't hate each other."

The door opened and saved me from more of the uncomfortable conversation. Rhys came into the room and pulled off a beanie to let his hair fall. Standing to hug him, I saw his gaze fall on Diana. Whatever flashed in his eyes, it wasn't pleasant but he pulled it back instantly.

"Diana," he said but didn't move to greet her. Knowing my sweet Rhys his lack of kindness was a clear indicator of how he felt about her. There was no time to see how awkward it would get because Tamela joined us and let us know it was time.

43

The office was starting to be one of my least favorite places. Ignoring the one sexy romp that had happened here weeks before, it seemed that only bad news was shared here. With no fire in the fireplace, it felt cold and more serious in there. I guess it was the perfect atmosphere for delivering unwelcomed information.

Diana had chosen to stand in the corner. I couldn't blame her, she again found herself the only of her kind with three vampires in a closed room. Sorin leaned back against his desk. Rhys and I flanked him on each side. I couldn't help but imagine what we looked like to her.

"Oh God, just spit it out," she spoke bravely. "Whatever it is I'll deal."

To Sorin's credit, he let the attitude go and didn't demand the respect he could have. "Diana, we decided together that you have the right to know something that came to our attention. We could have kept this to ourselves but didn't. We want you to see that we are not your enemies."

"Whatever, just tell me."

"First," Sorin began. "Would you tell us what you spoke to Henry Kunsman about? Kate said she saw you two speaking." I was impressed by how direct he was. There really was no point in just speculating. She may lie but even her reaction would tell us something.

Her reaction was annoyance. "He asked about all the nurses and doctors on the unit. He said that because I was new he wasn't looking at me but was curious about what I thought of you guys."

"And," I asked. "What did you say?"

"I told him I was busy and I didn't know anything about anything. I keep to myself for a reason."

Sorin must have been satisfied because he moved on. "Henry Kunsman is a hunter."

She leaned back against the wall and slid to the floor. Laying her head back, she laid both hands over her face and groaned. "Fucking great. Vampires and a hunter. I just wanted to make some money and mind my own goddamn business." She pulled her hands down and looked at him. "How do you know?"

"I overheard him," I answered. "He was on the phone in the stairwell and didn't know I was there."

"And, he's looking for shifters?"

I glanced at Sorin to see what I was allowed to say. He took over. "We don't know what he's looking for but it doesn't matter. Whether vampire or wolf, if he finds either it's bad for the other. They don't ask questions before they slaughter."

Visibly she mustered her courage and weighed her options. Hoisting herself up she faced us with shoulders squared. "So, what do you need from me?"

"I ask that you keep watch on him when he's in the hospital. Report to Rhys what he's doing or what you hear. You have the unique advantage of being able to walk in the sun and not currently in his radar. Rhys will be my representative in this and will report to me. I ask that you take a command from him as one from me."

"You're not my master."

My muscle clenched as I waited to see how he would respond. Everything in me wanted to lunge at her but I had to wait for his call.

"Your grandfather and I are friends. We have never had issues between us and even dreamed of uniting the pack and my people. I would not do anything to jeopardize you out of honor to him. I'm sure if you ask him, he will tell you that I am a man of great wrath but also great wisdom. I ask that you trust me to get us all out of this."

He spoke of her grandfather in the present tense to hide that we knew of his passing. If she came clean with us, it told us we could trust her. It also used him against her. I didn't know if what he said was true but it was very smart.

"Fine," she said without needing to tell us the truth. "I'm going to trust you. As for you and my grandfather, that's between you two and has nothing to do with me. Although, I question how well you know him. I do admit that he's spoken of you many times but never said anything to me about uniting us. I'll just tell you not to hold your breath."

Rhys took a step forward. "We may not like this but he's right. A hunter is bad for all of us. When it's over, you never have to talk to us again. There's plenty of hospitals to work at."

She crossed her arms. "I already said okay. That's the best you're gonna get. And, what does she have to do in all this?" She jerked her chin in my direction.

"Let me worry about that," Sorin responded. "If there is nothing more, we will be in touch with you."

Diana heard him loud and clear because she headed out of the room without looking back or uttering another word. From the way she was walking, I figured she couldn't get away from us fast enough. The front door slam was rough on our hearing but none of us flinched. It wasn't until the car started that I spoke.

"Do you think that was the right call?"

"I do," Sorin answered.

Rhys sat on the couch and leaned back. "She still didn't tell you about her grandfather or what's happening in the pack."

Sorin ran his fingers through his hair. "A problem for a different night. Let us survive the hunter and then we can address pack matters.

For now, we need to be together as best as we can. Rhys, would you stay here at night until this is done? I would like a report at the end of each night, as soon as you speak to Diana."

"Done," he said. "I always have a duffel of clothes in my car."

"Kate. We can't keep you here. You do have to go to work but you have to be safe. Don't show any powers, don't be around him if you can avoid it."

He was probably just as worried as I was that I'd be the one to get us caught. I was too uncontrolled, too new. I frantically thought of ways to get out of work but Sorin was right. I had to act like everything was the same as always. I replayed the last few weeks in my head and thought about how I'd probably looked to everyone. Honestly, if Kunsman had interviewed any of my co-workers about me he'd get an earful. I'd disappeared for a couple nights, returned with a new diagnosis looking better than ever, hooked up with an impossibly hot boyfriend, my best friend had been attacked and then I'd gone on a sudden two-week break. If he didn't know I was a vampire from that story- he was an idiot.

I tried not to give into the panic. "I can do that."

44

I'd spent the rest of the evening wandering around the house trying to get a handle on my worry. The difficult conversations with Jeremy and Diana had stirred up a lot of fear inside of me. I needed to talk to the girls but couldn't call them until closer to dawn. Calling them in the middle of the night would have worried them and I didn't want to do that. So, I'd wandered while the men had sat in the office to strategize.

During my wanderings, I'd found Edwin in the training room. He was beating on a punching bag like it'd wronged him in a past life. As much as I wanted someone to distract me from myself, I also knew what it was like to have to get all that frustration out so I left him with the bag.

Finally, I couldn't wait anymore. It was quarter to six and I figured that was good enough. They were early risers so they'd probably be close to get up or already up. The girls answered on the first ring. I thanked the universe for Facetime when their faces filled my screen and I could see they were okay. Both sets of eyes were bright, telling me I hadn't wakened them.

"Mom!" They were talking on top of each other so I waited a beat.
"Hi!" I said. "How are you guys?"

"Good," Olivia answered. "Where are you?"

"I'm at a friend's house. It's out in the woods and so pretty. Great for relaxing and getting some stress out." I paused waiting to see if they'd buy it or I'd have to face more questions.

"Can we come?" Ellie asked.

"Maybe someday," I answered, knowing that was never going to happen. "What have you guys been up to?"

The distraction worked. They told me about their sleepover and how Addison was teaching them tricks with the soccer ball. They talked about the Halloween costumes they wanted to buy and the parties they were invited to. That's when Olivia's demeanor changed. "Hey, Mom. Dad said that you don't want us going anywhere but school and his house. How come? I want to go to this party but he said I can't."

Thanks, Tom. Make me the bad guy. "Just being cautious, girls. There's a lot of bad things coming into the hospital. I want you guys to be safe. You can go to the party but Dad or Sarah has to stay with you."

"But, it's a sleepover! No one else's parents are staying."

"That's the rule. Dad or Sarah have to be with you."

My gut twisted. It was bad enough that I was never with them anymore but now they were on lockdown because of me. The howl from the vision ripped through my head and reminded me that this was the right call. It was better for them to be mad at me and alive than the alternative. I listened to their complaints but didn't cave.

"Someday," I interrupted. "You'll have kids and you can make the rules."

"I'll let them go anywhere they want." Ellie said defiantly.

"That's fine with me," I relented. "But you're my kids and I say not now."

"Whatever," Olivia grunted. "We have to go get ready."

It was obvious they were done talking with me. I wanted so badly to tell them they could go so that I could see them smile and have them not mad at me but I knew it wasn't worth the risk. I told them I loved them just as they hung up on me. I wondered if they'd ever forgive me for suddenly dipping out of their lives with no real explanation. Originally, I'd planned on telling them the truth when they were older but now, I thought that would likely never happen. Recent events had shown me that being brought into the world was dangerous, even for supernatural creatures. Humans didn't stand a chance. I only had to imagine Monica's broken body in the ICU to know it was true. Telling them the truth would be selfish, it would help me feel better. It wouldn't be in their best interest.

So, I have to get used to them hating me and not understanding.

Slowly walking up the stairs to the bedroom, I tried to imagine their perspectives of the last month. To them, their once very involved mom had abruptly not come home one night and hadn't been the same since. She was secretive and rarely available. She'd missed a band concert and couldn't be at any games or school events. She's at a stranger's house in the woods and won't let them go anywhere.

No wonder they were mad.

Opening the door to Sorin's room, I found the bed empty. The muffled worlds from the office told me they were still in there so I got myself ready for bed and lay down to stare at the ceiling. I had the impulse to text Monica and then remembered that she had enough to deal with. She didn't need to hear me whine about the kids or how unfair it all was, not after she'd been through what she had. It occurred to me that I didn't really have anyone to talk to about this. None of the vampires I knew had children and none of the humans I knew could understand my current predicament.

I was one of a kind and totally alone in this.

No single-mom-vampire-support groups for this girl.

45

The first thing I did when the alarm went off was to check for Sorin. To my relief he was next to me and safe. I'd fallen asleep without him, wondering how I'd ever get through all of this and wishing he'd come sauntering in to distract me. But, he hadn't. They must have worked in there until they couldn't anymore. I knew the office windows had very good light-blocking curtains but it was still hard to stay up after dawn. I still hadn't really tried it. Rhys and Sorin were older so they were stronger. I don't know when he'd come to bed but I was glad he was there.

Turning off the alarm, I headed for the shower and let him rest. To my dismay, there was no message telling me I didn't need to go in. Guess I should prepare myself for the night. After washing up, drying my hair and getting into my scrubs, I heard someone coming out from a room. Poking my head out into the hallway, I saw Rhys shuffling my way.

"Ready for tonight," he asked.

"I should be asking you. You're the one with an angry were-partner."

He rolled his eyes. "Don't remind me. What an attitude. The sooner we're through this, the better. Done in there?"

I stepped out and waved my arm into the bathroom. "All yours."

Making my way down the hall, I was pleased to see Sorin awake and sitting up. I jumped onto the bed next to him. "When did you come to bed?"

"Late," his voice was gruff. Until that moment, I didn't think he could ever look tired.

"Stay here," I kissed him on his cheek. "I'm getting you breakfast in bed."

After retrieving two glasses of warm blood from the kitchen, I returned to the room to see he hadn't moved. Laying against those pink pillows he looked like something an artist would step in front of a bus to be able to sketch. When he saw my bounty, he smiled. Handing him a glass, he gulped. "Thank you," he said when it was finished. "I don't think anyone has ever served me in bed. I admit, it's nice."

"Consider it a thanks. For working hard to keep us all safe. I wish I didn't have to go to work."

He patted the space next to him and I followed the command. "So, how did the talk go with Jeremy?"

I knew what he was referring to. He wanted to know if I'd given more thought to leaving my job. "He told me to trust my gut."

"That's all?"

"Basically," I answered. "He said he'd felt all the same things I'm feeling now but ultimately let go and just enjoyed the time he has."

Sorin set his glass down on the bedside table. "I've told you what I want. No need to continue to repeat it. I think you'd be safer away from the hospital and would be an asset to me and this city." I opened my mouth but he stopped me. "However, it's your choice. Do it if and when you feel it is right."

"That's just it," I jumped in. "I think you're right. It's like I know that I need to walk away but I just can't figure out the how and I'm afraid I'll regret it."

"Why?"

"Because it's all I know. It's been so much of my life for so long. I don't know how to not be a nurse."

"You'll always be a nurse, Katherine. No one can take that knowledge from you. And, you are more than that. Plus, you didn't know how to be a vampire a month ago and you're getting the hang of it very quickly. Anything you set your mind to; you can do."

He had a point and I felt my resolve fading. The truth was I was exhausted from all the lies it took to stay in my job. I wanted to stop all the charades and just enjoy my life. The only problem was if I even thought about hanging up my stethoscope, it made my stomach hurt. "I think it will be soon but not now. I'm just not ready."

"Okay, then. And speaking of which, I think you should probably be heading in. Please be safe and I expect a report at the end of the day. Do not ride with Rhys. Take the BMW. I can have the van brought here. I want you to have a way to leave that doesn't rely on another person and I don't think you should be seen arriving together."

He wasn't wrong so I didn't bother arguing. If I was being honest, I was actually starting to think of the car as mine and I liked it. Kissing him goodbye was hard. I consoled myself by remembering I was coming home to him in a few hours.

Rhys followed me in his car. We made a point to not use the same entrance to the hospital. I parked by my van so I could swing by Alex's office but he wasn't there. Using the stairs, I walked up to five and almost walked into Diana when I entered the break room.

"Hey," she said.

I waited for a snarky dig or her to blow past me but neither happened. She just stood there like she was waiting for something. "Hey," I responded.

"Listen. I was thinking about what I said at your boyfriend's house and I'm sorry." I didn't say anything so she kept going. "It's none of my business what you choose to do for your family. I wouldn't like it if someone gave me their opinion of my choices."

"Thank you." I wasn't sure what else to say. "I appreciate it."

"And, can you thank him for giving me the heads up? I mean he didn't have to tell me but he did. I thought about it when I left. If I was in the same boat, I don't know if I would have said something to you guys so, yeah, thanks."

I was speechless. An apology and gratitude in the same conversation was a lot from her. I knew it wasn't easy for her to admit any of it. "You're welcome. And, I appreciate your honesty. It takes a lot to say all that."

"I promise I'm not as awful as I seem."

"Neither am I," I admitted.

"Man, does your maker hate my guts, though. Bet he loves being teamed up with me." She opened a locker and found her water bottle. Taking a few gulps, she wiped at her mouth and put it back. I recognized the nervous gesture and felt bad for her.

"He doesn't hate you," I said. "He just doesn't know if he can trust you. I get the feeling he doesn't know a lot of… you know."

"Yeah, that's because there aren't many left."

I felt the room getting tense so I tried to lighten it up. "Well, then I guess I'm pretty lucky to have met you."

The tension faded. "I guess," she said. "Oh yeah, I'm also sorry for that shit I said about you having a choice. That was crappy and I know it."

"Thanks." Any more apologizing and I was going to have to walk out. It was too uncomfortable. I liked it better when she was being mean.

"Before you go to work, can I ask you something?"

"Sure," I said, bracing myself for whatever may come.

She took in a big breath and let it out. "How pissed will Sorin be if I've been holding something back?"

I figured she was talking about her grandfather but knew that, with her, it was hard to tell how many secrets she was holding onto. "Depends on the material. Is it something you should have told him?"

"Not me specifically but one of us, and since I've been in front of him twice, well.…"

"I see," I chose my words carefully. "I'll tell you this. He values honesty and bravery. The longer you wait and the more you're around him and don't say something -"

She shook her head. "Yeah, got it. Problem is, either I piss off my family or piss off him. But you guys did me a solid when you warned me and I feel like I should repay."

"Trust your gut." There it was again only this time I was saying it. I knew what she should do but how could I tell her that? She had to figure it out on her own.

"Got it," she held up her fist. At first, I didn't know what she was doing but soon realized. I pounded my fist against hers. "Well, I got two patients for you whenever you're ready. Let's try to get through this shift without getting hunted."

"Sounds like a plan."

46

After getting reports on my patients and not seeing any sign of Kunsman, I decided to press my luck and go see Monica. I didn't expect to see Alex at the bedside but, there he was. We met each other's eyes and I nodded. Monica looked better and there was a glow under her skin that could only be love.

"Hey Monica. Just thought I'd stop by and see how you were."

"Great," she lit up. "I was just telling Alex I get to go home tomorrow."

"That's great. I'm so happy for you. You must be thrilled." I shot a glance to Alex who looked apprehensive.

"When you have a minute," I nodded towards him. "I need to run something by you."

He stood. "Sure. I'll come now. I've got a lot to do. Monica? I will see you tomorrow. Get some rest and don't let them release you without talking to me first."

"You got it," she said up to him. "Although I don't know how much sleep I'll get. I'm too excited."

Before we left the room, I looked back at her. "Once you're home, just know that you can call on me for anything, okay?"

"Anything at night, you mean."

That one stung but I let it go. "Right but you know Tom would be willing to help too. Just ask."

I followed Alex to the conference room. Even with the door shut, I whispered. I didn't need anyone overhearing what I was going to say. "The DOH inspector is not DOH."

"What do you mean?"

"I mean, he's a hunter and he's here for vampires. He followed the murders and realized that this was ground zero. He faked the survey to get into the hospital and get access to us. It's only a matter of time before he narrows down on me, Rhys or both." I left out the info about Diana since it wasn't my secret to tell.

Alex dropped to a chair and let his head fall into his hands. "He was drilling me about when I got here and why I'm only here at night. He kept asking why did I choose hematology; he asked if he could look at my notes. I told him absolutely not."

"I don't know what to do, Alex. This guy's bad news for us all. If he catches wind of your search for the cure, figures out that you know about vampires, it's only a matter of time before he sees our connection."

"Did you tell Sorin?"

"Yes. He and Rhys are working on a plan. I don't know what it is. In the meantime, we have to keep him off our tails."

"I was worried about Monica going home. She doesn't seem strong enough," he met my gaze and I could see how exhausted he was. "But now I think it's best we get her out of here. She knows the truth which makes her someone we don't want him talking to. We definitely don't want him learning the condition she was in when she arrived. There's not too many people brought in with half their blood missing and bite marks."

"Oh God," I sat next to him. "I didn't even think about that."

"Let me take the lead on getting Monica discharged. You just worry about staying out of his sights. Tell Sorin, if there is anything I can do to help, I'm in this with you 100%."

"Oh Alex. I wish you didn't have to be. Monica either."

He stood. "But we are, Kate." And with that, he walked out of the room and left me to contemplate what that meant for them.

When I finally left the room, I knew I had to pretend it was just a normal night at the hospital. Each minute felt like hours while I moved through my night, trying to focus on the medications I was passing and the words I typed into each chart. How could everything be falling apart in my life but it be totally normal everywhere else? I was envious of the other nurses on the unit that night; jealous that they hadn't gone out to the cemetery one night and been changed forever. I hated that they could go into the sun if they wanted to and didn't need to worry about being hunted just because of what they were. Frustration boiled inside of me and I had to keep swallowing back screams when the reality of my situation would hit me.

Hours into the shift, I caught Diana's eyes across the unit. She looked just as upset as I was, struggling to keep herself together. I left what I was doing and crossed the space to her. "I'm taking a few minutes. I feel like I'm going to flip out if I don't get some air."

"Have you seen him?" she asked.

"Nothing," I said. "I guess it's too much to hope he's just left?"

"Take a break but don't go anywhere unprotected. Get Rhys if you have to."

I nodded in agreement but knew I wouldn't listen. If he saw Rhys and me together, it was too risky. Same for Alex. I didn't want him to connect me to anyone I really cared about. I figured I'd go sit in my car for a few minutes and just take some time to think. I could call Sorin and maybe he'd talk me down.

When I reached the parking garage, I saw that the van was gone. He must've had someone pick it up and take it to the manor. He worked fast, I had to give him that. Hitting the key fob, I heard the beep of the BMW unlocking and looked forward to my break. Coming to the driver's side, I froze.

The word "whore" was scratched in the side of the once perfect black paint.

47

Sorin picked up on the third ring. I didn't know how to start but I knew if I didn't talk to someone, I was going to burst into blood tears in the middle of the garage. He must have felt it somehow because he answered the phone with "What's wrong?"

"Evelyn is what's wrong." I launched into the story of the evening. I told him about my conversation with Diana, Monica's comment, her plan to go home and Alex's worries. The rant ended with the message on his car.

"Keying a car seems lowbrow for Evelyn. Her tantrums usually involved things more complex than that, more devious."

"Who else would scratch 'whore' into the car I've been driving?"

"Is it possible it was meant for someone else? Are there other BMWs in the garage?" I looked around. My shoulders fell when I saw two other black BMWs parked in two separate physician spots.

"Yes, there are. Wait, so you knew she might do something? And, what do you mean by more devious?"

"I didn't think she'd come after you, Katherine. I expected her rage to be directed onto me. I don't think this was her."

"Why are you defending her?"

His tone was calculated and careful. "I'm not. I will be contacting her and asking her about this. However, it just isn't her style."

I was getting more annoyed by the second. It felt like I was the one in the center of a shitstorm and he was sitting comfortably in his manor. While I was dodging hunters and crazy exes, what was he doing? "Well, good luck with that. I seriously doubt she'd admit to it but I guess it doesn't matter. I'm going to get back to work. I don't want to raise any suspicion with too long of a break."

I didn't wait for a response, just hung up. To my dismay, the conversation hadn't helped me get rid of the tears. In fact, they felt closer than ever. And, the one person I wanted to talk to—my best friend—didn't want to talk to me. So, I was on my own with a hunter on one side and a psycho bitch on the other.

The unit was quiet when I walked back onto it. Turning the corner to head to the nurse's station, I ran head-first into the chest of Henry Kunsman. "I've been looking for you," he said before I could back up.

"Sorry," I gasped and tried to keep my breathing in check. "I should've been looking." Backing up, I saw that he wasn't holding his usual clipboard and couldn't tell if that was good or bad.

"Can we speak somewhere private?"

I thought about my options. I could run which was pretty much the dumbest thing I could do. I could tell him I was too busy, but looking around anyone could see I wasn't. Plus, he'd just want to talk later. Or, I could get it over with.

"How about the conference room?" I led him to the same room I'd spoken to Alex in, trusting that he'd follow. Once we were in there, I started a mantra in my head. *Be cool. Be cool. Be cool.* Putting it on repeat in my thoughts, it was like a background hum. *Be cool. Be cool. Be cool.*

He sat in the same chair that Alex had occupied earlier in the evening. It felt like years had gone by since that conversation and I was overwhelmed with the wish that I hadn't hung up on Sorin. Henry crossed his legs and stared at me like I was supposed to say something.

I'd had enough for one evening so I took charge. "You asked to speak, Mr. Kunsman. I'm listening."

"You've been here for a long time, correct?"

"Correct." The more I told the truth, the better.

"Have you always been on nights?"

"I haven't. I used to rotate. I went to straight nights recently."

"And, why did you do that?" His face gave away nothing.

The more truth, the better. "Because it comes with $2 dollars more an hour, it allows for a set schedule and it's better for my kids."

The mention of my kids got a reaction out of him. He uncrossed his legs and leaned forward. "You're a mother."

"I am."

"So, tell me. How well do you know the other night nurses? I mean the ones who only work nights." His eyes were glued to mine and I refused to look away.

"Nurses come and go. That's the nature of the job. Lots of them end up going to straight nights because it's the only set schedule you can get. We become a family of sorts. I would say I know them well enough to trust my patients with them but not to hang out with them after work."

"Anyone of them seem different recently? Call off more or acting odd?"

I leaned into him and didn't break my gaze. "None. Every staff member in the hospital is the same person I've worked with all these years." Again, the less I lied, the better. "If I had concerns, I would have already told Jerry. Now, if you'll excuse me."

Without giving him the chance to stop me, I turned and left. I wasn't going to let this bastard get anything out of me that he could use to hurt someone. With every fiber of my being, I wanted that man out of my life. I had enough to deal with and my patience was growing thin.

48

It took every ounce of strength in my body to get through the rest of the shift. I was on the verge of my breaking point and if I hadn't needed to keep up appearances, I would have bolted. But, with so many eyes on the hospital staff, I needed to keep calm and focus on taking care of my patients. I was grateful that the tears I'd felt earlier were replaced with a boiling rage. I was getting more and more frustrated with the people around me. Monica had written off our friendship over something she didn't understand. Alex was more involved with Monica than with anything else. Sorin had quickly brought a request to quit my job, an unhinged ex-lover and the idea of forever into my once boring life. He hadn't believed me when I told him Evelyn was off her rocker and had worked on plans all night with Rhys but didn't bother telling me anything. Now I was wolf-sitting, avoiding psycho Barbie and trying to not end up in a hunter's crosshairs, all while missing my kids so much it hurt. I was barely holding it together and had never felt so close to giving up.

The smell of blood filled the air and snapped me out of my spiral.

Following the scent, I ran into one of the patient rooms to see a gowned older man on the floor. He was face first on the ground and blood pooled around his head.

"CODE," I screamed into the hall.

Rolling him over, I saw his eyes were opened but unfocused. He was whispering the same word over and over. "Fell."

I saw the gash on his forehead and held pressure to stop it from flowing. My fangs snapped into place but I was stuck. All I could do was make sure I continued to look down when I spoke. I couldn't leave him.

Nurses and doctors raced into the room talking on top of each other. "I was doing rounds and saw him on the floor," I shouted to the room of people.

Someone produced a c-collar and I wrapped it around the neck of the man still cradled in my lap. When the board entered the room, we worked together to get him onto it and strapped down. Someone called out for a "*STAT CT.*" When it came time to lift him to the stretcher, I crab-walked backwards and out of the way. It was one thing to keep my fangs hidden but with the adrenaline pumping through me, I didn't know if I could control my strength. I didn't want to toss him in the air by accident.

Looking down, I caught sight of the blood soaking into my scrubs and tried to slow my breathing. Standing up, I dropped my head and slid out of the room as they prepared the patient for transport to CT. Every muscle shook and my breath come out ragged. I felt like I couldn't get oxygen in, like I was choking. I saw blackness start to creep in from the edges of my sight.

Diana ran up to me in the hall and wrapped her arm around my shoulders, guiding me towards the breakroom. "Follow me," she whispered. "Kunsman is on the other side of the unit."

All I could see were feet as I kept my focus on the ground and pressed my lips together. I was putting my trust in a woman who despised me but there was no one else and I was desperate. I felt her throw her weight against the breakroom door and found the chair in the corner.

"We're safe," she said. "But we gotta hurry. You have to get those fangs in and calm down."

Hearing her say 'calm down' combined with the adrenaline leaving my veins had the opposite effect and my resolve came crashing down. The tears started to flow before I could swallow them back. With racking sobs, I let all the pent-up feelings come pouring out. I couldn't have stopped them even if I'd wanted to.

"Oh shit," she said. "Perfect timing. God, I hate that you guys cry blood. It's seriously creepy."

It made me laugh through the tears. "This from someone who gets furry."

"Touché," she laughed and tossed a set of scrubs on the table next to me. Pulling off my top, I found a spot that was clean and used it to wipe at my eyes.

Diana's head cocked to one side. "Incoming," she whispered and dove to lock the door seconds before it could swing open.

"Hey," I heard from the other side.

"Changing," I yelled back.

"I was just checking on you," came the voice from the other side. I wasn't sure who it was but it didn't matter. There was no way I was letting anyone in.

"I'm fine. Just give me a few minutes, please."

We both let out a sigh when we heard footsteps receding. Peeling off the bloody pants, I rolled the set up and threw them into a trash bag I found in the cleaning closet. Diana's scrubs were a little tight but they would get me through the rest of the shift. "Thanks," I said. "I'll get them back to you."

She produced a makeup removing cloth from her locker and indicated that I needed to wipe my face. Running my tongue over my teeth, I was relieved to see my fangs had receded. Finding a mirror, I worked at cleaning up what I could. Unfortunately, wiping off the blood meant the makeup went too. My skin was paler without the concealer;

my cheeks lost their blush. Just thinking about the amount of work it took to walk into work was exhausting and the tears threatened to return.

"Didn't you feed before you came in?"

"I did," I snapped. "I'm not stupid. But all the emotions and the adrenaline, it was too much. My fangs responded to more than just blood. I'm not an animal."

"Sorry," she said. I felt bad for snapping.

"No, I'm sorry. You're basically the only one helping me and I barked at you. Thank you for saving me."

"Want to repay the favor?" she asked.

I tossed the wipe in with my scrubs. "Depends on the favor."

"Can you get me an appointment with your boyfriend? The sooner, the better."

"Sure," I took a step towards her. "Should I tell him what it's about?"

"It's pack business," she answered. "And, can you be there when I tell him? You know, to make sure he doesn't kill me?"

I laughed. "I can try. How about tomorrow at sundown?"

She inhaled and let it out with a huge sigh. "Yeah. And, don't let me chicken out. Any advice for giving him kinda bad news?"

I did owe her one. "He can tell if you're lying so don't. Be honest and to the point. Address him with respect; it goes a long way. And, whatever he decides, it's best not to fight." Even as I said it to her, I knew she'd struggle with it. I know I did, and the more I got to know her, the more I thought she was a lot like me.

49

The clock let me know it was time to give report and get the hell out of the hospital. I would have just enough time to grab a few sets of scrubs at Walmart if I moved fast. The night had been one for the books and I wanted it over. Thankfully, every nurse was okay with a quick hand-off so I could be gone before running into Kunsman again.

When I saw the car, the anger returned. I climbed in, shut the door and started the engine. Rolling down the window, I found a rock station that matched my current mood.

The run for scrubs was my quickest yet, due in part to the recent frequency with which I was needing to replace them. I was in and out in ten minutes and didn't even have to use my vampire speed. Timing out my drive, I figured I'd have time to talk to Sorin about Diana's request. I knew we were going to have to hash out our little phone squabble. Frankly, I was annoyed that he hadn't texted to check on me or offered some consolation. It was probably because he really didn't think Evelyn was the one behind the message on the car. If I was being honest, I was having some doubts, too. Once I calmed down, I thought about it logically. She would've had to know where I worked, what car

I was driving that night, get to the hospital and scratch it into the paint without being seen. The parking garage had cameras and risking capture was seriously stupid for a vampire. Not to mention she had a lot to lose if she got caught. Also, it sounded like she was majorly busy trying to get ready for her fashion show. I remembered that Sorin had felt it was beneath her to vandalize a car, that she was craftier. That did feel right. Someone like Evelyn was definitely more of the conniving type.

Not to mention that I'd been working in the hospital long enough to know that affairs happen. Was there a chance that the message had actually been meant for another Beemer?

So, what was I going to say to Sorin?

Well, I guess it depended on what he said. I was fully prepared for a fight. Frankly, with the tension I was feeling all over my body, I needed a fight. I wanted to punch something—hard. It was only a matter of time before we had our first argument. I just wished it was over something I felt a little more confident about. As I got closer to the manor, I was becoming less and less sure that Evelyn was the vandal.

I needed to understand why I was really mad at him. Was I really mad because he didn't "take my side" when I called him? Was it the staying in his office all night? Was it that he came with so much history and expectations of me? Was it that he wanted forever?

Or, was I mad because his life seemed less complicated than mine? He had money and power. He was respected as a leader. He'd shared his bed with the most beautiful beings on the planet. He loved what he did and rarely had to hide.

Was I jealous?

But then he'd offered it all to me, too. He'd told me he'd take care of me and give me a job I didn't need to hide in. He wanted to give up all the gorgeous, passionate lovers and just be with me. So, why was I mad?

Because I wanted it. I wanted that uncomplicated life. It seemed intoxicating and wonderful to me. And, that made me feel like a horrible person. I wanted to walk away from saving lives to be a part of his world.

And, what did that mean for my kids? Would I walk away from them? Should I?

Pulling into the driveway, I saw my van off to the side. When the car was parked, I punched the steering wheel and screamed. Everything in me was at war. Nothing felt okay. I felt like I'd never be okay again. I jumped out of the car, needing to walk—to move. Leaving everything in the back seat and the door open, I ran for the trees and the little bench.

Staring at it, I could practically see the myself on the first night of my turning. I was in Rhys's clothes and looking around in wonder. It'd just started to see with vampire eyes and the lights in the trees were sparkling. Sorin came from my periphery with a glass of blood in his hand. The me from my past reached out for it and smiled. She didn't know who he was but she was having dirty images of climbing into his lap. She was feeling overwhelmed but had no idea what was to come.

A hand touched my shoulder and I whirled around. Sorin stood behind looking worried. Blinking to clear my head and pull myself from past to present, I wasn't sure what to say.

He spoke first, "Talk to me, Katherine. What is going on with you?"

"What do you mean," I asked.

"I mean what I said—talk to me. You keep slamming this wall of yours into place. I chip away at it and things start to feel right but, then that wall goes right back up."

All that anger was churning in my stomach. I felt like I couldn't breathe around it. "Well, I'm sorry but I have kind of a lot going on right now."

"It's happening to more than just you, Katherine. We are all in danger. We are all worried."

"Yeah, but you don't have to go to work and face it. You don't have to worry about what vision you may have next and if you can stop it. You don't have to worry that some wolf is coming after your kids. And, Evelyn is gunning after me not you."

"You're wrong," he yelled. "Stop thinking about it like you're in this alone. *If* Evelyn comes after you, she is coming after me, too. If the wolves start a war, it is with *all* of us. If the hunter finds one, it will affect us all. If something happens to your daughters.... I cannot think of it. I am terrified of what you are seeing and the idea that I cannot stop it, as is Rhys." I saw his face mirroring my level of fury. "We are in this together."

I took a step into him, matching his volume. "Then why doesn't it feel like it?"

"Because you won't open up," he screamed. "You won't let me in." My legs gave out and I fell to the ground. Sorin dropped next to me and grabbed my arms. I cried out into the sky, letting all the feelings inside of me become a guttural sound.

"Dammit, Katherine. Stop trying to take this all on yourself." He wrapped his arms around me as I screamed into his chest and pounded my fists against him. He took my blows, staying stock still.

"I'm so scared," I wailed as my cried died down to whimpers. "What if I can't stop it? Can't stop whatever happens to them?"

"We will. You have to believe that. It's the only way we're going to be able to hold ourselves up and move forward. Remember that you, truly, hold the power. What you do in the hospital, with your friends, with yourself—affects us all. I know you feel powerless but you are in control and you are not alone. We are with you."

There on the ground, he rocked me. It wasn't the first time he'd seen me fall apart. I seriously doubted it would be the last. It didn't mean I wasn't mad at myself for it.

"We need to get inside," he whispered.

He'd given me a few minutes post-meltdown to get myself together and had just held me in silence. Now, that I was calming down I was feeling a little overdramatic. But, the blood streaks on his once white shirt were going to make it hard for me to pretend it didn't happen. It also seemed stupid to try and act cool when I'd literally pounded on the man's chest. My one consolation was that he was an empath. If he'd felt half of what I was feeling, he'd understand the momentary loss of control.

Standing together, I took a deep breath and looked up. Those grey eyes had lost the rage I'd seen earlier and were full of sympathy.

"Let's go to bed," I said. "I don't think I can stand much longer."

Without a word, he lifted me into his arms and I relaxed against him. *Drained* and *hopeless* are the closest words I have to try and describe the way I was feeling in that moment. It only took a few minutes for him to get us into the house, up the stairs and into his room but it was the few minutes I needed to breathe. He was right. We had to believe that we could save everyone. The visions were for a reason and there had to be clues in them. We had the heads up on Kunsman and that was a victory. If I hadn't heard that conversation, we'd still be in the dark and that was also a victory. And, Diana was coming clean to Sorin which would help us prevent a war.

"Oh," I said when he set my feet down onto the bedroom floor. "I almost forgot. Diana is coming over at sundown. She asked me to set up a time with you. I think she's going to tell you everything. Maybe we can use it to get ahead of any issues."

"Excellent," he responded. "I hope you're right and she is not coming to tell us something completely different. I don't think any of us wants more surprises."

"Definitely not," I agreed.

We were stripped down and in bed when I felt the sunrise. I didn't want to sleep with unresolved issues so I rolled over to face Sorin. "I don't mean to put up walls, they just go up and then I don't know how the get them down."

He rolled to meet my gaze. "Like anything else, it takes practice. Eventually, you'll see and stop building them up."

"See what," I asked.

"That I'll just keep breaking them back down."

50

Someone was tapping my shoulder. Opening my eyes, I saw Sorin above me. I was confused that I hadn't heard the alarm when I remembered I'd forgotten to set it. As a matter of fact, my phone was still in the pocket of the scrub top on the floor.

"Hey," I said.

He produced a glass of blood. "Breakfast in bed. Diana should be here soon."

I sat up and took the glass. It was warm and I enjoyed the smell before drinking it down. "I have to run out the car. I left some clothes out there."

"Already brought in," he smiled. "Laying over on the couch. I wish you didn't have to go in."

"Me too," I agreed. "Soon this should be over and I can get back to my vacation."

Leaning in, he kissed me. It was a small, quick kiss but it was the reassurance I was craving. I knew we were okay. He'd seen me completely fall apart and hadn't run. He's laid down next to me, gotten up, gotten breakfast and woken me up. Totally normal and totally what I'd needed.

"Get dressed and meet me in the office. I'm assuming you want to be there?"

I nodded and didn't let him know that she'd asked for me to be there. It wasn't necessary.

"I have asked Rhys to be present. I believe he is already in the office."

Finishing my glass, I set it down and got out of bed to grab the new clothes. Once they were on, I retrieved my phone. No missed calls. I guess the girls were still mad.

I couldn't give Diana her scrubs back with blood and grass stains on them so I threw them into the hamper. Fluffing out my hair with my hands, I made my way to the bathroom to brush my teeth and meet Sorin.

When I walked into the office a few minutes later, Diana was already on the couch and she looked scared. My heart hurt for her. I knew she was making a very difficult decision and I hoped it was the right one.

Rhys leaned against the desk with his arms crossed. He looked at Diana, not hiding his distrust of her. I kissed my maker on his cheek. He looked to me and his expression softened. "Hey, kid."

"Perfect timing," Sorin said as I crossed to him and kissed him. He was in one of the merlot chairs. I thought about sitting in the other but decided to show Diana support and sit next to her. We might be different species but we we're both women. I believe in supporting women when they're in need.

She cleared her throat. "I need to tell you something that I should've told you earlier. For that, I will apologize right up front. When I'm done, I hope you'll understand my hesitancy." I was impressed with the way she phrased it, respectful and to the point.

He was frozen in that way that no human could do. I wasn't sure if he did it specifically to hide what he was thinking or if he just didn't realize he was doing it. The effect was unnerving and, while I'd gotten used to it–I wondered what she was thinking as she looked at him. To her credit, she didn't let it show if it upset her. She squared her shoulders and kept going.

"During the great battle between wolf and fang, my father and his four brothers were lost. Each of them was slaughtered by one of your own. My grandfather, our leader, survived but lost all of his children. He raised me and my cousins on stories of our fathers' brave acts. They wanted only to protect our ways."

I found Rhys. His hard expression was shifting slightly. I don't think he knew that she'd suffered so much loss. It explained her hatred of vampires and I couldn't blame her for not liking us in the beginning. Knowing Rhys, he was feeling the same as me. I turned to give her my attention again.

"My grandfather joined our ancestors a few weeks ago. This is why I returned to the area. My cousins are returning or are already here. One of us will take the place of master of our pack."

She paused and waited. Sorin appeared to be choosing his words but I knew that he likely already had them prepared. When he finally moved, I heard Diana let out a breath. "I am sorry for your loss," he began. "Gabriel was a great man and an ally. He valued peace, as I do. I wish I had known. Your rituals are private, I am aware, but I would have liked to have sent something to honor him."

"I thank you for the thought. He didn't speak much of you; however, when he did, it was with respect."

"Why wasn't I told?" he lifted his chin in a show of offense.

"This is where I want to be clear," she looked to me for assurance then back to him. "Telling you this is betraying my family. They will see this as me choosing your side. I am indebted to you for letting me stay and work when I didn't follow the treaty and for letting me know that Kunsman was a hunter. This is me repaying that debt."

He remained silent.

She finished quickly, trying to get it out before running dry on courage. "My cousin Diego is trying to rally the pack to defy you. He believes we should no longer honor the pact and wants to break the treaty. If he becomes our leader, he wants to rise against the vampires. There are others in the group who agree."

"How many of you have rights to be lead," he asked.

"The oldest child of each of the five sons of my grandfather. Myself and four more. The others are all male. I won't win." She sounded resigned and I laid my hand on hers out of instinct. She didn't pull hers away.

Sorin thought for a moment and asked another question. "How many of them agree with Diego?"

"Two more, Sebastian and Julian. Only myself and Marcos think the pact should remain. We follow the ways of our grandfather. We are trying to convince them this is bad for both sides but they won't listen."

Sorin was contemplating something so I took the moment to ask a question. "How do you choose? Is it an election?"

She turned to me and scoffed. "I wish."

"They fight," Sorin responded. "They shift and fight. The victor is the new pack master."

I grabbed her hand. "What? They could kill you."

"They should stop without killing. They only need to show dominance. And, we're strong in our animal form. But, they're male and much bigger than me."

I turned to Sorin and I'm sure he saw the panic. He shook his head. "We cannot interfere. Whoever wins, is the master. Diana, when does this happen?"

"Next full moon," she answered.

"That's next week," I interrupted.

Sorin leaned forward in his chair. "Will the pack follow the direction of their leader? If Marcos wins and tells them to continue the treaty, will your other cousins obey?"

"I don't know. It's our way to follow the commands of the master. They always obeyed my grandfather, even if they didn't agree. I can see how bad this is. We have children in the pack and my cousins expect them to fight against vampires. They'll die. And, our numbers are already small. We can't lose anymore."

"Will you tell them that you have spoken to me?"

"They'll be pissed but I can tell them tonight. I'm off."

"Don't," he responded. "It may put you in danger and they may not speak in front of you. I thank you for telling me. We need to plan for what to do if Marcos doesn't win."

"That's the other thing," she said. "Marcos won't fight. He's given up his right to master. I'm the only chance we have to not go to war."

51

I walked Diana out to her car in silence. I wouldn't have known what to say but it didn't seem like she wanted to talk anyway. She gave me one last look from her car before she pulled away. I couldn't tell if she felt relieved after telling us or more upset. Either way, I knew she had done something very difficult by telling us what she had.

When I returned to the office, Rhys was gone and Sorin was still in the chair. I sat in his lap and he embraced me. "What are we going to do?"

"I have a lot to think about," he said. "Diana is our one hope and while she is very brave, the odds are against her. We must plan for a meeting with the winner and attempt to reach an agreement without bloodshed."

"Do we trust her?"

"I felt her this evening," he responded. "She felt genuine. She's scared and in a very bad position. She's feels responsible for her pack and feels a connection to you."

"Is that good?" I pulled back so I could see his eyes.

"Yes. She feels a kinship with you. I don't know how but you've won her loyalty." He smiled. "I told you that you'd be a good lady of the city someday. You're already working you magic and turning enemies into friends."

"Maybe I should go try to win over her cousins," I laughed and his smile died.

"Don't go out there. We are not welcomed on their land and must be invited."

"I was kidding," I assured him. "I wouldn't just go to her house. My goodness, I'm not dumb."

He let out a sigh. "I never know with you."

"Well," I kissed him. "I have to go. I'm already late."

"Please be safe," he said looking more serious than I thought he needed to. Clearly, I wasn't comprehending just how bad this whole thing was. I told myself to ask more questions later but for now, I had to get to the hospital before red flags went up.

When I saw the BMW, I remember the lovely message on the side and decided I needed to return to my trusty minivan. I figured if that one got keyed then we definitely knew it was for me. Climbing into it, I caught a whiff of the girls. Their scents were fading but they were still there, embedded in the upholstery from years of sitting in their seats as we ran errands and went on weekend trips.

Thinking of them brought back the visions. I replayed them in my head and tried to take in every detail. The first had been outside at the park. It was the park close to our house and we'd gone 1,000 times. I'd heard their laughter and the sounds of soccer. I hadn't seen them but had seen other parents. It wasn't a memory because I'd been trying to get out of the sun so I'd been a vampire. It was fall, I knew from the smell of the leaves and the fact that everyone had been wearing light coats. That was all I could remember and none of it helped. Without seeing the girls, I didn't know what they had been wearing like I had with the vision of Monica so I couldn't even pinpoint a day. It'd been sunny, that's all I knew.

The second vision offered even less. It was at their school at night. No one was there. No sounds or lights in the school, no cars in the lot. The only thing had been the howl—a wolf's howl. But, now that I thought about it, was it a wolf's howl? It could have been a dog or a coyote. So, basically, I got nothing useful from that one either.

Smacking the steering wheel with my palm, I grunted. This was infuriating—visions with absolutely no way to stop them. What was the point?! It made me think of that Greek myth with Cassandra. She'd offered herself to Apollo in exchange for prophecy. He gave it to her and she'd backed out of the deal—refusing him. So, he cursed her. She'd see the future but no one would believe her so she could never stop the bad things from happening.

Only I'd been given the gift just because I was a vampire and people believed me but we couldn't do anything about it. All I could do was ask Tom to put the girls under house arrest but not explain why. And, I was well aware that wouldn't work forever. Eventually, he'd stop worrying and give in to them. He'd let them go to parties or the park and I couldn't blame him. He was a cop. I knew that he could sense I was holding back. It was only a matter of time before he'd pushed me for more information.

When I pulled into the garage, I decided it was time to start parking on a different floor. I'd been kidnapped and possibly vandalized on the previous floor. Time to use the stairs and find a new spot. I used a new elevator, too. Felt like washing myself clean of very old dirt.

To my relief, Kunsman was nowhere in sight. I got report from Jackson, Tiffany O and Tiffany H- the old crew. There was comfort in working with those three, even if they'd seen me post-tryst with Sorin. They'd never told anyone, to my knowledge and that bought them some serious brownie points in my opinion.

Looking at the patient names on the board, I saw that Monica had been discharged. Double checking my phone showed me what I already knew- she hadn't texted me. Going to my locker, I didn't find so much as a note telling me goodbye. Well, I thought, that was my answer. She was done with our friendship. Despite myself, I was happy for her. I pictured her looking through her clothes and planning out every moment of her date with Alex.

Speaking of Alex, where the hell had he been? Other than drawing my blood and me giving him the heads-up about Kunsman, he'd been basically MIA. Okay, that wasn't fair. He had stopped by the house to check on me. But things felt so different. He felt like he was drifting away and the thought of that caused a pang in my gut. It was silly because I'd practically despised him only a month before but it was true. He'd become very special to me very quickly and I didn't want to lose him if I was also losing Monica.

Selfish, I know.

The pang in my gut was replaced with what felt like someone grabbing my stomach and pulling forward. It was agonizing and insistent. Rhys' name filled my head and I had the sudden urge to find him. Just thinking about not doing it filled me with dread.

Heading for the stairwell, I ran down the stairs and into the basement hallway. Speed walking to the blood bank, I expected to see him on the ground or in some kind of distress. On the contrary, he was sitting behind his desk like always and looked perfectly fine.

"Rhys?"

He jumped up. "It worked!"

"What worked," I asked.

"I called you. It occurred to me that I'd never tried and what if it's an emergency and it doesn't work."

I grabbed the closest thing—a book—and threw it at him, careful to avoid the computer. "You dick! That was extremely unpleasant."

"Sorry," he said after dodging the book. "Never experienced it or if I did, I don't remember it."

"Well, it sucks. It feels like getting lead by the intestines. Please don't do it unless you have to." I went to the couch and sat. "You rushed out of the manor after Diana. You okay?"

"Yeah. Just feeling bad for Diana. Worried about what she said. You?"

"Not really but I'm trying to not freak out and just take things one at a time." I leaned back and rested my head on the back of the couch. "Just wish Kunsman would go away already."

"I get it. Have you seen him?"

"I did yesterday. It was quick. He was asking about people on straight nights and why I switched. I told him for the money and set schedule. He seemed to buy it."

"He was only in here once and hasn't come back. Thankfully, I didn't know what he was when he was here so I didn't panic."

I looked up and found his eyes. "So, what did you and Sorin come up with? You guys talked all night."

He came and sat next to me. "We did some research. He was right; no one named Kunsman works for the department of health. We couldn't even find an inspector named Henry. We found nothing on him. No birth records with that name match his age range. Couldn't find a driver's license with his picture. The guy doesn't exist on the Internet."

My heart plummeted into my stomach. "So, we got nothing."

"I'm sorry, Katie but if I can't find it on the web, it's not there. And, so far Diana has learned nothing. I know she's got a lot going on but she's terrible at gathering info."

It was unlike Rhys to be so unsympathetic. I figured after hearing that story he'd cut her some slack. Guess not. "Gotta get back." I kissed the top of his head and left him to his blood cave.

52

I made it to 4am without anything awful happening which felt like a literal blessing from the gods. I never thought I'd be so grateful for a boring shift. Jerry had come onto the floor around 3 o'clock to tell everyone that Kunsman was in an office looking at the charts of trauma patients that had come into the ED in the last three months. Part of me was worried he'd stumble onto something. The other part was happy he was in front of a computer instead of one of us. The director of nursing apologized to me again for making me come in when I was supposed to be taking a well-deserved break. His apologies were starting to wear thin. I reminded myself that he hadn't knowingly put my life in danger when he begged me to come in. And, honestly, I would rather have been here than have left Rhys alone with a hunter—but, still—I was allowed to be annoyed.

My phone dinged in my pocket. I pulled it out and said a silent prayer that it was Monica but I knew it was too late for her to be up. Maybe it was Sorin, checking in.

UNKNOWN: Come out back. I'm at the bench. <3

Did Sorin come to the hospital to see me? If so, why was he using an unknown number? I didn't think he had multiple phones. If he did, that was something we needed to talk about, for sure. It wasn't Rhys. He wouldn't have sent a heart at the end. Did Sorin know how to text hearts? I'm sure he did. I mean he was old not dumb.

When I opened the back door, the smell of the dried autumn leaves hit my nostrils. The vision of the park threatened to fill my mind as a reaction to the scent. I shoved it into the back of my brain and didn't let it take over. I'd already replayed it earlier. I didn't need a repeat performance.

Another scent was under the leaves. Expensive perfume and leather. "Fuck," I said into the night. "Where are you, Evelyn?"

I heard laughter from the tree line just as she stepped out from behind a tree. "Damn wind," she said. "Makes it hard to mask my scent."

As she moved through the graves towards me, I tried to remain still, the way I'd seen Sorin do it. She looked like something out of a movie—the tall, beautiful woman walking through the headstones. It was chilling, even to me.

I breathed in slowly to try and stop the boiling power I felt in my stomach. It was slowly climbing up, looking for a way out. "What are you doing here?"

"Just thought we were due for a little chat, woman to woman. We started off on a bad foot and I couldn't forgive myself if I didn't try to mend fences."

She reached the edge of the cemetery. Power was pulsing around her. I called bullshit on her story. There was no need to show power if you were here for a talk. "Close enough," I warned. "Talk."

"It occurred to me that you are very new and it's terribly unfair of me to have behaved the way I did." She was using that "50s housewife" tone and laying the sweetness on thick. "I didn't mean to overwhelm you. I also realized, once I had time to reflect, that you are not aware of my history with Sorin."

So that was her tactic, I thought, to tell me all about their escapades. "I don't need to know, Evelyn. He was around hundreds of years before me. I know he wasn't saving himself for me. I also don't care."

She smiled. "Oh, I'm not talking about sex. Although that was absolutely Earth-shattering. He told me I was incredible. No, I'm talking about the fact that every relationship he's been in he's ended as quickly as it started. Then he always calls me. He knows that we are better suited for each other than anyone else. Do you think you're the first one he's talked about running his city with? Or called his queen?"

Standing still was the best thing I could have done. Everything in me screamed to run or attack. To my credit, I did neither. "Anything else," I asked, not allowing her to see how much what she said had affected me.

"Just one more thing," she arched her perfect eyebrow. "And, don't answer tonight. You need to think long and hard."

"Hurry it up, Evelyn. I have a job."

"How much do you love Sorin? Is there a price tag on that love? I mean, it's only been a few weeks. You're not actually mated, yet. He can't mean that much to you already."

I was shaking with rage. I felt the heat of my power seeping from my pores like a fever and dancing around my skin.

"Now," she continued. "Think about a sum of money that could change your life. A million? Two? Or a set amount every month for eternity? Be out of debt and worry-free. Have anything your heart desired. I can make that happen for you. And, all you have to do is walk away from him—a man you barely know."

The ground below me caved in as I lifted off the ground. The heat that danced around me flared and her eyes doubled in size. "Get out of my sight," I growled. Her power increased its pace around her but her gaze told me she was thinking twice about what to do next. She bared her fangs at me, letting a screech come out of that flawless face and I saw the ugliness that makeup couldn't hide.

The door burst open and Rhys's voice hit the air. "Stop."

Evelyn turned and was gone in a blur. I dropped to the ground, feeling the impact of not controlling my descent. Footsteps ran up to me and he pulled me up. "What were you thinking," he whispered. "How could you be so stupid? There is a hunter inside. What if he saw you?"

The consequences of my actions hadn't occurred to me in the moment but they were clear as day now. I had majorly screwed up. I ran my gaze across all the windows of the hospital and didn't see anyone. It didn't mean no one had seen. Anyone witnessing what just happened would have bolted from the glass when I looked up.

"Oh God, Rhys. I wasn't thinking. She was here and I couldn't control myself. I'm so sorry. Oh god. What if he saw? If anyone saw?"

He hurried me inside the building and stopped a few feet from the door, at the base of the stairs. "Get your stuff and go. I will talk to you when I calm down."

Rhys had never been mad at me and I didn't know what to do. I wanted to fix it but I had to follow his command. He'd told me to leave and I'd already screwed up enough for one night. With my head hanging, I returned to my unit. After giving report to the nurses, I grabbed my bag and slowly walked to the garage.

Everything Evelyn had just said was slamming through my head. Deep down I knew she was trying to get me off-guard, upset me. But some of the things she had said stung. Sorin had said they'd only slept together once. Was that true? If not, why lie? He'd been so forthcoming with previous lovers, both male and female. The only reason to downplay Evelyn was because she really had meant something to him at some point. Had he really called her his queen, also? Was I really not the first that he'd used those lines on? Then, why offer to mate for life? Unless he wanted me with no one else but planned on being with others—No. That just didn't feel right. I knew that he meant what he said. He may omit things from time to time but he didn't lie. I believed him when he said he'd only been with her once. I also believed him when he said he wanted to be my mate. The only thing I was questioning was if he had called Evelyn his queen.

There was only one way to know. I had to ask him.

53

Even a new vampire could tell that the lord of the city was mad. It started when I pulled up the driveway; a wall of electrical heat around the manor. When I stepped out of the car it hit my skin like thousands of small currents marching across my body. My instinct knew instantly that the sensation was all Sorin. Walking up to the house, through the door and up the staircase was like walking through a storm without rain.

I didn't bother to knock, just opened the office door and faced my very angry, very powerful boyfriend.

At the fireplace, staring into the flames with his back to me he looked both beautiful and deadly. I braced myself for yelling but instead his words came out slowly—which was worse. "What were you thinking?"

Yep. Rhys had already called him.

"I fucked up, Sorin. I'm sorry." But even as I said it, I knew I wasn't really sorry and he was going to sense it. "Okay not completely sorry but I do realize how bad this is."

When he turned, I saw the storm clouds in his eyes. Normally, that meant he was excited but these clouds were dark with rage. "In public with a hunter in the building?" The same voice that he'd used to caress me now thumped in the air and sent a blast of heat against my chest.

"I know."

"Do you, Katherine? You are impulsive and flippant. You risked yourself, Rhys, Diana and every other supernatural creature in this city. If *anyone* saw you, he'd not rest until he found all of us. And, for what? Jealousy?"

So many vampires had warned me about Sorin's temper. Until that moment, I thought everyone was dramatic or they were such screw-ups they'd made him mad. Now, I saw it. He was furious and it was all my fault.

But it wasn't!

"Evelyn was at my hospital. She told me all about you two." It was out and I couldn't take it back. I may have been shaking but I was going to stand my ground. I took a step towards him to show him I wasn't backing down. "She offered me *a lot* of money to walk away from you. I could put my kids through the best colleges, pay off my debt, go to school, get rid of that shitty van and be set for eternity. And, all I have to do is let her have you. So, if you want her for your Queen, at least I'll get something out of it."

Steeling myself for his rebuttal, I lost my resolve when I saw his eyes. It wasn't rage; it was pain. I'd hurt him and wasn't bothering to hide it. It was now or never……

"Is that what you want?" I asked, squaring my shoulders and jutting out my chin. "Just tell me."

"I want to know exactly what she said—exactly." His voice was low and calm—making me take a step back to distance us. I didn't know how he'd react to the next part and I wanted an escape plan.

Steadying myself, I took a deep breath. "That you have gone back to her after every failed relationship. You've offered her to share in the ruling of the city. That your sex was incredible and Earth-shattering. That I could ask for any amount of money and she'd give it to me."

I gulped before I could say the last part. "That you've called her your Queen also."

The crackling in the air became audible. It had pulled back from my skin, thankfully, but I could hear it and sense it. He walked to the phone without a word and dialed. I heard the other voice on the line answer and knew it immediately. I didn't know how bad this was going to get but I knew it wasn't done.

"Do not speak, only listen," he commanded. "You will be at the manor tomorrow at sundown. That is an order from your master." He hung up. I couldn't imagine the fear Evelyn must be feeling when that line clicked and the ringtone hit her ears.

Facing me, I saw a mixture of emotions—anger, pain and fear. I wanted to take those away from him but didn't want to take a step towards him. I didn't need to because he was walking to me. "Please don't fear me," he said.

"You're scary when you're mad." Honesty was best, right?

"I'm scared, Katherine. Yes, angry as well, but you scare me, your recklessness scares me. I saw what you could do in the barn. I know you can protect yourself. However, you continue to be thrown into danger without the time to train your abilities. Another vampire is one thing but a hunter…"

He paused and gave me the chance to come to him. I took a tentative step in his direction, leaving only a few steps between us. I wasn't ready to close that distance.

He waited, continuing to calm himself. "You endangered yourself and everyone else tonight. I could not have saved you. I cannot be with you always and I hate it."

As the rage faded from his eyes, I took another step. Neither of us seemed ready to unite yet.

"Evelyn knows that you can fly. She has seen your power. She will not keep it to herself and that is exactly what I didn't want to happen. Not until you could control yourself. If Rhys hadn't been there—"

"I know," I yelled. "Okay? I know. I was so angry. I wanted to rip her apart. It was all I could think of and it just exploded out of me. I don't want to be like this—out of control and putting people in danger. I don't!"

With the blink of an eye, he was against me and crushing his mouth onto mine. I held onto him with a desperation I didn't know I was feeling. It was like I was floating in a dark ocean and he was a life-raft. His hands were in my hair, holding on with the same need for an anchor. In tandem we moved to the desk and he lifted me up to set me on it. It was Sorin who broke the kiss. *"Nu am numit-o niciodată regina mea.* I never called her that; never offered her to be at my side. I have only given my whole self to you."

He lifted my shirt over my head and ran his hand over the place where his bite had been. Matching his movement, I lifted his shirt off to lay my lips where my bite had been. He lifted my face to his. "Please don't leave me."

An ache rose in my chest. The thought of walking away from him sucked the air out of the room. "Never, we're forever."

This time the kiss felt less desperate and more of a reassurance, like a promise to each other. The ache in my chest spread to the rest of me and began to throb. I was frantic for the feel of him against and inside of me. Working at his belt without losing the rhythm of our mouths, I felt his pants fall to the ground and him step out of them. When the weight of my pants was gone, he pressed against me to feel that I was ready. Leaning back allowed for the angle he needed. He drove into me, groaning into our kiss. I had to pull my lips away from his to suck in air and focus my spinning thoughts. I felt his hands on my hips combined with the pleasure of him entering me and the loss of him pulling back. Our powers had joined between us without me realizing it. Lights spun around each other- a faint blue and a soft red. There was no chance to try and figure out if I was really seeing light or not. The throbbing in my core balanced between pain and pleasure. When I leaned forward to return my lips to his, it increased the friction between us and brought us to the edge of climax. I wanted to continue our kiss but was too overwhelmed by sensation to breathe. Pulling back, I saw his eyes—pupils swallowed by the dazzling grey. Raw desire filled those irises and could only see me. When the throbbing become one great cramp of need, I moved with him. The release brought a scream from me and he echoed it, arching back to thrust into me one last time.

The lights around us faded back into our forms—red to him and blue to me. "Did you see the lights," I asked when I could speak again.

"I did," he answered.

"Is that normal?"

"Nothing with us is normal, Katherine. I continue to be surprised by what we can do between us."

I laughed. "That's an understatement." I was contemplating a tandem shower when I felt warmth on my hand. Confused I saw a beam of sun on the desk and pushed him off of me. "Shit."

We glanced at the window to see the sun rising on the other side of the glass. "We might want to go to bed," he chuckled. "I guess this is a night of recklessness on both our parts. That's the second time you've lost control and risked your life in a matter of hours."

I slapped his butt. "But what a way to go." He chased me out of the office, down the hall and into the bedroom with us giggling and naked the whole way.

54

I was seriously sick of the alarm. While I may not wake up tired, it's unpleasant to be pulled into consciousness by an ear-piercing tone. When I was finally on vacation, I was going to see if I naturally woke with the sunset like Sorin and Rhys. Then I could be rid of that damn thing.

Sorin wasn't next me so he'd avoided the jolt- lucky bastard.

Before I could stop it, the memory of what was to come intruded on my thoughts. Evelyn was probably getting into her car. As much as I wanted to face her in a gown and jewelry, I had to go to work so it was pointless and a waste of time. I pulled on some scrubs, wrestled my hair into a bun, covered it in dry shampoo and set to using makeup to look worse. "Great," I said to the mirror. "She'll love this."

The doorbell ring told me two things: she was too scared to just walk in like usual and I was going to have to take my breakfast to go if I wanted to be full before seeing a patient. I glanced at my phone. Thirty minutes before I had to go. I could be there for the showdown and call the girls on the way to work while also drinking a meal. Easy.

Thankfully, I reached the office before she did. Sorin was waiting, seated in one of the chairs. I stood next to him without being told. I expected some kind of speech or direction, for him to lay out rules. But he was quiet. When she walked through the door, it wasn't with her head hung low. She entered with her spine straight and an outfit I expected had the tag removed an hour before. Everything about her said she was confident in what was about to go down.

I had to applaud her tenacity.

Sorin stood and I saw her hand lift a little in expectation of a kiss. It wavered and fell when she saw his face. He was always taller than me by several inches but, in that moment, he felt larger than ever. There was no power, just a very angry man. She moved to sit and he stopped her. "Do not take another step. This will be quick. Evelyn Blomgren, would you like a representative? Your business partner or maker will do."

That got a reaction out of her. For an instant, she looked like she would faint. The nurse in me was ready to respond, the woman in me hoped she break her nose when she passed out.

"Is that necessary?" she asked demurely. "I'm sure we can talk this out."

"Do you waive your right to a representative?" Sorin was not in the mood to play games. If Evelyn was smart, she'd stop the charade.

"Yes."

Tamela stepped into the room without needing to be called. When Evelyn looked up at her, it finally registered on her face that she was in serious trouble. Her gaze followed Tamela as she joined the other side of Sorin.

"I will begin to question you with Tamela and Katherine as witnesses." Sorin was cold in his delivery, almost business like. "Did you go to the Pittsburgh Medical Center last night and offer money to Katherine if she'd walk away from me?"

Tamela looked at me across Sorin and I nodded. Her eyes were wide so I was guessing Sorin hadn't told her anything beforehand. She'd just come as asked, not knowing what was going to happen. I wondered how many times she'd been witness to a trial of sorts.

"Yes," she answered, drawing our attention back to her.

"Did you tell her that we had shared a bed more than once and told her that I had offered you shared rule of this city?"

She held her head in place but turned her eyes to meet mine. I refused to drop my gaze. "Yes," she said.

"Was it a lie?" he asked.

"Yes," she said, clenching her jaw and breaking our stare down.

"Was your motivation to draw her into a fight or to cause her to display power?"

The pretty mask she'd been holding dropped. Her face contorted in defense. "She is more powerful than she should be and you know it. You're protecting her, allowing her among humans when you know she is a liability."

"Silence," he raged. His voice blasted from him and bounced off the walls. I had to clench my muscles and bend my knees to stop from being pushed backwards by it. Evelyn took a step back in her stilettos to balance herself.

"Yes," she answered. "I wanted her to show herself."

"Hear this, Evelyn Blomgren. I reject you. From this day forward, you will not enter my home. You will speak through Tamela for any business or city needs. I will not be at charity events if you are there. I suggest you let the board members know. You are dead to me."

She dropped to her knees. "Sorin, no... please. Don't do this. Please. What did I do to deserve this? All I did was love you."

"You attempted to break up mates. We may not have performed the ceremony but I told you my intentions. That is sacred and to come into it with the desire to destroy is punishable. By rights, I could cast you out from the city. I have shown you mercy but, Evelyn?"

"Yes?"

"If you come against me or mine again, you will be exiled."

"Sorin, my business is here—my home."

"Then I suggest," he stepped into her to look down and force her to look up. "You stay far away from Katherine and me. Now, get up and go."

She scrambled to her feet. She was acting shaken but there were no tears so I questioned just how hurt she really was. She clutched her stomach and laid the back of the other hand against her forehead. *Have some self-respect*, I thought.

When she saw that Sorin was not going to react to her damsel in distress routine, she stood tall, wiped her hands down her dress to smooth any wrinkles and cleared her throat. "When you calm down and change your mind, you know how to reach me." He growled and she held up her hands. "I get it. I'm leaving."

She was in the doorway when she glanced backwards. "I hope you're happy."

The sound of her heels on the stairs echoed through the house. No one was speaking or moving until she was really gone. When the front door shut, I saw Sorin relax. Tamela spoke without moving her eyes from the doorway. "I'm going to the need the whole story someday."

"It's one problem solved," Sorin said, maintaining the business tone. "We still have a few more to worry about. Kathrine?"

I turned to face him. "Yes?"

"To the best of your ability, please check in with me throughout your shifts. You've been abducted and now confronted at your workplace. I would appreciate knowing you're safe. If you have any inkling that the hunter knows of you, assure me you will run."

There was no doubt that he was worried. It was written all over his face. And, that worried me. I kissed him. "I promise."

"And, if you see or hear from Evelyn…"

"I know," I interrupted. "I'll walk away and call you immediately. Do you think she'll defy you?"

"I doubt it," he said and I prayed that he was right.

55

My phone rang before I could start my car or take my first sip. I answered without checking the caller ID. You think I'd know better.

"Kate?"

It was Diana. I didn't remember giving her my number but I didn't think it would be hard to find at work. We posted our numbers in multiple spots. I was just realizing how stupid that was but it was a little late now. She sounded worried and I was seriously over bad news.

"What's up?"

"I tried Rhys. He didn't answer. Are you with Sorin?" Yeah, she sounded worried.

"No, I'm on my way to work. Why?" I was at the end of the driveway and didn't see the need to turn around. I couldn't keep being late.

"Listen, my cousins are gearing up for something. I don't know what but I overheard them earlier. They were talking about making a move that would show you guys how serious they were. Sebastian said that it would force your hands and you would not refuse battle. I don't know what to do. If they know I'm talking to you guys—let's just say you'll need a new nurse."

I pulled the car over. "Are you safe?"

"Yeah," she assured. "I'm at work, waiting for you or Rhys."

I returned the van to the road and continued towards the hospital. I could go back but Sorin had enough to deal with and we didn't really know anything. Without solid clues, all this would do is send him to 100. "Okay, I'll be there soon."

When I pulled into the parking spot, I realized I hadn't called the girls and was out of time. I pulled up our group chat.

ME: I hope you guys aren't still mad at me. I miss you. Please call me when you wake up.

I gave it a few minutes but had no response. It was a little early for them to be sleeping but they could be preoccupied. I shoved my phone into my pocket, finished my warm blood and headed into the hospital. Once on the unit, I heard Alex's voice. When my bag was dropped on the nurse's station, I followed his voice. Standing outside the room he was in, I waited patiently for him to end his conversation with the patient. When he came out and saw me, he seemed surprised.

"Nurse Murphy." I don't know why he was being so formal but didn't care.

"Hey, stranger. You been avoiding me?"

Clearly, I'd confused him. "Why would you think that?"

"Because I've barely seen you the last week. I know you got a lot going on but I just want to know that you're okay; that we're okay."

He furrowed his brow. "Why wouldn't we be?"

I threw my hands up in the air. "I don't know. I'm just feeling a little sensitive and kind of alone. Monica is giving me the cold shoulder. Just need to know I still have one human friend."

Alex grabbed my arm and pulled me into an empty patient room. I was too shocked to react. He'd never been rough or angry with me. I wasn't sure what was going on. He shut the door and whirled around. "Stop saying things like 'human'. There's a hunter in the hospital. I'm keeping up appearances and doing my job. I'm staying away from you to keep you safe. But, Kate... it's not all about you, you know. Rhys is in danger; my research is in danger. Monica barely survived in the barn."

I'd never seen him mad and I never thought I'd be the one to set him off. As much as his words were stinging, I knew he was right.

"Try to not take this personally," he sighed. "You were not a part of my life for a long time. I owe you a great deal but you are not the only thing I need to worry about. If you need me, just call but I don't have the energy to hold your hand and tell you everything will be okay."

He gave me a last look before he walked out of the room and left me speechless. I should've stopped him but I didn't know what to say. It also didn't feel like the right time. And, to be honest, it would just be so I felt better which was the whole point of what he was trying to say.

I tried to forget the last couple hours and approach my shift like any other night. I'd get report, take care of my patients and get out as soon as I could. No need to worry about fixing things with Alex until we got the hunter out of the way and avoided a werewolf war.

Priorities, right?

I made it two hours before I saw Diana. She was clearly trying to get my attention but I couldn't get away from the patient in 504. She was talking my ear off and showing me her hundreds of pictures of her grandkids, birthday parties and cruises. Diana was practically dancing in my periphery, trying to get me to come to her. Finally, I told my patient that I heard a cardiac alarm and needed to check on someone. She let me leave and I hoped her sleeping pill would kick in soon. The rest of my patients had called it a night. She was the last holdout.

When I reached Diana, she whispered into my ear. "Go to the blood bank, I'll meet you there." Then she nudged me away and looked around. I didn't have the heart to tell her she seemed super suspicious. She was obviously proud of whatever she was about to share with us and I needed good news more than air.

Checking on each patient, I felt it was a good time for a break and followed her request. Down the stairs I walked again, wishing that all this stair work would burn some calories. I laughed out loud to no one, realizing I still had some human thoughts and it comforted me. When I made it to the blood bank, I was thrilled to hear music again. Either Jerry wasn't in the hospital tonight or Rhys just stopped caring. I wasn't sure which one I hoped for more. Tonight, was Kenny Loggins. Seemed silly to defy administration for Kenny Loggins but who was I to judge?

"Hey there," Rhys called out from his usual perch. He jumped up to meet me. "What's up? You okay? Did Sorin go easy on you last night?"

"We can talk about that later; no time now. Diana asked me to come down. Guess she wants to tell us something. Do you have lunch packed by chance? I'm hungrier than usual."

He pulled a thermos from his desk and tossed it to me. I gulped, trying to fill the pit in my stomach.

"She tried to call you earlier, you know?" I wiped at my mouth with the back of my hand. "You're supposed to be her partner."

He rolled his eyes. "I turned the ringer off and forgot to turn it back on. I figured we'd catch up today. She's been calling at the end of the shift so I can report to Sorin. But she never has anything. Honestly? She's useless."

"You won't be saying that in five minutes," she said from the hall. When she walked in, she tapped an ear. "You guys think you have good hearing? You got nothing on us."

In the corner of my eye, I saw Rhys clench. He wasn't going to apologize which was very unlike him. He was all about manners.

I watched Diana walk in and really noticed the way she walked for the first time. Most of the vampires I knew moved like dancers. Even the newer ones were graceful, carrying their weight in their hips. But Diana was different. Like the predator inside her, she stalked when she moved. Each step was calculated and seemed to come from her chest. She was waving her phone in her hand.

"Be ready to eat your words, leech."

Rhys groaned. "It better be good."

"How about pictures of the hunter's notes?"

56

I spit the blood in my mouth out and she ran to shut the door. "Good God," she cried. "That's disgusting."

"I'm sorry," I said, finding wipes and starting to clean up the results of my shock. "How did you get pictures of his notes?"

"I slept with him."

Rhys and I froze. "What," he said.

"I'm kidding," she laughed. "Jeez, what do you think of me? There's no dollar amount in the world to get me with that ape. He stinks."

I finished the chore, tossing everything in the trashcan and finishing the contents of the thermos. "So, how then?"

"He found me just after I spoke to you tonight; asked me to meet him in Jerry's office when I could. I didn't want to, I mean shit- was I sweating bullets just thinking about it. But, what could I do? Ignoring him would be worse. So, I grabbed some food and went to the office. Figured if he sees me eat, he'll know I'm not a bloodsucker and maybe he'll tell me something I can use." She crossed to the couch and sat, crossing her legs. "When I was there, he started to ask questions about if I'd heard any gossip about anyone in the hospital acting strangely. He said he wanted an outside observer's take. While I was talking, he pulled out this notebook from his pocket and started to write things down. The clipboard papers aren't what he's really here for. They're fake. He's got this notebook. While it was out, I got an idea and started to fake choke. He jumped up all bug eyed and tried to do the Heimlich—wrong by the way. I spit the food out and said "Can you get me some water? There's a vending machine in the ER? He left and the notebook was just there. So, I took pictures of every page, then was back in my seat before he came back."

"Holy shit, Diana." I held up a hand and ran up to high-five her. Her smile was so big, I thought her face my crack. It fell when she looked over to Rhys. I turned and his expression was far from impressed.

"Can we see the pictures?" He was stern. I made the mental note to talk to him later. It was unnecessary to call him out in front of her but I wanted to find out more about his issues with her. Was I missing something?

"I emailed them to you. Easier to see." She sounded like a kid that thought her parents would be proud but she was lectured instead.

He went to the computer and I followed close behind. I wanted to make Diana feel a little better but wanted to see the notes more. She stood. "I'm going to get back. I've already read them."

She was gone before he looked up. I slapped him on the back. A rock would have felt more but it didn't matter. It was the principle.

"You were so mean. What's your problem?"

"I don't trust her." He spoke without turning to me, clicking his mouse to open the email from a very disappointed woman that I was starting to consider a friend. "Have you forgotten about your visions? How much she hated us when she realized what we are?"

"There's stuff you don't know," I defended her.

"And," he faced me. "There's stuff you don't know. About our history with them; the multiple betrayals and the vampires lost to their jaws. It's easy to see her as human when you've just met her. But she is not—just like you are not. Don't be fooled."

"I'm not," I answered. "But I also don't look at her like a condition that she didn't ask for. I see a living being with a heart and a soul that you just crushed. No wonder they don't like us."

He shook his head. "That's a young person's outlook." He turned back to the screen.

I was starting to think everyone was in a nasty mood. First Sorin, then Alex and now Rhys. What was going on?

I saw the image fill the screen and leaned in to look. Curiosity replaced my concern or need to continue the argument. Instead, I focused on pages of scrawl. Whether due to penmanship or his use of abbreviations, it was impossible to read some of it. I looked for names I cared about and anything that I could use to understand how close he was—focusing in the things circled.

> Hunting grounds around hospital- ER point of contact? All victims tie back. Staff? Nearby?
>
> ~~Dr. K blood night shift. Eats and seen in the day on unit~~
>
> ~~MR- straight nights. Too much damage. Attacked by ??~~
>
> Blood bank- same 4—day/night set by ?—same for >5 years
>
> (Rs- straight nights/acts "weird"?)
>
> ER nurses- (Paul—set nights/ new/ never eats/long breaks?)
>
> ~~Denise—nights. Picks up daylight~~
>
> Diana—(new. Agency nurse. Possible informant/hunting recruit?) Strong, smart
>
> ~~Kate- switched to nights. "acting different"/looks better.~~ ~~Recent absence~~ Kids/MR has seen her in sun

"Shit," I said. "He's looking at you and Paul. It's only a matter of time before he rules out Paul. And, if he tried to recruit Diana..."

"She's toast," Rhys finished. "When they find out there are lycanthropes here, also, he will call for reinforcement. At least he's not looking at you."

"That doesn't make me feel better, Rhys. We have to do something."

"What," he asked. "What do we do? I can't stand in the sun to show him I'm not dead."

"But you can eat," I reminded him. "He thinks we can't eat—show him you can."

"It's worth a try. I haven't had food in decades, I don't know how it will go." He looked nauseous just thinking about it.

"Practice. Eat at home and see if you can handle it. I'll talk to Sorin when I get to the manor. Can you forward these to my email?"

He typed faster than humanly possible and I wondered how I'd never noticed when I was human, how no humans noticed. I guess they didn't want to. According to Kunsman's notes, people had noticed I looked better and was different but none of them wondered why. I think part of surviving is ignoring that there are things you don't understand—sticking your head in the sand. There weren't many people who really dug to find the scary truth. I figured that's part of how supernatural creatures had stayed hidden for so long. Unfortunately, individuals like Henry Kunsman did exist and wouldn't stop until he turned over every stone.

I saw the concern on Rhys's face but didn't know how to start addressing it. "I have to get back, Rhys. You okay?"

"Yeah," he snapped.

I kissed his cheek pulling his face to look at me. "We will figure this out. I won't let him get you."

"Aren't I supposed to protect you?" he asked.

"We'll take turns. Now it's my turn. I'll call you after I talk to Sorin."

"Okay," he whispered.

I left without telling him what Diana had told me earlier or what had occurred with Evelyn at the beginning of the night. I didn't want to worry him or lay more weight on his shoulders. Looking back, I should have taken the time to tell him everything. Leaving him in the dark wasn't fair and it definitely wasn't safe.

I would learn my lesson soon.

57

Stepping back onto the unit, I glanced around to be sure Kunsman wasn't there. No sign of the hunter so I walked the floor and check on my patients. They were all asleep; I thanked the universe and set to work charting for the shift. The ding in my pocket drew my attention as I was opening the last chart. I was surprised to see who texted.

MONICA: Can't sleep. Can you talk?

ME: Call you in 15?

MONICA: K.

I was able to finish my charting and slip into the breakroom by the fifteen-minute mark. I pulled up my previous calls and saw that we hadn't spoken on the phone in weeks. I was struck by how quickly your whole existence can change. Someone can be in your life 24/7 and then in a matter of minutes they could be gone, voluntarily or otherwise. "Please," I said to the empty room. "Please be my friend."

She answered groggily. "Hello?"

"Oh, I'm sorry," I said. "Did you doze off? Did I wake you when you'd finally fallen asleep?"

"No," she answered. "It's okay. I fall asleep then wake right back up."

"Why," I asked.

"Nightmares," she responded matter-of-factly. "And, too much on my mind. I can't stop my thoughts from racing."

"What can I do to help?"

She paused and I let the silence linger. I wasn't going to push her. "I need to get this off my chest so I can try to find some peace and move on."

That didn't sound good. I wanted to stop her, to give myself more time before she said what I thought she was about to say but my mouth was dry.

"I tried," she started. "I tried to think of you as the same Kate, my friend. We've been through so much and I didn't think anything could ever change that. But," she let out a sigh. "It has changed, Kate; you've changed. You're not the same person; you're not even a person. You can't go outside during the day, you drink blood, your heart doesn't beat and you look like you're ten years younger. You'll never get sick or worry about wrinkles or have a scar or need a birthday party. How can we be friends? What do we talk about or do?"

"Monica," I made sure I was talking quietly so no one could hear me. "I'm the same person. You're wrong."

"I saw you rip out a man's throat with your teeth," she yelled. "Your fangs! He drank my blood and was going to kill me just because I showed up at your house. You're not the same."

I couldn't argue. She was right but I didn't want to admit it to her or myself. I stayed quiet out of respect and pure agony. I was afraid if I started to talk, I would fall apart. The pain in my chest was crushing.

"There was a time that I would have died for you," she said through tears. "But now I'm afraid that being in your life means that I may have to die for you. I can't do it, Kate. I can't keep looking over my shoulder looking for monsters."

"I'm not a monster," I hissed.

I heard her uneven breathing and knew she was crying hard now. "I didn't say you were. I just said that you are not my Kate. My Kate died."

"I didn't ask for this, Monica." The crushing pain was still there but I was starting to get breath around it. If I didn't try to save this, I'd always wonder if I could. "It *happened* to me. I would never put you in harm's way. I can protect you. I'm strong and fast."

"Because you're not human. I'm sorry this happened to you, Kate. I want you to hear that part. I am so sorry it happened to you and I'm glad Rhys found you when he did. But it means I have to make a choice. It didn't happen to me. I can die, I can get hurt. I have to look out for myself. Please respect my choice. I don't wish you bad and I swear I'll keep you secret to my grave. You have to understand. I have a chance for a fresh chapter with Alex. I need to protect that."

I laughed sarcastically. "Alex comes with vampires. Did he tell you what he's working on—about his sister?"

"He did," she answered, her tears slowing down and her voice sounding cold. "I'll support his work but I don't need to be around it."

"And, Rhys? Sorin? I saw the way you were smiling at him."

"Again," she said. "I tried. I'm happy for you and Sorin. He's amazing but he's not human. And, neither of them was ever my friends. Not being around them will be easy."

"And work," I asked. "Are you just going to ignore me?"

She was quiet. I didn't think I was going to like the next thing she said. "I'm looking for a new job. I'm on FMLA for a while and by the time it runs out, I'll be somewhere else."

Everything around me seemed to cave in on me. What could I say? She was an adult and I'd know her long enough to know she didn't budge once she made up her mind. "Is there anything I can do?"

"No," she said and I knew she meant it.

"I'm going to miss you," I whispered.

"I already miss you but this is the right thing, a clean break. Good luck, Kate." The line went dead. I fought back tears and resisted the urge to throw my phone against the wall. I hadn't felt this helpless since I'd been locked into a crate by a psycho. Testing my legs, I stood and took a shaking step forward. I rallied my energy to give report to the nurses, gather my things and make it to the van.

Only then did I let the sobs begin.

58

When I pulled into the manor, I didn't think there was a drop left in me. Even with my preternatural vision, I had trouble seeing through my tears to drive. If I'd been pulled over, I was going to have to come up with a great story about why I left work covered in blood.

Thankfully, that didn't happen.

My tears had dried out and I was no longer sobbing but I was definitely not okay. I could feel that wall that Sorin had talked about starting to go up. Laying my head against my car seat, I took a couple deep breaths and visualized the wall coming back down. As much as I welcomed the promise of feeling nothing, I knew that wall was going to make things worse. Eventually, it was going to come down and I was going to have to face the pain. Pushing it off wasn't doing me any favors.

Walking into the manor had a calming effect. It was a place where I could be myself and was completely accepted. After my confrontations with Alex and Monica, I desperately needed it. The kitchen door swung open to reveal Tamela coming out with a glass. "Bedtime snack?"

She rushed up to me. "What happened?" She was running her hands over me to see if the blood had come from a wound. Finding nothing, she pulled me in for a hug. "Oh my god, Kate. Warn someone before you walk in covered in blood." She pulled back. "Are you okay?"

"No," I said and sat on the step at the bottom of the stairs. "Monica told me she's not safe around me. She never wants to see me again."

She sat next to me. "Oh, I see. Is it possible she'll change her mind?"

I chuckled. "I'd have a better chance of winning the lottery. Come on," I hefted myself up. "Where's Sorin? Might as well tell you both together."

"His bedroom," she answered. "Waiting for you."

"I'll meet you in there. Gotta wash my face." We walked up the stairs. Before I broke off and went to the bathroom, I reached out to her silently. She handed me the glass and continued to his room. I washed my face, pulling off the scrubs and tossing them to the corner. Wrapping the robe around me, I grabbed the glass to drink while I walked to his room.

When I stepped in, she was on the couch and he was leaning against the wall with her arms closed. They both looked worried. It was best to get it out fast. "Diana overheard her cousins planning something big to force us into a fight. She's trying to learn more. That's all she knows now."

Sorin stood and I continued before he could interrupt. "However, she was able to get pictures of the hunter's notes. I will send them to your email or you can look at them on my phone." His eyebrows arched. "He doesn't think I'm a vampire but he is looking at Rhys. He's also looking into a nurse in the ER but he's gonna figure out he's wrong. Unless Paul in the ER is a vampire?" I asked Sorin.

"Not to my knowledge," he answered.

"So, Rhys needs to eat in front of Kunsman. He thinks we can't eat food. He's going to practice at home to see if he can keep it down." That got a nod out of him.

"So that will get him off Rhys but we still have a problem," Tamela said. "He is going to look until he finds something. We have to get him somewhere else or out of that hospital."

"That's not the only problem," I let out a breath. "He's thinking about recruiting Diana. He knows she isn't one of us. But she can't be recruited. They will find out and that puts all of them at risk."

Sorin rubbed his temples and I paused to let it all sink in. One more thing and I was done. "And, Monica is done with our friendship. She assures me she will keep our secret but never wants to see me again. Seems silly when you say it at the end of all the other things."

He crossed the room and pulled me into a hug the same way Tamela had. Guess she'd learned it from him. "It has been a very long night. Email me the notes. I will look when we awake. I don't worry that Rhys cannot eat food. He is strong and will be able to convince the hunter. We can worry about Diana tomorrow. I trust that she will find out as much as she can. I can't wait to hear how she got pictures of his papers. Please tell me she wasn't seen."

"She wasn't," I said into his chest. "Rhys doesn't trust her."

"I know," he went to the door and opened it. "But I felt her and she is honest when she speaks. Tamela, you need to get to bed. Thank you for everything. We will talk more tomorrow."

She left quietly. I hadn't realized how late it was getting and it occurred to me I'd never seen her room. I had to be better about making an effort with her. Sorin crossed to the bed and pulled the covers back on my side. I kept the robe on, enjoying its comfort. When his weight was next to me, I rolled into him.

"She thinks I'm a monster," I said.

"Diana," he asked.

"No, Monica. She thinks that being my friend will put her at risk and she's right. What if I put the girls at risk?"

"If you ever believed that, you'd leave them with Tom and not look back. If you are still in their lives, it's because you know you are not endangering them."

"Shit," I rolled back. "They never called me. They must be seriously mad at me. They probably wish I *would* walk away from them."

"You've had quite the night. Try to not make any rash decisions until after you get some rest. We know what Kunsman is thinking and Rhys has a plan to get off his radar. That's a huge thing to celebrate. We will discuss Diana tomorrow."

"Okay," I sighed. "You're right." He was saying something smart about me telling him he was right but I missed it as I shut off the day and said goodbye to one, awful night.

59

Someone was shaking me but I was having trouble opening my eyes. I felt heavy, like I'd had concrete in my bones.

"Try to wake, Katherine. Fight against it and wake." Sorin was yelling and trying to lift me up. "It's the girls."

I eyes flew open and I shot up. "What's happening?"

Sorin was trying to put my phone in my hands but they weren't working. They couldn't grab anything. It was like my whole body had fallen asleep. I was waiting for the tingling to stop and my muscles to work again. He hit speaker.

"Kate!" It was Sarah, she was screaming. "Kate, the girls are gone. We told them they could go to the park. Nothing had happened so we thought it was safe. We told them to stay together with each other and Addison. They disappeared. It's been two hours. Addison says she went to the bathroom and they were just gone. We've looked everywhere. Tom has Tank in the park. He lost them in the parking lot. Please, please tell me you came and got them or sent someone to get them."

My body was on fire and everything lit up with adrenaline. I grabbed the phone trying to think. "It wasn't me, Sarah. I don't have them. Can we track their phones?"

"Tom has a cop working on getting into their accounts. They changed the passwords. Oh my God. We have to find them." She devolved into sobs and I was unable to understand anything else.

I looked at the time—4pm. I was trapped. I couldn't do anything until the sun fell. "Sarah, I'll call you back. Let me try a couple of things." I hung up before she could respond.

"Sorin, my vision. It's too late and we don't know where they are."

"Can you get into their accounts to find their phones? You know them. Can you guess their passwords?"

"Maybe," I said. I ran to the office, ignoring his warnings. The room was full of sunlight but I was too focused to care. I crossed the room, letting it burn my skin and pulled the curtains together. Dropping into his chair, I woke up his computer and pulled up the app to find their iPhones. He came in behind me, not bothering to mention that I'd walked into the daylight. Clearly, I didn't care. I punched in Olivia's email and the last password I'd remember her telling me.

Log-in denied.

Tom and I had told the girls to never change their passwords without telling us. I don't know when they'd started defying us but it was a moot point. I had to figure out the password now. I could chastise them later. I tried **Tank.**

Log-in denied.

"Think," I said to no one. I punched in **Soccer.**

Log-in denied.

Sorin stood behind me, squeezing my shoulders. "Something that's new and she's excited about; something recent. Is there anything she'd talked a lot about?"

I typed **UncleRhys.**

The screen switched to a large map. The dot was flashing and not moving so I took in a shuddering breath. It didn't look like a car. So, if they'd gotten in a vehicle, it was stopped or they'd gotten out. Zooming in, I manipulated the map to try and see streets. The dot was next to a large building so I hovered over that.

ELM INTERMEDIATE SCHOOL

I faced the man behind me and I saw that he'd seen it. "My vision. They're at the school. I can't breathe."

"Yes, you can Katherine. You know where they are. Call Tom."

"No," I insisted. "He's armed and has no idea about any of this. He won't know what he's walking into. He could get killed or kill them. I don't want them in a gun battle."

"You don't know this is related to anything supernatural. They could have just left or be with friends."

"Please, trust me. The park? The school? It's come true. Next is howling. We have to get them out of there by moonrise. But we can't go."

I knew what I needed to do. "Call Alex. I'm calling Monica." Sorin didn't ask, he ran for his phone. I pulled up my recent calls and hit send. "Please answer."

Whatever made her chose to not ignore me this time, I will never know and always be grateful for.

"Hello" she sounded confused and irritated.

"Monica, please don't hang up and listen. The girls are missing. It's been two hours."

"What," she screamed. "Where are they?"

"We tracked their phones, me and Sorin. Please don't tell Tom until we know what is going on. They're at the school—at least one phone is. Please, please go there. The second the sun is down I'll be out of the house and on my way. Please just let me know if you see them, I'm begging you. There is no one else I trust that they would go to. Sorin is calling Alex but they don't know him."

"I'm going now. I'll call you when I get there."

I felt 1,000 lbs lifted off my chest but my stomach was still churning. "Please, Monica. Please tell me they're okay."

The connection clicked off and I listened to silence. Everything around me was melting and out of focus. The very real possibility that I had put my human children in the middle of my mess was repeating over and over in my head. I'd been selfish and not wanted to let go even though I knew it was dangerous. Now, they could be paying the price.

Sorin interrupted my thoughts, "Stop spiraling. They could have walked off to a friend's house or the party they wanted to go to and you said no. You have to stay calm to get through this. If we need to fight, you need to be in control of yourself."

"I know you're right," I answered. "I can't slow it all down."

"Alex didn't answer," he explained.

"I'm calling Diana." I waited for him to argue. We both had been betrayed and knew deep down that she could be behind this. "If Monica is going into a trap, I want something non-human with her. I trust Diana."

"I do too," he said. "I hope we aren't wrong."

Diana picked up on the second ring. "Can you be up in the day," she quipped. I didn't have time for a comeback.

"I need your help," I remarked. "I am trusting you so tell me now if you're behind this. If you are and we find out, you're dead."

"Whoa," she snapped. "What the hell are you talking about?"

"Where are you," I asked.

"At the grocery store. What the fuck is going on?"

"Do you think your cousins would go after my kids?" I didn't see any reason to waste time with small talk. "They've gone missing. It's not a vampire since it's daylight. So, what are the chances it's one of yours?"

She was silent and I appreciated that she was taking it seriously. I heard her move quickly away from wherever she as and when she spoke it was in a hushed tone. "Kate, I don't know really know them anymore. I don't know what they're capable of. Tell me what's going on."

I looked to Sorin and he nodded. He looked as upset as I felt. "My daughters are 12 and 14. They're missing. I have visions and knew something would happen at a park and their school. They disappeared from the park and I tracked their phone to the school. My visions come true." I locked eyes with Sorin for support. "In the school vision, I heard a wolf howl."

I let that information hang in the air. She was silent. I didn't know if she was waiting for me or thinking. I kept going, "I thought it was you. I still don't know for sure what it means. But Monica is on her way to the school. She knows the truth about me but not you. Diana—she's human and injured. I'm scared for her and my daughters. Please go. I'm trusting you to save them. I'll owe you."

Sorin took the phone. "Diana, we will owe you." A moment of listening and he said "Elm Intermediate School." He hung up.

"She is on her way, twenty minutes away. She will call when she is there and facetime us so we can see. You have to hold tight until the sun is setting."

I stood, crossing the room and driving my fist into the wall. It caved under my blow but I didn't feel better. Ellie's face flashed across my brain. I imagined her holding onto Olivia, both of them sobbing, scared and being thrown into the wooden crate I'd seen Rhys pulled out of.

Running back to my room, I found the black dress hanging and threw it on. I didn't care about what happened to it or how I looked. I just knew I had to do something. Sorin was following behind. "Katherine, slow down and think. You have two people on their way to them. You have just under an hour until sundown and will be right behind them. Don't do anything rash. You dying in the sunlight will not help them."

I whipped around onto him, not in anger but in desperation. "You have to understand this, Sorin. They are my babies. Whatever happened, it was probably my fault. If I can make it to the car, I can stay behind the glass and out of the direct rays. But I'd rather burn than wait to see if someone else can help." Crossing the room, I grabbed his face with each hand. "I love you so much that it hurts but I have to do this. I'll never be able to look at my reflection again if they're hurt while I wait."

He pressed his lips into mine. It was a goodbye kiss and I knew it. He knew it. He'd accepted that I needed to do this and wouldn't fight me.

I held my phone up to him and called him. He answered with his eyes locked onto mine. "I love you," I whispered into the phone. "I love you," he mouthed inaudibly.

With bare feet, keys in one hand and my phone pressed against my ear, I ran down the stairs. Adrenaline pumped through my veins, telling me I was invincible. As I grabbed the front door knob, I let out a breath through pursed lips. Yanking the door open, I stepped into the late afternoon. The skies were the usual Pittsburgh over-casted gloom but I felt hundreds of needles running up and down my skin. "You have a few minutes," I heard the man on the other end of the phone caution. "Move fast."

I didn't hesitate. For the first time I didn't care about trying to look human, letting my speed propel me to the BMW. Fire ants marched down my back while I worked the driver's side door and swung it open. Agonizing pain was overcome by a mother's need to save her offspring. All I could feel was the desperate desire to reach them.

Once in the car, some of the pain subsided. I thanked Sorin for the light blocking windows but noticed that what came through the windshield was still branding what skin it touched. The engine roared to life. "Remain in control," Sorin said on the phone. "Do not go through all of this only to wreck the car on your way. I will follow in less than an hour. If you do not make it, I promise you I will."

"If I die, Sorin," I started but couldn't finish.

He did. "I will fight for their safety and they will want for nothing."

"And you'll never forget?" I couldn't help myself. I needed to hear it in that moment.

The silence made me think I'd chosen the wrong time to push. It turned out he only needed moment. The call had connected to the Bluetooth speaker when I heard his response all around me. "Never, my Katherine. Never."

60

There were times in that drive where the minimal amount of sun peeking through the clouds seemed to point in a different direction. In those times, I only had to block out the nausea and focus on driving. When I would turn the car in a way that directed the sun beams at my chest, the hot poker would return to my exposed flesh. A few times I screamed out in pain and returned to the labor breathing I'd used when giving birth. Sorin remained quiet on the phone, letting me know he was there but not wanting to distract me. I wondered how he'd felt—helpless in his manor—hearing me cry out. I wished he was next to me but also knew that both of us dying wouldn't help anything.

I didn't need a knight in shining armor… I needed someone of sound mind to be my team mate. He was the backup plan if mine went South.

The school was quickly approaching. I kept checking my phone for texts from Monica or Diana. Frustratingly, it remained silent to my secret pleas for information. I kept telling myself that the girls were okay and we were all overreacting.

When the sign for Elm Intermediate School came into view, it coincided with a new blast of sunshine and I screamed. "Talk to me," Sorin said.

"I'm okay," I choked out. "I can see the school." The smell of burning skin filled the car. Looking down I saw a black circle between my breasts, a result of the most recent sunbeam. Sunset was starting, so the rays were fading and dropping. "Please," I whispered. "Please go away."

"In 20 minutes," Sorin spoke through the car speakers. "I'm on my way. I will tell Rhys to meet you as well."

"Okay." I was too weak to come up with anything else. Just pulling the car into a parking spot was difficult. I felt like my coordination was sluggish and my energy was fading out of me. It was the cost of being in the sun. In the lot, I saw two cars and didn't recognize either. A quick look around showed nothing—no clue of who was here or if the girls were even nearby.

"Sorin? Check your computer. Is the phone still here?"

"Yes," he said after a minute. "It is still there. It hasn't moved."

"I'm getting out of the car now." I gathered my energy for one last sentence. "I'll love you forever." Then I ended our call, dropped the phone on the passenger seat and opened the driver's door.

Stepping out into the early evening air wasn't as bad I as thought it would be. The sun was dipping into the Earth and slowly allowing the night to take over. The marching ants were back on my skin but not as insistent as before. A glance down revealed that the charred skin on my chest wasn't better—but it wasn't worse so I considered that a victory. However, the extreme fatigue that had come over me was going to be a big problem if I really was walking into a fight.

Bending over, I let the nausea overwhelm me and heaved my stomach contents onto the ground. It'd been too long since my last meal so the dry heaving was more painful than helpful. Dropping to my knees, I tried to focus my spinning vision onto the white parking line below me. I was losing the battle against vomiting and dizziness when a scent hit my nostrils.

My daughters. It ripped through my head and pulled everything into sharp clarity. Adrenaline returned to surge through me. I could smell them—chocolate cookies, sunshine, grass and their shampoo. It was them.

Shooting up to my feet and ignoring the heat searing my back, I followed the scent to the woods on the edge of the parking lot. I knew them well. There was a hiking trail through them that teachers would take the students through on nice days. Someone in the community had even made a little area in the middle of the trees with wooden benches and a podium so the lessons could be done outside if an instructor was so inclined. My daughters loved these woods.

And, if my nose was correct, they were in there somewhere.

Without thought, I ran to the trees. The hard asphalt gave way to soft, wet ground under my bare feet. I was acutely aware that I had no weapons, my phone was in my car, I couldn't control my powers and other vampires were a good 45 minutes away. To be honest, I didn't even know if I was running up to my kids playing in the woods or dead on the ground. All I knew was I had to keep moving in that direction.

Relief overcame me as I was away from the last of the daylight. The burning subsided but was replaced with twigs and stones poking my soles, trees slapping at my burned chest and the sounds of the tiny creek in the distance pounding in my ears. "Be safe, be safe, be safe," I repeated out loud as I ran. "Be safe."

When the trail came into view, I leapt onto it and was able to move faster without the trees in my way. Other scents hit my nostrils and mixed with the smell of my daughters. There was cold metal, hot blood and sweat. One smell erupted over the others and gave me comfort.

It was Diana. She was in the woods too. I said a silent prayer to the universe that she had found them and was walking my daughters out of the woods. I quickened my pace towards the center of the dense forest, then came to a sudden halt as the woods cleared.

My hands came up into the air on impulse.

In the middle of the wooden benches were two small bodies, tied together and not moving. I couldn't register what my eyes were seeing. On either side of the podium, flanking my children's bodies, were two people I'd never seen. Each one had a gun in their hands and were pointing them in front of them and off to the side. I scanned the area to follow the trajectory of the barrels. To my right was Monica—hands in the air and shaking. To my left was Diana–mimicking Monica's stance but not moving at all. They both looked to me. Monica's eyes were pleading and Diana's eyes were cautious. I met both their gazes and then looked down to the pile I was afraid to witness.

Olivia and Ellie were both clothed and breathing. I let out a painful sigh and hoped that meant they were alive and had not been violated in any way. Their breathing was slow and deep, like they were sleeping. I hoped it was because they were drugged and had no clue what was happening. Ellie's hands were tied and down in front of her. Olivia's were tied but around her sister's back. I wanted to believe these people had tied them that way but deep down I knew that Olivia had been awake and aware—then wrapped her tied hands around her sister for comfort.

I could smell dried tears and dried blood.

Fury rose inside my chest. "Give me my children," I screamed in a voice that even I knew was terrifyingly inhuman. Both people shot their gazes over to me but kept their guns trained on my friends. It was only then that I really saw them. Both were younger—maybe in their late 20s but it had clearly been some rough years on this Earth. Both had fear in their eyes with a healthy mix of resolution. One was male and the other female. And both—were human.

"Stay there," the woman yelled. "You're not faster than a bullet. Whether your kid or your friend, I'll kill someone before you can flinch."

The man jerked his gun towards Diana and made a motion towards me. "Move over to her or I shoot you and then a kid. I don't care who."

Diana slowly side-stepped toward me and the man's gun followed. The woman took the prompt and repeated the same motion to Monica. There was no need for the command to be repeated. Monica turned and walked to my side. In a few seconds, all three of us were together. Monica whispered low enough for me to hear but no one else. "I don't know what they want. They told us we had to wait. That was it."

"Shut up," the man barked. "I told you before. Keep your trap shut."

Dropping my hands in a show of defiance, the women on each side of me mirrored my actions. Monica grabbed my right hand and Diana the left. A thought shot thew my head in a voice that wasn't mine. *I'm on my way.* It was Sorin. As much as I loved his voice and knowing he was coming—I also knew he'd arrive too late. Before I could process that thought, another voice filled my head. It was Diana. *I don't know if you can hear me but I have a plan. When it happens, get your kids and run. Don't look back.*

I turned to face her and saw the question in her eyes. Nodding yes, she knew I'd just heard her. A quick squeeze of her hand told me she was preparing for something but I wouldn't know what it was. We were interrupted by a voice behind us. Relief crossed both the humans' faces. They let their guns fall as their vision focused behind me.

"I was so hoping you'd be here when I got here. How did you arrive first, though? The sun wasn't down long enough."

I didn't turn because they didn't deserve whatever big moment they'd hoped for. I waited for them to come around from behind me and into my vision. I locked eyes with the voice and spoke with every ounce of hatred I felt.

"Fuck you, Evelyn."

61

"God, you are crass," she spat. "I will never understand what he sees in you." Even in the midst of kidnapping and whatever else she had in mind, she'd arrived in a pantsuit and stiletto heels. The rage I felt was making it hard to breath. I used my precious waning energy to calm my respiratory rate so she wouldn't see that she had affected me. She made her way over to her accomplices, stopping when my babies were at her feet. A pointed shoe pushed against Olivia's sleeping body, making her jostle. Diana pulled me back before I realized I was lunging forward.

She's too close to them, be patient. Diana's words slid across my thoughts. I squeezed again so she would know I heard her.

I needed to buy some time and get her away from the girls.

"What do you want, Evelyn? Sorin? You can have him. Give me my daughters and I'll leave. I'll move to the west coast and you'll never see me again."

She threw her head back and laughed. Her golden curls bounced in the air behind her as she made a show of her glee. When her head snapped back up, I saw a glow to her eyes. A light had flipped on behind her irises and they looked almost purple. What should have been beautiful was macabre when you thought about the two little bodies on the ground. She was evil. There was no other way to describe her.

"He won't ever touch me again," she hissed. "You made sure of that. You could die today. He could live alone for a millennia and, still, he would never look at me again. You destroyed any chance I had. You took him from me—the man I love." She reached down to grab the jackets of each girl. Hoisting them in the air, they looked lifeless.

Please stay asleep, I pleaded silently.

"Now," she screeched. "I take what you love." She let go, letting them fall to the ground. They didn't awake which I was thankful for but also concerned about. I worried about how drugged they were and how much damage they would sustain before I could get them away from her. I would not consider that I wouldn't get them away—I told myself it would happen.

Behind Evelyn, the man whispered. "Will you let us go now?"

She whipped around to him and he backed up. Whatever look she'd given him had told him he wasn't leaving.

The three of us stepped forward in tandem and she returned her sights to us. "First," she said to the people behind her without looking at them "you kill the blonde one. She's already kinda broken. She'll be easy. Then you shoot the brown one. Then," an evil smile crossed her face "you aim that gun at the black haired one. I am going to feed on these blood bags at my feet. If she moves, you shoot her."

I heard the heartbeats of the humans behind her speed up. I reached my mind out into the woman behind Evelyn. It was flurry of images—her with two little boys laughing in the sun, then her in a bathroom injecting something into her arm. It flashed to her in court and the boys crying while a man pulled them away from her. Then, a flash of her in alley with a needle in her arm and a tall, blonde woman approaching her—offering her the money she needed for rehab if she'd do a little favor for her. Then her asking my daughters to help her look for a lost dog. Then, my drugged daughters on the floor of a filthy car.

I fought back the scream welling up inside me.

Evelyn's head cocked to the side and stopped whatever tirade she'd been on. "What are you doing? I feel your power. Don't try anything."

I smiled and saw that it was infuriating her. "I'm not doing anything, Evelyn. I'm a month old. You know I can fly. What other powers could I possibly have?"

She seemed to think about it and be satisfied with my answer. While I had her off the subject of killing my friends and family, I wanted to keep her distracted. "So, what powers do you have? I haven't seen you do anything but host parties and whine. Can you do anything cooler than fly?"

She took the bait, stepping towards me and away from the comatose children. It was progress. As she carefully stepped over the wet ground in her Jimmy Choos, she held a hand in front of her–palm up. What flashed across those glowing eyes was something sinister as the air above her palm waivered and the gun materialized in it. The man behind her cried out. I assumed it was because she'd taken his weapon without being near him. I wondered if those poor, desperate humans behind her knew what they'd walked into.

She gripped the handle, righted her hand and aimed it at Diana without dropping her gaze from mine. The crack sounded through the air before we could register the flash from the muzzle. Diana's hand was yanked from mine when she fell to the ground. Monica screamed and my mind threatened to return to the barn. I focused instead on building that wall that I'd used so many times—the one Sorin had mentioned. I built it up around my shaking soul, visualizing my ribcage becoming solid, brick protection for all the feelings threatening to break out. I locked my mind into the moment I was in and refused to allow it to go back in time to the showdown with Will. The woman that had faced him down was the same women staring into Evelyn's dead, glowing eyes.

I would not let her win tonight.

Snapping in the trees behind us drew everyone's attention just as Rhys burst into the clearing. He was a blur at first but solidified into my maker with less than the time it takes to blink. The humans at the podium gasped. They'd clearly come to the realization that they were not among their own kind and were likely trying to figure out how to escape. Fear came off of them like a stench. But, my sympathy for them was lost when the woman trained her gun at my daughters.

Rhys's voice filled the dark clearing. "No!"

"Don't move," I yelled to him. "Evelyn and the humans have guns. She's shot Diana already." I took a shaking step into Evelyn and she didn't move. "Tell him your plan."

She chuckled. "I will make sure you both watch me feed on your disgusting spawn before I kill all of you." She'd said it like she was listing what she needed to buy at the store, devoid of feeling.

Rhys snarled. "No, you won't. You even touch them and you're dead."

Evelyn laughed again. "Oh, I don't need to." Throwing her voice backwards, she addressed the trembling addicts behind her. "Each of you get a kid."

I looked over her shoulder to see them look at each other for support. The man bent down and slid Ellie out from her sister's grasp, then threw her over his shoulder. The woman lifted Olivia and did the same. Both of them stood with one of my daughters draped over their backs like they were just completing a daily chore, waiting for the next command. The whimpering that filled the air around us told me that one of my children was waking up to witness this nightmare.

Evelyn started to walk backwards, gun aimed toward Monica. "I'm growing bored with this. I have a night full of work to do for my show so I'll need to finish this quickly. You understand, right?"

Her fangs snapped into place while she continued to step backwards toward the girls and the humans. I knew full well that she wasn't letting anyone leave this grove but I also could see that the kidnappers thought they'd get the money she promised and leave.

"Aim that gun at the blonde one," Evelyn said as she handed the gun back to the man. "And, you," she addressed the woman. "Aim yours at the kid in his arms. I'll take the one you have."

Before Evelyn could reach out and take Olivia, the sound of ripping fabric filled the quickly darkening woods. The tearing sound was coming from my feet. I instinctually side-stepped into Monica and away from the noise.

Dropping my gaze away from the kids and down to the ground, I saw Diana looking up at me. I expected a dead body with a bullet hole in the forehead and a dead gaze. Instead, I saw a woman that resembled Diana but the face was different–twisted in a way. Her irises were bright yellow and the whites of her eyes were disappearing under the growing irises. She was more than alive; she was changing and growing.

"Get the kids," she growled out of a mouth that was expanding and contorting.

I knew without knowing.

She was shifting and we needed to get out of her path.

62

While most of us were staring at Diana and trying to register what was happening, Rhys rushed to the man holding Ellie. He was almost too fast for me to notice so I knew the man was shocked when the girl was pulled from his arms. He wildly shot at the direction of the blur but missed. Evelyn whirled around to respond to the gunfire, only to see Rhys dart away with one of her meals. He was gone into the forest before she knew what had happened.

Her hand cracked across the man's cheek and his head shot sideways from the blow. A crack resounded as he fell to the ground. The woman was shaking violently as she watched him fall. She was trying to hold Olivia with one hand and the gun with the other but looked like she was going to collapse from the weight, the fear or both.

The tearing sound at my feet was replaced with a wet, squelching noise. I continued to take slow steps to the side and pushed Monica with me. My eyes were trained on the woman holding my daughter but I was acutely aware of the werewolf nearby. I had no idea what Diana was planning or even if she would retain her consciousness once she was full wolf. For all I knew, she was going to become an animal who'd eat anyone around. At the same time, I found solace in the knowledge that I was the only one who knew that I'd brought a werewolf to a gunfight. At the same time, I knew I needed to get my oldest daughter, my best friend and get the hell out of those woods.

A howl rang through the air—the howl from my vision.

Allowing myself to look away from the people in front of me, I glanced off to the spot I'd left Diana. I'd gotten about fifteen feet between me and her so I had full view of what lay there. She'd been replaced by a mass of wet, dark fur. It pulsed and twitched. I saw the limbs extend out from the core of the beast. As the feet hit the ground and the animal stood, it reached almost seven feet. A massive dark, brown snout lifted to the sky to fill the air with another long howl. The teeth that flashed in the rising moonlight were impossibly long and very sharp.

The woman screamed and I heard the thump of my daughter hit the ground. Snapping my head to the front, I took in the faces of Evelyn and her accomplices. All three looked up to the werewolf with terror in their eyes. Monica scrambled to the front to reach for Olivia but the man got to her first. He snatched her up and put the child in front of him like a shield. While, Monica looked between Olivia and Diana—not sure what to do next—the man extended the gun and shot at Diana.

Her shoulder jerked backwards with the bullet but she righted herself within seconds. She stalked towards the front, eyes set on Evelyn. The vampire turned into a blur and appeared behind the human woman, who screamed again and fired a shot at the werewolf. In her panic, she emptied the chamber but none of them landed on her target. As the wolf reached out and grabbed the woman by the neck, I sped towards the man and my daughter. He shot at me and I felt a stab in my stomach but kept moving. He threw the girl to the side so he could steady his gun with both hands and fire at me a second time. Monica ran to scoop up Olivia. I didn't see where they went but I hoped it was far from here. As I reached out for the man, I heard Rhys behind me.

"Get to the parking lot."

I assumed he was talking to Monica but didn't have time to find him in the chaos. Grabbing the man's face in each of my hands, I twisted and felt the snap. Before I could register what I'd just done, I heard a gasp. Looking around, I saw Evelyn on one of the wooden benches with Monica in front of her for protection. Olivia was cradled in her arms and pressed to her chest. Evelyn had two of the people I loved between her and us.

I didn't want to lose sight of the massive werewolf since I didn't know if she was aware of the difference between bad guys and good. I found her to my left, dropping the very dead woman to the ground like a bag of garbage. The beast found Rhys, who'd returned to the clearing without Ellie. I figured he was back to help but wished he'd stayed with her. He had his hands in the air, palms facing the lycanthrope. "Diana, it's me. It's Rhys."

It worked because the animal continued its search away from Rhys and found Evelyn with her human shields. It dropped down to all fours and stalked towards her. Evelyn aimed the gun, not at the wolf, but at the sleeping child. The beast stopped.

"You move and I will shoot her." Evelyn's voice waivered. She was scared. "I'm going to leave now. You get the kids and we all just walk away. Let's all survive the night, shall we?"

"You won't get away with this," I yelled.

"Oh," she smirked. "But, I will."

Simultaneously and in an instant, Rhys was knocking the gun out of Evelyn's hand, Diana coiled to attack and I screamed out "No."

With her vampire speed, Evelyn tossed Monica and Olivia into the werewolf as it lunged. It seemed like time slowed as I watched Monica throw Olivia towards me and land in the path of the charging wolf. She let out a cry when a claw tore into her bicep and down her arm. The wolf pulled back but it was too late. Monica was bleeding and Evelyn was gone.

Rhys scrambled to me, taking Olivia into his arms. "Run," I told him and he did.

Finding the werewolf and Monica, I prepared myself to fight the animal off of my friend and render first aid. Instead, I saw the blonde hair in the midst of the dark, brown beast. She was cradled in the arms of the creature. The head craned up to the sky and let out one more of those chilling howls. This time is sounded less like a warning and more like sorrow. It stood up, holding Monica who looked very confused.

Stepping towards me, the beast reached out to gently hand me the woman. I took her and nodded a thanks. Looking down, I could see she had pressed her arm into her chest to apply some pressure. A quick glance up and down her body showed that the gash was the only injury. "Are you okay to stand," I asked.

She nodded. "I'm shaking but not in as much pain as I should be. Did the girls get out?"

"Yes," I said as I let her feet hit the ground. I held on a few seconds to make sure she wasn't going to pass out. When she didn't, I let go.

Behind her, the wolf dropped to all fours and then collapsed to its side. Monica and I watched it writhe, twist and convulse. It was impossible to look away from the transformation of wolf to human. Whimpering rose from the shaking mass, then turned into the groans of a woman as the fur pulled back and skin rose out. Before our eyes, we watched Diana emerge, naked and shaking. She rolled to her side and vomited. Neither one of us knew what to do or say so we just watched her retch. When that was done, she shakingly stood and balanced herself with a step. Turning to face us, she weakly laughed.

"Awful, isn't it," she said. A few more seconds of gathering her energy and she closed the distance between us. "I told you to get out of the way when I turned."

I was taken aback by the sudden anger. According to my assessment of the situation, we'd gotten the kids out safely and killed two bad people. Yes, Evelyn had gotten away but, we'd leave her to Sorin. I didn't think she'd like what he would do to her.

"Hey, it's okay. We got the girls. Let's get to the parking lot before they wake up."

Diana looked at Monica and me. "We get them to somewhere safe and then we need to talk."

63

We emerged from the woods, as Sorin was climbing out of his car. Rhys was on the ground with both girls in his arms. He was rocking them and I knew at least one of them was awake. I heard his quiet singing but couldn't miss the sound of soft crying. Diana broke off from the group to her car. I ran to Rhys and dropped to the ground next to him.

Ellie turned to me, tears rushing down her dirty face. "Mom," she cried. I reached out and she climbed into my arms. "I'm sorry," she wailed into my chest. "I wanted to find the puppy. I know I shouldn't have. I thought the lady was nice."

"I know," I whispered into her hair. "I know. It's okay, honey. You're okay. Olivia is okay. We need to get you home to Daddy."

"Uncle Rhys saved me. He was so fast, like magic. I waited here and heard a wolf. I was so scared until he came back. I saw you too."

"How will we explain this," Rhys spoke. "To Tom?"

My daughter looked up now, to see everyone around us. She scanned Sorin, Monica and Rhys. Diana came up with gym clothes on so I assumed they were in her car somewhere. Or maybe she packed extra clothes in case of a shift. Ellie was confused and something like fear crept into her eyes. When she looked up at me, I knew she was figuring out that something was not normal. "Mom? Who are these people? How did you find me? What happened? What do you need to explain to Dad?"

"Rhys," I said. "Would you lay Olivia in the back of the car?"

"Sure," he said.

"Honey," I said to Ellie. "You know Monica and Rhys. This is my friend Sorin," I pointed up at him. "This is Diana," I pointed to her. "She's a nurse at my hospital. They came to help find you. You have so many people that care about you."

"What happened to your arm," she asked Monica.

"Scratched it on a branch," was the answer.

I could tell that Ellie was not satisfied with my answers and that things could get complicated very quickly. "Sorin," I asked. "I think we need to make her forget."

"Are you sure," he asked.

"Yes," I said, feeling her snuggle in tighter to me.

"What do you mean, Mommy? I'll never forget." She fell into a fresh round of crying, then buried her face into me once more. Hugging her tight, I kissed the top of her head.

Sorin dropped down to his knees and tapped Ellie on the back. She turned to face him. When his eyes locked on hers, the crying stopped and she froze. "Ellie," he said softly. "You were at the park and the lady came up to you?"

"Yes," she said in a robotic voice.

"Then what?"

"She said she'd lost her puppy and needed help. The puppy loves little girls so the lady thought the puppy would come to us if he saw us. We went to the parking lot where she saw him last and called out for him. Then it was black and I fell asleep."

I felt a tear roll down my face. I'm ashamed to admit it but I was glad those people were dead in the woods. I hated them.

"Ellie," Sorin continued. "You don't remember anything after that. You only remember waking up in the school parking lot with your mom and Rhys. They saved you. You never saw me or Diana or Monica. You didn't hear anything. You were very brave."

"I was brave."

"Now," he reached out and tucked her hair behind her ear. "Go to sleep and have a happy dream."

She slumped in my arms. "Thank you," I said to him. He laid a kiss on the top of her head and then on my lips.

"You did the right thing," he said.

"It doesn't feel like it," I responded. "Feels like messing with her head and keeping more secrets."

When I stood, he sniffed at the air then his eyes roamed over me. He reached out to press his hand at my stomach. I'd forgotten I'd been shot. It wasn't until he pressed that I actually felt any discomfort. "You're hurt," he said.

"Bullet," I explained. "It will heal right?"

"Yes, but we need to get the bullet out before it does. You have an hour at most."

"Shit," I said. "Just do it then."

Diana ran towards her car, calling back. "Hold on, I have a nurse's bag." She returned with large tweezers. "Lay down."

I did, sprawling out on the hard asphalt. She found the hole in my dress. "Hard to see, the blood looks like part of the dress."

"Yay for black," I joked.

"Brace yourself," she said and dug the tweezers into the wound. I screamed out and Rhys grabbed my hand so I could squeeze. The bullet came out with a wet, squelching sound. I sat up in time to see Diana hand the bullet to Sorin. He looked at it and angry flashed across his face.

"Get them to Tom's. I would like all of us to meet at my home, please. We need to discuss next steps. I assume we have bodies to hide." He climbed into his car and Rhys took Ellie to lay her in the back seat with her sister.

I stood to grab Monica and Diana, pulling them into a group hug. "Thank you. I don't know how I'll ever repay you." Pulling back, I saw that Diana was upset. "What's wrong?"

"I'll tell you later. Get them somewhere safe. I'll see you at the manor. Monica," she turned to face her. "I know you aren't a fan but will you come, too? You're a part of this now. Until Evelyn is caught, we need to be a team."

"Dammit," she answered. "Fine. I'll follow you but I really don't want to do this." She glared at me and I knew she was never going to forgive me after this.

Once they were gone, I met Rhys in the car. "Coming with me?"

"Yeah," he said. "We can get my car later. I'm not letting you guys out of my sight."

Pulling out, I dialed Tom. "Kate?"

"I have them," I answered. "They were in the woods by the school. I'm bringing them now."

I ended the call before he could start to grill me. There wasn't much distance between the school and Tom's house. I needed that time to get my head straight.

When I pulled up, the front door flew open. Tom and Sarah rushed out of the house and up to the car. Wrenching open the back door, Sarah pulled out Olivia and I could hear she was waking up. Tom was on the other side lifting up Ellie who was still asleep and would be for a while. "What happened? How did you find them?"

"We hacked their phones," Rhys answered. "Found them by the school."

Rhys and I were out of the car, watching the girls be rocked and squeezed. "Tom," I started. "They were kidnapped. A woman told them that she'd lost a puppy. Then she and a man drugged them. I don't know what their plans were but luckily Rhys and I got there first. We must have spooked them or they'd gotten cold feet because they weren't there when we found the girls."

"How do you know this?" Tom's eyes were currently a concerned father but I knew his brain was flipping to cop mode as he spoke.

"Ellie woke up enough to tell us."

Tom did look like he was buying the story. I braced myself for an argument when Olivia groggily spoke. "It's true, Dad."

Blinking back tears Tom pulled Olivia into him. "I was so scared," he whispered. "So scared." She wrapped her arms around his neck.

When his eyes finally met mine decades of knowledge sat between them. We'd been through so much together and he was searching my gaze for any kind of relief. Those cop eyes took in my light dress and bare feet in the cold October night, then landed on the charred skin of my chest. One look showed me that he didn't truly believe everything he was hearing but, he was willing to accept it for now. Without saying it to me, his eyes told me he would need more information later—for now, he was just relieved to have them home. We both knew a difficult conversation was coming soon.

I nodded and he seemed to accept it. Rhys got the same wordless exchange before we returned to the car. I watch the door to Tom's house shut me out, trying to find solace in the knowledge that my daughters were alive. Not surprisingly, it didn't feel good enough when Rhys started the engine to pull away from the home that protected my two daughters.

I knew then that I wouldn't be appeased until Evelyn was in the ground.

64

We entered the manor and started up the stairs but heard Tamela call from the solarium. Following the voice, we found everyone waiting. Monica looked pale and Diana was clearly upset. It was clear from the tension in the room that they'd waited for us to start talking about what just happened. Tamela handed Rhys and me glasses of blood. I sipped at it gratefully but stopped when I saw the disgusted look on Monica's face. Turning away from her, I finished my meal. As much as I wanted her to accept me, I was starving and needed strength for whatever was in my near future.

Sorin stood to address the room. "Diana filled us in on this evening. The most immediate concern is the two bodies left in the woods. Edwin and Naseem are on their way to retrieve those for destruction. Next, we need to find Evelyn. I have attempted to reach her maker to no avail. Once Evelyn is in our custody, her sire will be a part of the decision as she faces exile from the country or death."

I laid my empty glass on the table. "Exile isn't good enough. I don't want any chance of her ever coming after my children again. I won't spend the next 80 years watching out for her."

"I agree," Sorin said. "However, there is a way to do this right. Murdering her will only result in other problems for you and your family. Please trust me."

I didn't respond. He and I could have this fight later, by ourselves.

Diana stood. "I have to say something before this goes any further. I scratched Monica while I was in wolf form."

Sorin crossed to them. "Where?" he asked.

Monica held out her arm and gasped. The deep claw wound was gone. Dried blood remained but it was on healed skin. Running her hand over it she looked around the room to ensure we were all seeing it. I saw Sorin and Diana exchange a concerned glance before Diana dropped to her knees in front of the bewildered woman. "I'm sorry," she said. "I thought you'd run, that you wouldn't be around. I didn't worry about the rest since they can't be infected." Diana laid her hand on Monica's lap and bowed her head.

Monica jumped up to pull away from the woman. "Don't touch me. I don't even know what you are. You turned into a fucking animal."

Sorin stepped into her but stopped short of touch her. "She's a lycanthrope, Monica. She shifts from human to wolf. While she was born this way, others are created when injured by the claw or teeth of a lycanthrope in their animal form."

Monica shook her head then looked to me for assurance. I was just as shocked as her. She met Sorin's eyes, I think in the hopes this was a dream or joke. What she saw in his grey gaze was pity. "No," she said. "This is crazy. Vampires are one thing but werewolves? Seriously?"

Diana stood. "I'll teach you everything you need to know. I'll be with you for the first turn. You can be brought into the pack so you won't be alone."

Monica took several steps backwards until her back hit the wall. Her hand rubbed over the newly healed forearm like it was searching for the wound. She pointed at Diana. "You were my nurse. I confided in you, trusted you and this whole time—I thought I could trust you. I thought you were human."

Diana held up her hands. "Listen, you didn't ask for this; I get it. You're pissed, as you have every right to be. But it's already done. I can't take it back."

Monica wildly shook her head. "Nope. I would feel it, feel different. I don't. Maybe you're wrong."

Stepping into her, Diana reached out and took a bicep in each hand. "It's healed. Think about it, Mon. You're a nurse. You saw the gash. It was deep and now it's gone. You know that's not normal. It's because you're changed now—not human. You'll get stronger, faster. You won't ever get sick again. You're aging will slow down. It's not terrible if you think about it. The only bad part is that you sometimes go furry. Honestly, even that part isn't awful once you get used to it. Only the first couple shifts really hurt."

I crossed the room and stepped into the space. Diana let go of Monica and gave me the room to stand in front of my shaking friend. "Mon, look at me." She did. "I know what you're going through. Accepting it was the hard part. Once I realized it was really real, I made the choice to make it work. You can, too. Everyone in this room is going to have your back."

She pushed against my burned chest but I didn't budge. "Not this time," I continued. "You can try to push me away, say whatever you want— I'm not accepting it. You will need someone to help you through this."

Tears welled up in her eyes and she collapsed into me. I held on and followed her down to the floor. "But everything was perfect. I was going on a date with Alex and home. I was looking for a new job. It was my fresh start. I was going to leave all this behind."

"I know," I consoled her. "I know."

"This can't be real," she sobbed. "How can this be real?"

Diana dropped down beside us. "Monica, can I take you somewhere so we can talk? Please? Just hear everything and then you can decide if you hate me or want my help."

I looked to Rhys. He'd said something very similar to me the night he'd given me his blood and made me a vampire. At that time, I'd still had a choice to make but hadn't really believed any of it. Looking back, I don't know how I'd been able to deny all the facts. I empathized with Monica. I knew how she felt—teetering back and forth between utter disbelief and accepting the reality.

Monica met Diana's eyes. "Fine," she said and we all stood.

I pointed out of the room. "If you go up the stairs, to the right and down the hall to the last door on the left you'll find my room. It's got tree wallpaper. Take whatever time you need. We won't overhear you up there."

"Thanks," Diana said before the guided Monica out.

We waited for the sound of Monica's quiet tears to disappear up the stairs and into the room. When we heard the door shut, the four of us gathered together. Sorin laid his hand on my burn, which was already disappearing. "I cannot believe what you withstood to reach your children."

I rested my hand on his. "We have some other issues," I began.

"Indeed," Sorin agreed. "Are your daughters safe?"

"They're with Tom." I took a deep breath and let it out. "I want to tell him the truth."

"Explain," Sorin responded.

"He just saw me barefoot, half-dressed and charred in the cold. He's not stupid. A lot of questions are headed my way. I just keep building this web of lies and it's getting complicated. If I tell him the truth, he'll be better equipped to protect the kids. He'll help us, I know he will."

Sorin's expression gave nothing away. "He is a police officer."

"I know," I said. "But I've known him half my life. He'll be surprised and angry. Then, he'll ask what I need and what he can do."

"I must think on this," Sorin dropped his hand and turned. "Alex came to this city with the knowledge already. Monica needed to be told once she witnessed what she did and it put her in harm's way twice. Now, she is affected. Bringing another into our world is very risky, especially law enforcement."

"It might be good to have a cop on our side," Tamela interjected. "And, I trust Kate if she says he will not come against us."

"I have gotten to know Tom," Rhys added. "I also believe he will be of benefit and is an honorable man. He puts family above all else."

Turning to face us, Sorin returned to the group. He took my hand and pressed into me. Laying a kiss on my forehead, he whispered. "I trust you. I give you permission to tell him but ask we do it here and I be present."

"Me too," Rhys spoke.

"Of course," Sorin agreed. He stepped back so I could look into his eyes. "I would like to meet him."

"Okay," I conceded. Weight was lifted off my chest with the knowledge that I wouldn't have to keep up the lies with Tom. I believed it would be so much easier if he knew.

"Next," Sorin addressed us. "Is the topic of the hunter."

"Oh shit," I yelled. "I didn't go to work and I didn't tell anyone. I just didn't show."

Sorin pulled his phone from his pocket. "Call now."

When Jerry answered, I could tell he wasn't having a good night. "This is Jerry."

"It's Kate," I rushed out the rest. "I'm at Urgent Care with a kid. I forgot to call. I'm sorry. We're gonna be here a while. I'm not gonna make it."

"Damn, Kate. I already had one call off. Can you come in after you get your kid home? How late will it be?"

"I don't know," I answered. "But I'll come when I can. It may only be for an hour or two though. I have to leave before sunrise, remember."

"Shit," he said. "Forget it. See you tomorrow night."

The line went dead and I knew he was mad. It sucked, I know but, I had way bigger things happening. I couldn't drop everything and run into work. They'd have to figure it out without me. Upstairs, I heard a cell phone ring and would've bet my house that Jerry was calling Diana, Monica or both. I knew he was barking up the wrong trees. Neither one of them was going to pick up a shift tonight.

Sorin spoke and broke my line of thought. "The hunter," he continued. "We still need a plan for him. I have spoken to other city leaders and none of them are familiar with him. Any suggestions?"

"Let's not forget the coming battle with the wolves," I added. "We need him out of the city before anything like that happens."

"You're correct," Tamela agreed. "Sorin and I have talked about this very thing. We need to prepare for anything that may come. Getting him out of here is the most important." She turned to her master. "What if we lay our breadcrumbs that lead him away from us and to a different territory?"

"What do you suggest" Sorin pushed.

"I'm just thinking out loud but if we somehow lead him to a different set of clues that send him chasing vampires in a different state as far away as possible."

Rhys started to bounce on his feet. "I have an idea. If I created fake news articles of vampire like murders and they were sent to him via email…." He started to walk in a circle around the room and we all watched. "I could hack his email, send him the articles from an address he already knows. Make it look like a new assignment."

Sorin crossed his arms over his chest. "It's not a terrible plan. Can you create something and send it to me? Show me what it would look like."

"Sure," Rhys said. "I'll pull something from—say—the Washington Post then mimic it but with a string of murders. Throw in the usual 'drained of blood' or 'presumed animal attack'. Where do I send him to?"

"Wait," I said. "Is it okay for us to sic a hunter on another land? Won't we just be setting up another city for this?"

"As a leader," Sorin said. "We must protect our people. We have leaderless werewolves after a new one has just been made and Evelyn sending humans to kidnap humans. We cannot risk a hunter right now. Nor can we jeopardize Dr. Kitchner's work. I will alert the leader of whatever city we choose so they know what is coming. But, I assure you I care not about them—only ours. Rhys, please work on that as soon as possible."

"Can I use your computer? I need to download some things but I will ensure it's all safe."

"Tamela," Sorin turned to her. "Please show him to the computer and allow him access with your information."

They left us in the room alone. Rhys' face told me that what he was embarking on some of his favorite hobbies.

Sorin reached for my hand so I laid it in his. He pulled me into him, wrapping his arms around me. I had expected something else, something charming like the silent dance he loved or a stroll through the grounds. But, he went with a simple hug. Resting his chin on my head, he spoke. "You amaze and scare me."

I pulled back. "What do you mean?"

"To withstand the pain of the sun, allow yourself to burn, run through the woods to fight with nothing but your strength—you are like a warrior from the time of my youth. Yet, sometimes you seem so fragile. Perhaps it is because you mean so much to me. I fear that your spirit for battle will mean that I will lose you someday."

I wasn't sure what to say. I wanted to rest his fears but he was right. I was always going to fight for what I thought was right, always want to save people and always put the people I love above my own safety. I'd never known that I had this kind of strength inside of me but since becoming a vampire, I'd learned what I was capable of.

And, I loved that he thought I was a warrior.

"I can't imagine I'm easy to love. I also can't promise I will ever change. But, I promise to never stop coming back to you, as long as I am able."

He pulled me back into him. "I will take that."

I spoke into him, not sure what he would say. "We need to tell Tom tonight. As long as Evelyn is out there, he needs to know what he's up against."

I let the silence linger for a moment. He was thinking and I wasn't going to push my luck. "Are you sure this is right?"

"I am."

"Then call him."

65

When Tom answered the phone, he sounded amped up. I suspected he'd had a few cups of coffee and was playing the whole day over and over in his head.

"Hey," I started. "I need you to trust me again. I promise I'm going to tell you everything. Can an officer sit outside the house while you come meet me?"

"Yes. Where?"

"There's one more thing. Tell Sarah to not invite anyone into the house. No one."

"Kate, you better tell me everything. No more holding back." He was angry. I was very aware that anger was headed right to the manor to face me, hear the truth and meet my lover. I took in a breath to steady my shaking hand.

"No more holding back." I gave him the address before he cut the line.

Looking up at Sorin, I let my uncertainty show. "It is not too late to change your mind."

I shook my head. "No, this is the right thing. It will keep them all safe. But, what if he takes the girls? What if he never lets them near us again?"

Sorin didn't tell me I was crazy or feed me some fake line, he respected my fear. "Then we give him time to adjust and you hope he calms down."

I rose up on my toes to kiss him when Diana and Monica came into the room. "Get a room," Diana quipped.

When I faced Monica, I saw that her tears had dried. More than that, I noticed her little changes. The tiny wrinkles that had started to appear around her eyes a few years ago were gone. All the little sunspots, too. "I didn't know that you guys get younger when you turn."

Diana chuckled. "Not younger. We're aren't as lucky as you guys. Just damage repair. She'll continue to age just a whole lot slower."

Monica rested her hand against her forehead. "She said I could live to be 200. I still can't believe it's real but I looked in the mirror. I don't know how to explain it."

Taking a cautious step towards her, she didn't move away so I took it as a good sign. "Same thing happened to me. I wasn't listening to Rhys so he pulled me into his room to look into the mirror. That was the first moment I started to understand that something was different. I was in denial. But once you survive the turn, your fangs are out and you're drinking 0 positive, it's pretty hard to keep denying."

"Diana said the first turning is going to be bad."

"I don't know," I said. "Our turning is much different, I'm sure. It's like feeling yourself die while you're still awake. Then you're in your head seeing all these parts of your life. Each of us has to choose to come back or to die. When you're back, it's the same body but not."

Diana stepped in. "For us, the first couple times it's like having someone is ripping you apart but no one is touching you. The wolf kind of pulls out of you."

Monica wavered but Sorin caught her. He walked her to one of the chairs so she could sit. Diana knelt in front of her. "Then, it gets better. You can call it when you need it and fight it off. It's like the wolf becomes an outfit that you just put on and take off. When you're human, you're strong and fast. I've never had aching knees or a cold. And, you won't either. I'll be with you when it happens."

"When," Monica stopped herself, then found the courage to continue. "When will it happen?"

"The full moon," Diana answered frankly.

"That's in a few days," Monica laid back against the chair.

I gave her a minute to sit with it and turned to Diana. "How will you tell your family? Do you tell them?"

Diana raised up to face me. "Normally, we tell the leader of the pack. Since we don't have one, I'm not sure what to do."

"This may be a dumb question but if the fight for master is supposed to be on the full moon, how can you be with her and fight?"

Diana nodded. "I didn't think about that. I guess I need to tell them and ask for another day of peace. We can fight the next night."

I grabbed her by the arm and pulled her into the foyer. "If you die in this fight and one of your cousins wins, what does that mean for Monica?"

She looked back towards the room where her newest creation was being consoled by my ancient boyfriend. I couldn't believe how weird my life had gotten.

"She will not be welcomed. You will need to be there for her. Try to help her through and adjust. We may not be the same but the adjustment from mortal to supernatural is the same."

"I..."

The doorbell cut off my sentence. Tom was here and I was out of time. "Please go in with Monica. I need to handle this with Sorin. We will be back down when we can."

As I was talking, Sorin came out into the foyer to pass Diana returning to Monica's side. There was no time to talk. Tom's pounding on the door told me he was definitely still mad. Sorin whispered in my ear "You are a warrior and this is the right decision."

When we opened the front door, Tom stepped in. He took a moment to look at the man next to me, trying to figure out who he was and what the hell was going on. His eyes were wild making me think we should have let him sleep or calm down before calling him over. It was too late though so I needed to make it work.

Sorin extended his hand. "I am Sorin."

Tom looked to me, puzzled. "What's going on Kate?"

I reached out to touch his shoulder. "Sorin is my boyfriend. This is his house. We need to tell you some things. You'll understand why he needs to be a part of this soon."

I started to lead him back to the kitchen, talking to Sorin as I passed. "Would you go get Rhys and meet us in the kitchen. I'm going to get Tom some tea."

Sorin headed up the stairs while we walked through the swing door. I sat Tom at the island, moving around the room to find the kettle and some kind of relaxing tea. Tom sat but was not happy. "Kate, you need to talk now. I'm seriously over all the secrets and mystery."

"Let Rhys get here and I promise."

"Why does Rhys need to be here and who the hell is that man? Since when do you have a boyfriend and why does he look like a rock musician. Is he?"

"No, he's not," I answered without looking back.

Tom continued. "He's clearly loaded and he looks a lot younger than you. I don't think I like him."

"Give him time," I responded. "And, he's older than he looks." Tom *hmphed* in disbelief, which I ignored. Finding what I needed, I got the water started on the stove. While hunting, I'd discovered some cookies. I didn't know who they were for but I was grateful. Tom's Mom had always used tea and a sweet to calm him down. I wasn't above using that knowledge to my advantage. I placed a mug in front of him, dropped the tea bag in and laid the cookies next to it. It raised his suspicion.

"Is this bad?" he asked. "How bad is it?"

I stopped on the other side of the island. I wanted to be facing him but also wanted something between us when he heard what I was about to say. Sorin and Rhys entered the room to join me. Without speaking, they knew to flank me on each side. Tom let his gaze wonder over each of our faces, then landed his gaze on mine. The kettle squealed, giving me another minute of reprieve. Once the hot water was in his mug and the kettle was returned to the stove, I was back between my maker and my lover.

Our time was up.

"Tom," I began. "I need you to listen to the whole story and not say anything until I'm done. I also need you to swear to me that what I tell you remains among us and only us. You cannot tell anyone, even Sarah."

I paused, making it clear I wouldn't continue without the promise.

"I'm going to need to know what I am promising to keep secret, Kate."

"No," I said. "You don't hear anything else until you give me your oath. Remember that I've known you 20 years and have rarely asked you for anything difficult. And, know that what I am about to tell you puts us at risk but protects you and the girls. So, I'm trusting you with my life."

He pushed the tea and cookies to the side, rejecting my attempt to appease him. "You have my word, Kate. I would never do anything to hurt you."

Sorin laid his hand on my low back for support, to let me know he was there.

"Do you remember before my birthday, the night I was admitted to the hospital—the night I got sick at work?"

"Yes," he said.

"I didn't get sick. I was attacked."

He stood. "By who? Why didn't you tell me?"

"Please, let me talk and then I'll answer your questions."

He sat back down so I continued. "A man attacked me. He put me in serious condition and I was moments from death. Rhys found me. He saved me by giving me his blood. His blood is special, like Sorin's is special. It saved me but it changed me."

Sorin sent his thoughts into my head. *Tell him bluntly.*

"We're vampires," I told him.

He slammed his fists onto the island. "Dammit, Kate. This isn't funny."

"Use your eyes, Tom. You're not dumb. You said it the first time you saw me. I'm younger, I have no scars or wrinkles. I can't go in the sun. Tank doesn't want me near you. Think about it."

He did. His eyes looked over us again, this time he was examining and taking in details. When his gaze returned to me, I saw disbelief.

"Since then, Rhys and Sorin have been helping me adjust. But there are other vampires who don't like me. The one who attacked me and the one -" I took in a shaking breath. "The one who took the girls today."

Tom grabbed the mug and hurled it against the wall next to him. "God dammit. You put them in danger. I knew it."

We all remained still, allowing him to deal with this the way he needed to. Sorin spoke next. "What you must know is that I am in charge of the vampires of this city. They are out looking for her and she will face exile or death for this. She will not come near you or your children again."

"There's more," I said. "The two humans she hired to take the girls. We killed them."

Tom stood again and this time he was 100% cop. "Are you telling me that you committed murder?"

Rhys spoke this time. "I was there, Tom. They had guns on the girls, had them tied up and planned to kill them just to hurt Kate. We did what we had to do."

"Are they still there?"

"No," I answered. "We took care of it."

"What the fuck am I supposed to do with this information? How do I even know this is real? You've been doing nothing but lie for the last month."

I was out from the men and next to Tom in half a second. He stumbled backwards, away from me and fell over the chair. I reached down and lifted him up to his feet with one hand, letting him steady himself. "Believe me?"

"Yes," he said with a shaking breath. "Yes."

I used the same speed to return between Sorin and Rhys. "Classy," Rhys joked.

"I'm sorry to scare you, but we don't have time for you to decide if it's the truth. If you have questions, ask them." It was the nurse in me, going straight to the point.

"Do you drink blood," he started.

"Yes."

"Do you kill people to do it?"

"No," I said, turning around to open the warmer and pull out a pitcher of blood. "All donated. We're not animals."

"Who else knows?"

"Monica and Dr. Kitchner at the hospital. He's the one who faked the diagnosis for me."

"And, Rhys," he pointed at him. "He made you this way?"

"Yes," Rhys answered. "To save her."

"How old are you," Tom directed this to Rhys.

Rhys didn't skip a beat, "235."

He looked at Sorin. Sorin answered. "More than double that."

Tom dropped heavily to the chair. "You'll live forever?"

"If we're careful," I said. "We can die. Fire, too much sunlight, decapitation. Usual stuff."

"What about a gunshot?"

"I got shot tonight, still fine."

"What," he yelled. "You got shot?"

"During the rescue, one of them shot me. Shot at Monica, Rhys and Diana too. Thankfully, they were bad shots."

"What am I supposed to do with all of this, Kate? How am I supposed to just accept this? What about the girls? Are they safe around you? What if one of them gets a nose bleed, can you control yourself?"

Rhys laid his hand on my shoulder. "I work around blood every day, Tom. Rhys is in the blood bank. We can control ourselves."

"Why can't I tell Sarah?" he asked.

"Because it puts her and us in danger. If word got out that we exist… there's already a hunter in town. We can't afford any mistakes."

"Wait," he said. "An actual vampire hunter?"

"Yes," I said. "He's at the hospital as we speak. We cannot allow any more people to know."

Sorin stepped around the island to approach Tom. Tom's pulse started to race but he held his ground. "Just as you are a protector of the public, I have many vampires in this city to protect. I ensure their safety and that they follow our laws. I also hand down sentencing and see to it just punishment is given. The woman who took your children will be found; I promise you. In the meantime, we allow you this knowledge so you may protect your family. You not only know of our kind but how to kill us now. You hold all the power."

Tom sat quietly for a while and we let him. Rhys started to clean up the broken mug while I made him a new cup of tea. As he sipped at it, I could see it all running through his head. When he opened the cookies, I took it as a good sign.

"So," he began after his second cookie. "If she comes at night, light her on fire or take off her head?"

"Yes," Sorin answered. "If it comes to that, which I hope it does not, please call me. I will send someone for her body." They sounded like they were coming up with dinner plans.

Tom looked around to find me at Sorin's side. "And, you two? Serious?"

I took Sorin's hand in mine. "Serious. If I don't have the girls, I'll be here."

"I don't want them here, okay?"

"That's okay. But you should know one more thing." I sighed. "Ellie met him. She doesn't remember it though. She woke up during the fight, saw everything. Sorin used his powers to make her forget."

Tom shoved a cookie in his mouth and spoke around it. "You guys have fucking powers, too?"

"Yes," I answered bluntly. "We all have different kinds but we all have something."

"Shit," he said, gulping down the tea. "We're out there with guns thinking we can stop anything and freaking vampires are walking around unstoppable. What else should I know? Better just get it all out there, Kate."

"We have to be invited into human homes. That's why I told you to not invite anyone. You can also revoke the invitation so if you don't feel comfortable with me having access, you can uninvite me."

"I'm not going to do that," he said resigned. He looked like he was thinking hard about whether to ask the next question. "Why does this woman hate you?"

I laughed. "Stupid jealousy. She doesn't want me with him."

Tom laughed too. I think we were all emotionally exhausted and looking for anything to add levity to the situation. "She kidnapped my kids because she thinks you're hot?"

Sorin arched an eyebrow. "I guess."

That sent Tom into more laughter. I was worried we'd somehow broken his brain and sent him into a nervous breakdown. But his laughter calmed and he wiped at tears. "I can't believe this is happening. Honestly though, it makes way more sense than all the lies you've been feeding me. One more question?"

"Shoot," I said.

"What ever happened to the one who attacked you? The guy who tried to kill you."

"I killed him." It was blunt but I meant it when I said I was done lying to him.

He shook his head, finished his tea and plopped a cookie in his mouth. "Good," he said when he was done chewing. "Good."

66

I walked Tom to the door when Monica came out into the foyer. She ran up to him and gave him a hug. "Tom! What are you doing here?"

"I told him the truth," I started and saw her face fall. "About me," I finished.

"So, you know," she asked him. "You okay?"

"I need some time," he answered. "I need to let it all sit in my head for a day or so. How did you react?"

"Not good," she answered. "Pretty bad, actually. Still trying to deal with it all."

"Yeah," he responded. "I threw a mug, then ate a bunch of cookies. I gotta get home." He kissed Monica's cheek, then mine. Reaching out his hand to Rhys, he shook it. "Thanks for saving her," he said. Then, he let go and turned to face Sorin, extending his hand. "I'm not sure about you yet, but I trust Kate. If she thinks you're good, I'm gonna believe that til you show me otherwise."

Sorin took his hand for a firm shake. "I respect your honesty." With that, he opened the door and left the manor. When I heard the car rolling down the driveway, I relaxed.

"I think that went well," I said. "One problem down."

"You didn't tell him about me." Monica asked. "Why?"

"One, it's your business to tell," I answered. "Two, we do not get involved in lycanthrope stuff. That's something you need to talk to Diana about. Three, I think he learned enough for one day."

"Can we talk," she asked. "Private?"

"Sure," I said. "Where's Diana?"

"She went to get something from her car. I'm going to go to my place and pack some things, then stay with her. I need to meet her family, or whatever."

"Let's go to my room. Sorin and Rhys, can I meet up with you later?"

Rhys patted my back. "I'm going to go work on my little project. I'll find you." He darted up the stairs and Monica gasped at his speed.

Sorin laid his hand on my back. "I'm joining him. Find me when you're ready." He followed Rhys. I motioned in the same direction and Monica slowly climbed.

When we were in my bedroom, she sat on the end of the bed. As she spoke, I changed out of my torn, bloody dress. Before I threw it in the garbage, I took a moment to mourn it.

"I owe you an apology," she said. "I said such horrible things to you. I treated you like a freak. You kept saying how you didn't choose this and you were the same person but I didn't listen. Now, here I am—the newest freak."

Once redressed, I sat on the floor in front of her so her hanging head was a foot from mine.

"I didn't choose this but here it is. I'm a freak but I'm not. I'm still me, I just have this extra thing to deal with. And, you're being so supportive even though I let you go through this alone." She was crying again.

I reached up to grab her hand. I wanted her to talk but also wanted her to know I was there.

"I don't want to be this way and I haven't even had the bad stuff yet, only the good. But I want to be a human and go to dinner with Alex and have babies. I can't though. I mean I can have babies, I asked Diana and I can still go out in the sun and all but, I'm not human. How am I going to tell him?"

"You just tell him," I answered. "The same way I told you and Tom. Then, you hope it doesn't change anything."

She looked up. "Yeah, but I was your best friend and I was more than ready to cut you off. Alex *just* asked me out. How do you know he'll still want me?"

"I don't," I pulled her down to sit on the floor next to me so I could hug her. "But, if that's what he does, you have to be okay with it or you have to fight. That's all you can do. You can't control what he does but you can control how you handle it."

She squeezed me. "I'm so sorry, Kate. I had no idea. I was so naïve and selfish."

I rubbed her back. "It's okay, Mon. It's okay. And, I'll be with you every time you turn if that's what you need. Plus, you always have a place here to be yourself. I don't know how the other vamps will take it but we will figure it out later."

She broke our hug. "What do you mean?"

"Oh," I waved my hand. "It's a whole history. Vampires and werewolves don't get along. There was this war and a peace treaty and a whole bunch of stuff. I'm sure Diana will explain it all. But, it doesn't apply to us. We're friends whether they like it or not."

"Oh boy," she let out a huff. "There's so much to learn. So, do you really not have a heartbeat?"

"Yep," I arched my chest towards her and she laid an ear against it. When she looked up, she shook her head. "Wow. How's that possible?"

"Don't know," I answered. "That's what Alex is working on. How about you? Anything crazy about you? I don't know wolf stuff."

She jumped up. "Oh yeah! Watch this." She opened my drawer with all my beauty supplies. Pulling out my eyebrow scissors she crossed back to me. She opened the blades and extended her arm. Running one of the blades over her skin did nothing. "We have like tough skin. Hard to pierce."

I ran my hands over her forearm. "Holy cow. That's cool." I let the silence build between us then said what I was thinking. "I'm sorry that this happened but I'm so grateful for you going out to save the girls and I'm happy we're friends again. Please don't blame me."

She hugged me again. "I don't blame you for this or for the barn. Will is to blame for that night and Evelyn is to blame for tonight. I understand that now. I wanted to be mad at you because it was easier but the truth is I missed you."

After breaking the hug, we sat in the bed. "Are you scared," I asked. "About meeting the others or the change?"

"Yeah," she said. "But I'm getting calmer by the second, you know? Like I know it's going to be fine, no matter what. What about you? When you had to meet vampires for the first time?"

"Oh," I said. "That was here. The solarium we were just in was full of them and I had no idea. I was in Rhys' sweats. I went outside to wait for Rhys to bring me to Sorin but instead Sorin came to me—only I didn't know it. I just thought he was some random guys flirting with me. I had to like present myself to him and say any oath. I bowed instead of curtseying like an idiot. It was a disaster."

"Do I have to do that?"

"I don't know," I answered. "Like I said werewolf stuff is a mystery to me. Diana is the first one I've ever met."

"I definitely need to hear the whole story of you and Sorin," she smiled. "He's something. And this house."

"I know," I agreed. "And, you'll have to tell me what the pack is like and what you have to do."

She held up her pinky so I looped it with mine. "Pinky promise. I'll stay in touch and we will catch up. Vampire and wolf best friends... wonder if there's a necklace for that?"

I laughed. "I'm sure we could get it made."

"I need to get going."

"I know," I sighed. "Be safe, stay with Diana until this all blows over."

"I will," she conceded. "Love you."

"Love you too." She left me in my room to thank the universe she'd forgiven me for everything that happened and pray that one day I could forgive myself.

67

I found Sorin and Rhys in the office. "Where's Tamela," I asked. "Punching the bag downstairs," Rhys answered without looking up from the computer. "She couldn't really help here and she was just getting more rage-filled by the minute."

Sorin was pacing in front of the couch with a cell phone to his ear. His agitation was filling the room with that hot power that rolled off of him when he was mad. "You tell her to call me immediately. It's about her progeny. Tell her it's the Lord of Pittsburgh." He threw the phone onto the couch. "No one knows where Margo is. She's not answering her phone or emails. That was her assistant."

"Wait, rewind. Who is Margo?"

Sorin scrubbed his hand through his hair in frustration. "Margo is the Lady of LA and Evelyn's maker. Unfortunately, she has a blind spot for her progeny. I have been trying to reach her since Evelyn was banished from my home but she will not speak to me. I have already asked Charles, the Lord of Sacramento to travel to find her and insist she come to Pittsburgh. He will let me know when he arrives in LA." He dropped down to sit on the couch. Crossing the room, I sat in his lap. He laid his head against my chest then pulled back. "You smell like werewolf."

I laughed. "You don't like it?"

"Not particularly," he answered but returned his head to my chest. I ran my fingers through his hair to try and calm him.

"What do we do next?" I asked.

"We have vampires looking for her. She is not in her shop or at her home. Naseem and Edwin returned with the kidnappers. Their identities tell us nothing. Rhys already searched the internet. They were both addicts."

"I know," I said. "I read the woman's mind. She lost her kids and Evelyn promised her money for rehab and help getting her kids back. But I read Evelyn too. She was going to kill all of us, including those humans. They didn't stand a chance."

"Do you regret their deaths?"

"No," I said and realized I meant it. "They could have stopped, never taken my kids and figured out a different way. But they were both willing to watch Evelyn feed on my children if it meant a big pay out."

"We will find her," he said.

"I hope you're right." I stood. "I'm going to go shower off the mud and blood and werewolf smell. Then, I'm going to lay down. Rhys are you staying?"

"Yep," he answered. "I'll bunk here til this is all over."

"See you soon?" I asked Sorin. He nodded.

Before the bathroom, I found my cell phone in my room. Pulling up Jeremy's number, I called. He didn't answer so I left a voicemail. "I don't know if you or Logan have seen Evelyn but if you have, please let me know where she is. Don't tell her I am asking. Please be safe and smart around her. She's seriously deranged and I don't know what she's capable of anymore."

Stripping off the clothes I just put on, I wrapped a towel around me and made my way into the bathroom. When the water was running, I double-checked to make sure the ringer was turned all the way up.

Dropping the towel, my reflection revealed the part of my stomach that had been shot. In the center of the dried blood was a shiny, pink, round scar. It was hard to believe I'd actually had a bullet pulled out of me, let alone that it was only hours ago. Looking up at my face, I locked my stare onto the bright, glowing blue eyes in the mirror. No matter how many times I was reminded I was not human, I still had moments of shock remembering what I was. I thought about Monica and everything she was about to go through. My heart hurt for her.

I spent a few extra minutes in the shower, hoping Sorin was going to join but I knew he had much more important things to handle. When the water was cut off and I was wrapped in my towel, the phone rang.

It was Jeremy.

I answered. "Hey, tell me you know where Evelyn is."

"No," he responded. "What's going on?"

"Where's Logan?" I asked.

"At the shop. She was supposed to come help him but never showed. He's frantic trying to get everything done. I was going to go get him before he gets distracted and works into the daylight hours. Are you going to tell me what is going on?"

"She hired some junkies to kidnap my kids, Jeremy. They tied them up and took them into the woods. Evelyn showed up and told them to shoot me and my friends if we moved. She was going to feed on my daughters in front of me, then kill me."

"Tell me you're joking."

"Would I? About this? I was shot, my friends were hurt and we had to glamor my daughter so she won't need therapy for life."

"What about the junkies?"

I didn't think I needed to share this part. "They got away. So did Evelyn. She's on the run and desperate. She has to know what this means. Sorin's people are looking for her."

"I have to get to Logan," he said. "I knew she was crazy but this is seriously psycho level. If she shows up there, he won't have any idea what he's dealing with."

"Promise me that you'll let me know if you see her or her from her. She doesn't know we're friends. She'll never expect you to help us."

"Are your kids safe?" he asked.

"Yes.

"Go get Logan and be on high alert." I ended the call. I was worried that Logan would protect Evelyn and had just put the ball in their court.

Contacting Jeremy was my "Hail Mary" pass. I hoped it paid off.

68

I must have dozed off for a moment. When I felt Sorin's weight next to me, it brought me back. I didn't really think vampires took naps but I'd also been shot and gone out into the sunlight. Maybe I needed some extra rest. "What are you thinking about?" he asked.

"Do vampires nap?"

He chuckled. "Not exactly. But as we get stronger, we can rise from sleep much easier. That's all that you just did. You came out of your sleep."

"But you had to shake me this morning."

He laid his hand on my cheek. "And in the meantime, you've gotten stronger. I don't think you understand what you did today. You should not have survived the sun like that."

"It was very painful," I said. "And it burned me."

"Yes," he agreed. "But you are so very young. That kind of endurance comes with age. When I kissed you this afternoon, I believed I was saying goodbye. Yet here you are. Now, you are able to wake like someone a hundred years older than you."

"It's a good thing. When I slept like that, I'm so vulnerable."

"Katherine, I don't think you've been vulnerable since the night you died."

I sighed. "At the risk sounding very cheesy, I feel vulnerable with you. It's really the only time I feel like I'm—I don't know—hurt-able, I guess."

"Oh," he said. "You don't sound cheesy. In fact, I feel the same. Before you, I felt invincible. Now with you, I know I can be hurt. When you left today it was like having my insides carved out and taken way."

"That's very dramatic." I kissed him. "But I love it. Did you and Rhys get anything accomplished?"

He laid back against the pillow and stared at the ceiling. "We still have not tracked down Margo. Charles is there but not at her home. He will rest today and go this night. Evelyn continues to evade capture. Rhys has, however, created some very believable articles to send to our hunter. We will hack his email tonight and send them off. At the risk of seeming vindictive, I've asked the trail lead to LA. It is believable, far from us and serves Margo right."

I smiled and rose to straddle him. "I like this side of you."

He rested his hand on my hips. "Do you?"

"She needs to pay for what she did. I spoke to Tom before I fell asleep. The girls are still sleeping which is a good thing. Sarah has them both in bed with her. Tom is on the couch with a gun and the dog. He asked for an absence from work and won't return until Evelyn is gone. I hope telling him was right. He sounded scared. I hate knowing that I took some kind of innocence from him. I think it's easier to not know what's out in the shadows."

"It was the right thing. You've given him the best chance to fight, should he need to. I felt him. He's a honorable man. I don't believe we will betray us."

"Do you think Evelyn's left town?"

He ran his hands up and down my sides. "I've thought of that but it doesn't sit right with me. She would rather be banished than run away."

"I thought the same thing. She's not done and now she's got nothing to lose. I don't think she'll stop til we stop her."

He reached up to pull my lips to his, then wrapped his arms around me and pulled me as tight into him as he could. There was no agenda to the embrace. He wasn't trying to get any more from me. Just wanted to give and receive comfort and reassurance. I think we both needed it. So much was not in our control and so much was at stake.

"We need to rest," he said after a few moments of silence. "We must be ready for anything now."

"You're right," I agreed. "I wish you weren't but you're right. When this is all over though, I'd love a whole night in this bed—not resting."

He groaned and I felt him respond to the promise. "You have my word."

Even though we both went silent after that, I doubt either of us fell right to sleep. Thoughts raced through my head. I worried about where Evelyn was and what she was planning next. I worried who else was in danger—Rhys? Alex? Sarah? It was clear that Evelyn had no boundaries and would go after anyone. Which brought Monica back into my thoughts. She had a long, hard road ahead. As much as I would never have wished vampirism on her, now that she was changed, I did wish she was like me. At least then I could mentor her and be there for her. But I didn't know what she was really experiencing and had to trust Diana to care for her. What if she met the pack and started to really hate vampires? Would we ever really be friends again? And, what if she was scared? I wanted to call her but knew she needed time and space. I prayed Alex would accept her. If he couldn't handle this, it would kill her. I also couldn't help but replay my conversation with Tom over and over in my head. If he took the kids from me, it would kill me.

And, none of this was in my power to affect. I had to let it all play out. No matter what—I would have to get through whatever came my way. I'd had chosen this life and all I could do was live it.

No pun intended.

69

When I awoke that night, my resolve had returned. I felt less like someone who was waiting for something to happen and more like the badass woman I knew I was. I was going to figure out how to get control and put an end to the shitstorm that was swirling around us. Motivated by my returning fire, I got ready for work.

Sorin was already in the office with Rhys when I pulled on my scrubs and entered with a bounce on my step. Rhys looked up from the computer. "You look happy? Why?"

"I don't know," I said. "I just feel like I could take on the world, a feeling I much prefer over helplessness. You going in tonight?"

"I'm not scheduled. I can go though, to be with you if you need. I'll tell them I'm there to catch up on paperwork or something." The words came out over the frantic clicking on the keyboard.

"No. I appreciate the offer but she doesn't have the balls to come to the hospital again. I'm going to grab something to drink and then set to work un-prettying myself. Need anything?"

"No thank you," they answered.

Sorin crossed the room to me. "I don't feel good about this. I don't want you away from us while she's out there."

"I have to go and you know it. We can't raise any suspicions with Kunsman. And, Diana won't be there tonight. She's with Monica. I promise to call you if anything happens. Keep your phone on you."

He rested his forehead against mine. "Please be safe."

I laid my lips on his and left the room. It was getting harder to walk away from him each time. Deep down, I knew my time at work was coming to an end. As much as I didn't want to admit it, holding onto my old life was getting messy. Staying with him would be so much easier.

I'd cross that bridge we I reached it. Until then, I had to go take care of some patients and try to not get killed.

After a glass of B positive, applying makeup and a messy bun, I left the manor to see the BMW parked in the driveway. The scratches were gone. I was baffled by how he'd found the time to get that done but was happy to see it. My phone buzzed in my pocket so I answered.

Sorin was in my ear. "It's yours now. The key is already in it. Please don't argue. We both know the van needs to be retired. Honestly, I think it was always waiting for you. It rarely leaves the garage and deserves someone to use it and love it."

Fighting the impulse to argue, I conceded. "Thank you. I love it."

"I love you." The connection went dead.

When I slid into the driver's seat, it was different this time. Maybe it was because I knew it was mine now. Maybe it was another sign that my old life was quickly disappearing. Whatever it was, the sound of the engine sent my flames of determination into overdrive. Looking up to adjust the rearview mirror, I caught my eyes and spoke to my reflection. "You are a bad ass."

By the time I reached the hospital, I was fully believing it. I was a bad ass and no one was going to hurt the ones that I loved. They'd have to get through me first and that just wasn't going to happen. When the elevator dropped me in the fifth floor, the doors opened to the noises of IV pumps, heart monitors and call bells. There was a comfort in it. Even the old team was there—Jackson and the two Tiffanys. I was so happy to see them that I almost wanted to hug them when I got report.

I rounded on my patients to find out that my assignment that night actually wasn't bad. Most of them were overnight observations and all of them told me they didn't really want to be bothered once they fell asleep. I was starting to chart two hours before my usual time and was definitely thinking this night seemed too good to be true when my phone buzzed. The text was from Jeremy.

JEREMY: You need to call me ASAP.

I jumped up and made my way to the conference room in the fastest time a human could have done it. The ring in my ear was like a siren—I knew something was wrong.

He answered. "She's on her way. She just called Logan. She told us someone was after her and she needed some place to lay low. What do I do?"

"Where's Logan?"

"He's in the living room. I'm outside. I told him what she did and he's destroyed. He had no idea, Kate."

"Oh God," I said. "I never thought he did."

"We're with you. Tell us what you need and we will do it. I'll take her straight to Sorin if you want."

I had to think. "No. That will put both of you in danger. If she figured it out, she'd kill you both to get away."

Jeremy sighed. "Fuck. What do we do? It's against our law to kill her. I don't know if could. It's not like I'm a trained assassin."

That gave me an idea. "Can you text me when she's there? I might have a way to fix this. But. You need to keep this between us."

"You have my word."

I hung up and ran to my locker. Riffling through everything, I found what I needed in the back. Clutching it in my hand, I took a moment to think this all through. What I wanted to do could solve a few issues or it could go horribly wrong. I had no way of knowing what the outcome would be but I had to try something.

Unfolding the small business card, I dialed the number for Henry Kunsman, fake DOH inspector.

70

After I hung up, all I could do was wait. The timing had to be impeccable for this to work. Even a couple minutes off and this whole thing fell apart. I busied myself with charting, med passes and restocking med carts to try and pass the time.

The buzz in my pocket was the catalyst for it all.

JEREMY: She's here. Now what?

ME: Call me.

Seconds later, the phone lit up. Answering I cupped my hand over my mouth so no one would overhear. "Can anyone hear me?"

"No," he responded. "She's downstairs acting insane. She's rambling to Logan about being followed and how you've set her up to make her look like a killer."

"How far are you willing to go to get her out of your lives?"

"She tried to kill your kids, Kate. She's destroying Logan's sanity day by day and stealing his business out from under him. I will take this as far as it needs to go and then take the secret to my grave."

"Good answer," I whispered. "You're going to convince her that you're on her side. Tell her you want to help her kill me. Bring her to the hospital. Then when you're here, call me in front of her. Tell her you're luring me outside. I'll tell you where to go."

"Kate, this sounds like a bad idea."

"Trust me," I pressed. "Let me know when you're five minutes away so I can be ready. Then, when you get to the back of the hospital and see me–and Jeremy this is crucial—you need to get to the trees and hide. Don't be seen by anyone but us. And -" I hesitated but there was no backing out now. If he couldn't do it, I needed to know. "I need you to record everything after that on your phone."

"What are you going to do? I can help."

"No," I insisted. "You can't be seen here, by anyone. And, I need it all recorded. Do not leave those trees no matter what you see. Do you understand?"

"Yes," he said.

"Be safe."

"You too."

When he hung up, I looked around. No one had heard me. I'd already laid the groundwork with Kunsman. This call with Jeremy was the other big piece. The last of my plan relied on me being convincing. I needed to get myself together.

The bathroom was empty, cool and quiet. Opening the pictures on my phone, I pressed my back into the wall, slid down to sit on the floor and swiped through memories. I saw the girls playing outside, birthday parties, Tank as a puppy, Tom grilling something with Sarah laughing beside him, our house at Christmas and the girls with Rhys. I reminded myself that these people were why I was risking what I was. They all deserved more laughter and holidays and life to live. There were no other good options and no turning back. The plans were set in motion.

JEREMY: Leaving. There in 15.

Resting my head back against the cold wall, I looked up to think about whether to tell Sorin or not. He'd be furious to find out after the fact but he could ruin the whole thing. I could practically hear him in my head saying *I will meet you there and bring her in*. But that didn't solve so many other things. Not to mention, it put him at risk. He was much older and stronger that her but there was always the chance that she got the upper hand. With nothing more to lose, she was a desperate creature.

I wouldn't underestimate her.

Taking in a deep breath, I looked at the time on my phone. There was a solid chance that this would be my last hour on Earth. Just as I was aware that she could kill Sorin, I was aware that she had an even better chance of killing me. I was young and not in the wild state she was. I had a great deal to lose.

Standing up, I straightened my scrubs and texted Tom.

ME: Girls okay?

TOM: Yeah

ME: You okay?

TOM: Yeah

ME: Sorry I lied.

TOM: I get it. You could've told me sooner.

ME: I know. I was scared.

TOM: We'll get through this. We're still a family.

ME: Thanks. Good night.

TOM: Good night.

The roar of the water when I turned the handle snapped me out of my thoughts. Filling my hands with cold water, I splashed it onto my face and rubbed my hands over my cheeks.

The buzz of the phone told me that I'd lost track of time.

JEREMY: 5

Looking at the woman in the mirror, again I repeated my new mantra. "You're a bad ass." Then I left the bathroom to walk into a death match and try to survive to finish my charting.

71

Standing just inside the back doors, I waited for the call. When it came, I was ready.

"Hi Jeremy."

"Hey Kate," he said. "I'm at the hospital. Thought I'd surprise you."

"That's awesome! I'm just about to walk outside on my break. I'm headed out into the back, by the graves. Do you know it?"

"I'm sure I can find it. Wait for me."

"You got it. See you soon."

The graveyard spot was becoming way too familiar. Before all of this it had been a little retreat from the din of the unit. Now, it was more like a battle ground. I lifted up my phone to check the time. Then sent the text that would seal my fate.

ME: I'm in the back. Come out in 10.

The phone was dropped into my scrub pocket as I sat down on the little bench that had witnessed my death. The barren tree next to it had been full of autumn leaves during the attack. Now, it was naked and ready for the harsh Pennsylvania winter to come. I let my gaze fall onto the tree line, staring off to appear like I was taking a break. Cracking leaves to my left told me that two people were slowly approaching and time was up. I prepared to act my ass off and hoped I'd be believable.

"Jeremy?"

"Guess again." She sounded so proud of herself.

I jumped up in fear, facing her and backing away. Jeremy stood just behind her. Still wearing the same outfit from the night before, she'd lost that polished look I was used to. Her hair was falling out of its style in places and blood dotted down the front of her blouse. I locked eyes with Jeremy and sent a thought. *GO.* He turned and ran for the trees. I'd have to trust him to do the rest.

She was too focused on me to notice that her accomplice had fled. The way she was approaching me reminded me of the way someone plays a serial killer on TV. She almost seemed jerky when she stepped. I realized that her heels were sinking into the ground as she stepped, slowing her down. That was a good thing but I also had few precious minutes to get her riled up.

I took two steps towards her. "Get the fuck away from here, Evelyn. I'm going to call Sorin."

She laughed. "Do it. By the time he reaches you, he'll have to search for pieces. Wonder which one is his favorite. I'd like to light that part on fire."

"You already shot me and I'm still here. I'm not afraid of you. I'm not a poor defenseless child."

"Speaking of children," she hissed. "After I kill you, I will be going after them also. They smelled delicious."

Heat boiled in my stomach. *Don't use powers*, I thought. *No matter how angry she makes you. Control yourself.*

She sensed my rage and responded with her own. I felt the magic rolling off of her. It was a good start but I needed her to really get going and soon.

"So," I said and braced myself for what I was about to endure. "Since you're going to kill me, I might as well get this off my chest. Sorin said you were the lousiest lay he's ever hand, like a cold fish. We laughed about it in bed, after I made him scream with pleasure."

The heat blasted out of her and her hair flew up around her. In a flash, she was on me clawing and scratching. I grabbed each of her hands to stop her from ripping at my flesh. Her fangs snapped out and her eyes glowed with hatred. "I'll drink you dry and throw your insides around like confetti. He will have nothing left to mate. And, thanks to that bond—he'll feel you die. It will be agonizing. I just wish I could see the moment he knows your gone."

Wrestling to keep her hands from my body, I squirmed as she snapped her jaws at my face. I was strong but I knew I couldn't fight her for much longer. Without being able to use my powers, I was in serious trouble. The door behind me opened and I screamed.

"Help me," I cried out.

Evelyn's head jerked towards the sound and I heard a crack fill the air. She was thrown off of me and I rolled to my right. Scrambling towards the sound, I saw Kunsman with gun extended in front of him. I climbed to my knees and popped up in the most human way I could. Turning back at my enemy, I saw her raise her hand in the air. The gun materialized in her grasp and she threw it to the side. Kunsman slammed his hand against my chest to push me out of the way, and crossed the graveyard towards the vampire in his sights. Reaching behind his head, he slid his hand under the top of his shirt and drew a long blade from his back.

Evelyn shrieked and continued in my direction, ignoring the hunter completely. She was crazed and clearly not understanding what was happening right before her. Henry jumped to the bench and launched himself at her. The blade was swung through the air with deadly accuracy. He landed behind her on one knee, sword finishing it arc.

Evelyn took one more jerking step before she also dropped to a knee. Shock registered on her face just before her head slid from her neck and landed on the wet ground with a thunk. I watched her expression fall as the head rolled a couple feet and stopped in front of me. Staring at it, I remembered my role and screamed again. Kunsman got to his feet and retrieved the head.

"Stop screaming," he said, resting his hand on my shoulder. "I need you to calm down."

"Okay," I whispered, trying to make it look like I was trembling.

"Go inside. I'll get rid of this and find you."

"Okay," I repeated the whispered tone.

I gave myself a last look at Evelyn's head before I opened the back door and stepped inside. Retrieving my phone, I texted Jeremy.

ME: Sorin may have questions for you but this protects us all. You are going to tell them she forced you to drive her here and you didn't know anything. You ran and got it all on video.

JEREMY: It's over.

ME: Yes. Go hug Logan. Let me tell Sorin.

JEREMY: Let me know when you need me. I'll erase these texts.

I heard Kunsman on the phone. He was telling someone to come get the body in the back. My phone had just gotten into my pocket and I'd put a scared look back on my face when he came in. "Where can we talk," he asked.

"Down here." I gestured down the hall. Just past the blood bank was a call room for the residents. It had some beds and a TV for when they pulled long shifts. No one used it because the newer ones were upstairs but it was quiet and good for secret talks.

When I entered the room, I sat on a bed with my arms hugging myself and kept my head on the floor. Kunsman sat on a bed across from me. "Do you know what just happened?"

"No," I answered quietly. "I was outside waiting for you when this woman came around the corner and attacked me." I paused for effect. "She had fangs and her eyes…"

"She was a vampire," he said matter-of-factly.

I looked up, letting disbelief cross my face. "Vampires aren't real."

"They are," he answered. "And I hunt them. That's why I'm here. Five women were killed in the last year. The bodies were dumped elsewhere but it all leads back to here. I suspect she's the one who was using this hospital as her hunting grounds. I thought it was an employee but this makes more sense. If a vampire worked here, they wouldn't hunt here. Too dangerous for them."

I shook my head. "This is crazy."

"Crazy or not, it's real and you saw it with your own eyes. I suggest you keep this to yourself. The corpse will be gone in minutes and no one will believe you. But now you know."

"So, what does this mean? You weren't here to fire a bunch of people?"

He laughed. "Is that the rumor? No. I was here looking for vampires. No one is getting fired. I'll turn my report in tomorrow and no one but you will know the truth. Unless…"

"Unless what?"

"Now, that you know the truth—do you believe there are others? Maybe someone who works here? It would be stupid to kill where you work but I want to be sure," his stare drilled into mine.

I gave it some thought, showing him that I was really considering it. "No," I finally said. "I've known these people for years. Seen them out. Seen their families. Do you think she was going to eventually start killing some of us?"

He crossed his arms. "Likely. The victims have been people around here but she probably would have started picking you guys off, too. Looks like you were going to be her first. And I doubt you would have been the last. If I hadn't come out—wait, speaking of which—why did you want to talk to me in private?"

I looked down, pretending to be embarrassed. It felt gross but I was going to use his ego against him. "Never mind," I said to the floor. "I was going to ask you out but I see now that you weren't staying so it doesn't matter."

"I'm flattered," he answered. "And if I was staying longer, I'd say yes. But, with this done I'll need to leave. Besides, Diana is more my type to be honest."

I giggled. "Sorry," I replied. "She has a fiancée. But I get it. Thank you for saving me."

"You're welcome," he was really laying on the bravado. "Call me if you ever think you have a vampire problem in your city again. Most of our tips come from people who know the truth."

I pretending to wipe at a tear and winced when I stood up.

"You'll be sore tomorrow. They're very strong and I'm sure she bruised you."

"Thanks," I repeated and made a valiant effort to slowly walk away from the room, despite my desire to run.

Once upstairs, I found the other nurses and gave a quick report, telling them I needed to get home to my kids. I felt bad for bailing out on them early—again—but assured them my work was done and they'd only need to listen for call bells until morning.

My car felt a thousand miles away but I took my time walking out, even adding a small limp. If Kunsman had any remaining suspicions of me, he could be watching the security cameras. I wanted the show to be real. I didn't make it this far just get busted by a hunter at the very end.

Only when I was in my car and pulling out of the garage, did I let myself relax. Dialing Sorin, I fought the urge to speed back to the manor.

"Katherine? What is going on? I felt something and tried to reach for you but it was confusing and jumbled."

"Evelyn came to the hospital. She's dead. I'm on my way to tell you the whole story but please don't send anything out until we talk." I thought the call had dropped; it was so quiet. "Hello?"

"I hear you." He was mad. "I cannot wait to hear this."

And, the line went dead.

72

After everything I'd survived, I was seriously more scared to go tell Sorin the story than I was facing down Evelyn or Will. Now that it was done, I could see how stupid it'd been. I was very lucky that it had worked out in our favor. I could also understand why we was mad. We we're supposed to be a team but I'd done this without including him. I knew I'd done it to protect him but he was going to see it as me not trusting him.

He was standing in the doorway when I pulled up. Rhys was behind him on the stairs. They both looked mad so I suddenly felt like a bad kid coming home passed curfew.

When I was out of the car and heading towards them, Rhys pushed by Sorin to run up and hug me. "Goddammit, Katie. Why didn't you call us?"

"Let me tell you everything then decide how mad you are. But, I'm okay."

Sorin stood still in the doorway. We both turned to face him. Rhys grabbed my hand in a show of support. It was brave considering how angry Sorin looked. "Can we go to the grove? I'd rather be outside."

He gestured towards the grove but didn't say anything. I walked with Rhys to the bench, feeling Sorin behind me. It was one of those times I wished so hard for empathy. Honestly though, I didn't need it. I knew he was upset.

I held my hand towards the bench and Rhys sat. Pleading with my eyes, I looked to Sorin. The man in front of me was leader of the city, not my boyfriend, and I was about to admit to orchestrating another vampire's death.

If you're keeping track, yes—that's two vampire deaths on my shoulders in a single month.

To my relief, he silently sat next to Rhys, allowing me to stand and sort of have the stage. Taking a deep breath, I began.

"Logan is part owner of a fashion line with Evelyn. His mate Jeremy and I have become fast friends. Jeremy didn't trust Evelyn but kept quiet to help keep Logan's life as simple and stress-free as possible. Last night, when I went to shower, I spoke to Jeremy—asked him if he'd seen Evelyn and asked him to let me know if he heard from her."

I paused, wanting to ensure I had their attention. I did.

"I spoke to Jeremy tonight at work. He let me know that she'd contacted them and was at their home. She was accusing me of setting her up and claimed she was being followed. He said something about not being a trained assassin and it gave me an idea."

I knew even as I was telling the story, that was the moment I should have included them but didn't. Guilt was laying in the periphery of my feelings so I shoved it aside until I could finish.

"Jeremy agreed to help. He told Evelyn that he hated me too and wanted to help her, that they could grab me at the hospital. He gave me a heads up when they were on their way. Meanwhile, I talked to Kunsman—told him I needed to talk to him about something private and asked him to meet me out back when I could get away. I got the five-minute warning from Jeremy and waited outside the door. He knew to call me in front of her and pretend he was luring me out. That's when I texted Kunsman and asked him to meet me outside in ten minutes.

When Evelyn and Jeremy came around the back, I was outside waiting. I'd told him to hide in the woods and film it, to not come out no matter what. He listened. Then, just like I knew she would—Evelyn attacked me. Kunsman came out to see it. She was wild and full vamp. He killed her to save me. Jeremy got it all on video. Later, the hunter told me all about the existence of vampires and how he was there to save us. He's leaving tomorrow. He thinks Evelyn is the one who was using the hospital as her buffet line. He's gone, no longer looking and Evelyn is dead. It's a win-win. Plus, it's all recorded for you to show her maker. All our hands are clean."

I was done. Saying it out loud I could hear for myself now many things could have gone wrong: Kunsman could have not seen my text, he could have seen Jeremy or I could have vamped out and gotten killed. Jeremy could betray us or Kunsman could be lying and isn't really leaving. All that being said—it was done and I couldn't go back in time.

Waiting to see what would happen, I stood still, hands clasped in front of me.

"May I see the video?"

I pulled out my phone, pulled up the video Jeremy had sent and handed it over. Rhys and Sorin watched it together. I couldn't see it but I could hear it. It had been filmed too far away to pick up sound so no one would know that I'd verbally pushed her into a fight. They'd see her attack, a hunter emerge and her head being sliced off. When it was over, Sorin spoke without making eye contact with me. "I want to speak to Jeremy." He stood, putting my phone to his ear and sped away. I could have used my hearing to try and eavesdrop but that seemed real stupid given the situation.

Rhys joined me. "It wasn't a bad plan, per se. However, you should have included us."

"I know," I agreed. "It was reckless."

"But it was a good plan—complicated, but good. I'm proud of you for doing what you thought was right. I'm disappointed in you for putting yourself in danger, again."

"He's really mad," I said.

"He's a lot of things, Katie. Don't do him the disservice of boiling it down to one simple emotion."

He had a point. "When did you get so wise?"

Sorin was back before Rhys could continue. He laid my phone in my hand. "He will tell everyone that she showed up, demanded he drive her to the hospital but that she didn't tell him why. He tells me that was your idea. I believe that he will do this. She was a very big problem for them as well. He is coming here tomorrow so I can read him and be sure of his allegiance. He's very impressed with you. I believe you have gained his loyalty and respect."

"Can I say something." I knew I was pushing it.

"Leave us please Rhys."

Rhys bowed and we were alone a second later.

"Say it and then I ask that you listen to me." He returned to the bench to sit while I remained standing. I wasn't ready to be next to him until I said this.

"You want me to rule this kingdom with you. You're willing to give share of the safety of all of your people to me. Tonight, I was given a rare opportunity to move so I did. It was a calculated risk but one that I recognized as priceless and time dependent. We were able to end Evelyn's reign of terror and get the hunter to pack his bags with one action. I—and this part I want you to hear..." Crossing to him, I dropped to my knees in front of him, waiting for him to make eye contact.

"I am sorry I didn't call you. It was imperative that I moved quickly and have as few vampires involved as possible. I don't apologize for the choice I made. But I need you to know it's not because I don't trust you or think you can't handle yourself. I would never think that I don't need you. You and I are a team. But, sometimes, I'm going to do something—then tell you later. And, sometimes—you'll do the same."

I took his hands and scooted forward so I was pressed against his knees. "Know this, and it's not easy for me to say—you are the only one

I would ever give my complete loyalty to. You are my King." I laid my forehead on his thighs in a sign of submission and waited.

He didn't move for minutes. A pain in my heart was growing by the seconds, threatening to rip my chest open. I knew I had put him through Hell and not for the first time. For a moment, I hated myself for being so independent and I hated that stupid wall that continually put barriers between me and the people I loved. When his hand rested on the back of my head, some of the heart ache eased. He slid his hand under my chin and lifted me to face him.

What was in his eyes wasn't anger, it was a mix of admiration and pain. "You impress me while scaring me. You hurt me while making me complete. You make me feel powerless yet make me feel like I am greater than all. How could I have existed for half a century before you were even a thought from the universe and now you are my whole world?"

He slid himself down to the ground and matched me on his knees. "I was furious with you. Then, you say exactly what I need to hear without having the power of empathy. I hate that you don't need me. I hate that you are so strong and cunning. There's this desire inside me to protect you but you don't need protection. You leave me reeling sometimes, like I am out in a vast ocean at the mercy of the waves. Why, Katherine? Why do you hold such sway over me?"

"Sorin, I'm so sorry I scared you. I wanted to save us all, save my children. But I didn't want it to fall to you. I also want to protect you."

He looked confused. "No one has ever wanted to protect me. So many come to me for protection or what I offer them. None have ever put themselves between me and danger. I wanted to tell you to stop but at the same time, I love that you desire for my safety as I do for yours."

"I get that," I chuckled. "I always wanted to belong to someone but at the same time, I want to be independent."

"What a pair we are." He sat on the ground, resting his back against the bench. I climbed up into his lap, needing desperately to know he wasn't angry with me.

"What happens now?"

"Margo is on her way. She will be here tomorrow night and that's when I will tell her everything and show her the video. I will document that Evelyn died by the hunter and ensure he leaves town. Jeremy comes tomorrow and if he is found to be honorable, the truth stays with us for eternity. You will tell Tom that the hunter found Evelyn and let him sleep peacefully."

"Tidy," I quipped.

"Let's hope. Margo could cause a problem, want to look into things. We still need to deal with the wolves but this solves two problems."

"So," I smiled. "I did good?"

He shook his head and sighed. "It wasn't exactly the cleanest of plans but it did work."

"I will take that as a yes." I grabbed his face, intending to give him a celebratory kiss. What started out as a smack on the lips escalated quickly when he ran his hands into my hair and grabbed a handful on each side. Taking in a quick breath, he leaned forward enough for me to slide backwards with my back on the ground. He broke the kiss to hover over me and rip my scrub top over my head then pull off his shirt. Returning to my mouth, he was pressed above me and hard. The kiss was desperate; desperate for assurance that I was alive and that we were okay. I kneaded his back, enjoying the feel of his muscles bunching and releasing in rhythm. He was hungry for me. I worked at the tie of my pants, using my feet to pull them down and kick off my shoes. In minutes, I was naked on the soft grass, completely aware that this was the spot I'd first laid eyes on him. His pants were made of something soft and the feel of them against the most tender part of me was ecstasy. As much as I wanted him inside of me, his hard length under the satin fabric was too good to lose just yet.

For a second, it was like I left my body. I saw us writhing in the center of the grove; his pale skin on top of mine. The moon seemed to come out of us instead of shine on us. We were so natural, in the grass and the beauty of the night. The sight of us made my core ache. That brought me back to myself and the sensations around and through me. He rose up to his feet, looking down at me.

"You are the most enchanting thing I've ever seen."

Letting his pants join my clothes, he returned to me. I was ravenous for him, feeling like he could never be close enough. As much as I lusted for us to join, part of me already mourned the moment we'd come apart again. I let my legs spread to welcome him and he knew what to do. Coming to his knees, he let his gaze run up and down my naked form. Holding onto my hips, he raised me up to meet him. The tip teased at my opening and the arching of my back made every nerve in me come to life. "Please," I begged and he pulled my hips to sheath himself with my warmth.

Once he couldn't get further into me, he paused to lock his gaze into mine. "Your eyes," he gasped.

"Your eyes," I answered. "They're so beautiful."

"As are yours."

I let him be completely in charge that night. I knew he needed it and I knew I was utterly powerless against him. It was refreshing to be dominated and allow someone else to be in control. I showed him I trusted him as he manipulated my body to find the sensation he was searching for. I knew he'd found it when he'd pulled out and flipped me onto all fours. After that, his pace was frantic. Being outside and in this position made me feel primal. It added to the overwhelming need that was building inside of me. When he reached around to run his fingers over my throbbing flesh and matched it to the movements of him inside of me, it didn't take long for me to scream out in release. The jerking of my body, threw him over the edge and he mimicked my cries. As I felt the throbbing in the most vulnerable part of me, I also felt the weight of him fall onto my back. When he did slide out of me, I moaned.

Turning to lay back on the ground, he curled around me and laid his head on my chest. "We cannot stay out here much longer."

"I know," I sighed. "Just a few minutes more."

73

When I opened my eyes in our bed the next night, it took a second to remember the previous evening, then it was back in snippets. I flashed to the fight in the graveyard, the sight of Evelyn's head on the ground, the lovemaking in the grove and Sorin carrying me into the house and up the stairs—both naked. One thing I'd never stop loving about being a creature of the night was everyone's comfort level with sex and unclothed bodies. A month ago, I'd cringed at the thought of anyone seeing me naked. Now, I'd probably walk through the house in nothing. Best part—no one would even give me a second look.

I was pulled from my thoughts by the sound of my phone buzzing. A quick glance at the caller ID told me it was the hospital.

"Yes," I answered.

Jerry's voice on the other end sounded thrilled. "Kate!"

"What's up?"

"We got a perfect score from DOH. Guy just left! I owe you big time. Take your two weeks. I'll see you around Halloween."

"Thank you," I exclaimed. "That's great news."

I cut off whatever he was saying next because I was remembering everything we still needed to do. A quick search showed Sorin was already out of bed. I popped up and shuffled into my room. A quick search of the drawers showed someone had filled them with clothes. My money was on Tamela. Making a mental note to make the time to spend with her, I also made it a priority. She'd bared her soul to me and I wanted to honor that with some time.

The sapphire blue cotton sundress fit perfectly and was exactly what I needed. Running a brush through my hair, I thanked the universe I didn't need to get ready for work and could just be myself. After a few minutes of searching for my laundry, it occurred to me that my scrubs were out on the lawn. I was going to have to get them eventually but first I needed to eat.

My bare feet slapped on the stairs as I descended for something to eat, running right into Jeremy and Logan at the bottom. "Oh my God, I'm so sorry." They both were holding up hands to stop our collision. "Did I sleep in?"

"Guess so," Jeremy laughed. "It was a rough night. No surprise. We let ourselves in, is that okay?"

"Oh yeah," I answered. "I mean, it's not my house but a lot of people come and go. Plus, he's expecting you. Can you give me two minutes to find him? I was just going to eat. Are you hungry?"

"We're good," Jeremy answered. It was only then that I noticed Logan's face. He was obviously upset. Jeremy was doing all the talking so I hadn't caught it at first. I showed them to the living room and motioned for them to sit.

"I'll grab a glass and find Sorin. Make yourselves at home." I hustled for the kitchen and poured two glasses then headed for the office. I didn't know if he would be there but it was a solid start, which paid off. He was at his desk, scribbling onto some papers. When I came in, he looked up. Placing the glass in front of him, he smiled. "Good evening, *regina mea*."

"Good evening... wait. How do you say my king in Romanian?"

That brought a glow to his skin, which pleased me. "*Regele meu*," he answered.

"*Regele meu*," I tested.

He growled. "Oh, I like that."

I playfully slapped his hand as it reached for me. "No time. Jeremy and Logan are downstairs." He stood and this time we reached for my hand as his partner. I accepted it so we could walk down the stairs as a team. When we entered the living room, both men stood. Logan glanced back and forth between us. Jeremy gave a small bow.

"Jeremy," Sorin's voice filled the room with power but he kept it very subtle. "Please follow me. My mate will stay with yours if that is agreeable to you."

"Yes," he responded. They left the room to return to the office, leaving Logan and me alone to talk. I hated how upset he was and decided to face it head on since I didn't know how much time we had.

"Logan?"

He made eye contact but didn't say anything.

I continued. "I don't have the powers Sorin does but it's obvious you're struggling with something. Do you want to talk?"

He seemed to be taken aback by my abruptness but regained his composure quickly. "I don't know how to begin."

"Just talk," I said. "I'm a pretty good listener."

"Kate," he gulped. "You have to believe me. I had no idea what Evelyn was up to. I mean, I knew she was gunning for you and wanted Sorin all to herself. She's been after him for ages. But I thought it was jealousy. I thought keying your car would be the worst of it and she'd eventually move on. If I had *any* idea that she would go after your kids—I can't even think about it. I've been sick." I was too surprised to be sure what to say. He kept talking so I had time to think. "She made my life unbearable but I honestly thought it was just me and I could deal, you know? I thought eventually she'd move on and I'd have the company and be rid of her. Then, I saw you at the party- which I felt horrible about by the way—but I didn't know you so pretending to hate you was like this victimless crime. But, when I saw you at the house, I realized you were actually really nice. Then when Jeremy told me what she did…. I didn't sleep Kate. I just kept picturing two little girls, tied up and crying. What if I could have stopped it? If I had stood up to her years ago—maybe it wouldn't have happened. Oh my god, how could you ever forgive me?"

"Whoa," I finally interrupted. "That's a lot but let's talk about it. First of all, you have nothing to ask for forgiveness for. You didn't take my kids; she did. There is no way you could have known how evil she really was, I mean I didn't and Sorin didn't. Neither one of us thought to protect the girls, so you have to let go of that responsibility. As for standing up to her, can I tell you something?"

He nodded.

"I spent forty years trying to please people and be the person I though they wanted. I sacrificed myself day after day, interaction after interaction. It took dying for me to find my voice and start to stand up for myself. Just last night, I was apologizing for something really stupid that I did—which by the way put myself and your mate at risk—so I should be asking you for forgiveness."

"Listen," he perked up. "Jeremy told me the plan and I agreed with it. She was destroying my business and my relationship. Once I heard what she did to you—I was ready to kill her myself."

I was confused. "What do you mean, your business? I kind of thought it was hers."

He leaned back on the couch and put his hands behind his neck. "No. It's mine. I own 51%. I've been asking for years to buy her out and she kept saying 'Later, Logan.' I went to her for help and before I knew it, she had taken over. She came with all these famous people, so I let it ride for a little while. But they became my best clients and slowly gave me their loyalty, not her. She was like this leech—draining me dry. She was like that to everyone. I tried but I couldn't get out from under her. It was this abusive relationship. Every time the phone rang, my stomach clenched because I was afraid it was her." He leaned forward again, facing me. "You set us free, Kate. She's gone and I feel like someone just told me that my cancer disappeared. Its going to take a while for me to believe it but it's true. I saw the video. She's dead. How can I ever repay you?"

"Wow," I interrupted. "I mean, I'm happy for you, obviously. You and Jeremy deserve this—a fresh start. And, I don't need anything from you. Please, just enjoy your time and your upcoming show. I'd love to come see you work."

He clapped his hands together in glee. "Are you kidding? You have to come as my guest! I'll send tickets."

"I'd love that," I said, reaching for his hand. "We're good, okay?"

"Okay," he responded, squeezing my hand in reassurance.

I heard the office door opened and the combined voices of Sorin, Rhys and Jeremy talking. I rose to see them come down the stairs. Everyone looked pleased so I had hope that it went well. Sorin met my gaze and winked. We were good for now.

One meeting down; one to go.

As the men entered the living room, the front door opened. Edwin came into the room with Sorin's and my clothes bunched under his arm plus my phone. "I was doing my rounds. Found the phone buzzing upstairs and the clothes out on the lawn. I can just throw them in the laundry."

"Thanks, Edwin." I clutched the phone but wasn't ready for the next part. Before he left the room, he gave a bow and said "Of course, milady."

74

After saying goodbye to Jeremy and Logan, we'd returned to the office to debrief before our next guest. I started the conversation. "Jerry called. I'm officially on break. Mr. Kunsman left today."

"That's a relief," Rhys answered. "I won't miss him."

Sorin joined in. "Jeremy will keep our confidence. If asked by Margo, he will hold to his tale of how they ended up at the hospital and attest that he recorded the video for protection."

"I spoke to Logan," I continued. "The business is majority his. He takes over and when she's announced dead, he owns it outright."

Sorin nodded. "Have you heard anything from Diana? When is the fight for leader occurring?"

That reminded me of my phone which I'd discarded on the table. I found it and unlocked the messages. I'd had a missed call from Tom and Diana then follow up texts from both. Each one had asked me to call. I started with Tom.

"Hey," he answered. "I'm going nuts here. Where is she?"

"She's dead," I said. I saw no reason to waste time. "The hunter got her."

"That's convenient," he responded.

"Sure is." I paused but he was clearly waiting for more. "So, you can rest now. She won't ever hurt anyone again."

"I don't want the whole story?"

I huffed. "Definitely not."

"Thanks, Kate. I'll give them a kiss for you." The call ended and I dialed Diana. Sorin and Rhys sat still, waiting patiently for me to go through my business. I was struck by the understanding that—when time is no longer limited to 80 or so years—you can become very patient.

"Kate?" Diana was out of breath.

"Diana. How's Monica?"

"Good," she answered. "After this we're telling Alex. She wants to get it out now so she can go into the change with a clear head. I don't know how he'll take it but since he knows about you guys, we feel we can trust him. Meanwhile, everyone here loves her. It was kind of complicated trying to explain how I managed to scratch her without telling them all your stuff but its gonna work out. They're so excited to have new blood, I don't think they really care. She learning fast which is good because she's gonna turn tomorrow."

I dropped hard to the floor, ending up cross-legged on the office ground. "So soon?"

"Yeah," she answered. "And that's not the worst part. We are postponing the fight so she can turn with the support of the pack. But, the next night—my cousins will battle for dominance. I will need to fight or forfeit. And, if I don't win… Kate, they're still talking war."

"Shit," I sighed and shut my eyes. "That's it, huh?"

"That's it," she said. "I promise to be with Monica when she shifts. We will call you when it's over. She'll be fine, I swear to you. But, Kate—if they win the next night—a line will be drawn and we'll both have to choose between us and you."

"I get it." Ending the call, I found Sorin's concerned gaze.

"I heard it," he said. "Two nights and then we need to be prepared for battle."

"Sounds like it," I agreed.

"This will hurry our time with the California representatives. We need to get them out of town before they hear anything. If other masters think we cannot keep the peace, they will see it as weakness and challenge my position."

"Will Evelyn's maker already know she's dead? Can makers feel when their progeny die?"

He shook his head. "No. Only empaths can feel the deaths of those they make. The only death that all vampires feel is the death of their mate."

He paced in front of the fireplace. It was so unlike him to look like he didn't know what to do next. I realized then how much was on his shoulders. Local vampires, including me, found solace in the belief that he was always in control. Whether he knew what the next move was, he always gave off the impression that he was master of all—unbreakable. Seeing behind the scenes and knowing that even he couldn't fix everything had a simultaneous effect on me. I loved that he was felt free to drop the façade with me but also was scared that he was not infallible.

The sound of the doorbell changed it all in a second. The mask of the master was back and he wore his power like a cloak.

"They are here."

75

Margo was as blonde as her progeny and clearly, they had shopped at the same boutiques. It was possible the mint green pantsuit was one of Evelyn's designs as it looked like something she would have worn herself. Since both were the same size, it was also likely they just owned the same outfits. It was a good thing that Sorin was doing the introductions because I needed to few minutes to get my thoughts together. I had to wonder if Margo had turned Evelyn because they looked so much alike. It was kind of sick in a way—to make a mini-you.

Charles was the exact opposite. His bellbottoms were probably not retro from the mall but actually purchased in the 70s. The dark blue t-shirt framed him well and couldn't have been more than ten dollars. The gold medallion that hung from his neck was the only thing that told me he was a lot older than those jeans. His hair was so close to Rhys' color that I looked back and forth between them to see that Charles' hair was a little browner compared to Rhys' red. Just like my maker, Charles kept his hair less kept than most. Next to Margo's supermodel height, I judged him to be about 5'6". He would have seemed unimposing if he didn't have serious power radiating off of him.

Once in the solarium, Margo and Charles stood on one side; Sorin, Rhys and I faced them from the other. I wished there was something more than empty air between us. With glasses of blood in everyone's hands, Sorin began. "Lady Margo, I thank you for coming so far to see us. Lord Charles, I thank you for keep her company. We are honored you came to our side of the country and know your time is precious. I will make this quick so you may return safely to your hotel before dawn and catch your flights next evening."

The master vamps all raised glasses in the air like a salute, then drank. I noted Sorin drank first as the other two watched. They followed along a second later.

Sorin continued. "I asked you here to discuss your progeny, Evelyn Blomgren. When I reached out to you, it was with concerns regarding her behavior. Since then, circumstances have changed." He paused, giving Margo a chance to comment. When she didn't, he continued. "She has damaged my property, threatened Katherine at her place of work and shown power in a public place with humans nearby."

With this, Margo side-eyed me. Until that moment, she hadn't acknowledged Rhys or me. When Tamela had entered the room with drinks, Margo had given her the same cold shoulder. Finally, she had slid her glance to me. What I saw in those eyes was disdain. Since I was used to it, I don't think she got the reaction she'd hoped for. Instead of shrinking back, I met her eyes.

That was a point for me.

"Am I to understand," her voice was thick with an accent that I was pretty sure was Swedish. That explained the beauty and height. "That this new vampire is the one that Evelyn has come against?"

"Yes," Sorin answered coldly without offering anymore.

"What is she to you?"

Sorin's power crept off of him like a heater just turned on and warming up. "I have chosen her as mate."

Both Californian vampires turned to look at me head on. Margo did not hide her disapproval. To the contrary, Charles crossed over to bow in front of me then offer Sorin a hand. "Congratulations, Lord. I didn't think you'd ever be bound."

Sorin arched an eyebrow and allowed a tiny smirk before regaining his stoicism. "I thank you." Charles returned to Margo's side.

Margo didn't look happy and ripped her gaze from me to eyeball Sorin. "So, I will punish her accordingly."

I knew there was more to come and didn't envy Sorin having to tell her. Bracing myself for what I expected to be bad, I took Rhys's hand. He squeezed. Sorin finished, "Margo, the hospital that Katherine works at was being investigated by a hunter. When Evelyn showed her power, she could have gotten us killed. At that time, I cut ties with her. She knew the consequences for any more law breaking."

The hair on my arms rose in response to the change in the room temperature. Next to me, I could feel the heat of Sorin's power but from Margo, a coldness emanated. The contrast of the two was so stark that it pulled an instinctive reaction out of me. My own power bubbled in my stomach, wanting to join the mix. I had to use energy to focus on keeping it contained. Rhys squeezed my hand harder, telling me he felt it too.

"Where is she?" Margo's voice had its own frozen quality, like the words themselves were covered in icicles.

Sorin didn't look phased at all. When he finished the story, it was like he was reading a script. "She again went to the hospital to confront Katherine. This time she used powers and attacked. The hunter saw her, Margo. He knew what she was and destroyed her."

"Yet, she stands next to you. How was she not slain?"

"She followed my instructions to never show her power in public. She allowed your progeny to attack her without fighting as to not risk herself or others. I am thankful that she did control herself."

Even to me, that sounded like a passive aggressive jab at the deceased. While I still hated Evelyn, I didn't want her maker to be any more hurt than she had to be. I held my breath, waiting to see how she'd respond.

"I don't believe it," she spat.

Sorin didn't react. "She forced one of my people to drive her to the hospital under false pretenses. He was smart enough to hide and filmed the whole thing." Pulling his phone from his pocket, he worked quickly. "I have sent it to you so you may see."

Wild-eyed, she tore through her designer purse, found her phone and let the bag fall to the floor. While we watched them, Charles and Margo watched the video. My held breath came out shakingly when I saw the blood tears start to streak down her face. Considering the time they stared at the small device, I think they repeated it a few times. When she let her hands drop down, they both returned our gazes.

"I must tell you more," Sorin spoke before she could. "When she went to the hospital, we were already searching for her. I would like Katherine to tell this part, if you will allow."

Margo nodded silently.

I cleared my throat and stepped forward, locking eyes with hers. Just knowing what I was about to say was making me emotional. My own tears began. With a shaking voice, I started to tell a story I hoped I would never have to tell again. "Evelyn hired two humans who were addicted to drugs and at rock bottom. She offered them money to do something for her—kidnap my two, human daughters. I found them in the woods after they had been drugged, tied up and thrown onto the ground. Evelyn told them to hold guns on me and my friends while she drank from my children before she planned to murder us all. I was shot. My friend was hurt very badly. My daughters had to have their memories erased." I took one more step towards her. "They are 12 and 14."

Freezing to be ready for anything, I waited. Behind me, Sorin and Rhys also tensed. When she closed the distance between us, I didn't know how to react. She dropped to her knees and took my hands, pulling them to her forehead. "Forgive me," she whispered.

I pulled her up to face me while taking a step back. "Why do you need forgiveness?"

"I knew she was obsessive. It was a trait I enjoyed in her. She did not quit on anything that she set her sights on. Her determination made her a fierce force. However, I saw the dark side in her as, well." She looked down at the floor. "When she moved here, I thought it would be a fresh start for her. I didn't want to believe that she could be malicious. I didn't want to accept the wickedness in her. She was my child."

"I understand," I said. "You never want to believe that the one you raised could do anything bad." I put myself in her shoes. How would I handle it if I saw a video of Ellie or Olivia doing something terrible? If I heard about awful things they'd done?

Sorin came to my side. "Lady Margo. As your progeny died on my land with my mate as witness, you have the right to ask for a trial. Do you wish to challenge me or see the death investigated?"

She met my eyes. "No," she answered. "I am satisfied with what you have told me and what I have seen."

"I am witness," Charles said, laying his hand on her shoulder.

Margo picked up her bag and returned the phone into it. She pulled out wipes, handing one to me and wiping her face. When we were blood-free, she shoved the used wipes into her purse. Since she struck me as a woman who never would have dirty items in her purse, I knew she was still in shock. "There's been enough pain because of Evelyn. Let it end here."

"I agree," Sorin rested his hand on my low back.

Margo was quickly recovering her appearance of stoic beauty as she pulled back her icy magic. I assumed she was used to looking uncaring, so bringing the illusion back was like putting an old coat on. Just like Sorin, these masters had to shoulder the weight of a city on their backs without appearing to falter. I wondered why anyone would want to take on so much responsibility. It made me both sad for them and also so grateful for Sorin.

"If it does not come as offensive," Margo said, "I would like to leave now. I need to tell my other progeny they are—were very close to Evelyn."

"I am not offended," Sorin answered. "Please send my condolences to Ashley and Kristen."

Margo took my hand. "Congratulations to you two. I hope you visit us in California after you are officially mated. I would love to show you the city. And, enjoy your children. I was a mother before turning. Their time will go fast."

"Thank you," I said. "And, I'm sorry for your loss."

As Sorin saw them to the front door, I struggled to put that kind woman together with Evelyn. Was it possible that Evelyn had started good and then turned bad? Was it possible that Margo really hadn't seen it until it was too late?

Focusing my hearing, I heard Charles and Margo on the driveway, getting into the car and the sound of them rolling down the driveway. In addition to that sound was a second—another car coming up the driveway. Rushing to the foyer, Sorin and Rhys were standing in the open doorway. They had also heard the approaching vehicle. As far as I knew, we had told the vampires of the city that we were not having any get-togethers for a while and none of us were expecting anymore guests.

I smelled him before the car stopped.

What is Alex doing here?

76

"I didn't invite him," I said, anticipating Sorin's question.

"Me either," Rhys echoed.

When he stepped out of the car, I knew he hadn't showered in a few days. You can't hide a few days of filth from a vampire, no matter how much Axe body spray you lay on. He was still in his white lab coat, telling me he came from the hospital in a rush. Several days of stubble graced his jaw.

"What's wrong," I asked.

He rushed up. "I just talked to Monica. Where is she?"

Sorin tensed and I was afraid he would pounce on the approaching man. I held up my hands. "Whoa, Alex. She isn't here?"

"Where is she?" he repeated. "She wouldn't tell me. This is your fault." He jabbed his finger at me. "You put her in danger twice and now she's infected." Those words ripped open my gut.

Sorin stepped in front of me. "Calm yourself, Doctor." His voice felt like a caress, like someone rubbing your back when you don't feel well. Alex relaxed and the fire in his eyes dimmed but didn't disappear.

Alex turned and let himself fall down hard to sit on the step. His head fell to his hands in utter exhaustion. "She sounded so scared," he said into his palms.

I sat next to him. "She is in really good hands, Alex. Diana will be right by her side."

He looked up and turned to me. "Is it going to hurt her? To turn?"

"The first couple times," I answered, not seeing a reason to lie. Sorin stayed behind. I heard Rhys leave into the house. Alex returned his head to his palms.

I was completely at a loss for words. He was right, it was my fault that she was scared and facing something painful. Even with her forgiveness, I still carried the weight of guilt. Seeing what it was doing to Alex made that shame even heavier. Minutes of silence went by, finally broken by the sound of Rhys coming back and the smell of coffee. The hot mug was placed in front of Alex and he took it. Rhys sat on the other side of him with Sorin still watching over but not saying anything.

After a few sips, Alex spoke. "I am going to find a cure."

"I know," I said.

"No," he interrupted. "To lycanthropy. I'm putting the vampirism cure on hold—I need to help Monica first."

"Oh," I muttered. What did this mean for me? Did I even want the cure? I wasn't sure but I hadn't even considered that one day he would just stop or that he wouldn't find it. I think deep down I always assumed I would get to make the choice someday. What if he didn't ever go back to his work? Or, what if he did cure Monica? Would she run as far away from me as possible? If I was being honest, her being infected made us the same and I liked that. If she went back to human—I'd be the freak again.

Even as I was thinking it, another part of me was saying *Kate, that's so selfish*. Which I knew but I felt it anyway. I also wanted her to be cured so she and Alex could live happily ever after.

I realized Alex was still talking and tried to focus on his words. "If it's bloodborne like yours, then I can reverse it. This is what I do. I study viruses. I can use some of my work on vampires but apply it to werewolfism. Half the work is done. If I can get her blood and Diana's I can start."

"That's good," I said, not knowing yet if I was totally against it or for it. "In the meantime, can I ask you something? You don't have to answer if you don't want to."

He gulped down the coffee. "Sure."

"Are you still interested in her? Will you still date her?"

He met my eyes. "Of course," he answered, matter-of-factly. "She is the same person."

Letting out a breath, I was thankful. At the very least, Monica would still have her dream date with a man that I was quickly realizing was a really good one. If anyone could help her while also accepting her, it was Alex. A pang in my chest made me question if I was really being honest with myself when I said I was happy for them but I ignored it.

I changed the subject. "The hunter left. Moved on to some other unlucky city, hopefully far from here."

"That was lucky," he said dryly. "Guess he's not a very good hunter."

I wasn't certain what he meant but that but again ignored it. "Well, I'm glad for that. It put us, you and the wolves at risk, including Monica."

"Monica, too. I think it's going to take a while to really sink in," he sighed. "I've told so many families, so many diagnoses and watched them try to believe it. Now, it's me wanting to deny reality. That she has this condition, now."

"I'm so sorry, Alex."

He shook his head. "No. It's not your fault. That was really shitty of me to say. She told me everything. Why didn't you call me? I would have gone. I would have saved your daughters and protected her."

I was dreading this part. "We called you, Alex. You didn't answer."

He threw the mug into the woods. We were going to have to stop giving people drinks when we told them bad news. "Dammit. I was sleeping. It's the one time I turned off my ringer. The *one time* I took an afternoon for myself. Dammit," a guttural scream came out of him—a mix of a growling and a cry of pain.

"You couldn't have known," I reassured him. "None of us could."

"Your daughters?" he asked without finishing the question.

"Safe. They don't remember the worst parts but they remember enough to never follow a stranger again."

After he calmed himself down and regain his composure, he stood up to reach into his pocket for his keys. Staring out into the darkness, he addressed us all. "I promise, once I find out how to cure Monica, I will go back to my research for vampirism."

"We have time," Sorin said—the only thing he added to the conversation. "She must come first."

When Alex descended the stairs and walked to his car, he was hunched. In the midst of powerful creatures of myth, he was the only human and carried inhuman burden on his back. My heart broke for him. I fought the urge to run to him, to kiss him and comfort him but just watched him climb into the driver's seat. The red lights disappeared into the darkness with his departure. I wondered what was going through his head or if I should have said something different, something more. The night had been tumultuous, an emotional roller coaster that I wanted to get off of.

"Can we go to bed?" I asked Sorin, still down the driveway. "I'm done with tonight."

"Of course," he answered.

Too bad rest wasn't coming—I just didn't know it yet.

77

The smell of pine was so strong that it was on the edge of choking me. When I was human, I'd loved those evergreen candles. Now, with vampire senses in the middle of the dense forest, I didn't understand how I'd ever wanted that smell. It wasn't fresh and that was part of the problem. Under the pine needle scent was a mix of dead flesh, animal scat, rotting garbage from far away campsites and the growing bacteria in stagnant waters throughout. In the darkness, I could still see the scurrying squirrels as they prepared for the coming winter. As animals came and went around us, they eyed us with unsure glances. I knew where I needed to go but not exactly how to get there. Sniffing at the air, I found it—Monica's new smell. Running through the trees, I felt the ground under my bare feet. The sensation was familiar, the same I'd felt looking for the girls. And, now the mission was the same—save them.

Tree limbs scratched me as I ran, unsuccessfully trying to slow me down. The full moon made it easier to see what was coming so I could dodge large rocks and jump over logs. The sounds hit me before I could see anything: tearing of skin, snapping of bones, grunting and growling. I didn't need my eyes to know they were all shifting. I would, however, need my eyes to see how many there were. When the howls rose up to the sky, it was a chorus and still didn't give me a number.

The clearing opened up slowly with thinning trees first, then the path smoothed out and then a grove. In the center, a dozen werewolves stood with backs arch and mouths open to emit chilling calls to the moon. As they backed away, I could see a wolf standing in the center, hunching over the naked Monica. All the wolves were different colors and a variety of heights. The one above Monica was the smallest of them. Her dark brown fur made me believe that was Diana.

In awe, I watched her nose at Monica and whimper as the blonde's body started to convulse. She let out a scream of agony that pierced my eardrums. Throwing herself backwards, Monica started to seize. Something inside me told me to hold back and not interrupt this sacred time. Without knowing if it would work on lycanthropes, I reached my mind out to theirs. Voices filled my head like a crowded room full of conversation. Picking out individual timbres, I found Diana's thoughts. *You can do this. It's almost over and then we will run, child. Let the wolf free, don't fight.* I turned down the other voices but let them remain a light din underneath.

Twisting and arching her back, Monica thrust her abdomen to the sky. When I thought her spine would snap, her stomach ripped open to expose a furry spine arched in the opposite direction. Monica's screams continued as the wolf crawled out of her skin. What was Monica fell to the ground in a motion reminiscent of a snake shedding its skin. When the blonde wolf was free of its human casing, screams turned to howls. Shouts of joys filled my head when the pack realized that Monica had survived her first shift. Only then did I understand that some humans who are infected do not make it through the first turn. Diana hadn't wanted to tell me.

One thought weaved through the voices in my head: *it doesn't change anything. Diana and her spawn die tonight. I will be pack master.*

I didn't know what wolf the voice belonged to but knew deep down it was one of the cousins. I saw his plan in my head like a series of pictures. He was going to betray Diana, break his promise and challenge her to fight on the full moon for dominance. I opened my mouth to warn her but was too late. The biggest of the wolves, the one with silver fur, leapt onto Diana's back. She whirled around and threw him off. He stood, spread his feet and slammed his hands against his chest. A majority of the other wolves around him bowed. Three did not. The two black wolves lumbered forward to stand on each side of him, also slamming their hands onto their chests. Monica looked to the remaining wolf, the reddish one. After a moment of looking to her, he turned to the black wolf and bowed down. Somehow, I knew that this was the sign of challenge. Her cousins would fight for dominance amongst themselves but only after they made her submit or killed her. Reading their minds, I knew they had already discussed amongst themselves to not stop until she was dead, then claim they didn't mean to. They'd also agreed to fight each other until a winner was chosen but stop before a fatal blow. No matter what, whoever won—the vampires were next.

I screamed, "Diana!" But, no one turned. I wasn't really there, I understood now. I was in a vision or I was far-seeing. I didn't know which yet. While I tried to materialize in the forest, Diana backed up to protect Monica who didn't know what was going on.

"Run," she growled in a half-human, half-animal sound. And, Monica listened. She turned for the edge of the woods and stumbled at first. Once she got the hang of her four legs, she was gone into the trees. The silver wolf turned to one of the black wolves and it ran after Monica.

Diana stood tall, indicating that she would not submit. *Come and get me*, I heard her whisper in her mind. *I'd rather die as my grandfather, with honor, then cower.*

My work to be solid in the world was futile. Too many sensations overwhelmed me and I watched helpless. I could chase after Monica or stay with Diana. Either way, someone would suffer. When the silver wolf lunged, Diana dropped to her back on the ground and took the weight of her cousin with her paws. When on top of her, I could see how much bigger he was. Her limbs shook and she fought to keep his jaws away. Rolling to her side, he fell to the earth. She leapt up to all fours and snapped at her jaw only to have the other black wolf jump onto her back. He clamped his jaw around the back of her neck, pulling her back and exposing her stomach. When the silver wolf's claw ripped into her middle, it was too late. Her body went limp, being thrown to the side like garbage. I ran to the quivering animal. On my knees, I watched the light leave her eyes and I could swear she saw me.

The first black wolf returned from the woods. He lumbered like he had no place to be and licked at the blood mated to his snout. When he saw the dead beast, he howled to the sky. He knew he would still have to fight his cousins but at least now, whoever won, the vampires would finally pay. Joining in on the howls, his cousins sounded jubilant. Any of the wolves in the periphery dropped to all fours then bent their front legs to bow further. All of them knew what this meant for the pack and none had issue with the vampires but none of them were courageous enough to stand up to the three biggest wolves. They felt that diplomacy was best and risking their lives for bloodsuckers they'd never met seemed foolish. Only Marcos, the reddish wolf, howled in sorrow and wondered if he should have stood at Diana's side after all. He grieved for her and felt shame thinking that his grandfather was watching.

I let out my own howl of fury and heartbreak.

"Katherine." I opened my eyes and saw grey ones, full of storm clouds and worry. "What did you see?"

I grabbed onto him, a life-raft in the raging sea of my vision. I knew he was desperate to hear what I had witnessed but I needed a second to get my thoughts to calm down. I needed to be reminded that it was a vision, which mean it hadn't happened yet. I broke from him and grabbed my phone. It was close to sunset so we didn't have much time. Dialing Diana, I took a deep steadying breath. Only when she answered did I feel okay. I told her to come to the house now and bring Monica. To her credit, she didn't argue.

After I was sure the call was ended and they weren't listening, I looked at Sorin.

"Her cousins are going to kill them tonight and then we go to war."

78

It felt like an eternity before I heard the car pull up. I ran to the front door and Sorin waited in the office. He, Rhys and Tamela had already heard the whole vision. They'd asked questions but I could really only tell them what I'd seen and heard, no more. I kept reminding them that it was a future that we could change; we'd done it before.

When I yanked open the door, I grabbed them both into an embrace. I needed to feel them and see they were real. Diana spoke first. "We don't have long, Kate. We have to get back for the shift."

They followed me up the stairs. One look at the faces in the room and I think both girls knew something bad was happening. That was further evidenced when Monica said, "Best to just spit it out."

So, I did. They listened silently while I told them everything, not leaving anything out. Diana stood still but Monica dropped into one of the chairs about halfway through the story. Once it was over, Diana gulped. "I wouldn't believe you if you didn't describe what each of us looks like as a wolf and the ritual for challenge. Shit, what the fuck are we going to do? The moon rises *tonight*. I can't train Monica and I'm certainly not telling her to fight my cousins. I think she should stay here, shift here."

"That will raise alarms with your cousins," Sorin said. "And, we don't know the first thing about a first shift nor are we in a good area for a new werewolf."

"Shit," she said. "You're right. So, what do I do? I can't fight all three of them and from what you said, Marcos is backing down just like he said he would." She turned to me. "No one stood up for me at all?"

"No," I answered.

"And, they kill me?"

"Yes, quickly."

She turned her back to us. "Well, then. I guess that's my fate. I don't care about myself but we have to protect Monica. What if one of you is nearby? She can run to you and you can get her out of there?"

"They will smell us," Rhys said. "They'll know we are there."

"Not necessarily," she turned back. "Before shifting, our senses are haywire. We will be consumed by the coming change and they may not notice. Especially if they'd focused on waiting for the right time to attack me. Stay downwind and I bet they'd never know."

"Then, we will be there," Sorin spoke. "But, not hiding. We will stand for you, Diana. We will fight for you. You are allowed support in your challenge for leader, correct?"

"Yes," she responded.

"Must it be wolf?"

"It doesn't say that, only that we may have support. But no vampire has ever been involved in pack matters and you have to be invited onto our land."

"Then," he stepped into her. "Invite us. Your cousins are prepared to break your law and end you life during the challenge for dominance. So, we change things too. It is time for us to come together. With you as pack master, we can finally bring our two tribes together. We start by standing with you, by protecting you and Monica, by showing solidarity."

She stood silent, thoughts racing through her mind. She knew she would die if she said no but she was afraid of what the others would think. She was afraid we would betray her or try to take over the pack. Sorin must have sensed what she was feeling. "Diana," he extended his hand. "You saved Katherine's children. Let us save you. When you become leader, you and I can work together to end all this turmoil. The children of your pack will no longer go hungry or fear us. The others will follow your direction. Over time, they will see that we are not monsters."

Monica watched Diana like a scared younger sibling, waiting to know what was bad and what was good. After gazing at Monica, Diana glanced at me then Rhys and finally Sorin. Reaching out her hand, she laid it into his. "I invite you onto our land this night."

Sorin smiled and let his hand fall. "We have much to do before the moon rises. Let's work on your parts in this, then we will send you back to your family. Trust that we will be in the woods and let ourselves be known at the right time. Once the secret is out, it will move quickly. Monica, when it begins—you need to run. Someone will meet you in the trees and protect you—try to not maul them."

She laughed weakly. "I'll try."

An hour later, when Monica and Diana left, they knew their parts in tonight's showdown. We reviewed it twice to be certain that everyone had the plan down and there were no questions. Walking them down to the door, I hugged Monica and whispered in her ear "I will be there even if you don't see me."

Out of the corner of my eye, I swore I saw Rhys lay a soft kiss on Diana's cheek and smelled the blush rise in her face. The change of their scents told me that she was having a physical reaction to him and he was not unphased either. When we shut the door behind them, I turned to him. "I thought you hated her."

"I didn't know her." That was all he was going to say. I figured that hours before a major battle wasn't the time to push for gossip but if we survived the night, I was going to push until he broke.

79

We spent the next hour, calling those that we trusted to try and grow our army. Sorin felt that the more vampires who arrived, the quicker we'd end the fight and decrease the bloodshed. He and Rhys kept referring to the "original battle" which sounded like the first big blowout between us and them. They were trying to learn from the mistakes that were made and minimize the loss of life. Tamela was in before we even asked. Sorin didn't think we should ask Naseem or Edwin as it left the manor vulnerable and he wanted them here in case we didn't make it. He didn't say that but I caught some of his thoughts and he was thinking it. He also wanted vampires who could be trusted to be quiet. A showdown between wolf and fang was not something you wanted the whole city to know. I called Jeremy and Logan, knowing they could keep a secret. After a few minutes of explaining it all, Jeremy agreed but Logan wasn't sure. I told him I understood and would not be angry if he chose to stay back.

That was it—our master army—five vampires. My fear of the three colossal werewolves we were going to stand against was muted by the sight of Monica's blood on one snout and Diana's body under another. Losing this fight meant all vampires were in danger.

We would all rather die than not try to save them.

After deciding each person's role, there was no more time to waste. We had fed and the sun was long gone. The four of us went to the garage and climbed into the SUV; Rhys and Tamela in the middle seat, Sorin and I in the front. The door opened and revealed the full moon halfway to its peak. We needed to move fast to make it in time. While Sorin drove, we rode in silence. None of us knew what to say, knowing full well that this could be the last night for any or all of us.

I pulled out my phone and called the girls. They answered with their video so I could see their faces. Ellie had a faint bruise on her cheek. Olivia looked like she hadn't been sleeping well. "Hi guys," I said, trying to slap on a realistic smile. "How are you?"

"We miss you," Olivia said.

"So much," Ellie finished.

"Me too," I responded, fighting back tears so they wouldn't see blood rolling down my face. "How about I come see you tomorrow for a little while?"

They both perked up. "Yeah!"

"Okay, I will come tomorrow after sundown and take you home for the night. You can go back to Dad's the next day. Sound good?" They squealed. I waited for them to stop. "Hey," I said. "I love you guys so so so much. Forever."

"You too, Mom. See you tomorrow night." The screen went black.

Sliding my phone into the pocket on the door, I looked over to Sorin. "You'll see them," he said without me having tell him what I was thinking.

"I hope so," I responded.

"Are you sure you want to do this?" It was Rhys. They'd all heard my kids. Sorin rested his hand on my thigh. He was thinking the same thing but Rhys had asked first.

"I have to," I said resolutely. "I'm not the mother they deserve if I don't do something with my gifts. I've always told them to stand up for what's right. I have to live that. Plus, Monica and Diana risked their lives for those kids. I have to fight for them. And..." I paused before I could say the words out loud and make them real. "If I die, they have Tom and Sarah. They'll be loved."

I laid my hand over Sorin's and looked over. His face was unreadable. I didn't know what he was thinking but I knew he was affected. I was learning that he used that frozen mask to cover things, not because he was uncaring. It was the opposite—he felt it all.

When the city lights had faded and were replaced by trees, I knew we were close. Rolling down the window, I let the cold air hit my face and pull at my hair. It made sense to me now, why dogs put their heads out the window. All the smells hit at once and created a perfume of the outdoors. Closing my eyes, I replayed the vision in my head, trying to prepare myself. I already knew their plan which already ruined it. Finding comfort in that, I held on tight to that knowledge. *I know what you're up to and you won't get away with it,* I thought. I would do anything to save Monica and Diana–to see my daughters–anything. That fire in me was fierce. Letting the fire burn, I reminded myself that I was a powerful vampire, not a naïve human. At my side was an ancient master and behind me were warriors. We would prevail—I didn't accept anything else.

When Sorin turned the vehicle onto the wooded backroad, I knew we were close. The sickening pine smell from my vision was just as overwhelming in reality.

This was it—we were going to battle—and only one team would win.

As the gravel road gave way to dirt, he turned off the headlights. Vampire eyes don't need help and the beams would only alert people to our arrival. Pulling off to the side, the car came to a slow stop and the engine was cut off. We all looked to Sorin. "We walk from here," he said. "If the winds continue this way, they should not smell us."

A minute later, a car rolled up behind us and stopped. Without speaking, we opened our doors to meet Jeremy. Careful to shut them at the same time and quietly, we stood to await him. To my relief, two stepped out of the sedan. Logan had come and made us six. Each of us took a moment to embrace before Sorin lead the way into the trees.

Moonlight lit the way as we walked a mile into the dense forest of my vision. When the time was right, Logan and Tamela broke off to the left, Rhys and Jeremy went right, leaving Sorin and me to continue straight. Each member of our group had heard my vision. They were prepared with their individual jobs. But, no matter how many times I'd repeated it to them or replayed it in my head, the sight of the circular patch in the center of the woods took my breath away.

Seeing those people in the midst of the clearing made it pretty damn hard to deny that my vision was playing out right in front of us. That meant I had minutes before Diana would tell Monica to run and be slaughtered. I shot a thought out to the other vampires. *Be ready we have less than ten minutes. Once you hear howls, it all starts.*

80

Scanning the dozens of naked people in the clearing, I couldn't pick out anyone but Diana and Monica. Without them being in wolf form, I didn't know which men were Julian, Diego, Sebastian or Marcos. I carefully sent my mind into the crowd to try and pick out their voices.

Once she is dead, the others will fall in line. I found him. He was one of the largest men I'd ever seen. At least 6 and a half feet tall, his broad shoulders made him an impressive sight. I tried to not let his size intimidate me but couldn't help but remember that his wolf side as even bigger. His eyes were full of rage. I wondered how Diana wasn't freaking out. She knew what he was planning and looked completely unphased—all her focus on Monica.

On the other hand, anyone could see my poor friend was terrified. Sorin and I stood still on the edge of the trees, hidden in the shadows and grateful the wind was still protecting us. When the sounds of tearing flesh began, Monica's panicked gaze locked into Diana. She was hyperventilating as the people around her began to shift. I could make out what Diana was whispering to her but I prayed it was comforting. Deep down, I knew this may be the last thing she heard and I wanted it to be kind. Diana grabbed Monica and pulled her into a hug moments before her back arched and the wolf ripped its way out. Covered in blood, my best friend fell to the ground and onto her back. Agony filled her face, contorting her features.

It's time, I sent to our group just as howls tore through the silence of the night.

Monica writhed and seized. Sorin held my arm for both comfort and to ensure I didn't start forward. Every muscle in me was tense.

The dark brown wolf came to all fours to watch her newest sister change. The other wolves stayed on two legs around the shifting woman, waiting to see if she'd survive. While it appeared respectful, I knew three of those wolves were just waiting for the right time to enact their plan. As Monica's body arched and the blonde wolf came into the world, we prepared ourselves. More howls filled the skies to welcome their newest member and celebrate her survival. Listening to their thoughts, I realized most of the pack was excited for a new sister. They thought this was a sign that they may grow their numbers and be a happy family again.

They had no idea what was about to go down.

When the blonde wolf was on her four legs, she shook the blood and fluids off as her maker nuzzled her—back to her cousins.

The silver one dropped down and leapt on her back. Seeing it in slow motion, I witnessed Diana throw Diego off her back and him stand to beat his hand against her chest.

"Wait," I said to Sorin.

The two black wolves took their place on each side of Diego, making the sign of challenge. Just like in my vision, Diana turned to the reddish wolf but Marcos bowed to the others and Monica was alone.

"You challenge me?" Diana's words were her voice with a growl underneath. The combination of human and animal voice was unnerving.

"Yes," Diego answered in the same guttural speech. "Stand against three alone or bow down and live."

"I am not alone."

When Sorin and I stepped from the trees, Sebastian snarled. Diego roared in anger. Monica moved to stand behind Diana and looked to the right as Jeremy and Rhys stepped forward from the shadows. On the other side of the circle, I saw Tamela and Logan. All six of us faced the wolves, eyes glowing and muscles tensed.

The werewolves around the circle dropped to their paws and shifted nervously. They looked around to each other, not sure what to do. Reaching out into their minds, I didn't hear the anger I expected, but fear. They were afraid of us.

The silver and black wolves in front of Diana, however, were not. They were enraged.

"You brought bloodsuckers to our sacred space," Diego yelled. "You have soiled this ground and betrayed your family."

"You betrayed me," Diana answered. "You betrayed our grandfather—our ancestors—all that we stand for. You would kill your own to be in power and lead the whole pack into war."

"Never has a pack member used a vampire to fight. You would choose them over us? Your own?" This was from one of the black wolves.

"I choose to maintain peace amongst us. To protect our people. It isn't too late, Diego. We can find peace and start a new era where we work together. You don't even know them. They protected me—warned me of danger."

"They are vampires," Diego growled and let out a howl that sent shivers down my spine. "If you choose them, you are against us."

"You're wrong," she said. "Your way will be the end of us."

"We can end this now," Sorin spoke. His voice carried on the wind to all the wolves and sent reassurance with each word. His power seeped from him in summer-like breezes, just a hint.

"We create a new pact, choose a leader without killing and all walk away tonight."

The silver wolf turned his massive head slowly to us. "You do not have authority here. When I am leader, I will take you and your city."

In response, Sorin's warm power went hot but was still subtly dancing around the wolves. My own power reached out of my stomach to join his, hinting at what could come if they continued to fight. While the wolves in the periphery of the circle drew back further to get away from the magic and the imminent battle, the cousins remained in place and unphased.

Diana turned to Monica. "Run," she growled. Monica listened and the chain of events was set off.

We were anticipating the black wolf chasing after the small blonde one. Before he could make it to the tree line, Logan was already running to protect Monica. He knew his part in this and didn't hesitate. Tamela followed, jumping onto the black one's back as it lunged for Logan. Tamela rode the wolf, wrapping her arms arounds its neck and pulling it back. When it was in place, Logan bared his fangs and attacked the wolf, attempting to tear into the wolf. I lost sight of them when our attention was pulled back to the middle. Diego was on top of Diana.

Sorin, Jeremy and Rhys rushed in the center. Diego and Diana continued to struggle. The vampires reached the second black wolf before he could help his cousin kill Diana. They wrestled it to the ground, holding it on its back. Sorin held its jaw shut and yanked. The snap cracked through the night as the wolf went limp. A glance back to the edge of the woods showed Logan and Tamela standing over a bloody wolf. Logan's mouth was smeared with blood.

Go find Monica and keep her safe. We will meet you at the cars. Tamela and Logan were gone in a flash, their blurs lost to the trees.

When I found the center of the fight again, I saw Jeremy, Rhys and Sorin standing only feet behind the two wolves. They were on all fours, circling each other. Diana had explained to us the importance of her being to one to take down Diego—the pack wouldn't respect her authority otherwise. In an instant I was next to the men, knowing all we could do was watch. This part Diana had to do on her own.

In my periphery, I saw some of the other wolves start to inch towards us with teeth bared. We couldn't fight them all and we couldn't lose sight of the two in the middle. Without thinking, I shot my hand towards them and spun. My magic flared around us and a fire erupted—creating a wall of flames around the sacred circle to protect us from them and let the fight be a fair one on one.

Rhys let out a gasp. "Dramatic."

"Yet, useful," I quipped.

Diana and Diego were not distracted by the flames. They continued to stare at each other and circle. This close I could see the size difference between them and worried that all this would still end in Diana's defeat. I fought the urge send some of that fire to Diego's back. No matter what, we'd all agreed to prevent Diana's death but we knew that getting involved in the fight was a last option. Without Diana being the clear victor, we'd still face a possible uprising amongst the pack. We needed Diana to win.

We had to wait and watch.

When Diego leapt, none of us were prepared. We had less than a second to realize he wasn't heading for her but us. When his weight slammed into me, I hadn't understood what it was at first. All I knew was I was hitting the ground and couldn't breathe. The fire was inches from my head and the heat was overwhelming.

His breath was hot as the jaw snapped for my face and was pulled back at the last second. Sorin was on him and pulling but Diego was too big and too strong. He threw his body back and Sorin was gone from my sight. When his paws landed back on my stomach, I thought my spine may have snapped under the weight. I tried to suck in air but couldn't. My vision was getting fuzzy and I couldn't focus my thoughts to use power. Just when I was on the edge of losing consciousness, the weight was gone.

I rolled to my side and coughed, pulling oxygen in. When my sight was clear again, I shakingly stood up to find the wolf. The skin of his back was in Diana's jaw. She was struggling to maintain her hold as he shook his body. She spread her stance to try and absorb his movement. Sorin and Rhys stood to the right of them, waiting to see if they should intervene. I ran to them, keeping the wolves in my gaze. Diego twisted and threw his weight away from her. He lost a chunk of flesh but got out of her bite. She fell backwards and he rose up on two legs.

Diana recovered to mimic his stance, two legged and ready to pounce again. I could see the fatigue in her shaking muscles. She was exhausted but wouldn't give up. Suddenly, he lunged forward awkwardly and stumbled. Monica had jumped over the flames and onto his back. He frantically reached over his head to try and grab her behind him but her jaws were tight on the same raw spot Diana had just ravaged. Without hesitation, Diana pounced from the front and slammed her mouth onto his neck, using her weight to throw him to the ground. Monica rolled to the side and returned to snap at his stomach. The two she-wolves ripped at him—one on his jugular and one on his abdomen. When they reared back, ripping out vital parts of him, Diego's howling died.

Both women raised their heads to the moon and let out their own howls. These were not the sounds of victory or celebration but of mourning. Neither one of them had wanted to be killers. They'd both hoped for a peaceful resolution.

Reaching out to the flames, I pulled them back into my core. The fire circle left as quickly as it had shown up, revealing the shocked faces of the pack. One by one, the wolves bent their front legs to bow to Diana. They recognized the new pack master as a descendent of Gabriel—one who would follow the old ways. Without words, the knew that she would fight for peace but kill for them if necessary.

Logan and Tamela were at the edge of the clearing, walking towards us. Jeremy ran to meet his partner and they embraced, relieved to see each other. I rushed to meet Tamela. "I thought you were taking Monica to the car?"

She laughed. "No point in arguing with her. She wasn't running away. She's too much like you."

We all stayed a respectful distance from what was happening in the circle, understanding that this was not our moment but theirs. Diana walked around the space, touching her snout to each bowing wolf until she reached Marcos. His head was hung the lowest. She paused there, letting him worry that she would send him away. Instead, she nuzzled his neck. He stiffened and then relaxed into her, whimpering. Last, she stopped to face Monica who was also bowed down. Diana nosed at Monica's head to lift it up. Then bent her front legs to bow to her newest sister and friend. I knew they'd rule together and bring good things to the pack.

I turned to the man at my side, the man who'd asked me to rule with him and was overwhelmed with gratitude. The last thirty minutes had showed me what it takes to utterly trust someone and how carefully you needed to choose those that you let in. He'd chosen me. He trusted me. And, I wanted to be worthy of that.

Regele meu, I sent to him. He turned and whispered, "Regina mea."

"I think we should leave," I said to the group. "This isn't for us."

We turned to the trees. As each vampire disappeared in a blur, I looked back one more time. Three wolves lay dead and I felt a pang of regret for it. But, seeing the she-wolves in the center, knowing they'd protect each other, made the sacrifice worthy.

I sped from the circle and hoped I'd see Monica someday, but accepted that she was no longer my silly, love-sick friend.

She was a fierce creature of legend and we belonged to different worlds now.

81

At the cars, we said our goodbyes. I looked around the group and couldn't believe we'd all made it out. *Gratitude* seems like too weak of a word to describe how I felt. These people would have my loyalty for eternity.

The ride home was so much quicker than the one there. Isn't it funny how your perception of time can be changed by the mood you're in? Dread makes an hour feel like a day but joy makes the same hour disappear in an instant.

When the manor came into view, I realized how much like home it was starting to feel. Part of me missed my little house and the noise of the kids but the other part wanted to stay here forever. Pulling into the garage, I couldn't believe it'd only been hours since we left. Silently, we climbed out of the SUV and into the kitchen. Tamela was already pulling out a pitcher of blood so I grabbed glasses. I was starving and I knew everyone else had expended some serious energy, too. We all needed to recuperate.

It was me who broke the silence. "We just fought freaking werewolves."

"Yes, we did." Rhys raised his glass. We clinked all of them together and drank. Laughter bubbled out of me—mostly as a release of the pressure I'd been holding onto since my vision. But, once it was started, I couldn't stop. The other's joined in, laughing at my laughter and finally letting go.

A few minutes later, we were regaining our composure. Rhys finished his drink and took the cup to the sink. "I'm heading home, all. No offense but I want my shower and my bed." He crossed to me to kiss my forehead. "Call me tomorrow. I'd love to come see the girls."

"You gotta date."

Tamela followed behind him. "I'm heading to a hot shower and some rest."

"Tamela," I asked. She stopped and turned.

"In two nights, after I see the kids, I'd like to have a girls' night. You and me."

She smiled, "I would love that." Then, she was gone to get her well-deserved rest.

Sorin's arms came from behind me to wrap around my waist. "And, when may I have some time with you?"

Holding his hand, I walked through the kitchen door to the stairs and up. He followed behind, playfully pulled by me. It reminded me of the night he'd come to the hospital and allowed me to pull him into the supply closet—the night he'd marked me for the first time. I hadn't known then what this man would mean to me or that he'd risk his life twice for me and someone that I loved. On this night, I did know all that.

In the bathroom, I wordlessly filled the tub and started to strip off his clothes. He kept the silence and allowed me to do what I wanted. He trusted me.

When the bath was full and steam filled the room. We stood naked in front of each other, dirty and bloody from battle. The fact that it wasn't the first time and probably wouldn't be the last didn't decrease the sensuality I felt in that warm, tiled room. I climbed in, laying my back against the cold porcelain. Allowing my gaze to slowly slide down him and back up, I took the sight in like it was the first time. When clothed, he looked lean. But now I saw the intricacy of his muscled frame. He'd worked hard as a human, likely on the land. It'd given him a chiseled and hard body. His torso met his strong thighs with hard lines. His biceps swelled without him clenching. In fact, he was completely at ease while I ran my gaze across and over him. The sparkle of his eyes gave away his pleasure at my examination. That pleasure hit his center and I saw his start to swell.

Reaching out, I invited him into the hot water. He stepped in, moving to slide down and face me but I waggled my finger. "Turn around," I said and he did.

I opened my legs so he could sit between them and he could rest his back against my breasts. He sighed when I ran my hands over his chest. I let them glide across his pecs and down the ripples of his abdomen, stopping short of going any lower, then ran them back up and down his arms. His moan let me know I was on the right track. I didn't want to rush this—I wanted to enjoy his beauty and strength—revel in the fact that he was mine. For minutes, I repeated my slow worship of his upper body. Water rolled down those muscles and my hands followed. I could see that he was rock hard but I didn't let it distract me from the rest of him.

"Sit up," I said. Again, he followed my instructions without question. I took the cup on the edge of the tub and poured water over his hair, running my fingers through the dark length of it. I saw rivulets of blood roll down his back and stared. The muscles of his chest and thighs were impressive but they were nothing compared to his back. As I continued to wet his hair, I examined a back that could only be from hard labor. With awe, I followed the lines of his traps, the swell of his lats. I ran my hand over him. How could I have spent weeks in this man's arms and bed, and never really looked at him?

Breaking my trance, I squeezed the rose shampoo into my hand and lathered his hair, taking time to massage his scalp. With his hair gathered up in my hands, I saw his neck was as strong as the rest of him.

I wondered what kind of hard life had sculpted his body but quickly swept it from my mind. I didn't want his empathy to pick up on my questions and ruin the sensations he was experiencing now.

I gently pressed his shoulders down. He slid into the water, allowing me to rinse the last of the fight from that beautiful hair. When he rose, it sent the water up and some splashed out of the tub. He twisted as he came up, facing me and framed by the wet, dark locks I'd just washed. The look in his eyes told me that my time of playing with him was over. He reached his arms out to each side of my face, gripping the edge of the white porcelain. I stayed still, back against the cool surface and my head slightly back to rest on the rim. He kissed me, just on the brink of too much, and I relented to his need. I was very aware that all that playful exploration had pushed him to the brink of his control. Every nerve in his body was now alive with desire.

Laying my hands on his chest, I pushed him back against the other side of the tub. Without giving him time to respond, I straddled him and gripped his face. This time, the kiss was mine to lead. With the frenzied pace, I showed him what touching him had done to my sanity. I hoped his empathy felt what I was feeling—that he knew I desired him as much as he desired me.

When I lowered myself down to be filled with him, he broke the kiss and sucked in a mouthful of air. His hands grabbed onto my hips, holding me in place. When he returned his eyes to mine, the storm was raging and his pupils were gone. I knew he saw bright blue sapphires where my eyes had been. Several seconds went by and I started to rock. His lips returned to mine, his tongue finding mine and rolling with the movement of my hips. Using the last ounces of my reserve, I kept my tempo slow, trying to draw out the moment and not be lost in need. Water rocked back and forth with us, splashing up and over the tub as my movements slowly sped up. His mouth broke from mine and latched onto my breast, his tongue playing across the nipple. His fangs scratched at the sensitive skin, setting my body on fire. I moaned and arched back, driving him deeper into me. His hands dug into my hips and I rocked while holding that arch. It was too much. The pleasure in my belly was turning to something close to pain but I never wanted to stop. With a thrust, he sent me over the brink and I screamed in release. As the orgasm crested, his cry filled the room.

When I collapsed into him, he held onto me. The strong arms I'd been worshipping hugged me close against the chest I'd explored.

And, I was safe with the man I loved.

82

The next two nights were exactly what I'd needed. First night, Rhys and I had met at my house to walk down to Tom's and pick up the girls. When they saw he was there, they threw themselves into him. Tom had made a point to invite Rhys in and I knew he must trust the man to have done that. Tank had been locked upstairs. I didn't know if I'd ever be able to be around that dog again and it made me sad but it was a small price to pay.

We'd spent the night playing board games and talking. Ellie and Olivia kept begging Rhys to tell stories about Scotland. I was pretty sure he'd made up half of them—especially the one about one of his sheep learning to dance—but they loved every second and I didn't care what he said as long as they were happy. I'd bought them each their own pint of ice cream and they'd finished it off before finally falling asleep on the living room floor. Neither of them had asked about the night we'd rescued them. I figured they'd talk about it when they were ready.

An hour before sunrise, Rhys said goodbye and headed home. I texted Tom and told him I was heading to sleep, that the girls were in the living room. He said he'd come after lunch and make sure they got up and ate a decent meal.

When I rose that evening, I found a letter on the kitchen table. They had headed down to his house to play with Addison and wanted me to know what a good night they'd had. They ended the note with hearts and kisses. The bottom of the page had a picture of them, me and Rhys.

I folded the note up and put it in my pocket, then made my way to the manor. Tamela was in the kitchen. I was surprised to see her working on a crossword puzzle. I guess I didn't know her very well, after all.

That was the first night I saw Tamela's room. It was down the hall from the gym, furnished with art from all different artists and a multitude of eras. Each one had a woman in the focus. The women were a variety of ethnicities and ages. Every one of them was in the midst of an action—one breastfeeding, one working in a field, one fixing a car, one loading items onto a shelf in a grocery store and so many more. The effect of them all together was breathtaking and the message was clear—women can do anything.

On one side of the room were two giant beanbags and that's where we spent the night, talking about everything–our lives, our dreams, our fears.

Sorin only came down once, to give me a kiss and ask if we needed anything. He knew better than to interrupt a girls' night but had to see me. We shooed him away and he obediently left us to our talk.

Halfway through the night, Tamela asked if she could try some styles out on my hair and I gleefully agreed. I loved having my hair messed with and she obviously loved doing it. As she twisted and coiled and pinned, we talked. Every time she finished a style, she'd snap a picture, take it out and start a new one.

Through it all, I found out all the languages she spoke, the martial arts styles she knew, the skills she'd mastered and the loves she'd had and lost. I couldn't believe that this incredible woman had been in my life for a month and I hadn't taken the time to really talk to her. But I guess that's true for so many—people come in and out of your lives without you every really knowing them.

When I started to feel the lethargy of the sunrise, I thanked her for the wonderful night. "Let's do this like once a month—girl night."

She smiled and her eyes sparkled. "I would like that."

I hugged her and headed to Sorin's room, cracking open the door and peaking my head in. He was waiting up for me, propped against several pillows and reading. He patted the spot next to him so I stripped down and dove into that soft expanse. Giggling, I pulled down the covers to crawl under and next to him. "Read me to sleep." I said, laying my head against his chest. When he spoke, his rib cage vibrated against my ear.

"He spoke in a drawl as soft as velvet. The walls of the house were hung with portraits of European and American aristocrats—by Gainsborough, Hudson, Reynolds, Whistler. The provenance of this possessions traced back to dukes and duchesses, kings, queens, czars, emperors and dictators…"

With the cadence of his words and the hum of his voice in his chest, I fell asleep—grateful for a couple of normal nights with the people I'd chosen to be my new family. I didn't know how many of these nights I would get before the next big problem arose but I vowed to be more in the moment and find joy in all these normal nights.

83

In a rare moment, I woke up before Sorin. He was utterly peaceful when he rested, his white skin and black hair against the pink satin was like something out of a romance movie. For a moment, I was lost in him and this new existence I had. It felt too perfect, too good. I was certain that something bad would happen to take it all away. My spiraling was stopped when he opened his lids and locked his eyes onto mine.

"Beautiful," he whispered.

"I was just thinking the same thing," I answered.

"As much as I would love to keep you in bed all night, I have plans for us. You must get ready. Tamela has put the clothes in your room. I don't want to see you until we are ready."

"Wait," I started but was stopped by his finger on my lips.

"I beg of you—just listen to me this one night."

"Okay," I said against his finger. He pulled it back and replaced it with a quick kiss.

"Thank you." Then he was out of bed and rushing me out of the room.

Unexpectedly, Rhys was in the hallway with Tamela. They abruptly ended their whispering when I opened the door. Rhys was in an evergreen suit. His hair was actually styled which made me freeze for a second. He looked so handsome that I wasn't sure what to say. Next to him, Tamela stood in a long black gown. Her hair was braided and in a large chignon, studded with diamonds.

"Perfect timing," he said and clapped. "She will help you. I will get blood." Before I could object, he was down the hall and I was being shuffled into my room.

"What's going on?" I was a little panicked. I hated surprises, always had. The previous week had been a little too much for my psyche and I was holding back a freak out. Tamela must have seen it.

"If I tell you, will you promise to act surprised?"

"Yes," I relented.

"We are taking you to Logan's fashion show. Sorin wanted it to be a surprise. I told him that was a bad idea."

I felt my breathing calm and the terror inside of me subsided. "Oh, okay. That's fun! Alright, let's get me ready!"

Across my bed lay a white strapless dress with a diamond studded empire waist. I was not a huge fan of white when I was human. I always thought it made me look too pale. But, this night—as a vampire with flawless skin and someone who wasn't going to complain about an obviously expensive gown—I just smiled. "It's lovely."

When Tamela was done, my hair fell in think curls around my shoulders and down my back. A red rose was clipped just above my right ear. She clasped a necklace around my neck. When it fell, the simple gold chain ended with a red, ruby just above my breasts. Once the dress was on, I looked in the mirror. The touches of red from the flower and gem, mixed with my black hair and the white dress was amazing. Once again, she had known what to do. Arm and arm, we walked down the hallway to the top of the stairs. In my heels, I was closer to her height. Together, we must have looked stunning. The eyes of the men at the bottom of the stairs told me that was true. Rhys and Sorin stared up at us in wonder. Sorin has chosen a classic black tux and was the epitome of a romantic fantasy. A red rose graced his lapel. We descended the stairs to accept kisses from each man, just as three people stepped from the room to the left and into the foyer.

Diana and Monica were both gowned. Diana's was the same evergreen of Rhys's suit and Monica's was a soft pink. Alex's suit was grey with a pink rose to match Monica's dress. I rushed to them and pulled both into a hug. "You're here."

"Of course," Monica squealed. "I'm not going to miss a real fashion show." A chorus of groans and exclamations filled the room. She covered her mouth. "Oh no, I ruined the surprise."

"It's okay," I insisted. "I'm so thrilled that you're here; that's the best surprise of the night!"

"Ladies," Sorin said. "We need to leave. After you."

He opened the door to show us that the limo was back. Edwin stood in a black suit at the back of the car. Naseem stood at the driver's door. When we were all in, Edwin joined Naseem in the front and closed the partition between us and them. Glasses were raised—blood for us and champagne for the werewolves and human. We celebrated our survival, Alex's work, Diana's new position as pack leader and a future where the divide between vampire and wolf was gone. I watched Alex kiss Monica's cheek and her blush. Then, I caught a look pass between Diana and Rhys. Was it what I thought it was?

Sorin leaned into my ear and whispered, "Trust me."

Any attempt at getting more out of him was halted when the car stopped and the back door was opened. Jeremy's face filled the opening. "Finally, you're here!"

We climbed out of the limo, one by one, breaking off into couples: Sorin and me, Monica and Alex, Rhys and Diana. The men offered their elbows and the woman took them. Jeremy led the way down the red carpet. We followed. Inside the massive venue, music played from a speaker in every corner. The beats were heavy on the bass and lights of all different colors danced around. I heard shrieks and Jeremy side stepped to show me Tom, Sarah, Olivia and Ellie. They ran to me and I opened my arms to take them in.

"What are you doing here?"

Tom smiled. "Rhys and Sorin reached out. Once the girls heard 'fashion show', I was outnumbered." He wrapped his arm around my back and pulled me away from the group to step outside. Looking back, I saw the girls spinning in their dresses and my friends clapping. Tamela was helping Sarah twist her hair into something but I didn't see what because Tom was asking for my attention.

"Listen," he said. "I was freaked at first. I thought about fighting for custody." My heart plummeted into my stomach. "But I've had time to think. I've had time to talk to Sorin and Rhys, too. I realized something…" he paused and I waited. "They're safer with you than anyone else. You guys could literally take bullet for them."

I let out the breath I was holding.

"I still don't want them at Sorin's until I really get to know him. And, I don't want them to know the truth until they are *a lot* older. And, when you tell them—I want to be there. But I trust you. Don't make me regret it."

I held onto him, unable to stop the trembling in my muscles. "Thank you."

"And," he broke the hug and looked at me. "You and Sorin have my blessing." I laughed. I didn't really think I needed his blessing since it wasn't the Middle Ages but I bit my tongue. He was being very gracious and I wasn't going to ruin it.

We returned to the group to see that Sarah's hair was now in some kind of up-do with a flower in it. I didn't know how they did it but she looked very pleased.

"Shall we," Jeremy asked and motioned for us to go to through the door to our right. The music's volume went up in here. A long runway filled the center of the room. Hundreds of chairs were lined on each side. A quick perusal showed me that it was a mix of humans and vampires. I looked nervously to the kids and to Sorin. "They'll be safe," he mouthed.

I nodded and we found seats in the front row with our names on them. I couldn't tell who was most excited when the models started down the runway, strutting and turning to return down the walkway to the curtain. It was hard to look away. Each outfit was more stunning then the next. I saw Sarah and the girls stand to leave. She mouthed *bathroom* to me and I gave them a thumbs up. "I'll go guard outside the bathroom," Sorin whispered into my ear and I kissed him. He knew without me saying anything that I would have worried the whole time. With him on guard, I could enjoy the show. After fifteen or so more minutes, the music dimmed and Jeremy came on to the runway with a mic. At first, I thought he was modeling and didn't know why he'd need a microphone.

"Ladies and gentlemen," he spoke and his voice was rhythmic on top of the beats, almost like spoken poetry. "The designer and man of the hour—Logan."

Logan entered to the sounds of the crowd cheering, bowing along the way and thanking everyone. When he reached his partner, they embraced and walked back to the top of the runway. I thought that as the end but they stopped at the top. Jeremy raised the mic and kept going. "Tonight, we have some special models making their fashion debut. We are pleased to introduce something Logan has been wanting to do for a long time and now has the chance to—young adult."

From behind the curtain, two teen models entered and strutted down the runway. Ellie and Olivia wore matching dresses—one black and one white. They came down the long stage like they'd always known how to model. I stood to my feet and cheered. From behind the curtain, Sarah poked out her head to watch. Looking over to Tom, I could see he was both proud and completely terrified. At the end, they stopped back-to-back and waved at me. I waved back and blew them kisses. I wished Sorin had been there but knew he was probably in on the surprise and guarding them backstage. When the girls turned and walked back to the curtain, I was confused when they didn't go behind the curtain but instead stood next to Jeremy and Logan. Sarah came out to join them and I knew something else was up.

The music dimmed again, changing from a dance beat to a piano and a woman singing slowly about not wanting to fall in love but being powerless. The lights stopped swirling around the room and all focused on the end of the runway. Rhys stood and extended his hand to me. I took it and allowed him to pull me up on to the runway. He leaned in and kissed my cheek, then left the stage. I turned to Jeremy with confusion in my eyes.

From behind the curtain, Sorin emerged. He came down the runway with the confidence of a man who had it all and the grace of a dancer. I heard the silence fall across the crowd and someone gasped. I was frozen in place, my senses overwhelmed by the music, the lights, the eyes on me and the man coming towards me. I drew in a shaking breath. When he reached me, he took my hands and drew me in. Swaying, he started to dance with me and I followed his gentle lead. Suddenly, the room around us faded and all I could see was him. All I could feel was him.

He spoke to me like no one was watching. "I love you. I have never loved anyone like I love you. I want you by my side until we leave this Earth. What is mine is yours and what is yours is mine. Be my mate and I will protect you, care for you and worship you."

He slowly ended the dance and lowered himself down to one knee. A ring box was in his hand before I understood what was happening. He was combining human ritual and vampire—proposing to me while asking me to be his mate. The humans would see us as engaged and the vampires would see us as mated.

Looking around, I saw the joy in my daughters' eyes, the pride in Rhys', the love in Monica's, the agreement in Tom's and the respect in Diana's. Above all, I saw the hope in Sorin's.

That wall was ready to slam into place and protect me from the possibility of hurt. My mind told me that I was no good at marriage and this would end badly.

I pictured myself taking a hammer to that wall and watched the bricks crumble.

"Yes," I whispered, then yelled. "Yes."

He slid the ring on my finger and a roar erupted around us. Everyone was on their feet. The girls ran down the runway, followed by Sarah and they all wrapped around Sorin and me. I turned to find Rhys only to see him locked in an embrace with Diana, mouths together and arms entwined. Monica and Alex, too, were lost in their own love. The girls finally let go and ran down to their dad to show him their dresses. Sarah joined them, in a tableau of the perfect family.

From the speakers, I heard Jeremy's voice. "I dare you to find a fashion show more memorable. Congratulations to all this evening. Love will always win. Before we say good night, I urge you all to follow your heart and find your dreams. Good evening and goodbye from Logan and me."

The music rose and I wished that I had empathy and could feel the wonderful emotions that filled the room. Sorin laid a finger under my chin and lifted my face to meet his. "Over five hundred years of moments to choose from and this is my favorite."

I smiled, lost in him. "Here's to five hundred more years of memories just like this."

84

Now

It's hard to believe that was all just months before I sat down to write this. I mean so much has happened since. But, that's for another night and another journal.

Of course, because it's me and nothing ever comes easily, the whole bonding/marriage thing was not as simple as picking out a venue and the right color theme. Between us constantly having enemies, my trust issues, my wild magic, his responsibilities, problems amongst the pack and all the other things we contend with—well, let's say it's not exactly a Hallmark movie.

Rhys and Diana's relationship could be a whole separate book On its own. Come to think of it, that's actually not a bad idea. Maybe I'll write down their stories, too. Of course, only if you guys would be interested. And, I'd have to ask their permission, also.

Alex is hard at work on the cure for lycanthropy. As much as we'd like to see it made, I worry about little time off he takes. We haven't stopped looking for his sister, either.

Creating peace between the wolves and vampires was a lot harder than we thought it would be. That needs to be settled before we work on creating a union between us. Diana is doing a really good job as pack leader but she had a rough first few months. Monica is helping her clean things up and build trust among the wolves again. Turns out that her cousins did a lot of damage in that little time they were there.

Rhys and I are still at the hospital. I had actually turned in my notice and was ready to leave when the first case of the virus hit our city. Since then, I've been working alongside my fellow nurses in impossible situations. I see them burning out, sick, exhausted and losing their passion for this career. They're facing inhuman scenarios day after day, hour after hour. More patients than we can safely handle are walking through the door and there is no end in sight. As much as I would love to escape to a world of romance and eternal life—I can't walk away from them now.

Sorin understands. He would love to have me by his side all the time but knows how important what I'm doing is. I'm in school, working to be a nursing professor someday, when the pandemic is controlled.

We both dream of the day when I can walk out of the hospital for the last time.

The End.

Made in the USA
Middletown, DE
08 April 2025